NEIGHBOURS

A Contemporary Christian Romance
Series 1

by

Tracy Krauss

Fictitious Ink Publishing
Tumbler Ridge, BC

NEIGHBOURS A Contemporary Christian Romance

2nd edition published by Fictitious Ink Publishing,
Tumbler Ridge, BC, V0C 2W0
(1st edition published by Stardust Romance, a subsidiary of Helping Hands Press, 2014)

ISBN 978-1-988-447-10-0 (epub edition)
ISBN 978-1-988-447-11-7 (mobi edition)
ISBN 978-1-988-447-12-4 (paperback edition)

THE HOLY BIBLE, NEW INTERNATIONAL VERSION, NIV Copyright 1973, 1978, 1984, 2011 by Biblical Inc. Used by permission. All rights reserved worldwide.

Calgary skyline: copyright doranjclark

DEDICATION & ACKNOWLEDGMENTS

This series is dedicated to anyone who has ever had to pull up stakes and move, or to anyone who feels like they don't fit. As a person who has moved multiple times, I know how hard it can be. The good news is, if God moves with you, you're always at home.

Thanks to my writing colleagues and friends at Inscribe Christian Writers Fellowship. You are a wonderful source of inspiration and encouragement. Thanks to Priscilla Benterud, editor extraordinaire. To all my family, especially my husband Gerald, I acknowledge your support and love, without which I would have given up on this writing 'gig' long ago. Finally, I thank Almighty God, who has given me stories to tell. He hardwired me to write and has allowed me to follow that dream.

FOREWORD

I love people watching. Airports, waiting rooms, shopping malls - these are ripe fields for the student of human nature. It was during one of these 'research' sessions that I started a list of possible characters that might make an appearance in one of my novels. As I began to flesh some of these people out, it dawned on me that I had an entire community. I also realized that several characters had their own unique story to tell, perhaps not long enough for a full length novel, but perfect for a series of novellas. Thus NEIGHBOURS took shape. I hope you enjoy meeting this varied, sometimes quirky, cast. Welcome to the neighbourhood!

If you really keep the royal law found in Scripture, "Love your neighbor as yourself," you are doing right.

James 2: 8 (NIV)

EPISODE 1

NEW IN THE NEIGHBOURHOOD

*L*ate summer. The air was warm, but not oppressive. A slight breeze sent a shiver through the poplar trees lining the boulevard. Light and shadow danced together on the sidewalk as the sun's rays filtered down through the leaves. The 'whish' of passing traffic a few streets over underscored the relative silence on the quiet street, marked only by the melodic offerings of a songbird high up in the trees.

Honk! Honk! *"Hey! You're blocking the driveway! Get that rust bucket outta the way!"*

The tranquility was shattered. The impatient driver of the new BMW laid on the horn and craned his head around before jamming it into gear and backing up with a screech. Cranking the wheel, he swung past the offending blue pickup and U-haul trailer, coming dangerously close to clipping the front fender of the truck. The parting expletive and accompanying hand signal was not lost on the occupants of the rig.

"What's your rush?" Lester leaned out the window of the dusty truck and shook his fist at the retreating silver sports coupe. With a disgusted grunt he pulled his head back into the cab.

"We are blocking the street," Patsi noted, watching the now minuscule BMW. "I mean, couldn't we pull around closer to the front doors or something?" She surveyed her brother for a moment and then flopped back against the rather unforgiving bench seat with a sigh. "I forgot. You have everything under control."

Lester Ray Tibbett gave his young sister a withering look. "As a matter of fact, I do. No room to turn around. I don't know how they expect folks to move in and out of these blasted apartments with no room to maneuver a trailer."

The apartment block to which the brother and sister were relocating was a square, four-story structure situated on a narrow tree lined street in an older section of Calgary – if you could call any part of the city 'old'. The prairie city had boomed to such a degree in recent years that it was a miracle they'd found an apartment at all.

Lester inched the vehicle back a few more millimetres then pressed his foot against the brake. He put the truck in park while simultaneously engaging the emergency brake. He slammed out of the vehicle, keys in hand, leaving the tinny reverberations of the door to echo in his sister's ears. "Come on. We haven't got all day," he called over his shoulder.

Lester blocked up the U-haul's tires and unlocked the safety latch on the back doors. With a creak, he swung the doors wide, revealing the contents within. Placing hands on hips, he surveyed the stacks of boxes and furniture. He took off his cowboy hat and wiped his brow with the back of his checkered sleeve. His closely cropped brown hair was stuck to his head in a flattened ring where the hat had been, curling up at odd angles everywhere else. A day's growth of stubble darkened his jaw line until it merged with well-defined sideburns.

Patsi stood next to her brother and groaned. "This is going to take forever."

"No complaining. The longer we stand around the longer it'll take."

Patsi let out a dramatic sigh, but extended her arms to receive the first box. Lester piled two more on top before nodding his head for her to get a move on. He watched her for a few seconds as she strode to the building's entrance. Her blonde braid swung in time to her steps, mimicking the sway of her hips in the too-short jean shorts she insisted on wearing that day. She'd grown up right before his eyes, taking on a womanly shape that had him worried. His role as her guardian was sure to get more complicated once she started college. She was a good kid. Contentious as any teenage girl, but a hard worker. Both he and his sister were used to manual labor. Despite her petite figure and pretty face, she was tough as nails from doing chores and could hold her own.

Lester hoisted his own set of boxes and followed his sister. Several trips later they were both puffing from exertion. Lester had worked on the farm all his life and had the muscles to prove it, but so many trips up and down two flights of stairs was taking its toll.

"I need to take a break." Patsi bent over, hands on her thighs as she tried to catch her breath. "Any water in the truck?" Tendrils of hair were coming loose, framing her face with heat induced curls. The siblings had the same naturally curly hair, but Patsi's was a shade lighter than his. 'Dirty blonde' she called it while Lester's was a light brown. He, of course, kept his cropped short, but Patsi insisted on keeping hers long and tried to straighten it each day. It was a chore that made no sense to him, but girls would be girls.

"I think there's some in the cab." Lester strode to the driver's side of the truck and opened the door with a jerk. He rummaged around behind the seat until he came up with two bottles of water. He tossed one to Patsi on his way around the vehicle and she caught it with the quickness of an infielder.

"It's warm," she protested.

"Beggars can't be choosers." Lester downed the whole thing then wiped his mouth with the back of his hand before crushing the bottle in his fist and tossing it into the box of the truck among the other contents. "Okay, let's get this trunk out of here next." Lester jumped into the half empty U-haul trailer and tugged a large trunk toward the doors.

"It's too heavy for me." Patsi recapped her water and set it on the bumper of the trailer.

Lester shot her a frown. "Come on Princess. It's not going to move itself, and I don't see anybody else around, do you?"

Patsi sighed heavily and moved to take her place at the other end of the trunk. Lester took a hold of one of the corners and lifted, trying to shimmy the heavy burden so that Patsi could better grasp it by the handles. Suddenly the trunk slipped, jamming his finger between it and the open doorway of the trailer. With a yelp he snatched his finger away and squeezed it with his other hand. A few choice words escaped.

"I told you it was too heavy." Patsi cocked her head to one side in an 'I told you so' manner and raised her brows.

"Need a hand?"

Lester looked up sharply. A man was standing on his third floor balcony, overlooking the operation. He was tall and broad and was wearing a worn T-shirt and a dirty ball cap.

"Um... yeah. That would be great," Lester called back.

"Be right down." The man waved and disappeared through his sliding glass doors.

"My lucky day." Patsi beamed up at her brother. "Your new friend can take over from here."

"There's still plenty of small stuff," Lester said.

Patsi rolled her eyes. "I was joking."

Lester sighed. Sometimes his sister acted so immature. Okay, she was only seventeen, but she needed to start acting more grown up. He wasn't much older when he'd been thrown into more responsibility than most guys his age had ever dreamed of.

"Hi!"

Lester glanced back up at the building. Two small boys were watching from their own balcony two stories up. One had chocolate brown skin, while the other had straight black hair and an olive complexion. He just waved. Those little kids probably had nothing better to do, so let them watch if they wanted. He noticed the curtains moving in another window on the second floor. It was hard to remain anonymous in a place like this. Where everyone was all squished together like sardines in a can. Oh well. It was the best he could do.

The helpful neighbour was approaching so Lester turned his attention back to the matter at hand. "Thanks again for offering to help. Name's Lester Ray Tibbett." Lester stretched out his hand.

"Jed Malloy." Jed had a firm grip and his hand almost dwarfed Lester's.

"Good to meet you. Me and my sister are just moving in," Lester said.

Patsi rolled her eyes. "Obviously. Duh."

Lester pointed a thumb back at Patsi. "My sister Patsi Mae."

"Just Pat," Patsi mumbled, looking down.

Jed smiled. "Pleased to meet ya. I got a couple a sisters of my own back 'ome. You're mighty lucky to get the place. Ol' Tucker was 'ardly even cold when the place was advertised. A real 'ousing shortage these days."

"You from out east?" Lester asked. Jed's short clipped words, extended 'r' and lack of 'h' quickly betrayed his background.

"Yeah. Newfoundland."

Lester nodded. "Thought so. The accent kind of gives you away."

"I ain't the one with the accent. I keeps tellin' you westerners, but youse don't listen too well." They all laughed. "Well, we'd better get you moved in." Jed clapped Lester soundly on the back and then went straight for the trunk. "Where's this beast going?"

With a grunt the two men hoisted the heavy trunk and started lumbering for the entrance.

Jed was taller than Lester by several inches and at six feet Lester wasn't exactly short. Jed also looked to be broader and very muscular. Lester's own muscles were hardened by hard work and fine-tuned by riding broncos – one of his hobbies - but he wouldn't want to meet the other man in a fight. He just might lose.

The threesome had the remainder of the truck and trailer unloaded and into the apartment within half an hour.

"Thanks man," Lester puffed, winded from the last trek up the stairs with a particularly heavy chest of drawers. "I don't know how I would have managed with only Patsi for help."

"Hey, I'm no sissy," Patsi protested. "I could have managed."

Lester shook his head and snorted his doubts.

"I could have! Mostly…"

"No problem. That's what neighbours are for. I was glad to 'elp. I could use a cold one, though. As a thank you." Jed winked. He pulled off his ball cap to reveal a shock of dark hair that stood out at odd angles.

"Sorry," Lester apologized. "We haven't got anything to offer just yet. We could make coffee if we could find the coffee maker."

"Why don't you come over to my place?" Jed offered. "My fridge is always stocked with the essentials. Like beer, that is." He chuckled.

"Sounds good to me. I should move that rig out of the way first, though. I'll just be a minute."

"Sure. I'll just 'elp your sister move some of these boxes around."

Lester left Patsi and Jed to rearrange the boxes into their respective rooms while he moved the truck and trailer to a better location down the street. He returned in a few minutes to find them already waiting in the hall.

"A beer sounds pretty good about now," Lester said. "Got anything for my sister?"

Patsi stuck her chin out. "I can have a beer if I want. I'm not a baby."

Lester just raised a brow. "Only if I say so."

"It's not like I haven't had a beer before. Besides, I'll be legal in four months."

"Nineteen?" Jed asked.

Patsi shook her head. "Eighteen."

"Right. Legal drinking age is eighteen in Alberta." Jed shook his head. "No wonder the kids in the bar are looking younger and younger these days."

Lester and Patsi followed Jed down the hall to his apartment, three doors down from their own. It was a typical bachelor's pad – mismatched furniture arranged for optimal television viewing with dirty dishes and left over food littering every available surface.

"Excuse the mess," Jed apologized, going straight for the refrigerator and collecting three long necked bottles of beer. The first bottle let out a hiss as he twisted the top off. He handed it to Patsi and winked. "Ladies first."

"Thanks." Patsi looked pointedly at her brother and took a sip.

"Guess I can't say no now that you've put your germs on it," Lester said with a slight grin. "But don't get any ideas."

Jed distributed the remaining beer. "Have a seat." He did a wide sweep of the room with his free arm. Patsi and Lester found seats on the sofa and Jed stretched out in the armchair. "So? What brings you to the city?"

"Work," Lester replied. "That and my sister going to college."

"His idea, not mine," Patsi said with a sullen edge to her voice. She sipped tentatively from her bottle of beer.

"Education is a good thing," Jed said. "Something that can never be taken away. So my Ma says. Too bad I didn't listen." He grinned. "You seem kinda young for college, though." He squinted at Patsi.

"December baby," Lester explained. "Moving here should help her adjust."

"You talk like I'm not even here," Patsi protested. "Besides, I would have been just fine." As if to prove it she took a long drink of her beer. Suddenly she sputtered, choking as it went down the wrong way. Her diaphragm jerked as she tried to control the coughing and she glared at Lester, as if it was his fault she was choking.

Jed pointed with his free hand. "Bathroom's that way, if you want."

Patsi got up from the couch without looking at either man and headed down the narrow hall. Lester's eyes followed her.

"Where'd you say you come from again?" Jed took a long swing of his beer.

"Farmed near Coulee Creek," Lester said.

Jed nodded. "I know it. That's nice country."

"It's home. But there have been a few bad years. Drought. Poor grain prices. It costs about as much to put the crop in as any profits you might get. I figured I'd rent the land out for a bit. Let somebody else have all the headaches and just collect a pay check for a change."

Jed took another drink. "You gotta do what you gotta do. I came all the way across the country, so I definitely know."

7

"How long have you been here?" Lester asked.

Jed cocked his head to one side. "Let's see… Four years now? Something like that. Long enough that I 'ate to give up my job and move back 'ome. Besides, 'alf of Newfoundland is out west so's its not so bad. One of my brothers is coming out soon, too, or so 'e says."

"That's nice. Family is important."

Jed eyed Lester over the top of his bottle. "So it's just you and your sister?"

"Since our folks died, yes. Sometimes I feel more like her father than her brother."

"How long your folks been gone?" Jed asked.

"Nine years. She was only nine, so she's spent half her life without them."

"And there was no other family to take care of 'er?"

"I don't believe in shirking my duties," Lester responded quietly. "We had an old aunt in Saskatoon, but it was best for her to stay put in her own home. That's what my folks would have wanted."

"You must a been pretty young yourself."

"Twenty-three."

Jed let out a soft whistle. "Pretty young to have to take on that kind of responsibility. Took over the farm, too?"

Lester nodded. "I was planning on working alongside my folks anyway. It just happened sooner than expected."

"I see."

"It's a good life," Lester said. "On the farm, I mean. Good place to raise a kid."

"Keeps 'em out of trouble, I suppose," Jed agreed. "You might 'ave your 'ands full 'ere." He grinned.

"Not if I can help it."

"I know a thing or two about teenage girls. I've got sisters of my own and when they put their mind to somethin' they don't give in easy. I'd watch 'er if I were you."

"I intend to." Lester let out a sigh – one far too deep for a casual first meeting. "It's one thing I plan on doing right."

"Sounds like you're pretty 'ard on yourself."

Lester sat up straighter and tried for a smile. Trust a Newfie to skip small talk and go straight to personal. "So, what do you do for a living?"

"Construction. I know there's more money in the oil patch, but I don't care much for camp life. We're working on some big 'igh rise building downtown."

"You don't say. I'm starting up with a construction outfit myself. What's the name of yours?"

"Titan," Jed said.

Lester raised his brows. "Really? That's who hired me. My cousin put in a good word for me."

"Always pays to know the right people." Jed finished his beer and set the bottle on the side table. "Small world, ain't it?"

"True." Lester also downed the rest of his beer just as Patsi re-emerged. "Ready to go, Sis?" He stood and stretched.

She glanced at the full bottle of beer sitting where she'd left it. "I'm not done my beer."

Lester checked his watch. "I gotta get that trailer back before closing."

Jed winked at Patsi. "You can 'ave a rain-check sometime."

"Thanks again for the help," Lester said.

"Anytime. Whenever you two need anything, just 'oller."

LESTER RUBBED his right shoulder and did a few circular motions to try and work out the kinks. All that heavy lifting yesterday had him feeling muscles he'd forgotten existed. He and Patsi had stayed up late and managed to get the bulk of their belongings stored away. It didn't exactly feel like home yet, but it was one step closer.

"Do we have to go?" Patsi stood in her bedroom doorway, arms folded.

Lester stopped in the hall on his way from the bathroom and surveyed his sister's grimacing face. "Of course we have to go. You didn't think we'd just stop going to church, did you?"

"But, I don't have anything to wear." She gestured down at her black pants and nondescript maroon top.

"What's wrong with what you have on?"

"It's so... boring. How do I know what people are wearing in the city?"

"It's not about what you're wearing," Lester said reasonably.

"Okay, fine," Patsi huffed. "But if I don't like it I'm not going back."

"You're forgetting who puts a roof over your head. If I say going to church is part of the deal, then it is." Lester crossed his own arms and widened his stance.

"You're not fair, you know that?" Patsi shot at him.

"Nobody said life was fair."

Lester continued down the hall to his own small room. He'd given Patsi the bigger one as a concession. The apartment was tight compared to what they were used to. There had been plenty of room to spread out in the farmhouse.

Several minutes later they were heading out the door of the apartment building. Lester was wearing his one pair of dress pants and a white cotton shirt. He figured he might as well put his best foot forward.

"Hey, where are you going?" Patsi stopped on her way to the truck. Lester was already several steps in the opposite direction.

Lester shrugged. "I thought we'd try that church just down the street. No use driving to some mega-church if we can walk every Sunday."

Patsi threw up her hands. "But it's probably full of old people."

"How do you know? You haven't been there yet."

"I just know!"

"We'll see. But today we're going to try out the church in our own neighbourhood. Come on, at least give it a chance."

They arrived at the small community church and were greeted at the door by the pastor, a youngish man with a prematurely receding hairline. He was wearing all black except for the small white collar symbolic of his calling.

"Welcome. I'm Reverend Wallis."

Lester and Patsi shook the young Reverend's hand then found an empty pew and waited for the service to start. The congregation was small, although larger than their church in Coulee Creek. After three hymns the offering plate was passed and then the Reverend gave his sermon – a short discourse on the merits of being a good neighbour. All in all, it was satisfactory, as far as Lester could tell. The sermon was short and to the point and the minister seemed simple and unpretentious. Just what he liked.

After the service, the mostly elderly adherents filed toward the exit, waiting for their turn to greet the pastor on their way out the door. As Lester and Patsi waited, an elderly woman approached. She stopped directly beside them. "I believe we're neighbours." Her tone was clipped.

"Oh?" Lester turned his full attention toward the newcomer. She was almost as tall as he. Her mostly grey hair was smoothed into an iron clad pageboy with nary a wisp out of place. Her lavender suit was perfectly tailored, while the pearls around her neck drew attention to the cords of her throat.

"Yes. I live in suite twenty-four. I saw you moving in the other day. I'm Millicent Peacock. I've been attending this church since nineteen-sixty-five." She inhaled sharply through her nose and tilted her head up slightly, as if the information she'd given was of great importance.

"Pleased to meet you." Lester smiled and stuck out his hand. "I'm Lester Ray Tibbett and this is my sister Patsi Mae."

"Just Pat," Patsi threw in.

Millicent ignored the offered hand. "Your sister? Well, that's a relief."

"Beg your pardon?"

"I'm glad you're not one of those young couples just living together, although I should have known since you seem a bit old for her."

Lester blinked. He didn't even know how to respond. He glanced over at the minister to see if he could squeeze ahead in the line-up.

"I'm actually quite surprised to see you here this morning," Ms. Peacock went on.

Lester swung his gaze back to the elderly woman, his eyebrows raised in question. "Oh? Why's that?"

"All the ruckus when you moved in. I heard more than a few choice words coming from your mouth, Mr. Tibbett. I'm glad to see you have some fear of God in you after all. You may have to learn to tame your tongue, however." Her steely blue eyes dared his to stray.

Lester opened his mouth to respond but Millicent was already moving forward to shake the pastor's hand. Lester stood for a moment with his mouth open until Patsi elbowed him in the ribs. He jerked his gaze in his sister's direction. She had a smirk on her lips, the unspoken 'I told you so' written on her face.

With a sigh, Lester moved forward and shook Reverend Wallis's outstretched hand. "Good sermon, Reverend."

The minister smiled. "Thank you. Ms. Peacock tells me you moved into her building. I hope that means we'll be seeing you again next Sunday."

"Um, maybe," Lester mumbled. Thankfully, there were others waiting in line to shake the Reverend's hand.

When they were far enough away from the church Patsi finally spoke. "I told you it would be all old people. And the nerve of that old lady! She probably sits by the window spying on everyone in the building."

"Let her. I doubt we'll be seeing her much anyway."

"Not if you insist on going to that church every Sunday," Patsi pointed out.

Lester frowned. So much for a simple solution to keeping his sister's spiritual life intact. It had been a steep learning curve and he'd made some mistakes, but bringing her up in the fear of God was one thing he was determined not to mess up. Even if it killed him.

LESTER LOWERED himself onto a makeshift stool made of a plastic crate and gazed out over the cityscape. From this vantage on the eighteenth floor of the new concrete structure, he had an unobstructed view of the other high rises that made up the downtown core. There were no windows or finishes of any kind as yet, just cement pillars and gaping holes. The wind whipped pretty briskly up here, but he found he liked it. He'd never been afraid of heights and the freedom he felt at this elevation was something new.

It was lunchtime on his first day. He unscrewed the lid on his thermos and poured some steaming coffee into it, using it for a mug.

"Hey! What are you doing?"

Lester recognized the voice as Jed's and swivelled around to greet his new friend. "Thought I'd enjoy the view while I ate lunch."

Jed came and stood beside Lester, gazing past the large openings. "It is kind of cool." He looked down at Lester's thermos and lunch cooler. "I guess we think alike." He held his own lunch kit aloft. "Mind if I join you?"

"Not at all."

Jed set his lunch down and walked two paces to where another crate sat waiting. He kicked the dusty crate with his foot until it was near Lester and then he sat down on it. "Lots of the other guys go out for lunch."

"Can't afford to eat out every day."

"Same." Jed looked around the expanse of cement. "It's a nice view from up 'ere, but I guess we'll 'ave to wait and see if the finished product is any good. Sometimes these fancy architects don't take the practical into consideration."

"I guess if they hired him he must know something." Lester took a sip of his coffee.

"From Toronto, I 'ear. Chan or Chow or some kind of Chinese name."

"They couldn't find anyone local?" Lester asked.

"Beats me." Jed took a huge bite of his sandwich. "Mm-mm. I do love a good bologna sandwich!"

"Bologna, eh?" Lester surveyed the other man, obvious relish in the way he was chewing on his lunch. "I never cared for it much."

"Newfie steak, don't ya know," Jed said with his mouth full. He swallowed and gulped some juice from a bottle. "One day I'll take you to The Brew for lunch, though. They make the best Pastrami sandwiches around and their coffee is pretty good, too. It's just around the corner."

"The Brew? Sounds like a hangout for witches." Lester grinned and took a hefty bite of his roast beef sandwich.

Jed laughed. "Tamara and Carmen couldn't be witches. They're too easy on the eyes."

"The owners, I take it?" Lester took another bite.

"Yep. Tamara actually lives in our building, so I feel obligated to go to 'er café once in a while. " Jed stopped, finished chewing and then swallowed, all the while staring at Lester with his head cocked to one side. "I could probably fix you up if you want. She's a bit of a feminist or activist or some such thing, so she might be a 'andful. But you look like you could take it."

Lester frowned. "Then why don't you date her?"

Jed just laughed. "I'm not the settlin' down kind. No woman's gonna stick 'er claws into me. Not if I can 'elp it."

"Is that so? What makes you think I'd be interested?"

Jed rubbed his chin. "Are you?"

"Not at the moment." Lester kept his gaze straight ahead, out toward the wide-open air beyond the building's skeletal structure.

"You sure about that?"

Lester turned to Jed and gave him a withering look. "Absolutely. Now, change of topic. What does a guy do for fun around this city?"

"Depends on your idea of fun," Jed replied with a shrug. "What did you used to do for fun?"

"Work mostly. No time for fun."

Jed guffawed and shook his head. "Not buyin' it."

"Well, I used to do some rodeo riding. Broncos, mostly."

Jed's eyebrows rose and he nodded slowly as if impressed. "So, you're the real deal, then. A real Alberta cowboy."

"I guess you could say that." Lester smiled and looked down at his jeans. He felt suddenly embarrassed and slapped his hands on his knees before standing up. "I guess we better get back to work. Lunch break must be over by now."

Jed stood also. "I think I might know just the place for a cowboy like yourself to 'ave some fun."

Lester glanced at Jed and, by the look in his eyes, he wasn't sure he wanted to know. "I'm afraid to ask but go ahead and tell me, since you're going to anyway."

Jed leaned back and gestured with both hands at an invisible sign in front of him. "It's called The Urban Cowboy."

"You've got to be kidding."

"No joke."

"Sounds almost too cliché to be true."

"Ah, you laugh now, but it 'as one of those mechanical bulls. A leftover from the eighties or something. Vintage. Might be the only operational one in the city for all I know." Jed straightened and tucked his thumbs in his belt loops. "What do you think of that? Wanna try it out?"

Lester shook his head. "Those things are dangerous."

"Chicken? I thought you said you was a rodeo cowboy."

"I said I used to be. Big difference. I could break my neck. Besides, I've got Patsi to think about."

Jed started making clucking noises and tucked his hands up under his armpits like flapping wings.

Lester frowned. "Although, it might be fun to take a look..."

Jed slapped Lester on the back. "That's the spirit, cowboy."

"I'm not promising I'll ride the thing," Lester said. "So don't hold your breath. I just want to see what kind of machine it is."

"Awesome. Friday at eight."

LESTER LET the truck idle as he waited for Patsi to join him in the parking lot. He'd been thinking about his conversation with Jed the other day - the one where Jed kept bating him about dating. The truth was, he was lonely at times. But long hours on the farm and the weight of his responsibilities had kept him from pursuing anything past 'casual'. Now that Patsi was almost grown up, he just might consider a relationship – with the right woman, of course. It would have to be on his terms and not some random female that Jed picked out for him.

He spotted Patsi coming out of the main building on campus where he'd dropped her off earlier that day. She opened the passenger door with a jerk and then slammed it shut behind her.

"Hey. Everything okay?" Lester asked, surveying her sullen expression.

"Of course."

By the look of her folded arms and scowling face, he'd wager everything was not okay. "You sure about that?"

"I said so, didn't I?" Patsi snapped.

He held up his hands in a sign of surrender. "Okay." When she was ready to tell him, she would. He put the pickup in gear and started driving.

"You're not going to pick me up every day, are you?" Patsi asked.

"Is that what this is about? Me picking you up?" Lester looked over at her, trying to gauge her reaction.

"I feel like a total hillbilly. One of the Clampets."

"Sorry I can't afford a fancy new sports car," Lester shot back, gripping the wheel more tightly.

"I know. Sorry." She turned her head to look out the window.

"I just thought it'd be nice on your first day."

Patsi let out a long, drawn out sigh. "I just feel so… humiliated. Like I don't fit in."

Lester glanced her way again. "Change is always hard. You'll adjust."

Patsi shook her head. "It's not just the change. It's just, well…" She glanced over at him and then lowered her eyes.

"Spit it out," Lester commanded, not unkindly.

Patsi shrugged. "I don't want to hurt your feelings."

"I'm tough. You know that."

"Well, sometimes it's embarrassing. The way you're so cowboy-ish. So country-fied."

Lester let out a short laugh. "This is Calgary. The place is full of cowboys."

"I know." The corners of Patsi's mouth turned up slightly. "But you're the real deal, you know? And sometimes I feel it. Like I don't fit in. I mean, I try to dress normal. How everyone else dresses. To act normal so I just blend in. But then something happens and there I am. Right back where I started. The country bumpkin."

"Something happen?" Lester asked.

Patsi shrugged. "Nothing major. Just one of my Profs. She called on me in class by my full name. It was embarrassing."

Lester frowned. "What's wrong with that? It's your name."

Patsi rolled her eyes. "Who names their kids Lester Ray and Patsi Mae? Seriously. We're like a pair out of a country song."

"It's not so bad. Our parents liked them."

Patsi gazed out the window at the passing traffic. "I wonder what drugs they were on."

"No disrespect," Lester said firmly and shot her a warning glance.

"Sorry." Patsi sighed again. "Then I thought I overheard somebody saying my name after class. Mocking me. I couldn't get out of there fast enough."

"Ah." Lester nodded his head. "So that's why you were so upset when you got in the truck."

Patsi nodded.

"I thought you were calling yourself Pat these days?"

"I am. Except a certain someone," she looked pointedly at Lester, "keeps introducing me as Patsi."

Lester grinned. "Hey, you can't blame what happened today on me. I was nowhere in sight."

"True. It was Professor Chan." Patsi scowled. "She did it twice, even after I corrected her the first time."

"Tough luck, sister."

"Now you're making fun of me."

"If that's the worst of your troubles, I'd say you got it easy."

"Can you just try and remember to call me Pat from now on? Please?" Patsi asked.

He hesitated for a few moments as he concentrated on the road ahead. "Don't know if I can remember to do that. You've always been Patsi. I'm not sure I can change it now."

"Please?" she repeated, drawing out the word for effect.

"Next thing you know you'll be calling me 'Les'." He smiled over at her.

"Could I?" Patsi asked hopefully.

"Not a chance."

"Thanks - Les." Patsi sat back against her seat, a mischievous grin spreading across her face.

JED AND LESTER sat down at one of the high tables, drinks in hand, and waited for their sandwich order. At Jed's suggestion, they were taking their lunch break at The Brew.

"There's Tamara," Jed said. He waved at a strikingly beautiful First Nations woman who had just entered from the back room. She had long flowing hair and large feather earrings. She waved back. Jed leaned a little closer to Lester. "She's the one I was tellin' you about. She lives in our building."

Another woman brought their sandwiches. She was also pretty, with dark chocolate skin and large eyes. She wore a flamboyant, printed top, leggings, and a brightly coloured scarf, which was tied around her tightly curled black hair. Large hoops dangled from her earlobes. "There you go."

"Thanks Carmen," Jed said. "Busy today, eh?"

"You got that right. Both Tamara and I had to come in to help. We're so short staffed right now. Enjoy." She dismissed herself with a wave.

"She's the other owner," Jed informed just above a whisper.

"You're either very snoopy or very friendly. Either way you seem to know a lot about other people's business." Lester bit into his double-decker sandwich made on thick slices of homemade bread and chewed, savouring the first bite. "Mm, this is good."

18

"Told ya," Jed responded.

They were half way through their sandwiches when Tamara Spence joined them. "Sorry I didn't say 'hello' before now. We're pretty busy, as you can see."

"Yeah, Carmen mentioned it." Jed wiped the crumbs from his lip with a napkin. "By the way, this is Lester Tibbett. 'E and his sister just moved into our building."

Tamara turned her gaze to Lester and nodded. "I recognize you, actually, from the day you moved in. My son and his friend were watching from the balcony and I had to come out and get them."

Lester nodded as he swallowed the bite that was in his mouth. "I remember."

"Matonabee can be very curious. That's my son – Matonabee." Tamara paused for a moment. "Is your sister interested in a part time job, by any chance? We're really short staffed right now."

Lester shook his head. "I don't think so. She needs to focus on her studies."

"Let me know. Jed knows my number. I better get back to work." Tamara waved and walked back to the counter where there was another line up waiting.

"So? Either of 'em strike your fancy?" Jed gestured with his head to the counter where both Tamara and Carmen were working. "I know 'em both and could probably set you up."

"I told you before I'm not in the market, so you can stop trying to set me up with every random woman you know."

Jed shrugged a shoulder. "Just like to see my friends 'appy." He took a huge bite of his pastrami sandwich.

Lester couldn't help but grin. Jed was a giant of a man; talkative and a bit rough around the edges. But he had a heart of gold. He probably was genuine in his offer. "No thanks. I prefer to pick my own women. Not that I'm looking," he was quick to add. At least not yet.

LESTER WAS out in the parking lot doing some much needed repair work on his truck. He revved the engine several times, listening out the driver's window. After a few seconds he shut it off, got out of the truck and walked around to the front of the vehicle and looked under the hood.

"Hi."

Lester glanced up and saw the same two boys he had seen on moving day. They were leaning on the rail of a balcony, looking down at him. "Hi," he said and waved back.

"Whatcha doin'?" asked the native boy.

"Fixing my truck. Are you Matonabee?"

"Yeah… how did you know?"

"I met your mom the other day. That's a pretty cool name. Matonabee."

The little boy shrugged. "It's some chief's name or something. This is my friend Jason."

"Hi Jason."

"Hi." The little black boy waved in response.

"Well, I gotta get back to work." Lester raised his hand in salute and then ducked under the hood to make a few adjustments. A few minutes later he stalked back to the cab of the truck and started it up. He revved it a few times, listening intently out the open window.

A minute later Jed sauntered up to the truck. "Need some 'elp?"

"Sure. Could you keep it going while I check under the hood?"

"No problem."

Jed switched places with Lester behind the wheel, and Lester went to the front of the vehicle, leaning in over the motor as Jed roared the engine. Lester was just wiping his hands on a rag when Patsi arrived. "Can you give me a ride to the mall?"

"Are you meeting someone?" Lester asked.

"Are you a cop or something?" She sighed dramatically. "Never mind. I'll take the bus."

"Don't be silly. This'll only take a few minutes." Lester raised his hand in the air. "One more time," he called to Jed.

Patsi leaned again the side of the truck box and crossed her arms.

Jed poked his head out of the cab and turned to Patsi. "Your brother tell you about the job offer at that café downtown?" He spoke louder than normal in order to be heard over the motor.

Patsi frowned and her eyes flashed to where Lester's head was hidden under the hood. "No. What job?"

"Oops. Maybe I wasn't supposed to mention it."

"Lester!" Patsi yelled. "Jed says someone wants to hire me at a café downtown."

Lester bumped his head as he stood up and grimaced. He pushed the ball cap he was wearing toward the back of his head and made a 'cut' signal with his other hand. Jed let off the gas.

"Why didn't you tell me about the job at the café?" Patsi demanded.

Lester slammed the hood down into place, and narrowed his eyes at Jed. Then he swung his gaze back to his sister. "It's nothing. The owner of this coffee shop happened to mention they needed more waitresses. But I knew you'd want to focus on school, at least until you get into the groove."

Patsi put her hands on her hips. "When are you going to quit trying to run my life?"

"I'm not trying to run your life. I'm just trying to make the transition easier for you."

"I never asked you to make my life easier. What's wrong with me getting a part time job?"

Lester tossed the greasy rag he had just wiped his hands on into the cab of the truck through the open window. "For one thing, that café is downtown. Who's going to drive you to and from work?"

"I'll take the bus."

"What about late at night? That's not safe."

"Sorry man." Jed raised both hands in apology. "I guess I should have kept my mouth shut. Last thing I want is to get in the middle of a family fight."

"We're not having a family fight," Lester said.

"Yes we are," Patsi countered.

"If you really want to make some extra money why not do something closer to home? Like babysit?" Lester suggested.

Patsi rolled her eyes. "Great. Who do you suggest I babysit for? I don't know any kids."

Lester turned and looked up at the balcony where Matonabee and Jason still stood watching. He waved. "Hey boys. Either of you ever need a babysitter?" They both shrugged. "My sister here is a real good sitter. Tell your moms."

A dark skinned woman appeared on the balcony and scanned the ground below until her eyes pinned Lester.

"Hi," Lester called. "I was just telling the boys my sister here is a real good sitter if you ever need one."

"Thanks," the woman called before ushering the boys into the apartment.

"And that was Goldie. Jason's mom," Jed said under his breath. He rubbed his hands together. "Did I tell you she's also single?"

Lester let out a frustrated breath. "I'm not interested. Quit trying to set me up."

"Maybe you should let him," Patsi put in. "Then you wouldn't be so uptight all the time."

"She might be onto somethin'." Jed grinned and clapped a hand on Lester's shoulder. "In any case, good luck with your discussion. I gotta go."

LESTER GOT out of the taxi as Jed shoved some bills at the cabby. It was Friday night, and as promised, they were heading for The Urban Cowboy to check out the mechanical bull. "Thanks!" Jed said with a wave as the cab driver drove off.

Jed had insisted on taking a cab 'just in case' even though Lester had tried to assure him that he wasn't going to be over indulging. "I hardly drink. I'd rather take my truck."

"The parking is terrible downtown," Jed had said. "Besides, better safe than sorry I always say."

Lester hadn't liked leaving Patsi alone, but as Jed also pointed out, she wasn't a baby.

They approached the neon sign that said 'The Urban Cowboy' in scrawling '70s script and Jed opened the door. A blast of country music met their ears.

"This way." Jed waved for Lester to follow. The interior was like a flashback to the seventies. Neon and wood paneling; large framed posters of cowboys in designer jeans. Lester shook his head as he passed. Those models had probably never seen a real horse, let alone a bull. Jed led the way to a long bar that took up one whole wall. Mirrored glass behind made the place look larger than it really was. They perched on two stools and Jed ordered two beers.

"What if I didn't want beer?" Lester asked.

"They're both for me," Jed said with a grin.

Lester laughed out loud and ordered his own beer from the bartender.

"Eh, Jacques," Jed called to one of the bartenders further down the line. "Come over 'ere a sec."

A tall and lanky fellow approached. His dark blonde hair was slicked back into a ponytail and he sported a goatee and moustache.

"This is Jacques," Jed introduced. "Lives in our building, too. Lester and 'is sister just moved in."

"Pleased to meet you." Jacques had a distinct Francophone accent. "I believe I heard the ruckus on moving day." He smiled congenially and Lester couldn't tell if he was miffed, teasing, or serious.

"Sorry about that," Lester apologized.

"It is nothing. I sleep late, that is all."

"Jacques 'ere is from Quebec, but I don't 'old that against 'im," Jed confided in a staged whisper. "Not to mention he's the best barkeep around. Can make anything. Can't you, Jacques? Go ahead. Ask 'im anything and 'e'll know 'ow to make it."

"I'll just have my beer thanks," Lester said.

Jacques bowed his exit and went to serve another customer.

"So? Where is this mechanical bull you were telling me about?" Lester asked.

"Around the corner in back." Jed gestured in that general direction with his lofted beer bottle.

23

"So there's more to this place than meets the eye," Lester said with a nod.

"Exactly. Pool tables, some retro arcade games, and the mechanical bull, of course."

"Of course."

"The place isn't actually that old. They just decorated it this way to make it fit with the name. We'll check it out after I finish this beer." Jed downed the contents of the bottle and let out a satisfied burp.

"Nice," Lester observed with a raised brow.

Jed just grinned. "Thanks. Wanna share some garlic ribs? Maybe some Buffalo Wings? This place 'as great appies."

"No thanks. I ate at home. Barbecued burgers."

"And you didn't invite me?" Jed grinned widely. He glanced around and then elbowed Lester in the ribs. "Check out the hotties that just walked in."

Lester frowned. He didn't like some of the slang used to describe women, but he did glance in the direction Jed pointed. The girls he was referring to were indeed attractive, but they knew it, too. Typical oil-town girls looking to flaunt themselves and get a few free drinks, as far as he could tell. Too much makeup and clothing that was too tight and too short. He turned back and faced the mirror behind the bar.

"I'm gonna talk to 'em. You comin'?" Jed asked.

"Thought you were hungry."

"Not anymore. Come on." Jed gestured with his head toward the girls.

"Not my type. You go ahead." Lester took a sip of his beer.

"Suit yourself. You may end up taking a cab alone, if you get my drift." Jed winked and stood up.

Lester watched Jed's retreating figure in the mirror and shook his head, a slight smile on his lips. His gaze shifted and caught another pair of eyes watching him in the reflective surface. She was sitting just two stools down from him. As soon as she realized he'd noticed her watching him, hers dropped downward. Lester turned his head to take a closer look at the real thing and when their eyes met again, this time without the mirror as a go between, he nodded and smiled.

Here was a woman who wasn't trying too hard. She was pretty, yes, but in an understated yet exotic way. Her distinctly Asian features were petite and perfectly formed with a small, straight nose and compact lips. Her eyes were slanted upward; luminous and dark, and her hair, which hung to her shoulders, was jet black, shiny and straight.

"Sorry about my friend," Lester said as an opener.

Her perfectly arched brows raised a notch. "Why should you be sorry? You can't control the behaviour of others."

"True." He smiled again. "I'm Lester, by the way."

"Hello, Lester."

He glanced at the empty counter in front of her. "Can I buy you a drink?"

"No thank you."

Lester blinked, not quite sure where to go from here. "Oh. Okay. Um, you come here often?"

"Not really." She didn't exactly smile, but he thought he saw the corner of her mouth twitch just a bit.

"I see." He twisted the bottle in front of him and focused on the wall ahead. Big mistake. She was looking at him in the mirror again with that same mixture of interested aloofness.

"I'm meeting someone," she said to the mirror.

"Ah." His head bobbed up and down. "Right." There didn't seem much else to say. He downed the rest of his beer and set the empty bottle on the counter with a decisive clunk. "Well, nice to meet you, uh... what was your name again?"

"I never said," she replied.

He laughed and shook his head. "Right again. I guess I better quit while I'm ahead. I hear there's a mechanical bull in this place with my name on it, so I guess I better go check it out."

Her composed mask slipped just a bit. "Really? I didn't know that."

"So my friend tells me." Lester gestured with a nod to the table where Jed was sitting, an arm around each girl.

The pretty Asian girl beside him shivered. "I'd be too afraid to try something like that. Isn't it dangerous?"

Lester sat up a little straighter. "A mechanical bull? It could be, I suppose, if you don't know what you're doing. You might pull a muscle or two. Now riding a real animal, that's a whole different story."

"And you have?" she asked.

He nodded. "Broncos, mostly."

"So you're a rodeo man." It was more a statement that a question.

"Not so much anymore. I got hurt a couple years back and decided it wasn't worth it."

"Yet you're still going to ride the mechanical bull? That doesn't make sense."

Lester could see the disapproval in her face and didn't quite know why it mattered. He just shrugged. "I haven't decided yet."

He saw a well put together Asian man approaching in the mirror, and apparently, so did she. "My name is Sherri, by the way," she said quickly. "Sherri Chan."

Before Lester could respond, the other man was behind her, placing a familiar hand on her shoulder. She smiled up at him and he kissed her on the cheek. Lester swung off the stool without looking back and headed toward the games area of the club, or at least where he thought the games area would be.

Sure enough, just around the corner from the main bar, the establishment opened up into a much wider, larger room. At least six pool tables took centre stage, with blinking arcade games straight from the eighties lining the circumference. At the far end, roped off and with plenty of room for viewing on three sides, was a mechanical bull. A padded floor ensured soft landings.

Lester strode straight to the roped off area and leaned on one of the padded posts. He hadn't seen anything like it since he was a teen. There had been one set up as an exhibition ride at a rodeo he'd gone to once, and he'd tried it out then, just for fun. If memory served, it was a piece of cake to ride once you watched its rhythm for a bit. Not like a real animal whose whim dictated the strength of each thrust and twist.

"Would you like to try it?" a male voice asked from behind him.

Lester turned to see a young black man smiling at him. Lester's brows rose slightly. The man had dreadlocks and a definite 'gangster' vibe. Not the kind of person he'd expected to see in a place with such country flair.

"Um, not sure. I was just admiring it for now. Definitely brings back memories."

"You ever ride one of these things?"

"A few times." Lester smiled.

The man stroked his chin and nodded. "I bet you go for the real thing. A real rodeo cowboy."

Lester just shrugged, but he couldn't help smiling.

The other man stretched out his hand. "Cory Roberts. I'm part owner of this joint."

Lester's eyebrows rose for real this time as he took the other man's proffered hand. "Pleased to meet you. Lester Tibbett."

"I know what you're thinking." Cory's eyes twinkled. "What's a brother like me doin' in a place like this? The answer? I'm a closet cowboy. Don't let the looks fool you."

"I see."

"So? You ready to take it for a spin? My partners said I was crazy when I installed it, but maybe if we could get someone to show us how it's done, more people would start using it. First ride's on me."

Lester thought about it for a moment, and then nodded. "Let's do it."

Lester climbed over the ropes followed by Cory, who then proceeded to show him how to mount and where the hand straps were located. Lester already knew, but figured the other man needed to go over it for insurance purposes. "I'll keep the speed down for this first one," Cory said. "Once people hear it, they'll come running."

"Great." The word got whisked away when the bull jumped into action. Lester felt his head whip back and he tightened his knees. He'd almost forgotten how it felt to ride a bucking bronco, or in this case, a mechanical bull, and he tumbled to the mats after only three seconds.

He stood up, only slightly winded, and brushed at his jeans. Of course, there was no dirt or debris on them, but it was a habit that had come rushing back instinctively. "Again," he said.

About ten people had already gathered around the perimeter of the ropes. Lester ignored them and mounted the bull with one fluid jump. Now that he'd had a taste, the rush of bronco riding had come flooding back and he was determined to conquer the thing.

The whine and grind of the bull started up again and this time he was ready. He secured the reins tightly around his one hand and allowed the rest of his body to settle into the jolting rhythm that was rodeo riding. Stay loose, let your body become one with the animal. That was the secret to not getting bucked off.

He raised his free thumb and Cory increased the speed. This was a piece of cake. He could do this all day. Somewhere in the recesses of his mind he was aware of a loud Newfoundland brogue cheering him on. Jed. He grinned and gave him the thumbs up.

The hand signal was also the sign for Cory to increase the speed again, which he did. Then Lester saw her, pushed right up against the ropes. Sherri Chan, she'd said.

The momentary distraction caused him to lose his centre of balance. Two more jolts and he was catapulting from the bull's back, his head thumping on something on the way down.

Then the buzzing room became a hazy grey of softness.

EPISODE 2

STUCK IN THE NEIGHBOURHOOD

*F*amily dinner. It was a Chan tradition that took place around eight pm every Sunday at the Fortune Cookie Restaurant. The restaurant was one of two Chan family businesses that were as much a part of Sherri Chan's heritage as Chinese New Year. She, her twin brother Sherman, and her three cousins had worked, eaten their meals, and done their homework at the 'Fortune Cookie'. In many ways, it was more home than the apartment her parents still kept over their convenience store.

Sherri entered the dim interior of the restaurant through the glass front door. The décor was the same as it had been for the past thirty years. Red velvet, gold braid, Chinese lanterns, and pictures of pagodas decorated the wood panelled walls. She'd suggested an update on more than one occasion, but the older generation wasn't in favour. Even her brother Sherman, an architect, couldn't convince them. They didn't adapt well to change.

She spotted Uncle Dave behind the counter reading a Chinese newspaper. He seemed content at his post and didn't notice her entrance. Sherri strode in his direction, stopped at the counter and tapped the paper with one finger. "Hi, Uncle Dave."

Dave jerked his head up and nodded silently. He was a man of few words; gentle in his mannerisms. He only spoke when absolutely necessary.

"I'm just going to head to the kitchen and see if I can help." Sherri gestured with her head in the direction of two double doors near the back of the restaurant.

He nodded again and then went back to his paper. Dave was a confirmed bachelor, brother to Sherri's father, Joseph. There were the three original Chan 'boys' – Joseph, Dave, and their youngest brother Ed. Together, they ran the family businesses. Sherri's parents, Joseph and Lani, spent most of their time at the convenience store. Dave, Ed, and Ed's wife Joanne, were responsible for the restaurant. Of course, all the offspring had jobs at one establishment or the other – a ready-made labor force that tended to be fairly fluid.

On her way to the kitchen Sherri waved at her youngest cousin Lily, a petite girl of 18 who was bustling by with a tray of steaming food. The place closed early on Sunday nights, but someone still had to work until the last customers took their leave. There was only one table of six left.

Sherri's grandmother sat in her usual spot at the table right beside the kitchen doors, folding napkins. She was tiny and frail, her skin a wrinkled parchment hung on high cheekbones. Despite her age, she insisted on doing something useful to contribute to the family business. Sherri bent to kiss her on the cheek. "Hello Nai-Nai."

Grandmother smiled and nodded, her grin toothless.

"I'm just going to see if they need help in the kitchen."

Keeping with the rule to always enter on the right side of the swinging doors, Sherri pushed her way through into the clatter of pots of pans. "Hi Uncle Ed, Auntie Jo. Need any help?"

Ed shook his head. Aunt Joanne offered a huge smile. "Sherri! So good to see you."

"Let me take those plates for you," Sherri offered, walking over to her aunt. "Are we eating in the main restaurant or the private dining room tonight?"

"Dining room," Joanne replied. When Sherri tried to take the plates, Joanne resisted. "No, no! I can do it. You go sit with Nai-Nai."

Sherri frowned and looked around the kitchen. "Where is everyone else?"

"Never mind! You go keep Grandmother company until I say."

Something was up. "Okay."

Sherri exited through the 'out' door and slid into a seat beside her grandmother. She grabbed a few napkins and started to fold. A few minutes later, her mother, Lani Chan, appeared, coming from the private dining room.

"Hey, Mom." Sherri waved between folding motions. "Auntie Jo won't let me go into the dining room. What's up?"

Her mother ignored her. "Thank goodness for Sunday night. Otherwise I would never see you no more. So busy! Too busy to visit your own mother, huh?" She smiled as she said it. As if on automatic pilot, she started refolding the pile of napkins that Grandmother had already done.

"I'm sorry, Mom," Sherri offered. "You know how it is."

"Sorry? Sorry! Me, I only have two children! And they never visit. Too busy. Always too busy. And no grandchildren! Who will look after me when I am old? Huh? Tell me that?"

Sherri sighed. "Please, not this again. I really am busy. I have classes to prepare. Marking to do."

"Too busy." Lani shook her head. "Too busy to get married. How much longer you think Clarke will wait? How am I ever going to have grandchildren? You almost too old. Thirty! Too much longer and he won't want you. Then no grandchildren!"

Sherri frowned. "That isn't fair, Mom. Clarke isn't ready to settle down yet, either."

"Clarke is a good boy. What does his mother say?"

"We're adults, Mom. What Clarke and I decide to do is not his mother's business, just like it's not yours. Goodness!"

"Of course it is my business. That's what mothers do. At least he is a good Chinese boy."

Sherri focused on the folding. "Now you're being racist."

"The sooner you marry Clarke Ling the better. Then we have grandchildren."

Sherri clamped her mouth shut. There was no point arguing with her mother. She and her brother had been drilled since childhood about the merits of a good education, but now that Sherri was the youngest professor on staff at the university, all her mother cared about was grandchildren.

"Why you being so quiet?" Lani asked.

Sherri invoked her most cool and controlled voice. "Please don't talk like this in front of Clarke."

Lani's eyes widened and a smile spread across her face. "Clarke is coming for family dinner? That is good!"

"Mom!" Sherri rolled her eyes. "It's not like this is the first time he's come for family dinner. And when he gets here, no more talk of babies. You know how shy he is."

Grandmother said something in Mandarin which Sherri didn't catch. She raised her eyebrows inquisitively at her mother.

"She says soon it will be too late for babies."

Sherri laughed and patted Grandmother's tiny, arthritically twisted hand. "Don't be silly. Thirty is not too late for babies. These days, most people are having children later."

"Not good." Lani shook her head. "Too dangerous. I know."

"Momma," Sherri said gently. "Just because you and Pops had some bad luck in that department, doesn't mean that I will. And there's still Sherman. I don't hear you bothering him to get married."

Lani shook her head. "Your brother. He is even more stubborn than you. He tells me nothing. Off living in Toronto. I don't even know if he has girlfriend or not!"

The front door opened again, and Clarke stepped over the threshold. Clarke Ling was just the kind of catch Sherri's parents had been hoping for. Smart and hardworking, he was also handsome. He was about five foot ten with a slim build and was wearing a tailored grey suit, white shirt, and a tie – the typical uniform for an up and coming corporate lawyer. They had been together for two years now. It was a comfortable relationship, if not full of fire. It was enough. Until recently.

Sherri gave her mother one last warning look, and excused herself from the table.

Uncle Dave made it to the front door first, however, and locked it behind Clarke before switching off the 'Open' sign.

"Hello." Sherri and Clarke exchanged a peck on the lips before they retraced her steps to where mother and Nai-Nai sat folding napkins.

Clarke bowed at the waist. "Hello Mrs. Chan. Grandmother."

"Clarke!" Lani smiled widely. "Finally you come to dinner. You will have to get used to Sunday dinner if you are to be part of the family."

"Momma!" Sherri scolded under her breath.

Lani waved a dismissive hand and stood up. "We will go to the dining room now." She switched to Chinese. "Those slow customers are finally finished eating. They will be leaving soon. Come now. Our surprise has been waiting long enough."

"Let me help you up, Nai-Nai," Clarke said in perfect Chinese to the elder Chan. "I will escort my two favourite ladies to the dining room."

With Clarke's assistance and much effort, Grandmother got to her feet. Sherri and Clarke flanked her as they made their way in small, shuffling steps to the dining room doors. "I suppose I'm the only one out of the loop?" Sherri gave him a sidelong glance.

Clarke flashed a smile. "My lips are sealed."

"Oh. So that's how it is." She smiled.

After what seemed like an eternity, they reached the red cushioned double doors that led into the fine dining area reserved for large groups. Clarke released Grandmother's arm and held the right door open so that Sherri could escort Nai-Nai into the dimly lit interior. She was so intent on making sure her grandmother didn't stumble that she didn't look up until someone cleared his throat.

"Hey, Sis."

Sherri's eyes flew to the voice. "Sherman!"

Sherri's twin brother Sherman bolted forward to take Grandmother's other arm, laughing all the way. "Surprised?"

"Are you kidding? I had no idea! What are you doing here? When did you get in?" She stopped and turned to Clarke. "You knew?"

Clarke nodded his head. "I had orders from the top not to tell." Clarke pulled out one of the dining room chairs and Sherri and Sherman maneuvered Nai-Nai into it.

Lani wasn't far behind. "See? What a surprise!" She set a platter on the table and scurried back toward the kitchen.

"Come here. I haven't had my hug yet." Sherman enfolded his sister in a bear hug. They rocked back and forth for a few moments.

Sherri pulled away and looked at him. Her brother was slightly taller than Clarke and broader across the shoulders. His hair was short but stylish and the latest trend in glasses was perched on his nose. Trust her brother to look great – relaxed, fit and fashionable. "You didn't answer any of my questions yet," she said.

"I have to have a reason to visit?" Sherman asked.

"Toronto isn't exactly down the block."

"Remember the project I was telling you about? The high rise going up downtown? I'll be back and forth quite a bit checking on the progress," Sherman explained.

"Whatever it is, I'm glad you're here." Sherri gave him another squeeze around the middle.

The rest of the family was beginning to file into the dining room, laden with various serving dishes. There was Uncle Ed and Joanne, their children Lily, Rod, and George, Uncle Dave, and bringing up the rear, Sherri and Sherman's father, Joseph, who was pushing a cart.

Soon they were absorbed with the food. The meal was traditional Chinese fare, not the kind that was passed off as Chinese food in the restaurant. There was much to talk about and everyone, it seemed, was talking at once in both English and Chinese.

Sherri was most interested in catching up with her brother. They had always been close, but lately it seemed that their busy careers kept them from talking as much as they used to.

"I just can't believe you didn't tell me you were coming," Sherri said for the tenth time. She gave Sherman a playful swat. She was sitting in between him and Clarke. "I wasn't expecting you until next week."

"Thought it would be a nice surprise." He popped another morsel into his mouth with his chopsticks.

"Speaking of surprises." Clarke cleared his throat and then said in a loud voice, "Can I get everyone's attention, please?"

The din of voices and cutlery diminished until the room was eerily quiet.

"Clarke?" Sherri turned to look at him. Her body felt suddenly stiff.

"Yes. Well. I thought this would be a good time, with all your family here and everything…" He cleared his throat again. "Sherri." He stopped and pushed his chair out.

With the precision of a slow motion replay, Sherri watched as Clarke stood and then got down on one knee. Apprehension was crawling up her spine, but her mind had frozen. She realized she was holding her breath but somehow it was impossible to start breathing again.

"Sherri." Clarke's voice penetrated through the fog that had infiltrated her brain. "Will you marry me?"

Sherri's eyes swept the table. Expectant faces peered at her, their mouths open. Her mother was grinning like a fool, her hands clasped dramatically under her chin. Sherri turned back to Clarke and blinked. "Yes," she heard herself say.

Suddenly real time kicked in again. The family struck up their usual cacophony of Chinese and English. Clarke was hugging her and she was hugging him back. She found herself on her feet, moving from embrace to embrace in a receiving line of laughter and well wishes. Her mother was crying outright, making no attempt whatsoever to hide her joy.

A sickening wave rolled upward from her stomach. Of course she'd said yes. What choice did she have?

SHERRI STOOD on the other side of the panelled door and took a steadying breath. She was on the verge of a panic attack, but having an emotional outburst in front of her students was simply out of the question.

She was still reeling from last night's events. Marriage was the next logical step in her relationship with Clarke. She didn't believe in living together first. It went against her family's traditional Chinese ways as well as her own beliefs as a Christian. She should be happy. Then why did she feel as if her life was ending?

Because she didn't love Clarke.

Not that she knew definitively what love was supposed to feel like. She was comfortable with Clarke, and for all she knew, it could be love. But lately she'd been having fantasies about cowboys. Well, one certain cowboy, to be exact. Ever since she'd run into a handsome man at Sherman's friend's nightclub. That didn't sound like something a person in love would do.

The man in question had been hurt while riding some ridiculous mechanical rodeo machine. Her heart had jumped right into her throat. He'd knocked himself out for a few seconds, but came to and went home in the charge of his rather raucous friend. She'd wanted to rush to his side, but of course that wasn't possible. She hardly knew him and Clarke had been right there. It was the first time she'd measured Clarke up to someone else and found him lacking.

She shook her head to clear the mental images of the rugged cowboy with his curling brown hair and twinkling eyes. "You can do this," she whispered under her breath, adjusting her chin to a higher tilt as she straightened her shoulders. After all, she was a professional. As the youngest professor among an old boys' club, she had proven her mettle, despite three strikes against her. She was young, a female, and Asian. She had never run from a challenge and she wasn't about to start, even if that challenge was getting past her own errant emotions.

With one last intake of air, Sherri opened the door that led out onto the lecture platform. Rising in front of her were rows of students, all seated at inadequately small desks whose tops folded out of the way for easy access to their attached seats. Her heels clicked on the wooden flooring and she set her briefcase on top of a long table.

As the murmur of voices gradually faded, the snap of her briefcase latch sounded ostentatiously loud.

Sherri straightened the hem of her grey blazer and smoothed her hands over the matching pencil skirt. She scanned the room and cleared her throat. "Hopefully you've completed the problems from our last session. I expect all assignments to be handed in electronically and on time. However, I'm not your babysitter. Choosing to pass this course is completely up to you. Today we're reviewing quadratic equations."

She opened her laptop, and then picked up the remote that controlled the 'Smartboard' hanging behind the podium. With a few deft clicks she was able to access the day's lesson.

As soon as the familiar numbers and symbols appeared, she felt herself relax. She loved the logical nature of mathematics. It was so much easier to manage than personal relationships. There were no surprises and certainly no need for subjectivity. The answers were right or wrong. Just the way she liked it.

Several minutes into the lesson, Sherri stopped. She turned away from the Smartboard to peruse the crowd. "Is there anyone who can tell me what step we take next?" Her gaze swept the faces, most of which now had a glazed look about the eyes. There were no volunteers.

She ran her index finger down the printout of registered students, looking for someone she hadn't asked yet. She noted her own printing beside one name where she had stroked out 'Patsi Mae' and wrote 'Pat' instead. She couldn't blame the girl. After a few more seconds of scanning the paper, she lifted her gaze. "Joshua Bordeaux?"

There was a shuffling noise near the back of the room as the student adjusted himself in his seat. "I... uh, I'm sorry. I don't know."

Sherri pursed her lips and expelled a lengthy breath from her nostrils. "Well, I see we'll need to pay closer attention if we hope to pass the course."

It sounded snarky, even to her ears. Too bad. She wasn't here to make friends with the students.

∾

SHERRI and her brother Sherman sat at the small table, sipping lattes. The Brew, a trendy downtown café, was near the site of Sherman's latest building project. It offered a wide variety of coffees and teas as well as specialty drinks, sandwiches, Panini's and homemade soups. They sat at a high table near the window. Sherman set his mug down and scrutinized his sister. "You alright?"

Sherri flipped a few strands of her straight, black hair behind her shoulder. "Of course. Why wouldn't I be?"

Sherman shrugged. "Seems like you're not as excited as I'd expect from somebody who just got engaged."

"Of course I'm excited." Sherri set her teacup down with a clatter.

"You sure?"

"Clarke and I have a lot in common. Everyone is very happy for us."

"The perfect match," Sherman said, his voice laced with just a hint of sarcasm.

"Exactly." Sherri sat up straighter. "We share the same culture. There will be no issues of him fitting in with the family. Besides, Mom is over the moon."

Sherman let out a small laugh. "She'll be expecting babies soon. Watch out."

"Hopefully the wedding will keep her occupied for a while." Sherri turned the cup around in its saucer, aligning the pattern on the handle with the pattern on the rim of the plate.

"I'm glad it's you and not me," Sherman said.

"Your turn is coming. Once she gets me married off she'll be turning all her attention on you."

"Thanks for the warning." Sherman laughed.

Sherri cocked her head to one side. "Which reminds me… anyone special that I should know about?"

"Don't start."

"You're my twin. I'm entitled."

Just then a pretty waitress swept by their table, holding a tray laden with dirty mugs and other dishes. "Can I get anything else for you two?" she asked, pausing for a moment. The woman was in her mid to late twenties, had a dark chocolaty complexion and very short curly hair that grew close to her head. She was wearing some kind of flowing, brightly printed top with a definite African flair and had large earrings that swung when she moved her head. Her bright red lips parted in a friendly smile, showing perfect white teeth that were in stark contrast to her dark skin.

"No thanks," Sherri responded. She looked over at her brother.

"Um… I'm good as well," he said.

Sherri raised a brow as she watched her brother following the waitress with his eyes. "Just as well you don't have a current girlfriend. She wouldn't be pleased with the way you're staring at the waitress."

"I wasn't staring." Sherman straightened his shoulders and angled his body away from the woman. "Anyway, back to Mom and Dad. I was thinking I'd like to build them a new house. They've worked too long and hard to be stuck living above the convenience store. What do you think?"

"I think you'll have a hard time convincing them to move," Sherri said.

"It's the least I can do, after all they've done for me."

"They won't go for it and you know it."

"I could say I'm building it for myself and I need someone to live in it for a while until I move back to Calgary," Sherman said.

Sherri laughed. "No use lying to them. You're not moving back to Calgary."

Sherman shrugged. "How do you know?"

Sherri stared at her twin. "You're serious? You might be moving back?"

Sherman toyed with his mug. "It was just a thought. I fly all over the place as it is, so it would be just as easy to make this my home base as Toronto."

She scrutinized him with a smile. "I'm all for it. Mom and Dad could turn all their attention on you for a change. Then I won't be the only one whose life they try to control."

"You mean you wouldn't be happy to see more of me?" Sherman leaned forward with a twinkle in his eye.

"Of course, that, too."

"Building a house for them is actually a brilliant idea, if I do say so. Nai-Nai is getting too old for them to look after properly. She can hardly maneuver those stairs anymore. You should have seen her today when I was there for a visit. The new house would be all on ground level."

Sherri nodded. "That might convince them. I've been noticing that myself. About Nai-Nai, I mean."

Sherman rubbed his hands. "The more I think about it the more I like it."

"You're crazy," Sherri said with a laugh.

"We should go out and celebrate tonight. What do you think?"

"Celebrate?" Sherri frowned. "You've only just thought about building them a house and now you want to celebrate?"

Sherman rolled his eyes. "While that is a good reason, I meant we should celebrate your engagement. Have you been to The Urban Cowboy yet? Cory Roberts is part owner."

"I was there last week, as a matter of fact. Cory didn't tell you?"

Sherman shook his head. "I haven't had much chance to talk to him this time around." Cory Roberts and Sherman were long-time friends.

"Maybe with all the other excitement he didn't think to tell you I was there. With Clarke, of course," she added.

"What excitement?" Sherman asked.

Sherri shrugged and traced the pattern on the tabletop with her finger. "Some guy fell off the mechanical bull and got knocked out."

Sherman's eyes widened. "That can't be good for business."

Sherri shrugged. "He seemed okay after. Anyway, I'll have to pass. It's a school night."

"Come on," Sherman coaxed. "I'm not in town that often. Indulge me for a change."

"That doesn't change the fact that it's a school night."

Sherman turned to the waitress and spoke loud enough for her to hear from where she was clearing a table not far away. "Can you try and convince her that it's okay to go out on a school night? Especially if it's a special celebration?"

The woman ceased wiping and stood up with a smile. "That depends. What's the occasion?"

"An engagement," Sherman said.

She nodded at both of them. "Congratulations."

"Not us," Sherman was quick to correct. "This is my sister. She's the one who got engaged."

The waitress looked at Sherri. "Oh. Well, congrats to you then."

"So? You going to help me convince her or what?"

The waitress sauntered to their table, rag in hand. "I'd say that is a good excuse, even on a work night."

Sherri cut in. "We already had a big family dinner. He just wants an excuse to go out before he has to go back home."

"You're not from Calgary?" the other woman asked, directing her large chocolate eyes at Sherman.

"I live in Toronto, but I'm originally from here. I'm thinking about moving back though. Sherman Chan, by the way." He stuck his hand out and she shook it. "And this is my sister Sherri."

"Carmen Lamont. The Urban Cowboy is definitely a good choice." She smiled sheepishly and her gaze flickered down to her toes for a second. "I was eavesdropping."

"You should join us," Sherman suggested.

Carmen's eyes widened when she looked up. "Oh. Well, thank you. Maybe I will." She fumbled with the dishcloth. "Well, I better get back to work. Nice to meet you." She waved before turning to walk away.

"You're doing it again," Sherri whispered once Carmen was out of earshot.

"Hm?" Sherman turned an absent gaze toward his sister.

"Staring at her."

"Was not." He straightened and downed the rest of his now cold coffee.

❧

SHERRI SCANNED the dim interior of the club for Sherman. She and
Clarke didn't frequent bars as a rule, yet they'd been to The Urban
Cowboy twice in less than two weeks. If it weren't for the fact that she
wanted to spend more time with Sherman before he headed back to
Toronto, she would have insisted on staying home.

Actually, she missed her twin more than she would ever let on to
anyone – even Clarke. The mythology that twins had some kind of
secret bond wasn't far from the truth. Sometimes she woke up in the
night thinking about him. She hoped he really did decide to move
back to Calgary.

The place was packed for a weeknight. There was a country tune
playing in the background - just audible over the din of multiple
conversations. A long well-polished bar with a black granite top ran
the length of the room.

Clarke stood behind her, his hand on the small of her back. She
was dressed in jeans and a sweater, but Clarke was still wearing a suit
and tie, like he'd come straight from the office. His uptown look had
appealed to her once. Now she found it stuffy.

Sherri spotted Sherman when she saw him wave and she and
Clarke headed toward the small table where he sat with his long-time
friends Cory Roberts and Steve Russell. They used to call themselves
the United Nations, since Sherman was Asian, Cory was African
Canadian, and Steve was Caucasian. Cory was sporting a head full of
dreadlocks these days, which hardly seemed the best image for the
owner of a country bar. Still, Cory had never been one to follow the
status quo. He was a bit of a maverick and standing out in a crowd
was what he did best.

"Hey, Sis. Clarke. I was beginning to think you weren't going to
show."

"Sorry," Clarke apologized. "I had to work a bit later than
expected."

"Good to see you two again," Cory greeted both Clarke and Sherri
with a knuckle punch.

"Hi, kids," Steve Russell said with a wave. Steve was good looking
in his own way, with brown wavy hair and blue eyes. He was a news-

paper journalist, and was always on the lookout for a story. The fact that he was still wearing his suit, minus the tie, made Sherri feel less critical of Clarke's attire.

They sat down with the group and Cory lifted a hand to signal one of the waitresses to come their way. "Sherman tells me we're celebrating tonight. What'll it be? It's on the house."

"Oh, I think I'll just have a ginger ale," Sherri said.

Cory screwed up his face. "What? That's no way to celebrate. You gotta have something stronger than that. On me."

Sherri sighed. "Okay. Just one. But I don't drink much, so I really don't know what to order."

"One of those fancy, girlie drinks," Sherman suggested.

Cory laughed. "One fancy, girlie drink coming up." When the waitress came by, Cory ordered for the whole bunch.

A few minutes later, Sherri found a rather large stemmed glass in front of her. "My goodness. This is rather large." The contents were quite pretty – ruby red liquid at the bottom of the hurricane glass gradually blended into orange, like a beautiful sunset. It was topped with a slice of orange on the rim and a maraschino cherry.

"Here's to the happy couple," Steve said and they all clinked glasses.

Sherri forced a smile and kept her eyes fixed on the contents of the glass. When she took a sip it was surprisingly delicious. She'd never cared much for the taste of alcohol, and she certainly didn't believe in getting drunk and losing control of her senses. Still, this cocktail was quite good.

Clarke smiled and took a sip of his drink. "Thanks everyone. I'm just glad she said yes." He put his arm around Sherri's shoulders and squeezed her against his side. Sherri smiled dutifully and took another long drag from her straw.

As THE EVENING WORE ON, Sherri found another drink in front of her and then another. She couldn't quite remember how many, but it didn't really matter. She was having fun. Felt relaxed. In fact, she wasn't sure why she'd been so tense before. Clarke was a good guy. The perfect guy.

At least her family thought so.

She smiled as she watched Sherman and Clarke talking animatedly about Sherman's latest project. What was love anyway, other than a choice to commit to someone? Clarke would be a loyal companion and they would be very happy together.

The crack of pool balls from the nearest table made her jump. She squinted in an attempt to focus. A couple of redneck types were just starting a game. One wore a ball cap, the other a cowboy hat, but they both sported checked shirts and jeans. She smiled despite herself. Even with the nondescript clothing she couldn't help but notice the broad shoulders and bulging biceps. They exuded a raw male virility that she suddenly found appealing. Not that Clarke wasn't good looking. He kept his body in great physical condition. But these men were untamed. Rough.

"What do you think about that?" Clarke broke into her thoughts.

Sherri blinked back to her companions. She hadn't heard a word. "What?"

"I said, what do you think of investing in that new town-home development in the south?"

Sherri frowned, not sure what he was talking about. "Um, what?"

Clarke sighed. "Sherman says it's bound to increase in value. We could go in as partners."

He placed his hand on top of hers and she stared at it for a few seconds.

"I'm thinking of investing myself," Sherman said. "I'd like you to take a look at it, though, Sis. You're smart when it comes to crunching the numbers. What do you think?"

"I think..." Sherri hesitated and then looked up at both men with a grin. "I think I want to play pool."

Sherman laughed. "I think you've had a few too many. When's the last time you went out drinking?"

"She really doesn't drink much," Clarke offered.

Sherri frowned. "How would you know? You don't own me." She giggled.

Clarke's eyes widened.

"I don't care much for pool," Sherman interjected. "You always beat me cause you know all the mathematical angles and such."

"Scared?" Sherri asked.

"Never."

"Okay then. You're on." She stood on wobbly legs and straightened her sweater. With deliberate movements she turned and sauntered to the nearest pool table. She slapped a bill on the table's edge. "I'd like to use this table, please." She'd seen that in a movie once. Or at least she thought she had, minus the 'please'.

"Don't ya know the rules?" The man with the ball cap had a distinct Newfoundland accent, much like an Irish brogue. "Ya gotta play the winner for it."

Sherri blinked. "Is that so? Okay." She smiled.

She watched as the man who spoke took his next shot and missed. Then it was the cowboy's turn. He was shorter than the other one, but probably at least six feet tall with broad shoulders. His red plaid shirt was rolled up at the sleeves and he had well defined arm muscles and curling brown hair that covered his forearms. The hair on his head was brown, too, and curled out beneath his cowboy hat with longer than normal sideburns. There was a darkened stain of stubble on his cheeks and chin. Her eyes strayed to his backside as he leaned over to make his shot and she couldn't help that her smile widened.

The man in question flashed her a grin and then pocketed the next ball with a decisive clatter as it dropped to the underside of the table. Several shots later he stood and leaned on his pool cue, having sunk the eight ball for the win.

"Nice game," the Newfoundlander said, slapping his companion on the back. "I was thirsty anyway." He turned to Sherri. "Looks like you're up, little lady. I wish you luck. You're gonna need it cause Lester here seems to be a pro when it comes to pool."

"Lester." Sherri rolled the name off her tongue and frowned. Something in her memory was fighting to resurface, but she just couldn't bring it forward. She shrugged and grabbed a pool cue from the rack under the table. Next, she chalked the end of the cue with extra concentration. When she looked up she noticed that the man named Lester was staring at her.

"We met before. Remember?"

Sherri let out a laugh that sounded more like a snort. "Wow. That's original."

Lester grinned. "I mean it. You're…" He hesitated for only a second, then snapped his fingers. "Sherri Chan, right?"

Sherri's eyes widened and she blinked her surprise. "How do you know my name?"

"I told you. We met before. Here at The Urban Cowboy."

It all came rushing back. Their conversation at the bar. Him riding the mechanical bull. And then the fall. "You're okay." It was an obviously stupid thing to say.

He laughed. "Appears so. Well, let's get at it, shall we? Good luck." He stuck his hand out for a friendly shake and she took it. It was square and calloused, hardened by manual labor. So very different from Clarke's well-manicured hands.

"What are you doing?"

Sherri looked to her left. Clarke had sidled up beside her. "Kicking this cowboy's butt at pool," she replied.

Lester chuckled. "Big talk for a little lady. You haven't even made one shot yet."

"I'm Clarke. Her fiancé." Clarke said the word with extra emphasis.

By this time, Sherman had joined them.

"Challenger breaks," Lester said.

"Since when?" Sherri asked.

"Since I said so. Gentleman's rules."

"Because I'm a woman?" Sherri placed her hands on her hips.

Lester just smiled. "Go."

Sherri shook the hair off her shoulders and bent to take her first shot. Despite her slightly inebriated state, it was a decent break and she managed to land one of the striped balls. She made the next shot as well and only missed by a hair on the third.

"I'm impressed," Lester said.

"My sister is a mathematician," Sherman said. "She knows all the angles."

"Got a few nice curves, too." Lester's big friend had joined them again, beer in hand.

Clarke frowned.

"Ignore my friend," Lester directed at Clarke. "Jed doesn't always filter what comes out of his mouth."

Good-natured banter continued as the game progressed. Sherri noticed Clarke's deepening scowl, but the possibility that he was jealous made her feel powerful. Was she flirting? Yes. Did she care? No. Clarke didn't own her and maybe it was time he saw that other men might find her attractive. Lester won the game and she challenged him to another.

"Um, I think we should probably go now," Sherman suggested, placing a gentle hand on her shoulder. "School night. Remember?"

Sherri tried to focus on his face. "Why? I'm having fun."

"Maybe too much fun," Sherman mumbled.

THE LAST OF her students was filing out of the lecture hall, the scraping of their feet like nails on a chalkboard. A nagging headache plagued the back of Sherri's head, even after a pain pill, and she felt decidedly ill. Self inflicted, but none-the-less real.

She packed up her briefcase as quickly as possible and headed for the parking lot. She needed to call Sherman. With her cell phone pressed to her ear with one hand, she used the other to pinch her nose between her index finger and thumb as she waited for him to pick up. The last thing she needed was a lecture, but she knew things had gone sideways last night and she needed to talk to him before she talked to Clarke.

Sherman answered just as she was sliding into her car. She shut the door with a click and leaned back against the seat, closing her eyes.

"I was wondering when you would call," Sherman said. "That was quite the performance last night. Not sure I've seen you that wasted in... well, in a really long time."

Sherri groaned. "I feel terrible. Have you talked to Clarke today?"

"No. Why would I? He's your fiancé."

"I know. But I was just wondering... Exactly what happened last night? My head is a little foggy."

"Besides the fact that you were throwing yourself at some redneck? Oh, nothing."

"Define, 'throwing' myself."

"Well, let's see. Ignoring Clarke altogether while you flirt with another guy?"

"Define 'flirt'."

Sherman laughed. "It's hard to define. Just the way you women do, you know? Batting your eyes and complimenting him on how strong he is. Stuff like that. An intangible language we guys recognize."

Sherri let out a frustrated sigh. "I am so embarrassed."

"Yeah, you should be. I'm just glad Clarke and I were there to get you home safe. Who knows what bed you might have ended up in."

"That bad?" She winced.

"Mmhm."

"Was Clarke mad?"

"What do you think? I managed to convince him it was the booze talking. That you really didn't have a clue what you were doing. I got you into your apartment and flopped you on your bed. Seemed like he didn't really want to have anything to do with you at that moment."

"Oh dear."

"And by the way. I met those two guys you were flirting with at The Brew this afternoon. They were having lunch."

Sherri groaned again. "Did you talk to them?"

"As a matter of fact, yes. Turns out they work for Titan, the main contractor for the new building I've designed. Fortunately, they didn't seem to hold your behaviour against you. I made sure I apologized for you just in case."

"Well, that's a relief." Her voice was sarcastic.

"If I were you, I'd say you have some major sucking up to do."

"With them? I don't even know them."

"No, silly. With your fiancé. Sheesh."

"Of course. I'll do my best." Sherri hesitated. "You busy later?"

"Why?"

"I just thought you might be able to come along. As a buffer."

"Sorry, Sis. You're on your own this time."

After she hung up, Sherri called Clarke's cell. It rang several times and then his voice mail answered.

"Um, hi hon," she began. She bit her lip and then continued. "Sorry about last night. Not exactly sure what happened, but Sherman says you're probably upset. I'd like to talk about it. How about dinner? My treat. Call me back." She hesitated. "Love you."

She hung up, leaned her head against the headrest and closed her eyes. Did she really love Clarke? She didn't know, but right now she had to concentrate on making herself believe so.

THE LITTLE BELL above the door rang as Sherri pushed the solid wood and glass open. The convenience store her family owned and operated had not changed in the thirty years that she could remember. It was cluttered; almost antique in appearance, and situated in the very heart of Chinatown.

Her father sat in his usual spot behind the counter reading a Chinese paper. She could understand many of the Mandarin caricatures, but mostly because of her own insistence, not because her parents had forced it upon her. Their greatest desire was to see their children become successful. Westernized with good paying jobs and fancy possessions. It was all well and good except there were still certain strings attached. Like marrying a good Chinese boy.

"Hello, Father." Sherri placed a kiss on his cheek and he nodded his acceptance, although he hardly looked up from the paper. "Mom upstairs?"

He nodded again. Of course she was. Where else would she be

unless she was here working in the store or at the restaurant? That was one thing about her family. They worked hard with very little time for hobbies.

Sherri headed toward the back of the store. Her immediate family still lived in the apartment above. It was a three-story brick building, square and featureless except for the colourful Chinese neon sign on the street. Her parents, along with her grandmother, and her father's single brother, Dave, lived there. It was cramped and outdated and it was a miracle that Nai-Nai could still maneuver the stairs. No wonder Sherman wanted to design a new home for them.

Lani Chan was standing at a small butcher block in the cramped kitchen, chopping celery. She looked up in surprise as soon as Sherri entered. "This is a surprise. You usually don't visit during the week. I am just making some soup for Nai-Nai. She didn't feel up to going to the restaurant tonight. Would you like to join us?"

"Um, sure. That would be nice." Clarke hadn't called back yet so she had no dinner plans. She sat down on one of the worn chairs. It was made of tubular chrome whose surface was peeling off in places and the vinyl seat had been repaired with duct tape. "Where is Nai-Nai?"

"Lying down. She not feeling well these days." Lani shook her head.

"Have you ever thought about moving?" Sherri asked. "Somewhere that would make it easier to look after her?"

"This is my home!" Lani exclaimed. "Besides, it is so convenient. The store is just downstairs."

"Auntie and Uncle live in a decent house. They don't live at the restaurant. Why should you live here?

"What wrong with this house?" Lani chopped more vigorously.

"You and Dad have worked hard. You deserve something better."

"This good enough."

"But what about Nai-Nai? It must be hard to get her up and down the stairs."

"Moving too difficult. Besides, store is convenient, like I said."

"You could always sell the store. The restaurant is busy enough for everyone. And with the profits, you could buy – or build – a nice house."

Lani waved a dismissive hand. "You talk silliness. We not sell the store. It belongs in our family."

"But who is going to run it when you, you know… can't do it anymore?"

"Someone." Lani bobbed her head with assurance. "It belongs in the family."

"Mom," Sherri said gently. "Neither Sherman nor I want to run the store. You made sure of that. You're the one who wanted us to go to school – to get good jobs. We couldn't just leave those to run a store."

"Then maybe one of Ed and Joanne's kids."

"You know as well as I do that Auntie Joanne's children don't want to run it either. This store is in a prime location. You could make really good money on it."

Lani pointed her knife at Sherri. "No more. I not talking about it no more."

Sherri sighed. "Okay. Sorry to upset you." She stood up and gave her mother a kiss on the cheek. The small woman remained stiff and Sherri sighed again. "Maybe I'll go see how Nai-Nai is doing."

Sherri tiptoed into the small room that Nai-Nai called home. It was really little more than a closet but it had a single bed, a dresser and a wardrobe all crammed into the tiny space. The elder woman was curled up on her bed in the fetal position under an afghan. It smelled in the room. A mixture of lavender and unwashed body. It was obvious that soon someone would have to force the issue of getting proper care for her.

Sherri went back out to the kitchen. Why had she stopped here anyway? She was searching for someone who might understand the unsettled feelings she'd been bottling up ever since Clarke had proposed. Marriage seemed so final. So permanent. Was it just cold feet or was she really having second thoughts about spending her life with him?

Sherri watched her mother as she stirred the simmering soup pot. Her mother had agreed to an arranged marriage and left her home and family in Hong Kong to settle with her new husband in a foreign land. Even though her father had been born and raised in Canada, he was still very much a traditionalist and had succumbed to his parents' wishes when it came to finding a wife. Only a nice Chinese girl would do and he allowed his relatives to do the search for him.

It seemed to work. Her parents genuinely cared for one another and they had been together now for more than thirty years. Still, it wasn't a route she could follow herself. Yet, in many ways it seemed like she was doing just that. Clarke was a good 'Chinese' boy, one that her parents approved of. In the end, did it really make a difference?

"I am glad you are staying for supper and we can have some time alone." Lani set the wooden spoon down on a plate near the stove. "We must start making wedding plans."

"There's no rush," Sherri said. "We haven't even set a date yet."

"Why not? You must hurry before he changes his mind."

"What makes you think he's going to change his mind?"

"Men don't like waiting. I know."

"Mom." Sherri rolled her eyes.

"You must decide soon. We invite all of our relatives from Hong Kong. They need time to make travel arrangements."

"Is that necessary? I don't even know them."

Lani silenced her with a stare. "Of course. It is the way."

"I was hoping for something a little simpler."

"A Chinese wedding simple?" Lani laughed and turned back to the stove to give the soup another stir. "You will want a church wedding, but also a traditional Chinese ceremony. We must start looking at dresses. You will need at least four. One for the church, one for the traditional ceremony, one for the tea service, and one for the banquet."

"Four dresses! Now you're getting carried away. Whose wedding is this anyway?"

"You are my only daughter. Of course we want the biggest and best wedding we can afford."

Sherri's eyes widened. "It's too much! And I would never expect you to pay for all that."

"It is our duty. Out gift to start you on your right foot. When I married your father my family paid for everything. It is the way."

"But I can't let you do that. You can't afford all the things you're talking about. Besides, what if I don't want four dresses?"

Lani's mouth tightened into a line. "It is settled. And you talk of building a house! We need all the money for the wedding."

"This is ridiculous." Sherri rose from her chair. "I need to talk to Dad about this."

"Your father and I already talk. We will get a second mortgage on this property. So you see, we cannot sell the store."

"I won't let you go through with it. Maybe Sherman can talk some sense into you."

"You would disgrace us by not allowing us to make a big wedding for you?" There were actual tears glistening in her mother's eyes.

Sherri sighed deeply and pinched the bridge of her nose between her thumb and forefinger. "Sorry. I didn't mean to upset you. I... I just wasn't expecting all this, that's all."

Lani put her arms around Sherri's shoulders. "We want the best for you, our only daughter. Allow us to do this for you."

"I don't know. I can't say for sure right now. Just let me think about it a bit, okay?"

"Not too long. The relatives in Hong Kong..."

"I know, I know." Sherri checked the watch on her wrist. She suddenly felt claustrophobic. "Um, listen, I actually have to get going."

"So soon? Aren't you going to have soup?" Lani's expression was worried.

"I just remembered. I have to meet Clarke." Sherri swallowed. It was a lie, but anything to get out of these oppressive surroundings.

Lani's face lit up. "Ah! How is my son-in-law?"

"Fine. Just fine."

"Good, good. You go to him, then." Lani made a shooing motion with the wooden spoon. "But soon we must plan the wedding."

As soon as she got out onto the street, Sherri called Sherman. She held the cell phone to her ear as she crossed the street, listening to the ring as she jogged across. He answered just when she was about to hang up. "Hi. Can we go somewhere to talk?"

"I was just on my way over to The Urban Cowboy. I thought it would be fun to hang out with Cory and Steve once more before I have to head back to Toronto."

"Oh." Disappointment flooded through her. "That's okay, then. Maybe we can talk tomorrow."

"Why don't you come by?"

Sherri laughed. "After what happened last time? You think that's wise?"

"You don't have to drink. You can be the designated driver."

She hesitated for a moment. Did she really want to show her face at The Urban Cowboy so soon? Then again, she really needed to talk to Sherman. "Okay. I'll see you in half an hour."

SHERMAN MET her right inside the door of the club and they settled at the bar, Sherri with a glass of ginger ale and Sherman with a beer.

"So what's up?" Sherman asked.

"I just came from Mom and Dad's." Sherri sighed after she said it.

"And?"

"Mom is putting on the pressure about dates and dresses and guests coming from Hong Kong."

"It is kind of big deal for them," Sherman pointed out as he took a drink of his beer.

"I know. But it's got me wondering if I agreed to marrying Clarke more for them than for me. I'm just not sure I'm ready, you know?" She turned to Sherman for support.

"Everybody has misgivings," Sherman said. "Or so I've heard. Wedding jitters, cold feet... you know."

"What if it's more than that?" Sherri asked.

"What do you mean?"

"What if Clarke's not the one?" Sherri shook her head. "I thought I cared about him – I do care about him – but since he asked me to marry him I've been thinking. I don't even know if I really love Clarke. That can't be a good way to start a marriage."

Sherman shrugged. "I suppose it depends on how you look at it. I'm not sure there really is just 'one' person out there, waiting for each of us. Maybe love is a choice. Mom and Dad had an arranged marriage and it's worked out pretty well for them."

Sherri looked at her brother with skepticism in her eyes. "Is that what you want? To settle for someone and 'choose' to love them, even if you don't really feel anything?"

Sherman laughed. "I didn't say that and we're not talking about me. I'm not planning on getting married anytime soon. I like my freedom. You, on the other hand, already said yes to a really decent guy who seems to love you even if you don't return the sentiment."

Sherri looked down at her hands. "It's a mess. And I'm a terrible person."

"Not terrible, just confused." Sherman patted her hand. "Does Clarke know how you feel?"

"No." Sherri hung her head.

"Don't you think it's kind of important that you talk to him about it?"

"Yes. But I just don't want to hurt his feelings. He's decent, like you said."

Someone sat next to Sherri and she turned her head to see who it was. Her eyes widened when she recognized Lester's friend Jed.

"Sherman Chan and…" Jed furrowed his brow for a second then snapped his fingers. "Sherri, right? We're practically best buddies by now, the way we keep bumpin' into one another."

"Right…" Sherri turned and looked at Sherman with a question in her eyes.

"I told you I met up with Jed, here, and his friend Lester at The Brew. Remember?" Sherman said.

"Oh right." Sherri nodded.

"Your brother explained that you don't normally drink much." Jed winked.

Sherri could feel the heat rising in her cheeks. This is exactly why she shouldn't have come here. "I hope you won't judge me based on that performance."

"No worries." Jed took a long draught of his beer.

Sherri peeked around Jed's massive shoulder. "Is your friend here as well?" Now why had she asked that?

Jed shook his head. "Not tonight. 'E doesn't drink much, either." Then he grinned. "'E'll be awful sorry 'e didn't once I tell 'im you was 'ere."

She didn't know what to say. Did that mean Lester liked her? That he'd spoken about her with his friend? She shook her head. "Oh. Well, say hi." That sounded lame. She turned her attention back to Sherman. "I should go find Clarke."

"What are you going to say?"

Sherri shook her head. "I guess I'll know once I say it."

SHERRI PULLED up in front of Clarke's condo and let the car idle a bit while she gathered her thoughts. Just what was she going to say to Clarke? She closed her eyes. "Okay, God. I know I haven't been the best Christian lately. I've been kind of preoccupied with my work and you know all about last night. But I really need some help here. Am I supposed to marry Clarke or not?"

With a sigh she opened her eyes. She hadn't prayed much lately. Hadn't attended Mass as regularly as she used to either. She'd been so preoccupied with her reeling emotions she'd forgotten to even consult God in the matter.

Some Christian she was turning out to be. She'd always believed in God, and started going to a protestant church when she was in college after going to a rally. But she found she liked the liturgy and symmetry of the Catholic Church better, so she switched back since she'd gone there some as a child. Now she had all but abandoned her faith. It was time to get back to that place of peace and security.

She shut off the car and got out, looking up at the light shining through Clarke's living room window onto the street below. He was home and there was no turning back. God was going to have to give her the words, because at this point, she was totally at a loss.

CLARKE OPENED the door the moment Sherri knocked, almost as if he had been expecting her. After a cursory, "Come in," he closed the door behind them and stood waiting for her to make the first move.

Sherri took a deep breath and then dove right in. "Do you love me?"

Whatever he was expecting it obviously wasn't this. He scrunched his eyebrows into a frown. "Oh course I love you. I should be asking you that question."

She sighed, then without warning, grabbed his face between her two hands and kissed him fervently on the mouth. It was a test but she wasn't sure what the correct answer was.

He responded after a moment and then drew back, holding her at arm's length. "Is this an apology?"

"I don't really know what it is," she admitted.

"You had me kind of concerned last night. Sherman assured me it's just stress."

"He's probably right." She ran a hand through her hair and slouched. "Can we sit down?"

"Of course." He ushered her into the chic living room with its leather sofa and large abstract painting over the fireplace. "What's going on? Are you okay?"

Sherri lowered herself onto the couch. "I don't think so. I went to see my parents today and then I talked to Sherman. I'm... I'm very confused right now. Ever since you proposed."

Clarke interrupted. "Is your mother making you uncomfortable about the wedding arrangements? If she is, we can just elope."

Sherri shook her head. "That would kill her."

"She'd get over it." He smiled and placed his hand over hers.

Sherri stared at their hands for a moment and then slowly and gently slid hers out from beneath his and placed it in her lap. "Actually, what I have to say might kill her anyway." She took a deep breath. "You're a good guy. A decent guy and my family loves you."

"You're scaring me," Clarke said.

"I'm scaring myself. Maybe that's the whole thing. I'm scared." Her eyes pleaded with him.

"Everyone feels wedding jitters. It's natural."

"I'm sorry, Clarke." Sherri looked directly at him.

"Are you saying you want to call the wedding off?"

"Yes." It was barely above a whisper.

"But why? What happened?" He seemed genuinely puzzled.

"Once you proposed, I started wondering if this is what I really want for my life."

"If it's time you need, I can do that. There's no rush."

"I'm not sure if time is the answer."

Clarke's eyes narrowed. "Or maybe you found someone else? Is that it?"

"I think I should go." Sherri stood up.

"Tell me, Sherri. Is this about another man?" He was standing also.

Was it? She didn't really know. All she knew was she suddenly felt a burden lift that she didn't even know she was carrying.

"You're a good man, Clarke. Just not the right man for me."

EPISODE 3

SNEAKING AROUND THE NEIGHBOURHOOD

*P*atsi Mae Tibbett slid into a vacant seat, trying not to make eye contact with anyone else in the packed lecture hall. If she did, they might know she was a fraud. She'd always hated Math, and calculus was the worst. She just didn't get it. If she had her way, she'd drop the class, but her older brother Lester wouldn't hear of it.

She and Lester had just recently moved to Calgary. Lester said it was so she could attend college, but she knew it had more to do with the farm not doing so well. He loved the country and it must have been hard for him to leave it behind.

The farm had been left to him when their parents had died nine years ago. Lester was considerably older than she was – fourteen years older in fact - and was more like a father than a brother. He'd raised her from the time she was nine years old and she supposed she owed him a lot. He'd made a lot of sacrifices over the years for her sake. Still, it was becoming increasingly difficult to handle his over-protective ways now that she was practically an adult.

Just wait until later that year when she turned eighteen. Then he couldn't stop her from doing what she wanted.

Ms. Chan, the Math professor, entered through a door at the front of the room. It was a theatre style auditorium with the lecture area at

59

the lowest level while the seats rose upward toward the back. Patsi sat up straighter. Ms. Chan seemed to be happier lately. Less robotic and uptight. Patsi had heard something about her being engaged, so maybe that was it. No amount of pleasantries on Ms. Chan's part could make calculus palatable, however.

A latecomer maneuvered her way down the row of seats and Patsi moved her legs to the side so the girl could slide by. With a smile of thanks the other girl sat down and settled herself. She had bouncing brown hair with just the right amount of highlights and was wearing a trendy outfit that screamed 'money' without being gaudy.

Patsi turned her attention to the onslaught of numbers. Not that it would make much difference. Ms. Chan could be talking Chinese for all Patsi understood. The pun made her smile in spite of herself and she settled into her seat. Chinese torture - that's what I was.

Fifty minutes later, the shuffle of zombied feet woke Patsi from her daydreams. She glanced at her notebook and sighed. The doodles on the paper didn't bring back any recollection of the lecture. She stretched and then chanced a look around. From what she could tell from the mass exodus, calculus sucked the life right out of most people.

"I've seen you in class before."

Patsi's gaze darted to the girl beside her. "Oh... yes. Been here every day – unfortunately."

The new girl swung her purse strap over her shoulder. "I'm Megan." Her fingers fluttered.

"Pat," Patsi said quite deliberately and sat up straighter. "I actually don't remember seeing you before. I guess it is a pretty big class."

Megan shrugged. "I skip a lot."

Patsi's eyebrows rose and then she blinked. "Oh."

"But then my parents found out and... here I am." Megan shrugged her shoulders daintily. "My father says if I don't start attending classes he's going to cut me off."

"My brother would kill me if I skipped," Patsi said.

"Your brother?"

Patsi nodded. "He's my legal guardian. My parents passed away when I was a kid. But only for another eight weeks," she added. "Then I'll be eighteen."

"I turned eighteen last summer." The girl flashed a smile as if remembering something pleasant. "I had a crazy party at the house. My parents were so mad." She readjusted the books in her arms. "Well, nice to meet you. See you around."

Patsi doubted it. They obviously ran in different circles. Patsi watched as Megan floated up the stairs toward the exit. What would it be like to live that kind of privileged life?

PATSI LAY ON HER BED, calculus text open in front of her. The symbols were literally dancing before her eyes. With a frustrated sigh, she slapped the book shut just as a knock sounded on her bedroom door. "Can I come in?" Lester's voice asked on the other side.

"Sure." She swung her legs around and sat up as her brother entered.

"There's a lady in our building who's looking for a babysitter. She's a nurse and sometimes has to work nights. I told her you might be interested." He passed her the corner of an envelope with a number scrawled on it in a feminine hand.

Patsi surveyed the number and then looked up at her brother. "Who is it?"

"Her or her kid?"

"Both."

"The kid's name is Jason. You might have seen him hanging on the balcony railing a time or two. Him and his friend. His mother's name is Goldie Harper." He gestured to the scrap of paper. "I met her a few times in the lobby getting the mail. It'd be a way for you to make some spending money."

"Something regular might be better." She looked up hopefully. "Like that waitressing job Jed mentioned."

Lester's stance was unmoving. "School comes first. Take what you get." He glanced down at the textbook lying on her bed. "Homework?"

"Calculus." Patsi sighed. "I just don't get it! Professor Chan goes so fast. She expects everyone in her class to be a Math whiz or something."

Lester cocked his head to one side to better see the title of the book. "Maybe I can help."

Patsi rolled her eyes. "This isn't high school Math. Besides, things have changed since you went to school."

"Well, sorry for offering," Lester bit back. He straightened.

"She says I should go to some stupid tutorial group."

"That's a good idea."

"None of them line up with my schedule. I'd be waiting around for hours after my other classes or going there way early or way late. And I know you won't want me riding the bus after dark."

"I could drive you," Lester offered.

Patsi let out a scornful grunt. "I doubt it. It might cut into your bro-mance with Jed Malloy."

Lester frowned. "Bro-mance? What is that supposed to mean?"

"You and Jed. Always off 'playing pool'." She made quotation marks in the air with her fingers. "And then you tell me not to drink!"

"We are playing pool - mostly," Lester defended. "And as an adult, I'm allowed to have a life."

"But I'm not?" Patsi raised an eyebrow.

Lester sighed. "I don't want to fight about it. Right now you need to concentrate on school. And if your teacher says you need help in Math then we'll figure out a way to get you some help. Just don't make everything so difficult."

"You can get out of my room now." Patsi's tone was sweet but her eyes were narrowed.

Lester turned and left. Patsi knew he was only trying to help, but her big brother was taking his guardianship just a bit too seriously these days. She was almost an adult and it was about time he started treating her like one.

MEGAN SAT beside Patsi again in Calculus. "That was the longest Math class ever," she sighed when it was over. "Ms. Chan is so… prickly."

"You think so? She's actually getting nicer," Patsi said. "They say she's getting married."

Megan grimaced. "Really? To who?"

Patsi laughed. "She's not that bad. She's actually kind of pretty."

"Yeah, if you like business suits and last year's pumps."

Patsi glanced to where the professor was cleaning up her desk. She actually looked nice, in Patsi's view, but she didn't say anything more.

Megan led the way up the ramp toward the exit. Patsi hoisted her school bag onto her shoulder and followed, half a step behind her new 'friend'. Megan was so fashionable. So confident. So cool.

When they reached the outer hall, Megan surveyed Patsi from head to toe. "Where'd you get your outfit?" Her face was a perfect mask with no hint whether she approved or disapproved.

"Um… I don't remember." Patsi felt herself flush and looked down at her clothing. It was a new outfit she'd just bought at the mall.

"I didn't mean it was bad," Megan clarified. She surveyed Patsi for a moment longer. "Wanna hang out for a bit? Come over to my place?"

Patsi checked the time on her phone. "Um, I guess. As long as I get home before my brother. What are the busses like from where you live?"

"Forget the bus." Megan waved her hand dismissively. "I'll drive you home."

"You own a car?"

"Of course." Megan looked at her as if she were from the moon.

Not only did Megan own a car, but it was a sporty red BMW Z4 Roadster. Patsi had never been in such a luxurious car - or one that went that fast. "Nice car," Patsi said for lack of any other comment.

Megan just shrugged. "Last year's birthday present."

The drive to Megan's house took about half an hour. Megan filled the time with random chatter about the latest celebrity gossip - a topic which Patsi knew very little about. She mostly nodded and smiled.

The homes only seemed to get larger as they approached Megan's neighbourhood. Her family lived in an upscale area full of large homes with even larger garages. Patsi purposely closed her mouth and tried not to gape. She had figured Megan was well off, but nothing like this.

When they entered the house through a set of grand double doors, Megan deposited her books on a side table and simply dropped her purse on the floor. "Just throw your stuff wherever," Megan said. After a moment's hesitation, Patsi set her books on the table as well, but kept her purse slung over her shoulder.

They walked past a spacious formal living room and down a hallway before reaching a large open kitchen with an eating area and family room attached. The finishings were sparkling and sleek and there was a large fireplace and the biggest television Patsi had ever seen.

"Want something to drink?" Megan opened the stainless steel fridge and peered inside. "Cola, ginger ale or lemonade?"

"Cola is fine," Patsi responded.

Megan took out the drinks and handed one to Patsi before cracking open her own can of ginger ale. "Let's go outside."

Megan led the way to a set of French doors. As soon as she opened them the sound of male laughter filtered in. Megan rolled her eyes. "My stupid annoying brother has friends over."

When they stepped out onto the large deck, Patsi saw exactly where the noise was coming from. A hot tub occupied its own corner of the adjoining patio, bubbling like a cauldron. Three males lounged in its depths.

Patsi gave a tentative smile to the group and then focused on following Megan to a set of outdoor furniture positioned under a pergola.

"Who's your friend?" one of the males called.

"None of your business," Megan called over her shoulder. "Just ignore them," she added more quietly to Patsi.

Patsi took a sip of her cola and looked around. "You have a really nice place."

Megan shrugged. "Yeah. I suppose."

"We live in a two bedroom apartment. Our house back on the farm is a lot bigger, but nothing as nice as this."

"Where did you say you were from again?" Megan asked.

"Coulee Creek," Patsi replied.

Megan looked puzzled.

"It's a little town south of here. You probably never heard of it." Patsi looked down at the drink in her hands.

"Do you miss it?"

"Not really." It was actually a lie. So much of her new life in the city was unfamiliar and lonely. But she couldn't tell someone like Megan that. She would think she was a hick. Sometimes she felt like it, too, but there was no use confirming it. She sat up straighter. "What do your parents do?"

"They're both lawyers." Megan sniffed. "They aren't home much."

"Oh." Patsi glanced at the boys in the hot tub and then away again.

"You wanna join us?" one of the males called. "No bathing suit required."

"Ew. And risk your germs?" Megan called back. She grinned at Patsi. "They are such morons."

A few minutes later the distinct smell of marijuana wafted by. Patsi purposely avoided looking at the hot tub, but she knew what was happening. "Won't your parents mind?" she asked in a hushed voice.

Megan just shrugged. "What? The Maryjane? They won't be home for hours." She hoisted herself from the lounger. "Come on. Let's go up to my room and leave these losers alone."

Patsi followed Megan back into the house, the deep timber of male voices following her until the French doors were securely closed behind them. She let out a sigh of relief, despite herself. "My brother would flip out if he caught me smoking pot."

"My parents don't mind as long as we're discreet," Megan said. "They even like to do it on occasion, but don't tell them I told you so. They think I don't know."

Patsi's eyes widened.

"Don't look so shocked," Megan said with a laugh. "Don't tell me you've never smoked weed before?"

Patsi shook her head. "No, I haven't." Misgivings rolled in Patsi's stomach as she followed Megan up a flight of stairs. She had always lived a fairly sheltered life, and although she sometimes resented it, right now she wasn't feeling very comfortable.

"Excuse the décor." Megan made a sweeping gesture with her arm as they entered her bedroom. "I went through a pink phase. There doesn't seem much point in updating since I'm moving out soon." The room was rather juvenile with lots of pink ruffles. Megan flopped down on the bed and hugged one of the many stuffed animals to her chest. "Although, I am rather attached, aren't I, Teddy?"

Patsi sat down on the edge of the bed. "When are you moving out?" She ran her hand over the coverlet and let her eyes wander over the designer everything. It all matched. She had never had anything like this, even as a child.

"I don't know. Just sometime, when I feel like it." Megan sat up and tossed the bear. "So what do you want to do?"

Patsi shrugged. "I don't know."

Megan cocked her head to one side. "Have you ever thought about wearing a little more makeup? You have pretty eyes and I think a little bit of eye shadow would really bring out the color."

"I have trouble getting up in the morning so I don't have a lot of time to get ready." The truth was, back home she was more interested in riding her horse or playing sports at school. She just hadn't thought about makeup much.

"Do you mind?" Megan was already up and rummaging through some makeup on a dressing table.

"Uh… go ahead, I guess." Patsi's stomach gave a flutter but she couldn't tell if it was nerves or excitement.

"Okay. Come sit here. It'll be fun."

Patsi moved to sit in the chair at the dressing table and Megan proceeded to apply some eyeliner. "You know, I could totally take you on as a project. Not that you're not already pretty," she quickly added, "but I could make you stunning. Sort of a 'before and after' thing. After I'm done your makeup, I'm going to straighten your hair."

"I straighten my hair sometimes…"

"Cool. When we're done you can try on one of my outfits and see what you think."

Quite some time later, Megan proclaimed she was finished. "Voila!" She spun her to look in the large mirror over the dressing table.

Patsi squinted at herself and then her eyes widened. She'd never really thought of herself as pretty before, but the woman staring back at her looked attractive – sexy even. Megan had even managed to do something with her normally unruly hair. In its natural state it was dirty blonde with lumps and waves that refused to be tamed. Even when she straightened it there were fuzzy spots. Now it lay sleek and chic. "I can't believe it. Especially the hair."

"I thought you said you straightened it sometimes."

"It never turns out like this." Patsi touched the top of her head and let her fingers glide down the perfectly straight surface.

"It's probably one of those cheap straighteners. You need a good, professional one."

"Oh. Okay." Patsi's gaze flickered away from where Megan was staring at her in the mirror. "You're really good at this."

"I just like doing it. I've thought about going into aesthetics as a career, but my parents don't think it's good enough for the daughter of lawyers."

"I think people should be allowed to do whatever makes them happy." Patsi looked up to catch Megan's eye once again but the other girl was already packing her makeup into its carrying case.

"Tell that to my mom. It would be too embarrassing for her. Imagine having to tell people her daughter did nails for a living." Megan snapped the lid down and closed the latch. She straightened and smiled. "Now for something different to wear."

"Oh, I couldn't," Patsi protested.

"Not listening." Megan walked to her closet and flung the double doors wide. She stood for a moment with her hands on her hips and then started rummaging through the rack. She held up several selections, cocked her head to the side as she considered the merits of each one, and then tossed them on the bed. "Here, try this."

Patsi took the V necked T-shirt, short skirt and mini cardigan. "Um… where should I go to change?"

Megan laughed. "I didn't take you for the shy type. If you don't want to change in front of me then go into the bathroom next door."

Patsi smiled sheepishly but went to the bathroom anyway. She was used to stripping down in the locker room when she'd played school sports, but she didn't want Megan to see her faded bra and utilitarian panties.

The top was very tight and the V dipped much lower than she felt comfortable with. Still, she felt kind of sexy in the outfit. She turned and inspected herself in the bathroom mirror before opening the door and venturing out into the hall.

As soon as she stepped out of the room she bumped into a young man. His hair was tousled and he was still wearing wet bathing trunks. His chest was bare except for the towel that was slung around his neck and she couldn't help but notice the smooth, well-formed muscles of his torso.

"Sorry." She forced her gaze down and stepped to the side to let him pass.

He did the same thing simultaneously and they were in each other's way again. They both laughed.

"Since my sister didn't have the decency to introduce us earlier, I'm Brett."

"Pat."

"Nice to meet you. Well, I guess its ladies first." He gestured for her to pass.

She smiled and did so, but could sense his gaze lingering as she went by.

"Look at you!" Megan exclaimed as soon as Patsi entered the room.

Patsi smiled and looked down at herself. She could feel the heat rising in her cheeks. "The top's a little tight."

"Are you kidding? If you got it you might as well flaunt it, and you definitely got it. Now we just have to take you somewhere to show you off."

Patsi's eyes widened and she shook her head. "Oh no, I couldn't do that! I should probably get home soon anyway. My brother worries. I'll just take these off." She turned to scurry back to the bathroom to change, but Megan interrupted.

"Keep them. You look great and I never wear any of it anymore."

Patsi looked down at the skirt and smoothed her hands over the material. Then she glanced up. "Really? Are you sure?"

"Of course. I wouldn't offer if I didn't mean it. Next time we'll go shopping and see what we come up with when you don't have to wear my old hand-me-downs."

"That sounds fun… except I'll have to wait until I get some money. I'm going to start babysitting."

"Whatever. I'll lend you some money or something."

"But -"

"No buts! How can I invite you to the party this Saturday if you don't have something new to wear?"

"You're inviting me to a party?" Patsi's eyes were beginning to hurt from opening them so wide.

"Don't look so surprised," Megan said with a laugh. "You sound like you've never been to a party before."

"I've been to parties," Patsi said quickly. Mostly church youth group parties, but Megan didn't need to know that. "I just don't know if my brother will let me go."

"Then don't tell him." At Patsi's frown Megan added, "Or tell him you're staying at my house. That should work."

"He likes me to go to church with him on Sunday."

"My goodness. Well, can't you get out if it? Just this once?"

"I'll see what I can do."

"Would it help if I came up to meet him when I drive you home?"

Thoughts of their shabby apartment sprung to Patsi's mind. "Um, no, that's okay. He'll probably be fine with it."

Megan shrugged. "Okay. Whatever."

Patsi's mind was racing, but she forced herself to pause and look directly at Megan. "Um, do you mind if I ask you a question?"

"Sure."

"Why are you being nice to me?"

Megan blinked. "Am I? I don't know. I think you're nice. Different."

"Different than what?" Patsi asked.

"Different than my other so called friends." Megan gaze shifted to her lap and she picked at one of her nails. "Most of my friends dumped me last summer when I was… going through a rough patch. When I saw you sitting by yourself the other day I thought you looked lonely, like me. It seemed like a chance to make a new friend. Start fresh." Megan laughed and looked up. "Sorry. That sounded totally sappy. Let's get you home."

Patsi laughed, too. "It's okay. It sounded honest. Maybe we need each another."

THE NEXT DAY Patsi and Megan headed to one of the big malls for some serious shopping. Patsi hadn't felt so excited about anything in a long time. Megan pulled Patsi along behind her until they reached a trendy store that catered to hip young twenty-somethings. "We'll start here. This is my absolute favourite store."

Megan was like a shopping machine, pulling items off racks and shoving them into Patsi's waiting arms ready to be tried on.

"What about you?" Patsi asked.

"I have lots of clothes. Shopping for you is way more fun. You're like a blank canvas."

Patsi wasn't sure whether to be pleased or offended by the remark. Once in the change room, Megan continued to throw more items over the door until Patsi felt like she couldn't keep up. She modeled each outfit except for a few that were so revealing she absolutely refused.

"I can't afford all of this!" Patsi wailed, surveying the pile of garments in the tiny change cubicle.

"Let's see." Megan stood just outside the doorway. "Well, which ones do you really like? If money was no object, I mean."

Patsi chose a few that she thought she could afford - if she saved for a month. She picked them up and folded them carefully.

"I said, 'If money was no object.'" Megan reminded, her hand on her hip.

Patsi added a couple more items.

Megan sighed dramatically and scooped up several more items. She marched from the change area, arms full. "We'll take all of this," she called to a passing salesgirl.

"Certainly." The girl did a one-eighty on her high heel and followed Megan and Patsi to the check-out counter.

"I can't afford all this!" Patsi hissed in Megan's ear.

Megan dug in her wallet for her credit card. "I know. Consider it a gift."

"I can't do that!" Patsi squeaked.

Megan cut her off by pointing a finger in her face. "You can't stop someone from buying you a present. Besides, this is fun for me, okay?" She held up the credit card and then handed it over to the salesgirl.

Patsi was still feeling a little panicked. "What will your parents say?"

Megan just shrugged. "My mother calls it Retail Therapy. They want me to be happy."

Once the purchases were made, the girls headed for the food court, both laden with shopping bags. "I feel really guilty about this. At least let me buy you lunch."

"Deal." Megan smiled widely. She almost seemed giddy. "I'll have a Japanese veggie roll with no dressing and a Chai Latte - half soy, half skim, extra foam."

Patsi rehearsed the list in her head while Megan found a table and sat down with all the bags. Patsi had been eyeing up the burger joint, but headed for the trendy looking Japanese booth instead. When she returned with the low calorie food and drinks, Brett and his two friends were sitting at the table right next to Megan. This time they were talking and laughing quite sociably.

Patsi smiled and set the tray down.

"Pat, this is my brother Brett," Megan introduced.

"We met," Brett said and smiled.

Patsi thought her stomach was going to land right in her shoes. He was just as handsome with dry hair and clothes as he had been yesterday barely clothed. His hair was blonde and styled, and his eyes were a dark brown with long lashes. "Hi."

Megan looked puzzled. "You met? When?"

"In the hallway when I was changing," Patsi explained. Her gaze dropped to the tray of food and she could feel her cheeks heating up.

"And these are Brett's friends, Scott and Brian," Megan continued.

"Only Brett's friends?" the one named Scott guffawed. "Geez, thanks, Megan."

"Yeah. I thought we were your friends, too," Brian teased.

Megan rolled her eyes. "Whatever."

After more good-natured banter, the boys got up to leave. "Nice to meet you, Pat." Brett caught Patsi's gaze with his own and he smiled, showing perfect white teeth.

"Right. You, too," she stammered.

"Hopefully we'll be seeing more of each other."

Patsi watched as a silent message passed between Brett and his sister and then the three males took their leave.

"What does your brother do again?" Patsi fiddled with the remains of her wrap.

Megan laughed. "Besides smoke pot, play video games and hang out with his friends? Nothing."

Patsi frowned. "Oh. I though he seemed older than you."

"He is. He's currently taking some time off from college while he decides what he wants to do with his life." Megan squinted at Patsi. "Don't even think it. You cannot fall for my brother. He's a player and I will not allow him to take advantage you."

A nervous laugh escaped from Patsi's lips. "That's not going to happen." She sat up straighter and flipped her hair off her shoulder.

"I mean it, Pat. Just ignore him."

Patsi produced a confident smile. "Got it." Inside, she knew that might be easier said than done.

"So, you're sure you're going to be okay with Patsi?" Goldie Harper was down on one knee, eye level with her six year old son, Jason.

Patsi watched as the little boy nodded his head up and down vigorously. "We'll be fine," Patsi assured. "Won't we Jason?"

Goldie gave the boy a quick hug and then stood up. "I'm just so glad I ran into your brother the other day at the mailboxes. I've been praying for a good sitter. I hate taking advantage of my friend Tamara. Jason and her son Matonabee are good friends, but she's really busy with her café, and expecting her to take him for overnight is just a bit too much."

Goldie was a nurse and a single mom. She was a pretty African Canadian woman in her mid-thirties and Patsi was glad she'd decided to take the babysitting job. Keeping up with Megan was going to need some funding.

Goldie waved one last good-bye and left the apartment.

"So, what should we do first?" Patsi asked.

"I like Lego," Jason said.

"Okay. Let's go."

Patsi followed Jason to his bedroom. It was compact, seeming even smaller because of the furniture that took up most of the space. A single bed, a small dresser and a large set of shelves were all crammed into the room along with what looked like a homemade coffee table with an old tube TV set on top of it.

Jason dug a tub of interlocking blocks out from the bottom of his closet and plopped down on the floor beside his bed. Patsi got down on the floor beside him and they proceeded to build.

"I'm making a house," Jason said.

"Cool. Me, too."

They worked for several minutes with Jason filling in the silence with chatter about what he was building. Without warning he threw a curve into the conversation. "Do you think my mom is pretty?"

"Um... yeah. Why?"

"Do you think your dad thinks she's pretty?"

Patsi frowned. "My dad...?" The light bulb went on and she laughed. "Oh, you mean Lester, my brother."

73

"Yeah, him."

"Why do you ask?"

Jason shrugged and kept his eyes on his creation. "I just thought maybe he'd make a good dad."

"Oh…" Patsi shifted her position on the floor. "It's not always that easy with adults."

"Hey, look at mine!" Jason held up his house for inspection. He seemed to have forgotten all about his earlier question. "Do you like it?"

"It's great. You should save it and show your mom." Patsi set her own house on the floor and stood up. "We should probably clean up now. It's your bed time soon."

"Can't I stay up a little longer?" Jason asked, a slight whine in his voice.

"Sorry, buddy. Your mom gave me strict orders. Besides, I have homework."

Jason's eyes were wide. "You still have to do homework?"

"Sure. I'm at college and we have tons more homework than in regular school."

"I'm never going to college then," Jason said.

PATSI WAITED OUTSIDE near Lester's pick-up. He was under the hood again, tinkering. Megan was scheduled to pick her up and there was no way she wanted the other girl to see the inside of their apartment. This would work out better, anyway, since Lester was being anal about meeting her new friend.

Patsi heard Megan's sports car even before it rolled into the parking lot. She pushed off the box of the truck and waved.

Lester emerged from under the hood just as Megan drove up. "Pretty fancy set of wheels." He wiped his hands on a dirty rag. "What did you say her parents did again?"

"Lawyers," Patsi said.

"Hm." Lester's face took on a concerned look - the one he used just before refusing a request.

"Stop being a snob," Patsi shot his way before stalking toward Megan's car.

Megan had unfolded herself from the driver's side by this time and Patsi had a sinking feeling in the pit of her stomach when she saw the short skirt the other girl was wearing. Lester was right behind her.

"You must be Megan. I'm Lester, Patsi's brother. I'd shake your hand but mine are pretty dirty." He held one up for inspection.

Patsi cringed when Lester said her name, but Megan, if she'd noticed, didn't say anything about it. "Nice to meet you."

"She tells me you're having a few girlfriends over for a movie night." By the look in Lester's eye, he was gaging the truthfulness of Megan's cover story.

"You know. Chick flicks." Megan smiled, never missing a beat. She was a pro.

"Well, have fun." Lester waved and turned away. Suddenly he stopped and swivelled around. "Be home at ten-forty-five in time for church, remember?"

Patsi rolled her eyes. "Of course."

She stocked to the passenger side of the car and let herself in, careful not to slam the door the way she felt like doing.

"Your brother is cute," Megan said as she revved out of the parking lot.

Patsi stared at her friend. "Excuse me?"

"I said, he's kind of cute. For an older man, that is."

"Ew. He is ancient, as in thirty-two, and besides that, he's my brother."

Megan shrugged. "Sometimes I'm attracted to older men. They definitely know how to treat a lady."

Patsi screwed up her face. "You've dated older men?"

"A couple. No biggy. They don't mind spending their hard earned money."

Patsi studied Megan's profile as she maneuvered the car into heavier traffic. She wondered how many guys Megan had dated and how far she'd gone with each of them. She wanted to ask but didn't want to sound naïve.

"You're quiet," Megan observed.

"Just thinking."

"About what?"

Patsi hesitated. "Just a school project I'm working on," she lied.

"Boring. When we get to my place I am going to blow your mind with the dress I'm going to wear tonight. I hope you brought that one I suggested? The purple one we bought the other day?" Megan glanced over at Patsi, a worried look on her face as if not bringing the right dress was a national tragedy.

Patsi patted her backpack. "In here."

"Phew! Just wait till I get you fixed up. You'll be a knockout."

Patsi surveyed her reflection in the full-length mirror in Megan's room. If Lester could see her now, he definitely would not approve.

"So? What do you think?" Megan asked, bouncing excitedly behind her.

"I don't recognize myself," Patsi said truthfully.

The dress was clingy in 'all the right spots', as Megan would say; definitely too low cut and too short, accentuating her long legs made to look even longer by the heels she was borrowing from Megan. Her hair was piled on her head in a wildly elegant style, and Megan had done a superb job of applying her makeup. She looked like a different person all together.

"You're gorgeous," Megan declared. "I can hardly wait to take you to the party."

Patsi turned to look at her new friend. "I don't really like a lot of attention."

"That ain't happenin' tonight, sister. Just wait until everybody sees how beautiful you are."

"It almost sounds like you're using me," Patsi said with a laugh. Inside she felt less confident.

"Of course I am." Megan smiled unashamedly. "You're way prettier than any of my other friends, and way nicer, too. They'll be so jealous."

"Oh." Patsi looked down at her painted toenails.

Megan put an arm around Patsi. "It's not a bad thing. You are way more fun than any of my old friends anyway."

"So what happened with your old friends?" Patsi asked.

Megan sighed and sat on her bed. She patted the spot beside her for Patsi to sit also. "I wasn't going to tell you, but I suppose it'll come out eventually anyway. You have that effect on me. Make me want to be different. Honest. And nice."

Patsi laughed. "You're nice already."

Megan shook her head. "Not the old Megan. I used to be the biggest snob ever, if you can believe it. I would purposely do things to hurt people and I'd make fun of anyone who was different."

"What changed?"

"I started doing cocaine," Megan said bluntly.

Patsi's eyes were wide. "Oh."

"Don't freak out or anything. A lot of my other friends were doing it, too, but for some reason, I… well, I went way overboard. When I tried to quit it started making me depressed and then I started cutting."

Patsi glanced down at Megan's perfect forearms. For the first time she noticed that Megan always wore long sleeves or wide bracelets. Megan removed one of the bracelets and Patsi could see the scars – red lines that ran perpendicular to her arm.

"I ended up in rehab. Nobody wanted to hang around with me after that. Some of the girls started spreading rumours that I was sleeping with guys for money. As if!" Megan let out a pent up breath.

"Why would they do that?" Patsi asked. "Hurt you more when you were already hurting. I don't get it."

Megan smiled. "Which is why I like you. I could tell right away that first day I sat by you in class that you were different."

"Cause I was wearing clothes from a department store?" Patsi asked with a grin.

"Maybe."

They both laughed.

"Seriously," Megan went on, "I just knew you wouldn't judge me. And you looked like you needed a friend as much as I did."

"I guess I did," Patsi admitted.

"Anyway, I imagine lots of those girls will be at the party. It's the first time I've gone to one since I've been better."

"How long ago was that?" Patsi asked.

"Over the summer."

"So not that long."

Megan shrugged. "I'm better, though. So don't worry." Megan slapped her knees and stood up. "Now, we better get going. I can hardly wait to see the looks on their faces."

Patsi wasn't sure she wanted to be the object of some mean girls' scrutiny. Still, she was excited to be going out to a party in the city. She hoped Brett was going, too, but she couldn't ask after Megan's warning the other night. No matter how good she looked, his approval was the only one she cared about.

THE PARTY WAS at a bonafide mansion. Patsi knew there were plenty of millionaires in this city - most of them rich from the oil industry - and of course, they had to live somewhere. But to actually be at a home that looked like something out a movie – well, that was something else all together. People milled about the whole house – the main great room, the dining room, and even spilled out onto the patio.

Megan waved to several people as they circulated through the crowd. Patsi felt like a new prize on display. Somewhere along the line a drink got pressed into her hand. She smiled and accepted it, but Lester had drilled her on the dangers of the date rape drug over and over again, so she just held on to it and didn't take a sip.

Megan didn't have the same misgivings about taking alcohol from random strangers, however. Soon her friend was dancing up close and personal with a cute guy who had dark hair and olive skin. Patsi stood on the edge of the crowd, feeling very out of place. A yawn escaped her lips and she placed her hand over her mouth. It had been a long day and suddenly the party didn't seem that exciting anymore. She set the untouched drink down on a table behind her and hoped nobody would notice.

"Well, if it isn't Pat. My sister's new friend."

Patsi turned to her left. Brett was standing next to her, smiling.

"Hi." She waved.

"You look forlorn," he said.

"Do I?"

He nodded and took a sip of his own drink. "Or bored. One of the two."

Patsi just smiled. "Tired, actually." She looked down at her toes, feeling silly all of a sudden.

"Looks like my sister has abandoned you." He gestured with his glass to where Megan and her dance partner were rubbing up against one another on the dance floor.

"She's having fun," Patsi offered with a shrug.

"She likes to do that, all right."

They watched for a few more seconds before Brett spoke again. "You like to dance?"

"Um... I guess. I'm not a great dancer, though." Truthfully, the only kind of dancing she had done was two-stepping at weddings and school dances.

"Let me be the judge of that."

Brett downed the rest of his drink and held out his hand. Patsi took it and he led her into the fray of bodies moving to the music.

Two songs later, she had relaxed and was enjoying herself. When the third song started, Brett grabbed her around the waist and brought her closer, moving seductively against her. She was alarmed at first when she could feel his arousal, but he just smiled at her and she let herself get into it. It was a new experience for her, to have that effect on a guy.

The song ended and the music went straight into another. Brett had quit smiling and was instead staring at her with such intensity that she had to look away. She pulled back and then disentangled herself altogether. "Um... I think I need a breather."

He shrugged and followed her off the dance floor. "Need a drink?"

She nodded.

"What'll you have?"

She wanted to say a beer but thought that sounded too provincial. "Um... I don't know. What are you having?"

He winked. "Stay right there. Be right back."

Patsi fidgeted for several minutes as she waited for Brett to return. When he did he had two small glasses in one hand and a bottle in the other. He handed her a glass and proceeded to pour clear liquid into each one. "Tequila shots," he said. "Ready? On three."

This is what she wanted, right? No turning back now. He counted to three and they both shot back the fiery liquid. Patsi coughed into the back of her hand and then gasped for air.

"Easy," Brett said with a laugh. "You okay?"

She just nodded and held out the glass, expecting him to take it. Instead, he filled it again. He counted to three a second time and they downed another shot. She was more prepared for it this time and it went down easier. One more shot each and then he set the glasses on the table beside her other untouched drink.

Back on the dance floor, Patsi soon felt much less inhibited by Brett's seductive moves. At some point they were kissing and then all of a sudden she felt a tap on her shoulder. It was Megan.

"Can I talk to you for a sec?"

Patsi stumbled after her friend, smiling widely. Megan stopped in a semi-secluded alcove and swung around to face her. "What are you doing?"

Patsi blinked. "What do you mean?"

"I just saw you kissing my brother."

"Oh. That." Patsi stifled a giggle with the back of her hand.

"Didn't I tell you not to get involved?" Megan asked angrily.

"You were having fun. Why can't I?"

"But this is totally different. Brett is my brother. He'll use you and dump you but you'll still run into him because we're friends. Then it'll ruin our friendship because you'll feel awkward."

Patsi tried to focus. "It's not like we're going to sleep together or anything."

"Oh yeah? I know my brother, okay?" Megan sighed and crossed her arms over her chest. "I suppose we'll have to leave now. Oh well. I think we made an impression, anyway."

"Is that all I am to you? Your pet project?" Patsi squinted and tried to focus on Megan's face.

"Don't be silly."

"Hey, what's going on here?" It was Brett.

Megan turned on him, pointing a finger at his chest. "I thought I told you to stay clear of Pat."

"She didn't seem to mind," he returned.

"She's not like your usual girls," Megan said.

"I'm right here," Patsi put in, waving a hand.

"We're leaving now," Megan said. "And just so you know, she's staying over. So smarten up."

Brett's eyebrows rose. "You're not driving I hope."

"Of course not. We took a cab," Megan said.

"Great. I might as well catch a ride and save on cab fare." Brett grinned.

Patsi couldn't help but smile.

FOR A MOMENT, Patsi didn't know where she was when she woke up on Sunday morning. Unfamiliar pink ruffles filled her vision when she opened her eyes. It was the large canopy over Megan's bed. When she rolled to one side a sudden queasy feeling assaulted her stomach and a nagging pain in the head told her she had had too much to drink the night before.

"Psst. You awake?" Patsi whispered, gently shaking Megan's shoulder.

Megan just groaned.

Patsi checked the clock on the nightstand and saw that it was already nine o'clock. Lester was expecting her home in time for church. Patsi sat up and slowly swung her legs over the side of the bed. She waited for a moment until her head quit spinning and then stood up.

Her head really hurt and she felt like crap. A shower would hopefully help her to feel human again.

A shower and a few headache pills she found in the cabinet helped some but her stomach still felt queasy and she was parched. She changed into her regular clothes and stuffed the dress and all her toiletries into her backpack. She hated to just abandon Megan, but her friend didn't seem to be waking up and she really needed to get going.

Patsi descended the stairs and risked going into the kitchen for a drink. A middle-aged woman sat at the granite island sipping coffee. Even in a tracksuit and wearing glasses, she looked stylish. She did not say anything but raised an eyebrow and then directed her gaze to Brett, who was bare chested and rummaging in the fridge.

"Mom, meet Pat. Pat, this is my mom, Elaine."

"Hi." Patsi waved and tried to smile. The woman's stony face did nothing to make her feel welcome and Patsi lowered her gaze.

"Sleep well?" Brett asked, a bottle of orange juice in his hands.

"Um, yeah."

Brett laughed. "Looks like you could use a glass of this. Sit down."

"Thanks." Patsi took the glass of orange juice he offered. He gestured for her to sit at the table.

"Can I speak to you for a moment?" Elaine directed an icy stare at her son.

"Sure." He smiled a Patsi and sent her a wink before following his mother into the hall.

"I've told you how I feel about you bringing random girls home overnight." The older woman made no attempt to soften her voice. Patsi nearly choked on her juice.

"Relax, Mother."

Brett reappeared in the kitchen, all smiles and minus his mother.

"Why didn't you say something?" Patsi asked. "She thinks I came home with you."

"You did."

"Along with Megan," Patsi countered. "Why didn't you tell her I was Megan's friend, not yours?"

"I'd like to think we're friends, too."

Patsi closed her eyes. Her head was far too sore for an argument. "You know what I mean."

"Don't worry. I'll set her straight later. I just like to irritate her a bit."

"That's terrible." Not to mention disrespectful, she thought. What would Lester say about all of this?

"I know."

Patsi opened her eyes. "You bring a lot of girls home I take it?"

"Not recently." His smiled was disarming.

Patsi felt her defences beginning to melt and concentrated on drinking the rest of her juice.

"For the record I had fun last night. With you," Brett said.

"Um, yeah... about that. I'm not used to drinking hard alcohol. So..."

"It's okay. I didn't mind."

"I'll just bet." This time it was Patsi's turn to smile.

There was a second of silence as they looked at one another until Patsi looked away. "Well, I guess I better get going. Um... what's the transit like from here on a Sunday?"

"Transit?" Brett asked.

"You know, as in bus or train...?"

"I wouldn't know. I've never taken a bus or train."

Of course not. "Oh. Well, I suppose I could check online. Being Sunday they might not run as regularly." In her mind she was calculating the cost of a cab and didn't think she could afford it.

"I can just drive you," Brett offered.

Patsi looked up from her phone search. "That would be too much trouble. I don't expect -"

"I want to," Brett said, standing up. "Just give me a minute to throw on some clothes."

"So you and my sister met at college," Brett opened the conversation once they were on the road in his electric blue Mazda RX-7.

"That's right. Calculus, if you can believe it," Patsi said.

"No kidding! Now, that I find hard to believe, since my sister isn't exactly college material."

Patsi smiled. "Me neither."

He glanced at her briefly. "Is that so? Then why are you going?"

"My brother thinks it will be good for me." She screwed up her face.

He nodded, still concentrating on the street ahead. "Siblings. I get it. I suppose my sister told you that I'm a total deadbeat. That I flunked out and now I just hang around the house sponging off my parents."

Patsi tried not to laugh. "Something like that. Is it true?"

"The sponging part, maybe." He smiled and glanced her way before focusing on the road again. "But I do have some ambitions. I'd like to get into DJ-ing more. I've done a bit, but…"

"Like that guy from last night?"

"Well… not really. He was mostly just playing top forty. I'm more into composing my own electronic music. Mash-ups, scratching. You know."

Patsi shook her head. "Actually, no. I haven't a clue what you just said."

Brett grinned. "Sorry. It's where you remix a song with a new beat, maybe add a bass line or speed it up. Make it more danceable. My friend Cory Roberts has a really sweet system and we've spun together a few times. It's something I'd like to do more of."

"So why don't you?" Patsi asked.

"Are you kidding? My parents are both corporate lawyers. Imagine the disgrace if their one and only son ended up spinning at clubs for a living."

"Sounds like a family disease," Patsi said.

Brett frowned. "What?"

Patsi smiled and waved a hand. "Just something Megan said about wanting to be an aesthetician."

"Oh, yeah. That. Our parents have high aspirations for us both. It's tough to live up to their expectations."

"And here I thought I was the only one. My brother is strict, but when it comes down to it I know he'll be okay with whatever I choose."

When they arrived at her apartment building, Patsi was feeling much better – both physically and mentally. Brett McMillan seemed genuine, not the player his sister made him out to be. When she got out of the car he said, "See ya around," as if he meant it. She hoped it was true.

THEY WALKED the few blocks to church, Patsi trailing slightly behind her brother. Lester didn't see any point in driving to some 'mega-church', as he called it, when there was a perfectly good place to worship just down the street.

At the end of the service, they were waiting in line to shake the pastor's hand at the door when Millicent Peacock, an especially nosy neighbour, sidled up beside Lester.

"I heard some rather rough language coming from your apartment last night. Is everything alright?" Her smile was saccharine sweet.

"Excuse me?" Lester turned to her. "Rough language? I doubt that. It must have been someone else." The rest of the crowd at the door had become eerily quiet.

"Well, perhaps it was just the yelling."

Lester clamped his mouth and turned away, sticking his hand out to shake with the pastor. Patsi followed behind, trying to keep the grin off her face. If there was one thing Lester hated, it was the way Ms.

Peacock kept rapping on her ceiling every time the TV was too loud or there was some other noise above a whisper.

Outside the church, Patsi almost had to run to keep up to Lester's long strides. "What was that about?" She asked as soon as they were out of earshot.

"Nothing. Just had a few friends over, that's all."

Patsi's eyes widened. "You? Had a few friends over? I need details!"

Lester scowled in her direction. "Jed and a couple of other guys from work. It's not like it was a party or anything. We had a couple of games of cards. Drank a couple of beers." He stopped talking for a moment to return Patsi's stare. "What?"

"Just the fact that my perfect brother isn't so perfect after all."

"WELL, everything is ready for supper. All you have to do is pop it in the oven." Goldie slipped a jacket over her nurse's uniform.

"Okay," Patsi said. She was babysitting Jason again that evening. "Have a good night at work."

"Oh, and there's an apple crisp in the fridge, too, left over from yesterday. You can have some for dessert." Goldie hesitated by the door, her hand on the nob. "You know, I'm off next week. Maybe you and your brother would like to come over for dinner."

"Um, I'll ask him." Maybe Jason's mother had been having the same thoughts as her son about finding a new dad. "So... whatever happened between you and Jason's dad? If you don't mind me asking."

"He didn't want to be a dad. Simple as that."

"Did you ever think he was 'the one'?"

Goldie smiled. "Actually, I think I was just lonely and I thought I could change him. It didn't work. Anyway, I better go."

Patsi locked the door behind Goldie and clicked the deadbolt into place.

Patsi and Jason shared the spicy macaroni casserole Goldie had made, apparently Jason's favourite, played a video game, and then Jason went to bed. Patsi tried to concentrate on some homework but found herself sliding further and further into the depths of the couch until she fell asleep. Suddenly, an unexpected buzzing noise woke her with a start. She sat up and fumbled to find her cell phone. "Hello?"

"Hi. Can I come up?"

Patsi frowned. The voice was familiar but she couldn't quite place it and the number was an unknown caller. "Who is this?"

"Forgot about me already?"

Her mind ran through all the possibilities and then her mouth opened in realization. "Brett?"

"Expecting someone else?"

"No. How did you get my number?"

"Easy. My sister leaves her phone lying around all the time. Meet me outside and we'll go somewhere."

"You're at my apartment building? But how..."

"Did I know where you live?" he finished. "Why else do you think I insisted on driving you home?"

"Right... Listen, I can't. I'm babysitting."

"Oh." He hesitated for only a moment. "So, I'll come up."

"Well..."

"Come on! I'm freezing out here. What's the number? Buzz me in."

Patsi gave him Goldie's apartment number before hauling herself off the couch. She went to the outdated intercom on the wall which also served to remotely unlock the front security doors. She pressed the button and then waited, butterflies flitting in her stomach until she heard a quiet knock on the door.

She peeked through the security peephole then unlocked the dead-bolt and swung the door open. "What are you doing here?" she asked just above a whisper.

"Coming to see you." Brett was staring at her with a goofy grin on his face. "You are really beautiful, do you know that?"

She was flattered and alarmed all at the same time. "Um, thanks." His glazed eyes told her he was slightly drunk, a fact that made her feel somewhat uneasy, but she let him step inside anyway. "Want a drink? Coffee? Tea?"

"What I want is a kiss."

Patsi sidestepped his somewhat awkward lunge, but had to grab his arm to keep him from toppling over. Make that more than slightly drunk. "I think we should sit down." She slipped her shoulder under his arm and maneuvered him to the couch.

He flopped back against the cushions. She considered her options for a moment and then sat down on the couch beside him. She doubted he would be too dangerous in this condition. "I hope you didn't drive."

"Scott dropped me off," Brett said.

"Good." Her parents died in a car accident and drunk driving was not something she took lightly. "Then you'll have to call a cab when it's time to go."

"I was hoping to stay the night." He grinned. "Or at least for a while…"

Patsi blinked. "What? But… I'm babysitting. It wouldn't be right."

"The kid's asleep, right?"

"Um, yeah…" Sometime during the conversation Brett had moved closer. She stiffened and moved over a millimetre. "But Jason is right next door and Goldie didn't say anything about visitors."

"You talk too much."

He was leaning in for a kiss and even though her sensible side was telling her to stop, there was another small part that nudged her to meet him halfway. "We really shouldn't…"

Brett silenced her completely with his mouth. A whirlwind of conflicting emotions ran the gamut of Patsi's body as everything she'd been brought up to believe melted away in the heat of Brett's wandering lips and hands.

"Who's that?"

A little boy's voice jolted them apart.

Patsi catapulted off the couch. "Jason! You're awake!"

EPISODE 4

WORKING THE NEIGHBOURHOOD

Tamara Spence sat at the small desk in the back room of the coffee shop she co-owned with her friend Carmen Lamont. The 'office' was actually a corner of the storage room. Boxes of supplies were piled high along the metal storage shelves and a freezer hummed nearby. Hardly the best atmosphere to take care of the business end of things, but it was the best they could do at the moment.

The Brew had been open for about a year and in that time they had built up a successful clientele of local business owners and young executives. It was a dream come true for both women. Tamara, in her early thirties and the older of the two, was a single mother from the Blood First Nation just south of Calgary. Her business partner, Carmen, was twenty-eight; an African Canadian woman who gave up her dream of making a living as an artist for something that would put bread on the table - literally. They had met a few years ago at a vigil for victims of abuse and had become fast friends once they discovered that they shared so many interests. Not only did both women have a well-developed social conscience, but they both loved art and they both loved to create in the kitchen. Thus, the idea for a trendy café in the heart of downtown that could become a hub for artists, musicians, poets and anyone with a heart for social justice, was born.

The two had plans for expansion that included space for artists to display their work, a place for live performances, and maybe even a platform for interest groups to launch their campaigns. The current space was limited at this point, however. They didn't even have room for a proper office.

"I'm just going to slip next door." Carmen Lamont stuck her head around the corner. "My niece is coming to town and I wanted to get her a little something before opening night."

"Renee?" Tamara looked up from the paperwork.

Carmen nodded. "She got a part in a local production and is going to be staying with me for a month."

"That's cool." Tamara pushed her office chair back from the desk. "I was sick of trying to figure out this invoice anyway."

Tamara logged off the computer, stood up, stretched and then went into the café. It was their slow period between the lunch rush and afternoon coffee break. Still, there were several patrons sitting at the high tables or lounging in leather armchairs that were placed around the room.

One of their regular customers, Steve Russell, a newspaper columnist, was sitting at his usual spot near the front window. He came almost every day during their slow time and drank exactly three cups of plain coffee while reading the 'Globe and Mail' on his phone. He wrote for one of the local papers and was known for his satirical take on local politics.

"Thanks for your mention of The Brew in yesterday's column," Tamara said as she brought a fresh pot of coffee to his table and filled up his cup.

"No problem. I call it like I see it." Steve was good looking in a 'slick' sort of way. Every hair on his head was in place and he always wore a suit and tie.

Tamara flipped her long, straight hair off her shoulder. "I suppose now we'll have to put up with all you journalist types. Since this is such a great place to connect with your muse, as you say."

"Hopefully not unwanted business," Steve said.

"Of course not." Tamara smiled. "I'd even welcome a few politicians or an oil baron or two. We'll serve fair trade coffee while you try to outmaneuver one another."

Steve frowned. "Outmaneuver? I'm not following."

Tamara cocked her head to one side. "I haven't decided which of you are more crooked – government, big business, or the media."

"Ouch." Steve smiled and shook his head. "I'm the guy trying to get at the truth. You really lump me in with those other snakes?"

"I call it like I see it," Tamara repeated Steve's own line, her lips turned up slightly.

"Listen. We should definitely get together some time and talk this through. I think you may have misjudged me." Steve smiled disarmingly.

Tamara blinked. Was he flirting? Was she? She sobered instantly and schooled her features into a noncommittal mask. "Sorry. My social calendar is full. Too many protest rallies." It wasn't far from the truth.

Steve laughed. "Of course. I should have guessed."

Tamara turned away, heading for another table that needed a refill. Steve Russell was definitely not her type, she decided. Charm and good looks were not enough. He was far too entrenched in the establishment to merit her interest.

TAMARA TRUDGED up the stairs of the apartment building, a reusable cloth bag full of groceries in one hand and her purse in the other. She never used the elevator unless absolutely necessary. She lived one more floor up, but she had to pick her son Matonabee up from her friend Goldie's place. Matonabee and Goldie's son Jason were best friends and Mat often went there after school until Tamara was off work.

Tamara knocked on the apartment door, and within seconds,

Goldie swung it open. "Come on in," Goldie said, gesturing for Tamara to enter.

"I really can't stay," Tamara said. "There's a small protest at city hall that I want to attend. Matonabee!" she called. "Get your stuff. We need to go!"

Matonabee materialized around the corner from the living room. He had an action figure in his hand. Jason wasn't far behind, flying his own super hero through the air with accompanying sound effects. "Can't I stay?" Matonabee asked.

"Sorry, kiddo. We have a rally to get to."

"Aw! I hate stupid rallies!" Matonabee exclaimed.

"I've got a sitter coming," Goldie said. "I'm on nightshift and she should be here soon. I don't think she'd mind an extra for a little while. It would probably keep Jason occupied, too."

Tamar considered this. "I hate to just dump my child on your babysitter. Especially since I've never met her."

"She's a college student. Just moved in not that long ago," Goldie said. As if on cue, another knock sounded at the door. "That's probably her now. Why don't you ask her yourself?"

Goldie opened the door to a blonde girl on the other side. She looked young, with long wavy hair.

"Pat, this is my friend Tamara Spence. Is it okay if her son Matonabee stays for a while?"

"I shouldn't be more than two hours," Tamara added.

"Sure." Patsi shrugged. "No problem."

"Of course I'll pay you." Tamara's brow furrowed slightly. "Have we met? You look familiar."

"I don't think so," Patsi said. "We moved in last month. My brother Lester and me."

"I know you!" It was Matonabee. He'd come into the kitchen. "I seen you in the parking lot."

"That's 'saw'," Tamara corrected. "I saw you in the parking lot."

Matonabee just shrugged.

"Pat's my new babysitter," Jason piped up proudly. "She's fun."

"Actually, I do recall seeing you." Tamara turned back to Patsi.

"And I believe I met your brother, too. He came into The Brew once with Jed Malloy."

Patsi nodded. "If he was with Jed then that would be him."

"I mentioned to him that we are really short staffed at the moment. If you're interested in a part time job, let me know," Tamara said.

"Um, okay. I'll think about it." Patsi smiled and then looked down at the floor.

"Well, I better get going, then," Tamara said. "Nice to meet you. And I'm serious about the job." She turned her attention to her son. "Come give me a hug. And be good for the sitter."

TAMARA APPROACHED the small band of protesters gathered on the steps of city hall. Most of them held placards above their heads as they shuffled in a semi-circular conga line up and down the steps. She waved when she saw Carmen and picked up her pace.

"Glad you could make it." Carmen held one of two placards out for Tamara. "Where's Matonabee?"

Tamara looked at the sign. It read, *"Jail is not the answer!"* in big bold letters. "He's at Goldie's. He and Jason were having fun and the sitter said he could stay." Tamara held the sign aloft.

"Probably for the best." Carmen lifted her own sign proclaiming: Johns are the real criminals! "It might be tough explaining to him what this is all about."

They got into step with the two-dozen other protestors, some of whom were scantily clad despite the cooling fall temperatures.

"He knows what prostitution is," Tamara said. "And he knows that I don't agree with it as a lifestyle choice simply because of the degradation to women. But I won't support a government who refuses to look at the other side of the equation."

"Hey, you weren't kidding when you said your calendar was full with protest rallies."

Tamara swung to the left where Steve Russell had fallen in step beside them.

"What are you doing here?" Tamara felt her frown reaching all the way to the rim of her knitted hat.

"Researching a story," Steve shot back with a grin. "I could be asking you the same question. Here to support your fellow working women, I take it?"

"I don't support women having to sell their bodies as a way to make a living." Tamara flipped a strand of her long hair behind her shoulder. "But some of these girls don't have a choice."

"There is always a choice," Steve countered.

"Not if you're hooked on drugs, homeless, or controlled by a pimp," Carmen spoke up. "Besides, putting these women in jail for longer periods of time isn't solving anything."

"But it's keeping them off the street, at least for a while," Steve reasoned.

"Most of these women are victims," Tamara said. "The government should be targeting the real root – the men who pay for their services. Without customers, they would have to find another way to survive. And it would crush the pimps who control most of these girls in the first place."

"You don't have to convince me." Steve gestured with his head toward the large cement building on whose steps they marched. "It's mayor and council who've proposed the tougher legislation."

Tamara was about to respond when she tripped and fell forward onto the cement steps. Pain shot through her wrist as she landed with her full weight on her outstretched hand.

"Are you okay?" Steve was by her side almost instantly, his hand under one elbow.

Tamara nodded and looked away. "I just need a minute." She grimaced as she twisted her body so that she was sitting on the step instead of kneeling on it. Carmen took the somewhat crumpled sign while Steve sat down beside her.

"Are you sure?" Steve bent to look into her eyes. His gaze met hers, genuine concern shining out of their dark blue depths.

Tamara blinked and lifted her chin. "It's nothing. Probably just a little sprain." The pain was actually quite severe. She took a deep breath and tried to calm herself like she did during yoga class.

"Maybe you should go to emergency," Carmen suggested. "Just to be sure."

"Good idea. I'll take you." Steve stood up and helped Tamara to her feet as well.

"This is silly, I really don't need -"

Steve cut Tamara off by holding up an index finger. "Sh. Stop talking and let me get you to my car."

"Text me later to let me know how you are," Carmen called to their retreating figures.

Tamara allowed Steve to maneuver her through the protesters as she cradled her wrist in her other hand. His car was parked about a block away – a silver sedan that looked neither fuel efficient nor fashionable. "Hm," she commented as he held the passenger door open for her and she slid in. "I would have pegged you as the sports car type."

"Still judging me?" Steve said with a laugh. He went around to his own side of the vehicle and got in. "You of all people should know better than to make assumptions."

"Why is that? Because I'm native?" Tamara asked coolly.

"No, that is not why," Steve shot back. He gave her a look that clearly displayed his disapproval then started the engine with a roar. "It's because you say you're all about social justice and equality. You attend rallies for goodness sake! Yet you insist on judging me, for what reason I know not."

He pulled out onto the street. There was silence in the vehicle for several minutes as Steve concentrated on driving. Tamara felt shamed into submission and her wrist throbbed terribly. Still, she couldn't bring herself to apologize. She had been judgmental when it came to Steve Russell. But letting her guard down now might be dangerous – for her more than him.

They arrived at the Foothills Hospital and Steve parked the car in the emergency parking area. Tamara had her own door open and was out of the car before Steve could come around to her side. "How's the arm?"

"I think I'll live," she clipped. "This is probably unnecessary."

"We'll let the doctor decide," Steve said. He placed his hand under her elbow and they walked to the emergency doors, which swished open upon their arrival.

Tamara waited in a small lineup at the reception desk and filled out some preliminary paperwork. Then she was directed to take a seat in the waiting area. "I hope this doesn't take too long. My son is at the sitters, but I wasn't expecting to be gone for more than two hours."

"At least he's looked after," Steve said.

"You really don't need to wait with me," Tamara said. "It could take a while judging by the room full of people. I can find my own way home."

"It's okay. I've got nothing better to do."

Tamara doubted that, but kept her mouth shut. She picked up a magazine with her good hand and rested it on her lap as she flipped her way through. If Steve Russell insisted on staying then he could wait in silence.

After about fifteen minutes, a nurse called her name. Tamara tossed the magazine onto the pile and stood up, following the nurse into a small examining room. After another few minutes, a doctor with white hair and a neatly trimmed beard to match entered the room and shut the door behind him. Another half an hour, an initial examination and some x-rays later, he gave his prognosis. It was just a bad sprain.

Prescription in hand, Tamara made her way back to the waiting room. Her injured wrist was in a tensor and she wore a skin coloured foam sling to keep it somewhat elevated. Steve was still sitting there. He looked up as soon as he saw her approaching figure and stood up. "So? What's the verdict?"

"Just a sprain." Tamara shrugged.

"Enough to warrant some pain meds, I see." Steve's gaze went to the small piece of paper in her good hand.

"We'll see. I don't like taking pharmaceuticals if I can help it."

"Of course you don't."

Was he mocking her? She straightened her shoulders. "Well, thanks anyway. For the lift. I can find my own way home, though."

"Don't be ridiculous," Steve said. "I'll drive you."

"You don't have to do that." They were already heading toward the exit.

"I know. I want to. Besides it's dark now and I'd hate to see you taking a train or a bus this late at night."

"I do it all the time," Tamara said.

Steve grinned. "Of course you do."

They emerged into the night air. Floodlights lit the parking lot so that it was almost as bright as in the daytime, but darkness crept around the perimeter and cast long shadows beneath the vehicles.

On the drive home Steve asked questions about how the business was going, about Matonabee, and about Tamara's interest in social justice. She kept her answers short and to the point. At the back of her mind was the knowledge that he did this for a living – interrogated people, and he was very skilled at making her want to open up to him. But she was onto his game and wouldn't allow him to get past anything superficial.

"Anyone ever tell you that independence can be taken too far?" Steve asked.

"Meaning?"

"This whole stand-offish vibe. Underneath I know there's a really interesting woman. You just seem afraid to let anybody in."

"Not anybody. Maybe it's just you."

Steve laughed. "Touché! I guess I walked right into that one."

"I don't like being interrogated." Tamara looked at his profile. Straight nose - perhaps a little longer than it should be; full lips; brown hair combed slightly to the side. She didn't like the feelings she had when she was this close.

"Is that what you think I'm doing? Interrogating you?" He glanced her way before focusing on the road again.

"Aren't you?"

"If interrogating means getting to know you better, then maybe I am."

"My apartment building is just right around the next corner," Tamara changed the subject.

"Street side or parking lot?" Steve asked as they approached the building.

"Street is fine," Tamara answered.

Steve pulled up in front of the building and let the vehicle idle.

"Thanks for the lift," Tamara said as she opened the passenger door.

"No problem. Now I know where you live." Steve grinned.

Tamara stood for a minute, not sure how to respond. She decided on slamming the passenger door and heading to the building.

"SORRY I'M a little later than expected," Tamara said to Patsi once the teenager had opened Goldie's apartment door.

"No trouble. The boys fell asleep watching a movie, so I just moved Matonabee onto Goldie's bed."

"Thanks." Tamara held up her bound wrist. "I didn't plan on being so late, but I had a little mishap."

"Oh my!" Patsi exclaimed. "Is it broken?"

Tamara shook her head. "Just a sprain, thankfully. I really can't afford to take any time off work. Although I'm not sure how efficient I'll be."

"Um… I was thinking about what you said earlier." Patsi's gaze shifted downward before rising to meet Tamara's again. "About the part time job?"

Tamara nodded. "We sure could use someone, especially now."

"What would the hours be?"

"Well, we've been closing in the evenings since most of our clientele are business people. But we'd like to start staying open in the evenings, too, if we can get staff. Obviously, I don't want to work in the evenings as much because I've got Mat to think about. But if we could get staff to cover during the day, Carmen – that's my partner –

would take over some evenings. Goldie said you were a student. What kind of schedule do you have?"

"I'm pretty flexible. I could give you a schedule of my classes and work around that." Patsi glanced down at the floor again. "Except my brother wouldn't like it if I had to take the bus home after dark, so I guess evenings is out."

"You could get a ride home with me," Tamara suggested. "And if not, I would make sure to pay for your cab fare or whatever. We'd work something out. I'm really just desperate for reliable workers at this point. Why don't you come down tomorrow sometime and fill out an application? Then we can take it from there."

Patsi beamed. "Sounds good."

"Well, I suppose I should get my son and get him into his own bed."

PATSI DID AS PROMISED and arrived the next day to fill out an application. When she was finished she brought it up to the counter where Carmen and Tamara stood.

Carmen scanned the document and nodded. "How soon can you start?"

Patsi's eyes widened and she shrugged her shoulders. "Now, if you want."

"Great. There's an apron right on one of those hooks." Tamara pointed at a row of aprons hanging behind the counter. "Put it on and we'll get you started."

Before long the lunch rush hit and Tamara and Carmen were both so busy they had little time to coddle Patsi through their routine. While they were busy filling orders, Patsi cleared tables and made the rounds with the coffee pot. An hour later, they were all exhausted, and every table in the place was full of dirty plates and leftovers.

Without being told, Patsi grabbed a plastic tub from under the counter and started to clear away the debris.

Carmen leaned closer to Tamara. "She's fantastic. Where did you find her?"

Tamara held her wrist in her free hand. It had started to throb. "She lives in our building. She's the one who was babysitting last night for Goldie."

"I wish we could find a few more like her," Carmen said.

"Exactly." Tamara took off the large, clear plastic glove she had placed over her bandage and started to unwrap the tensor.

"What are you doing?" Carmen pointed to Tamara's bound hand.

"Dishes," Tamara answered.

"Didn't the doctor say to take it easy for a few days?" Carmen asked.

"Yes, but -"

"Then listen for a change. Or I'll send you home." Carmen's tone was light but her eyes had that no nonsense look. "As soon as Pat has cleared the tables she can do the dishes."

"Good advice."

Tamara glanced at Steve Russell. He was standing at the counter. She hadn't seen or heard him come in and it was a bit earlier than his usual time. "Coffee?" she asked, deciding to ignore his comment from the night before.

"Of course. I can carry it to my own table, since it looks like you two are run off your feet."

"Thanks a lot," Carmen said with a grin. She filled a cup of coffee and handed it to Steve. "Now, why don't you two go sit down for a bit? Tamara needs to rest that wrist."

"Sounds like a good plan," Steve said and smiled in a way that sent Tamara's insides a flutter.

Tamara focused instead on the countertop. "Sorry. I've got paper-work to do in the back."

"Not a chance. I'm heading back there now. Rest." Carmen gave Tamara a pointed stare and then turned to leave.

Tamara waited until Carmen was out of earshot, then she looked at Steve. "We're training a new girl. I can't sit just yet." By this time, Patsi had finished clearing all the tables. Tamara deliberately turned her back on the journalist, and proceeded to instruct her new employee on the proper method of rinsing and sanitizing dishes. "One day we hope to get a dishwasher, but for now we do it the old fashioned way."

Several minutes later Tamara heard the door open and turned to see who had entered. It was her neighbour Jed Malloy. "Hi Jed," Tamara called. "What can I get you today? Your usual?"

"Yup. Give me a bowl of soup to go with it." Jed was a giant of a man, his boisterous Newfoundland brogue filling the air as much as his frame filled the room. He plunked himself at one of the high tables. His feet touched the floor quite nicely despite its height.

"Coming right up." Tamara slipped a clean plastic glove over her bandaged hand.

"Is that my neighbour Patsi Mae Tibbett workin' behind the counter?" Jed called from his spot.

Tamara glanced at Patsi and saw the girl visibly stiffen.

"Hi Jed." Patsi responded as she continued to wash the dishes. She looked at Tamara, almost apologetically. "Just call me Pat. I hate my full name."

"What's that brother gonna think when 'e finds out you're workin'?" Jed asked. As was often the case with folks from Newfoundland, Jed dropped the letter 'h' at the beginning of most words.

"None of your business," Patsi called back.

Tamara looked at Patsi. The girl was obviously flustered. "Is there a problem? Something I should know about?"

Patsi shook her head. "No. My brother just wasn't in favour of me getting a job, that's all. But he'll get over it."

"You're sure?" Tamara frowned as she slid a stack of Pastrami on Jed's sandwich. "I don't want to be the cause of any friction between you and your brother."

Patsi nodded. "It'll be fine. Really."

Tamara turned away. She certainly hoped so. They were in desperate need of more staff and Patsi seemed like she was a hard worker.

Next, Tamara filled a bowl with their soup of the day – vegetarian split pea. When the sandwich was done she put both on a tray and brought it over to Jed's table. "This is a bit late for you. Don't you usually take your lunch break earlier than this?"

"Rumour 'as it the architect from Toronto is coming back to town to inspect. We 'ad a few things to tidy up before 'e showed." Jed took a big bite of his sandwich and sighed. "Mm. that's good. If I was the marryin' kind I'd sweep ya off yer feet if you'd promise me a sandwich like this every day!"

Tamara laughed and shook her head. "Whatever. Enjoy." As she walked past Steve's table, he reached out and touched her arm. She stopped. "Yes?"

"Should I be jealous?" He glanced at Jed, who was still in the process of eating his sandwich with gusto.

Tamara screwed up her face. "What a question." She marched back to the counter and pretended to be busy by making more coffee.

The door opened again and Tamara glanced that way. The attractive black woman who entered The Brew looked vaguely familiar. Her hair was straightened to about shoulder length and she wore form fitting jeans, a sweater and a fashionable scarf. She was pulling a travel suitcase and had another large bag slung over her shoulder. "Just sit anywhere," Tamara called. "We aren't busy at the moment."

It was true, except for Steve and Jed the place was empty.

"Actually, I'm looking for Carmen Lamont. Is she here?"

Recognition dawned on Tamara's face. "Of course! You must be Renee, Carmen's niece. She's just in the back."

"I can get her," Patsi said as she dried her hands on a towel.

A few moments later, Carmen came rushing from the back and she and Renee locked themselves in a bear hug. "You look so great!" Carmen gushed.

"You too. I can't believe it's been a whole year," Renee exclaimed.

"How was your flight from Vancouver?" Carmen asked, stepping back.

"Fine. It's been raining there all week, so it's kind of nice to get somewhere dry."

"Is this all you brought?" Carmen gestured to the travel suitcase.

Renee laughed. "I'm trying to turn over a new leaf. Besides, it's only for a month. Thanks for letting me stay with you, Auntie."

Tamara smiled at the endearment. Renee looked to be only a few years younger than Carmen.

"No problem," Carmen said. "Here, let me put your stuff in the back room for now. Have you had anything to eat?"

"I ate on the plane," Renee said. "I was thinking I might just take a cab over to your place right away, if that's okay. I would have gone straight there but I didn't have a key."

"Of course. Or you could take the train. There's a stop right around the corner from here and my apartment is only two blocks from where you get off. Let me just get my spare key." Carmen bustled into the back room and returned a minute later with a key in her hand.

Carmen handed the key to her niece and then proceeded to explain the directions for getting on and off the train.

"Excuse my intrusion, but wouldn't it just be easier to take the cab?"

All three sets of female eyes swung to Steve Russell.

"My thought exactly," Jed piped up. He wiped his mouth with a napkin, the paper rasping against the stubble on his chin.

"I don't mind the train," Renee said. "It's a lot cheaper."

"Plus, public transit is much better for the environment," Tamara put in.

Steve shrugged. "Suit yourself. I'd offer to drive you myself but I don't suppose you'd agree."

"Um..." Renee's gaze darted from Steve to Carmen to Tamara.

Tamara placed her hands on her hips. "And why would you do that?"

"Just being civil." Steve raised his hands in a gesture of surrender. "I'm not up to anything devious, if that's what you think."

"I wouldn't put it past you," Tamara said under her breath.

"He's right," Carmen said. "A cab is way easier. I'll pay the fare if money is an issue."

"I couldn't let you do that," Renee protested. "I have money. Just give me the number to a cab company and I'll be on my way."

Steve recited a number off the top of his head and Renee punched the numbers into her phone.

It was a strangely intimate moment as the group of near-strangers sat silently listening to Renee make the arrangements with the taxi company. Carmen cleared her throat and turned to Steve. "I enjoyed this morning's article. About the city counsellor who is a proponent of the stricter prostitution laws and then was caught using the services of a prostitute."

"Told you I was doing research last night." Steve caught Tamara's eye. "Politicians. Those are the guys you should be suspicious of. Not journalists."

Tamara glanced away.

"I read that article, too." Jed joined the conversation. "Nice piece of work. Expose the scoundrels, I always say."

"Indeed," Steve said.

"How do you get away with it and not get sued?" Carmen asked.

"That's why they pay me the big bucks." Steve laughed. "Seriously, though, we cover our butts pretty well. I didn't mention any names, so if the man in question actually came out and tried to sue us, it would be like admitting it."

"Clever," Carmen said.

"More like sneaky," Tamara added.

Steve smiled. "Still a skeptic? Oh well. Someday you'll see my true colours. For now, I guess I better get back to the grindstone." He rose from the table and fished in his back pocket for his wallet.

Tamara turned away and headed for the counter. For some reason she felt flustered and she didn't like it one bit. Steve Russell was a smooth operator and she didn't trust him as far as she could throw him – no matter what he said.

Later, after Renee had left in her cab, Carmen came into the back room where Tamara was checking through some invoices.

"I think this tip was for you." Carmen tossed a ten-dollar bill along with a business card onto the desk.

Tamara looked at the money and the card. Steve Russell, journalist. Her nostrils flared but she purposely re-focused on the stack of invoices. "Just put the money in the tip jar and we'll share it later."

"Read the back of the card." Carmen folded her arms over her chest and waited.

With a sigh, Tamara took the card and turned it over. It read, *"I'd like to do a story on you sometime. Call me."* She tossed it back on the desk. "That'll be the day. Steve Russell takes pleasure in making fools of people. I'm not interested."

"No? Well, I think he is. Interested, I mean." Carmen grinned like a Cheshire cat.

Tamara looked up sharply at her friend and frowned. "Don't be silly. Steve Russell is just on the lookout for a story. That's it."

Carmen shook her head and laughed. "For someone so smart, you sure can be naïve at times."

"MOM! Come play ball with us. Puh-leeze?" Matonabee dragged out the word for effect.

Tamara shielded her eyes from the afternoon sun as she turned her attention toward her son. He and his friend Jason were tossing a softball between them. "I hurt my wrist, remember?" It was Sunday afternoon and one of the few days she had off.

"Aw!" Matonabee wasn't shy about sharing his disappointment. "Jason isn't a very good catch."

A smile tweaked at the corners of Tamara's mouth. True, the ball was rolling on the ground more than it made it into their gloves. She turned to Goldie, who was sitting on the park bench beside her. "Are you up for it?"

Goldie sighed, but stood to her feet anyway. "So much for a few minutes of down time while the kids play."

Tamara watched as Goldie sauntered to where the boys were playing. She took the ball and with an exaggerated underhand movement she tossed it toward her son Jason. It bounced off his oversized ball glove and went rolling in the opposite direction.

"Hi neighbours."

Tamara glanced toward the newcomer's voice and nodded in greeting. "Hi. Lester, right?" The cowboy had sidled up to the park bench.

He nodded. "Surprised you remembered. I've only been to your café once." He had his hands jammed into his jeans pockets and he smiled.

"I never forget a face," Tamara said with a smile of her own.

"Or a name, apparently."

"Actually, I met your sister the other night. She watched my son Matonabee for a few hours while she was sitting for Goldie. She mentioned you." She purposely omitted the fact that 'Pat' was also her newest employee.

"Ah. That explains it." Lester let his gaze sweep over the playground and rest on Goldie and the boys. "Nice afternoon for a game of catch." He gestured with one hand to the threesome, keeping the other hand in his jean's pocket.

"They're trying," Tamara said with a slight laugh. "I'd help but I hurt my wrist." She held up the bandaged limb.

"Maybe they need a relief pitcher," Lester said.

"I'm sure Goldie would be thrilled."

Tamara watched as the lean cowboy with the brown curly hair and sideburns sauntered toward Goldie and company. A few seconds later, Goldie was handing over the ball, a grateful smile on her lips. She stepped back to give Lester more room.

"Okay, boys," Lester called. "Mat, you need to move a little to the left. Jason, you stay right there. First, I'll toss it to Jason and then he'll throw it back to me and then I'll toss it to Matonabee. Got it?" The boys nodded, their faces alight with excitement. "Now, hold your gloves up nice and high. That's it." Jason lined up and Lester tossed the ball at him. The boy shrank as it approached and it bounced off his glove again and dribbled to the ground.

Lester turned to Goldie. "On second thought, why don't you pitch and I'll help Jason with his catching technique?"

"Um, okay." Goldie stepped back into place and Lester walked a few paces to stand behind Jason.

Lester grasped the glove, Jason's hand still in it. "Don't be afraid of the ball," Lester advised. "Let it go right into your glove."

Goldie lofted the ball high, and Lester maneuvered the glove underneath so that Jason 'caught' the ball. The boy wore a huge grin.

"Way to go, buddy!" Lester high-fived Jason and Goldie clapped her hands. "Easy, see? We'll try it again after Mat has a turn."

The game of catch continued for several minutes until Lester finally had to take his leave – but not before Goldie had invited him and his sister for dinner that evening. "I'm making barbecued ribs. Not to brag, but I make a pretty mean rack of ribs."

"Ribs are my favourite," Lester said. He tipped his hat, waved one more time at the boys, and sauntered away from the park.

Goldie's eyes followed him for a few minutes before she turned to the boys. "That's enough for now. You boys go play on the monkey bars or something." She walked back to the bench and sat down beside Tamara.

"That was awfully nice of him to stop and play with the boys like that," Tamara said.

"I know." Goldie nodded.

"Nicely done, by the way," Tamara added, gaging her friend's reaction out of the corner of her eye.

"I don't know what you mean," Goldie responded, her lips pursing coyly.

Tamara laughed. "Like heck you don't. Inviting the new neighbour over for dinner tonight? Good one."

Goldie shrugged her shoulders. "I saw an opportunity and I took it." She smiled and looked at Tamara. "You don't think that was too forward, do you?"

"It's about time you started dating again. What I want to know is how did you know ribs were his favourite?"

"I asked his sister," Goldie admitted.

Tamara laughed. "Now I am really impressed. He is rather good looking, I will admit."

"He is, isn't he? And his sister says he goes to church, which is exactly the kind of guy I'm looking for." Goldie grinned at Tamara. "If things work out I can see if he has a friend."

Tamara shook her head. "No thanks. I don't have time for men."

"So how did your dinner go the other night at Goldie's?" Tamara asked Patsi the next day at work.

Patsi's hands were in a sink full of sudsy water. Her eyebrows lifted slightly. "Fine. How did you know we were going to Goldie's for dinner?"

Tamara smiled. "Oh, Goldie and I are friends, that's all."

Patsi chuckled. "It was a bit awkward."

"What do you mean?"

"I think Goldie likes Lester – which I don't get at all - but then Jason asked him if he wanted to be his new daddy. Talk about awkward!"

"Kids." Tamara shook her head. "They are so transparent." She glanced out of the corner of her eye toward Patsi's profile. "What makes you think your brother isn't a good catch?"

Patsi shrugged. "I don't know. He's just old. And I don't think he's ready to settle down. He seemed kind of uncomfortable and he sure high tailed it out of there after dinner."

"Poor Goldie." Tamara shook her head again.

Carmen appeared in the doorway from the back room. "Tamara, can you come back here? The delivery truck is out back and there is absolutely nowhere to put any more stuff."

"Be back in a sec," Tamara said to Patsi and followed her partner into the back.

"This is why we need to expand," Carmen said. "There is absolutely no room back here for all these boxes. Where are we going to put them?"

A gust of wind snuck by the delivery truck driver as he stood just inside the back door which led out into the alley. His dolly was loaded high and he was leaning on the top box with his elbow.

"We just have to get creative," Tamara said.

"I don't know how much more creative we can be. We're already practically climbing over boxes back here as it is." Carmen threw up her hands.

"Just leave it right there." Tamara gestured to the floor directly in front of the delivery man.

Carmen shook her head and disappeared back into the front. Tamara waited for the man to offload the stack of boxes and then signed the necessary paperwork on his clipboard. Once he had taken his leave, she shuffled a few boxes around and shimmied the new stack out of the direct line of the back door. It would have to do for now.

"We're going to have to do something about the lack of space," Carmen said as soon as Tamara re-entered the front.

Tamara pasted on a smile and turned to Patsi. "Can you fill up the napkin holders, please?"

Patsi grabbed a bag of napkins made of recycled paper and scurried to do as she was told. Tamara waited until Patsi was out of earshot and then focused on her partner. "I don't like employees witnessing an argument between us."

"It was hardly an argument." Carmen folded her arms against her chest. "I was just stating the obvious. We've outgrown this venue."

Tamara sighed. Yes, space was tight, but she seemed to be the only one in this partnership who understood they couldn't afford to expand right now. "We'll get Pat to do a major restock out here and that should free up some space. I'll go shift a few more things around so she knows which things we want restocked."

Carmen shook her head. "No, I'll go. You should go attend to our regular customer." She gestured with her head to where Steven Russell sat at his usual table.

Tamara let her gaze swing to the newspaperman. "He comes here every day. He doesn't need 'attending.'"

"How do you know?" Carmen asked. "Looks like he could use a refill to me."

"Let Pat do it." Tamara stopped and then narrowed her eyes. "Are you trying to manipulate me?" It wasn't an accusation exactly. She couldn't help but let the corners of her mouth turn up just a little bit.

Carmen rolled her eyes. "Moi? Manipulate anyone?"

"I don't need your help in that department," Tamara said quite firmly. "Besides, you know I'm not looking and if I was, he is all wrong."

"So says you, but don't think I haven't noticed."

Tamara frowned. "Noticed what?"

Carmen raised a brow. "I know you secretly like him. Admit it."

"I don't know what you're talking about. Besides, I would never be interested in a guy who works for the establishment like Steve Russell."

"The establishment? What does that even mean?" Carmen asked.

"You know. People who make a living on gossip and speculation, feeding off the misfortune of others."

"Oh. That's what it means." Carmen's exaggerated nod just added fuel to Tamara's rising ire.

"I'll go rearrange the back room now." Tamara swung her considerable length of long black hair off her shoulder and swept past her co-worker.

Carmen could speculate all she wanted. She, Tamara Spence was not going to get trapped into a relationship unless it was on her terms.

"TAMARA?"

Tamara rolled as far as the office chair would allow in the cramped space and leaned past some boxes to look at Carmen.

"The boutique next door is up for sale." Carmen waved a real estate flyer above her head.

"So?" Tamara asked. She rolled back to her desk and focused on the order she was preparing on the computer screen.

"Well, we have been talking about a way to expand the business. This might be our chance. Just think. Room for more art, live music… a proper office." Carmen looked around at the boxes piled high around the make shift office space.

"I guess it depends on how much they want and how much a 'reno' would cost." Tamara paused for a moment, blinking into thin air. "What we really need is an engineer or an architect. Someone we could ask about the feasibility."

"An architect, huh?" Carmen said. "Doesn't Steve have a friend who's an architect? He was in here a while back."

"You mean Sherman Chan?" Tamara shook her head. "He lives in Toronto."

"Oh, right." Carmen glanced down at the floor.

"Although, I do remember that big Newfie, Jed, saying something about him coming back for an inspection or something. He's behind that new high-rise that's going up nearby."

"Oh. That's right, too. I forgot."

Tamara squinted at Carmen. "You forgot, eh? Now who's keeping secrets?"

"What do you mean?" Carmen's tone had a defensive edge.

"If I recall, a certain rather interesting Asian man may have taken a liking to one Carmen Lamont." Tamara leaned back in the chair and folded her arms.

"Don't be silly. Besides, you're a fine one to talk when you won't even admit you have the 'hots' for Steve Russell."

"I do not have the hots for Steve Russell!" Tamara exclaimed.

Patsi appeared around the corner. "Um, I just thought you might like to know Mr. Russell is here with his friend. A guy named Sherman Chan? They specifically asked for you."

Tamara and Carmen exchanged a glance and then both burst into adolescent giggles.

"Okay, fine. So neither one of us has been getting any satisfaction, lately," Carmen said.

"Speak for yourself," Tamara countered. "I haven't admitted to anything."

Carmen smoothed her flowing top over her flat stomach and schooled her full red lips into a demure line before exiting the back room.

Tamara saved the file she was working on and then took a deep breath. If her own attraction to Steve Russell was as obvious as Carmen's was for Sherman Chan, then she really was in trouble. It was a silly physical thing and nothing more. She really would have to get ahold of herself. She stood up and tossed her straight long hair off her shoulders. At least the other couple would deflect some of Steve's attention away from her.

Steve was standing up to the counter with a good-looking Asian man with a trim, muscular build, dark hair and designer glasses.

Carmen flashed a smile at Tamara. "Look who's back in town."

"Sherman Chan, right?" Tamara asked.

"Glad you didn't forget about me." Although it was directed at Tamara, Sherman's gaze was locked on Carmen.

"The usual?" Carmen asked Steve, her voice sounding suddenly out of breath.

"Please," Steve said with a nod. He glanced over at Tamara and she quickly looked away, busying herself with pouring his coffee.

"I might want to try something different to drink," Sherman said.

"Like what?" Carmen asked.

"Surprise me." He smiled. "Oh, but I will have a piece of that carrot cake. It looks good."

"Go ahead and sit down. We'll bring it over," Tamara said. The men nodded and turned to head for Steve's table.

"I'd love to surprise him, alright," Carmen whispered near Tamara's ear before lifting the lid off the cake tray.

Tamara suppressed a giggle. "The apple spiced tea will go good with the cake."

"Should I ask him about the expansion?" Carmen asked. She placed an extra large slice of cake on a plate and then replaced the glass lid on the display stand.

"Might as well. We might not get another chance - although, I would say that is highly unlikely."

If it wasn't for Carmen's dark skin, Tamara was sure she was blushing.

Carmen delivered the drinks and the cake a few minutes later. "Apple spice. I hope you like it. We thought it would complement the cake." Tamara loitered nearby, wiping an already clean table.

Sherman made a production of stirring some honey into the small teapot and then pouring the tea. He finally took a noisy sip and nodded. "Good."

"Glad you like it." Carmen waited another moment. "Say, do you mind if we pick your brain about something? Something to do with the business?"

Sherman looked up in surprise. "Sure. Anything."

Carmen gestured for Tamara to join them and then perched on the empty stool next to Sherman. She waited until Tamara was standing nearby.

"Looks menacing." Steve looked from Carmen to Tamara. "Should we be nervous?"

Tamara ignored the jibe and took a deep breath. "We've been talking about expanding for some time and now the boutique next door is up for sale. We need to get an expert's opinion on whether it's even possible."

"Almost anything is possible – if you have the money," Sherman said.

"Of course," Carmen said with a nod.

"I'd need to look at the blueprints, first," Sherman continued. "See what we're dealing with. Even then, until you actually start tearing down walls, it's often hard to tell what the actual scope will be."

"I see."

"Of course, I'm no expert when it comes to the business end of running a restaurant." Sherman paused and laughed. "Although my family does own one. But you'd need someone to help you crunch those numbers to make sure it would be worth it financially. My sister is good at that sort of thing."

"All in the family," Tamara quipped.

"It's true," Steve said. "She's a Math professor." He turned to Tamara. "What's your budget like?"

"Minimal," Tamara said.

Carmen laughed. "Let's just say that it's a point of contention between us at the moment."

"You've got to spend money to make money," Steve offered.

"Exactly." Carmen looked pointedly at Tamara.

"Forget about money for now," Sherman said. "What did you have in mind?"

"It would be easier to show you." Carmen grabbed a napkin. "Anyone have a pen?" Steve produced one from his inside pocket and Carmen started making some quick concept sketches. Sherman leaned in, intent on what she was drawing.

"I should probably get back to work." Tamara rose from the stool.

Sherman looked at his watch. "Oh! Me, too. But we should talk more about this. I am definitely intrigued."

I'll just bet you are, Tamara thought, but she smiled congenially.

"I have a friend at public works who has access to most of the blueprints for the buildings in the downtown core. I'll see if I can get ahold of them and then I'll call you."

"Perfect. Here's my number." Carmen recited her number for Sherman to put into his telephone contacts.

"Thanks." Sherman smiled up at Carmen.

Tamara kept her lips clamped tight. Sherman was pretty slick. Must be why he and Steve Russell were such good friends.

Suddenly Sherman's phone beeped, signalling an incoming call. He pressed a button and held the device up to his ear. "Sherman Chan." The rest watched as his face visibly changed from cool and pleasant to one of grave concern. "Got it. I'll be right there." He cut the call short. "Sorry. I've got to go." He stood, obviously in a hurry to leave.

"What's up?" Steve asked, his own forehead marred by a frown.

"There's been an accident on the job site. One of the workers fell three stories down an elevator shaft."

Tamara and Carmen both gasped. Patsi dropped a glass plate behind the counter and all eyes turned toward her.

"Are you alright?" Tamara rushed to Patsi's side.

The girl was statuesque, as if in shock. "Did... did they say who it was that got hurt?"

"Not sure," Sherman said. "One of the new guys. I better go."

"My brother Lester works there," Patsi said, her voice barely above a whisper. "He's a new guy."

"Can you call and let us know?" Carmen directed at Sherman's retreating figure.

"I will," he called over his shoulder. Next thing he was out the door.

Tamara put a steadying arm around Patsi's shoulder. "It's going to be okay. It probably wasn't your brother anyway."

Patsi started to cry. "I never should have lied about this job," she said. "What if he dies and I can't say I'm sorry?"

"Now you're over dramatizing." Tamara put on her best motherly voice. "We don't know for sure who it is, so there's no use worrying. Everything is going to be fine." She looked over the girl's head and made eye contact with Steve. His steady gaze seemed to say she was saying and doing the right thing, and that gave her strength. Even if she was not at all sure about the truth of that statement.

EPISODE 5

BACK IN THE NEIGHBOURHOOD

*I*t was a harrowing day for Sherman Chan. He'd just arrived back in Calgary after a long flight from Toronto when he got the news. One of the construction workers on site had fallen three stories down an elevator shaft.

Lester Tibbett was an awfully lucky man. Somehow he'd managed to avoid any broken bones – a miracle in itself. He was pretty bruised up, though and would need to spend the night in hospital and several more days resting and recovering before he could come back to work. At least there wouldn't be any 'Workman's Compensation' issues.

But now the real test of Sherman's mettle was about to begin. Visiting his parents. Not that he didn't love them. He did. But his father and mother were old school. Steeped in traditions that somehow didn't fit with Sherman's modern lifestyle. They didn't know he was coming. It was better that way. Less fuss.

Sherman stood outside the small convenience store for a few minutes staring up at the Chinese characters that flashed in red neon above the door. It was a three-story brick building, square and featureless except for the blinking sign. One of two family businesses built with sweat and much sacrifice. With a sigh, he pushed the door open and was met by the jingling of a little bell. Things hadn't changed much. It was cluttered - almost antique in appearance.

There sat his father, Joseph, in his usual spot behind the counter reading the paper. It was a Chinese paper, the caricatures mostly indecipherable to Sherman, raised as he was to be a success in the 'Western' world. He felt cheated, sometimes, because his family's hard work had almost precluded any real interaction with his own culture. "Hello father," Sherman greeted in Mandarin.

Joseph Chan nodded calmly. "Hello son," he responded in perfect English. Joseph was a second generation Canadian, born and raised in Canada, although his upbringing was quite traditional. Never one to show too much emotion, he didn't seem surprised to see his son. He folded his paper carefully, and rose slowly from his stool behind the counter. "When did you get in?"

"I just arrived this morning," Sherman replied. "I stopped at the job site first."

Joseph nodded. "That high rise seems to be coming along very well."

"Yes," Sherman agreed. "Everything is on schedule."

"I see. Does your mother know you're here?"

"No," Sherman replied sheepishly. "I should have called, but... I didn't have a lot of time before I left Toronto, and well, you know how it is once you're in flight." It sounded like an excuse, even to his ears.

"Your mother is upstairs," Joseph said, as if that was the reason Sherman had come home.

Sherman nodded and headed toward the back of the store. Sherman's parents, along with his grandmother, and Joseph's single brother, Dave, lived on the second floor. Sherman wanted to design a new house for them someday. They deserved something better after working so hard and sacrificing so much so that he and his twin sister Sherri could get a 'good' education. Besides that, Nai-Nai was getting old. It was traditional in his culture to look after one's parents, but getting grandmother up and down the steep stairway was becoming increasingly difficult. It might take some convincing on his part, but moving his parents to a more suitable location was top on his list of priorities.

Lani Chan, Sherman's mother, looked up in surprise as soon as he entered the small apartment kitchen. "Sherman! You no tell me you coming for visit!" She rushed to her son and squeezed him tight, then held him at arm's length. *She* had no trouble displaying emotion.

"I wanted it to be a surprise."

"Good! I make dumplings. You sit now and I give you some." She opened a cupboard door and reached for a bowl.

Sherman didn't bother objecting. He knew his mother. She would insist he eat. To her, food was the answer to everything.

"Mm. Smells good. You are the best cook in the world."

"You have a girlfriend yet?" Lani demanded as she ladled soup into the bowl.

"Um, no. Nobody special."

"Special? Why it has to be special? Just get a girl and get married. Then have grandchildren."

Sherman laughed. "You are so funny. You know that? You would not be happy with just any girl and you know it. You want me to marry the perfect girl. Which is impossible, because she would have to be like you and you are one of a kind." He kissed her cheek and she batted it away playfully, laughing.

"Such a bad boy! So mouthy! You go to Hong Kong and find a nice girl. That's how your father found me."

"I know. But you raised me to be a modern man, remember? How can I just go and pick out a bride from a group of strangers?"

"Not strangers. My relatives know someone," Lani said pointedly.

"Sorry, Mom, but that's not going to happen." Sherman sipped at the soup sitting in front of him on the table.

"It's up to you now," Lani said, pointing the ladle in his direction. "Your sister has made a mess of things with Clarke. Such a nice Chinese boy! I don't understand!"

"Maybe she didn't love Clarke," Sherman suggested.

Lani made a dismissive sound with her lips. "You learn to love someone. That is how it was for your father and me."

"Times have changed." Sherman focused on the soup in front of him. He had definite visions of a certain girl he would like to get to know better and she wasn't his mother's choice at all. The one disadvantage of moving back home was he would now be his mother's new favourite target. Maybe things hadn't changed after all.

SHERMAN WAS MEETING his long-time friends Steve Russell and Cory Roberts at The Urban Cowboy, a local downtown bar with a retro atmosphere that had become a trendy hotspot of late. Cory Roberts was part owner of the bar. He fancied himself a bit of a ladies' man, and with his dreadlocks and suave mannerisms, he was probably correct. Steve was a newspaper journalist. When they were kids they used to call themselves the three musketeers. Then they changed it to the United Nations. Cory was black, Sherman was Asian, and Steve was white. They had a lot of fun with the metaphor.

"What'll you boys have?" Cory asked Steve and Sherman when they sat down at one of the high stools along the long bar that took up one whole wall in the pub. "Whatever you want. It's on me."

"The usual," Steve said and leaned his elbows on the counter.

"Jacques!" Cory called to the other bartender. "Three beers on tap." He turned back to his friends.

"Three? Aren't you working?" Steve asked.

"I'm the owner. I can do what I want." Cory leaned on the counter, propping himself on his elbows. His beaded dreads swung forward.

"We should have ordered something expensive," Sherman said with a laugh. "He's paying."

"What'll it be, then?"

"Beer's fine." Sherman adjusted his glasses and looked around the room.

Jacques, a slender Frenchman with blonde hair and a goatee, served up a frothy stein of beer for each of the three. Sherman nodded his thanks and took a long swig.

"That was some crazy business this afternoon at the job site," Steve said to the other two after taking a sip of his beer. He looked at Cory. "Did he tell you? Some guy fell three stories down an elevator shaft. Hardly got a scratch."

Cory raised his brows. "I never heard. Anyone I know?"

"He's been in here a time or two, I think." Sherman chuckled. "Actually, my sister was hitting on him pretty hard one time just before she and Clarke broke up."

"Ah, I know who you mean. Real cowboy. Likes to ride the mechanical bull. Hangs around with a big Newfie guy."

Sherman nodded. "That's him."

"Actually, did I tell you I was thinking of hosting a bull riding tournament?" Cory asked. "Hope he's not too banged up. I figured he'd be a shoe in for sure."

"If he does enter, don't tell my sister," Sherman said.

They all laughed.

"So how long are you here for this time?" Cory asked.

Sherman took another drink before answering. "Actually, I'm here to stay." He smiled smugly as he waited for his friends' reaction.

"What?" Steve turned to Sherman and gave him a slug in the arm. "We had coffee earlier today and you never said anything?"

"I thought I'd wait and surprise you both at the same time," Sherman said. "If I told you first, it might cause a problem."

"No kidding?" Cory asked. "You're really moving back to Calgary?"

Sherman nodded. "Yeah. My belongings should be arriving in the next week or so. By that time my apartment will be ready and I can tell my parents."

Steve frowned. "They don't know yet?"

"No. I'm staying at a hotel downtown. Easier for now." Sherman shook his head. "I love my mom, but she would be all 'up in my face' and want to know why I'm relocating."

"So what are the reasons why?" Cory asked.

"A lot of reasons, actually," Sherman said. "Our firm is getting more and more business out west. Since I travel a lot anyway, it makes sense for us to set up a permanent office here."

"And?" Steve prompted.

"And... I plan on building a house for my parents in the spring." Sherman shrugged. "I figured my being here would help them accept the inevitable." He downed the rest of his beer.

"I can't imagine your mom going for that," Cory said. He signalled Jacques to bring another round.

"She has to face reality sooner or later. They aren't young anymore and it's time they sold the store and retired to just one business. And my grandmother can't be kept in that second story apartment any longer. They're either going to have to put her in a nursing home or move to somewhere more suitable. Since I can't see them doing the first one, the latter is the only option."

"So that's two reasons," Steve said. "Any others?"

Sherman looked sideways at Steve. "What is this? An interview?"

Steve shrugged. "Sorry. Just thought there must be more to it." He tapped the side of his head. "My inquisitive brain."

"Well... last time I was here I realized I missed it. I miss my family, Sherri, and you guys of course. I just feel like it's time for me to move back, that's all. Unfortunately, my mom is focusing her attention on me now that Sherri and Clarke broke up. Know any eligible Chinese girls?" Sherman grinned.

Steve raised his brows. "I'd say you had your eye on a different girl this afternoon, if I'm not mistaken."

"Maybe." Sherman shrugged and took a drink from the full mug sitting in front of him.

"Keeping secrets?" Cory asked.

"Hardly. I just got back."

Steve leaned forward. "Carmen Lamont, one of the owners of The Brew downtown."

Sherman flicked his gaze at Steve. "I wouldn't talk if I were you. You seem to have a thing for her partner, Tamara."

Steve shrugged. "Not denying it. So?"

"Isn't this just like high school.?" Cory laughed. "Next you two will be going on double dates."

"I'm game," Steve said.

Sherman surveyed his friend for a moment in the mirror that lined the wall behind the counter. He wasn't sure if Steve was joking or serious. He turned back to Cory. "I'm not denying Carmen has a certain... appeal. I offered to do a little research for them on a building project. They're thinking of expanding their café into the building next door and asked if I could take a look at the feasibility."

"Oh, I get it. Work your way into her heart," Cory said. He paused. "Get it? 'Work' your way...?"

Sherman shook his head, but laughed despite himself. "Lame. Stick to DJ-ing or bartending. You suck as a comedian."

"I'm wounded." Cory placed his hand over his heart.

Steve's eyes flickered to another area of the room. "Listen, I see a guy I need to talk to over there. I've been trying to get ahold of him all day."

Sherman glanced over to where Steve had gestured. A man in his fifties sat at a table alone. He wore a rumpled brown suit over an equally rumpled shirt and sported a moustache straight out of the seventies. "Go ahead. This conversation was getting old anyway."

Cory and Sherman watched Steve wind his way to the other man's table and sit down.

"Vinny Kirkpatrick," Cory said. "An ex-cop who now works as a private investigator."

"He looks like something right out of an old movie."

"Except he's the real deal," Cory said.

Sherman shrugged. "You know Steve. Always looking for a story."

"True."

"So, you gonna tell me more about this Carmen woman, or do I have to beat it out of you?"

"How about I beat it out of you, as in a game of pool?" Sherman asked and stood up.

"If I didn't know better, I'd say you were avoiding the subject," Cory answered with a grin.

Sherman just shrugged and smiled. Maybe he *was* avoiding the subject. His attraction to Carmen Lamont was something that had taken him by surprise. He had noticed her the last time he visited, but work and distance had made the memories fade. This afternoon when he saw her at The Brew it all came rushing back. She was definitely a lady he would like to get to know better.

~

SHERMAN DRUMMED his fingers on the desk as he waited, his cell phone pressed to one ear. The architectural firm's new Calgary office had a decent view, situated as it was on an upper level floor of a downtown high rise. If he leaned forward just a bit, he could see the arm of the huge building crane being used to build their latest project. In the far distance was the craggy blue outline of the Rocky Mountains. He'd managed to convince the firm that they needed a permanent western office. What had once been a temporary ad-hoc space was now his permanent domain. It wasn't big but it was a start.

He looked up and nodded as the office manager brought in a rolled up file and set it on his desk. "Thanks," he mouthed.

A sultry female voice suddenly came on the other end of the line. "Hello?"

Sherman sat up straighter and transferred the phone to his other ear. "Hi. Sherman Chan here."

"Oh, hello. I was hoping you'd call."

Sherman smiled at the comment. He could hear the bright smile in Carmen Lamont's voice the moment she recognized him on the line. "Yeah. I managed to find those blue prints. We should look them over together."

"Okay. When?"

"Your call," Sherman said. "Evenings actually work best for me, but whenever it's convenient for you is fine."

"After hours is best for me as well," Carmen responded. "We could meet tonight if you're not busy."

Sherman smiled. "Perfect." In his mind he was cancelling his plans with Steve and Cory.

"Do you want to meet here at The Brew? Seven o'clock? That way we could actually look around the place as we talk. Take some measurements or whatever you need to do."

"Sound good. See you then." Sherman hung up. He had never been this excited about a business meeting before in his life.

"Nice digs."

Sherman swung around in his office chair. "Sis! Glad you could come down and see the new office." He jumped up and met his sister Sherri halfway with a bear hug. Once he released her he gestured to their surroundings. "What do you think?"

Sherri Chan surveyed the small space and then walked to the window. "Not exactly grand, but the view is nice."

"Exactly!" Sherman joined her. "It'll be all uphill from here."

Sherri turned and gave her brother a smile. "I am so excited that you've decided to move back to Calgary. I just can't believe you haven't told Mom and Dad yet. They're going to be mad when they find out you kept it from them."

"Then don't tell them." Sherman went back to his desk chair and gestured for her to sit in the one opposite.

"I'm not sure how you're going to keep something like that a secret."

Sherman shook his head. "Easy. As far as they are concerned I'm staying in a hotel – which I am. I just need a little bit of time to get myself settled before Mom starts horning in on my life."

"Welcome to my world," Sherri said with a slight laugh.

"The only down side to moving back."

"That's a terrible thing to say," Sherri scolded, but there was a smile on her face. "So, tell me about things. How has the project been going?"

Sherman shrugged, not sure he should tell her about the accident. "Good. On schedule."

"You want to go out tonight? We could go to the Urban Cowboy. I haven't seen Cory and Steve in a while. And I haven't really been out much since... well, since Clarke and I broke up." Her mouth turned up at one corner. "I promise I'll behave."

"Um, actually I've got other plans."

Sherri's brows raised a notch. "Oh?"

"I told the women down at The Brew I'd help them with an expansion plan." Sherman focused his eyes on the shiny surface of his desk.

"You did, did you?" Sherri nodded knowingly. "As I recall, you did seem awfully interested in one of the owners last time you were here."

"Yeah, well, it's kind of early in the game, but I'm hopeful. Just don't say anything to you-know-who. She'll flip if she thinks I'm dating a non-Asian girl."

"You know me better than that. Your secret is safe with me."

He knew it. That was one thing he could say for his sister. She understood the dichotomy he faced on a daily basis. The pull of his family and culture was strong, but the pull of his own heart was even stronger.

WHEN SHERMAN PULLED up in front of The Brew, he could see Carmen waiting at one of the tables near the front windows. Thankfully there was a parking spot right in front, and he pulled his black Lexus into it and cut the engine. When he got out of the car he wrapped his overcoat around his body just a little tighter. The buildings downtown created their own wind tunnel, and the temperatures had dropped recently as winter approached.

As soon as he was on the other side of the glass doors, Carmen was there to unlock the deadbolt and let him in out of the cold. "It's getting chilly out there," he commented.

Carmen nodded her agreement. "I know." She locked the deadbolt again behind him. "Just throw your coat on one of those stools if you want."

He did just that, and looked around the interior of the little café. It seemed different from what it was in the daylight. It was cozy. Intimate. Of course, the lights were turned low since it was now closed. He cleared his throat and held up a cardboard tube. "I brought the blueprints."

"Oh, yes." She seemed out of breath. "Let's spread them out on one of the tables and take a look."

Sherman followed as Carmen led the way to one of the larger tables. Her hair was a closely cropped mat of black kinks, not the extensions or styled and straightened coiffure many other black women preferred. It suited her. It was the perfect understated backdrop for her bright smile, accentuated by flaming lipstick, and the chunky earrings and flowing African print dress she wore.

"This should do." The bangles at her wrists jangled as she gestured to the table.

"Perfect." He meant that she was perfect, but of course, he couldn't say that.

He opened the tube with a pop and tipped the container so he could grasp the rolled up document. "Do you have something to hold down the corners? Salt and peppers, a sugar container?"

"That would be the day you'd find white sugar in my café," Carmen declared with a grin. "I'll go see what I can find."

While she went to look for something, Sherman unrolled the blueprints and spread them out with the flat of his hands. Carmen was back a few moments later with some small glass bowls. "Will these do?"

"Perfect." He smiled.

They spent several minutes perusing the blueprints. Carmen had lots of questions and Sherman was more than happy to answer them. He inhaled her aroma, but not too deeply so as not to draw attention. It was a mixture of baked goods, hand soap and a mildly musky perfume.

"This is how I saw the space getting transformed." She pointed at a spot on the paper. "A large archway right here into the new part would mean we could have a lot more seating, but it would still seem cozy." She looked up at him and their eyes met for a moment.

"In theory it looks good, but this is a structural wall." He traced a line on the blueprint with his finger.

Carmen let out a small sigh. "So it can't be done?"

"I didn't say that." He looked up at her and smiled. "It will just cost more."

"Oh." Her face still held disappointment.

"Let's take a look at the real thing and then come back to these," Sherman suggested. "There might be other options we're not seeing here."

"Okay. Follow me."

Sherman kept a pace or two behind Carmen as she took him through every space in the cafe, including the small office and storage room in the back. He enjoyed the tour as much for Carmen's animated descriptions as for seeing the actual building.

"We need to take some measurements," Sherman said once Carmen had talked her way through the place.

"Do you have a tape measure?"

Sherman laughed. "Do I have a tape measure? What kind of architect would I be without one?" He produced a small retractable measuring tape from his back pocket.

They spent the next forty-five minutes measuring up various parts of the café. When they were through, they went back to the blueprints. "Do you have any paper?" Sherman asked. "I have an idea. It would be nice to do some concept drawings."

Carmen disappeared into the office and came back a few minutes later with some paper and a couple of pencils. She sat down at the table across from Sherman. He started sketching a rough floor plan but got distracted when he glanced over at what Carmen was doing. She was drawing a surprisingly realistic interior layout. "You're a good artist," Sherman said as he watched her ideas take shape on the page.

She smiled up at him. "I have a background in theatre arts – set designing to be exact."

"Is that so? What made you stop?" Sherman pushed his glasses up further onto the bridge of his nose and leaned in closer to her artwork.

"Lack of food." She laughed when he frowned. "I needed to make a living so I could eat and there wasn't enough demand for set design around here. I did a few odd jobs - department store windows and the like, but it wasn't steady."

"That's too bad. You're good."

She shrugged. "It's okay. I still do art. And I love working with Tamara. I've learned a lot from her about business and things."

"I like going to the theatre," Sherman said, "if that counts for anything."

"Good to know." She smiled. "It kind of runs in the family. My niece is an actress. She's staying with me this month. She's in a show that is playing until Christmas, so it will be fun to see her while she's here."

"Where is she from?"

"Vancouver. That's where all the action is, or so I'm told." Carmen added a few finishing touches to her drawing. "There."

Sherman inspected the drawing. "Very nice. Here's mine."

She leaned closer to look at his idea. "Explain it to me."

"Okay. Expanded back room with a proper office, larger prep area, and more seating, of course."

She nodded. "I like it…"

"But?"

"We really want a designated area for local musicians and such." She pointed to her own drawing. "Here's what I mean. Nothing major, but…"

He squinted at her rendering and pushed his glasses up. "That's valuable real estate that could be used for more tables."

"True, but it's been a dream of ours to support local artists, writers, activists… Tamara and I are both passionate about it. It's one of our main reasons for wanting to expand."

"Besides not having room to turn around?" Sherman grinned.

"Yes, that too." She smiled back.

"How about this?" Sherman made a few strokes with the pencil on his own sketch. "It could double as a stage area in the evenings but still be used for seating during the day when you need it most."

Carmen cocked her head to the side as she surveyed the altered floor plan. "Of course! How smart."

"I am an architect, after all," Sherman teased.

"What about cost?" Carmen asked.

"I'll do a rough estimate. Of course, it all depends on the price of the boutique. That's not something I can control." There was a moment of silence as neither one had anything else to add. He picked up both drawings. "These will definitely help me come up with a design."

"How long do you suppose it'll take?"

Sherman furrowed his brow. "A few days, maybe? I'm not sure. I'll call you as soon as I'm done."

Carmen laughed, a nervous sounding tinkle. "How presumptuous. Oh course you're busy and you have other, more pressing things to do, I'm sure. Take as long as you need."

"It's no problem. I want to do it."

Carmen kept her eyes lowered. "Thanks."

"My pleasure." Sherman cleared his throat. "I suppose I should be going, now. It is getting late."

"Okay. Thanks again. Call me if you need to clarify anything."

"I'll do that." Sherman had a feeling this job was going to take more consultation that normal.

On Friday, Sherman returned to The Brew with some actual plans. He had wanted to visit sooner, but demands at work had kept him occupied. When he got to the counter he held up his tablet. "Want to see?"

"The plans?" Carmen asked, her eyes twinkling with excitement.

"Mmhm."

"I can hardly wait. Tamara!" Carmen called over her shoulder. The other woman came around the corner from the back. "Sherman has some plans to show us." She wiped her hands on a towel.

"Pat, can you look after things for a bit?" Tamara asked their young employee behind the counter. The girl nodded.

Sherman led the way to an unoccupied table, followed closely by both women. He sat down, and with a few deft taps on the screen, brought up some plans for the renovation. "Here it is. Just swipe to see the next slide. I did some 3D imaging as well as a flat floor plan."

Sherman let them peruse the plans without any interference, amid their 'oos and ahs'.

"This is incredible!" Carmen finally breathed. She looked up at Sherman with wide eyes. "Just what I had in mind."

"I listen." Sherman tapped his ear.

Tamara pointed to the screen. "What's this?"

Sherman proceeded to explain the plans in detail. Both women nodded their heads as they listened, throwing out the odd question now and then. A few minutes later, Steve Russell entered the café and headed straight for their table. "What's up?"

"Sherman has drawn up some plans for our expansion into the building next door," Carmen told him excitedly. "Want to see?"

Steve stood behind Tamara and bent a little closer in order to see the small screen. Sherman smiled to himself. He wasn't the only one taken with one of the 'Brew' sisters.

"Did Carmen tell you we talked to the bank yesterday?" Tamara asked. "As much as I hate to take on more debt, it looks like we'll be able to secure a loan."

Sherman's eyebrows rose slightly. He was actually surprised that the women had managed to put their financial house in order in such short time. "That's good news."

"Well, there is a catch," Tamara continued. "We also spoke with the realtor and the seller wants the possession date put off until after Christmas so they can take advantage of the season's sales."

"I can see their point. It's probably for the best, though. It gives us more time to finalize the plans," Sherman said. "Get an engineer involved. And for you to save up."

"Is that going to be a problem?" Carmen asked. "I assume you're going back to Toronto sometime in the near future…"

"No, actually. I'm moving here."

"Is that so?" Carmen's eyes literally lit up.

Sherman couldn't help smiling at her reaction. "Mmhm. Once you finalize the paperwork and we get a permit from the city, we can start in earnest."

"Is that going to be a problem?" Tamara asked.

"What?"

"Getting permits?"

"I don't think so," Sherman said. "I deal with the boys downtown all the time, so they'll know they're dealing with someone they can trust."

Tamara rolled her eyes. "The old boys club?" She was smiling though.

"Just be glad this old boy is on our side," Carmen put in.

Steve laughed. "We old boys can come in handy once in a while."

"We'll need to talk some more. Want to meet somewhere later so we can go over the entire plan?" Sherman looked from Carmen to Tamara and smiled in what he hoped was a casual way.

"Sounds good," Carmen agreed almost immediately. She turned to Tamara. "Can you get a sitter?"

"It's kind of short notice. You two go ahead and fill me in later."

"You should probably go ahead and get that sitter," Steve advised. "You wouldn't want them making decisions without your input."

Sherman frowned ever so slightly in Steve's direction, but smiled at the women. "It probably is better to talk to both of you at the same time."

Tamara's brows descended. "Maybe my neighbour Goldie wouldn't mind – again. I'll have to give her a call first."

"Oh!" Carmen suddenly exclaimed. "I forgot I told my niece Renee I would spend the evening with her. We've hardly had a minute together since she's been here, what with her rehearsal schedule and everything."

"Bring her along," Sherman suggested with a shrug. "The more the merrier, so they say." He flashed Steve 'the look'.

"I SAID you guys would be double dating before long," Cory teased as he set two frothy steins of beer in front of Steve and Sherman. They were sitting up to the bar at the Urban Cowboy, waiting for the women to arrive.

"Yeah, thanks for cutting into my alone time with Carmen," Sherman said. He held his mug aloft in a mock salute.

"This is hardly the place for alone time, my friend," Steve replied. "Besides, I saw an opportunity and I took it." He glanced over his shoulder.

"Are you okay?" Cory asked Steve. "You seem a little edgy."

"Me?" Steve dismissed the comment with a snort. "Ridiculous. Probably just working too hard."

"Now that would be a miracle," Sherman teased. He had noticed Steve's jumpiness, too, however, as soon as he joined them at the bar. He wondered if it had anything to do with Vinny Kirkpatrick, the private investigator Steve had been talking to when Sherman first entered the establishment. Vinny had since left, but now there was a rather unsavoury looking man with a shaved head, goatee and tattoos sitting alone that Steve kept glancing toward.

Sherman looked over his own shoulder and saw Tamara, Carmen, and another woman with a dark complexion, arriving together. Seeing Tamara should put Steve out of his funk. Sherman raised a hand to wave them over and then turned to Cory. "Maybe we should move to a table. Easier to discuss things if we aren't sitting in a row like this." He frowned when Cory didn't respond and snapped his fingers. "Earth to Cory."

Cory's attention jerked back to Sherman. "What? Oh yeah. Sure." Cory made his way around to the other side of the counter to join Steve and Sherman just as the women arrived.

"Hi. This is my niece Renee Tucker," Carmen made the introductions. "Sherman Chan, Steve Russell, whom you've already met, and... I'm sorry but I don't know your friend." She looked from Cory to Sherman.

"Cory Roberts," Sherman introduced. "He's part owner of this place."

"Pleased to meet you." Cory took Renee's hand but instead of shaking it he bent and kissed it. His dreadlocks fell forward as he did so.

Renee suppressed a giggle. "Um. Likewise."

Cory flashed his best smile at Carmen and Tamara. "I've been to your establishment. Very nice atmosphere – from one owner to another."

"Thanks," Tamara said. "So? Are we going to discuss the plans?"

"This way." Cory gestured for them to follow him. He wound his way past several tables and around a corner to another part of the club that housed pool tables and the mechanical bull. He stopped at a large, round table. "This okay?"

"Fine," Sherman said with a nod. He pulled out Carmen's chair and noted that Steve managed to sit next to Tamara while Cory sat next to Renee.

"Drinks are on me," Cory said. "How about a round of my signature Margaritas?"

"One and that's it," Carmen said with a slight laugh.

"I thought you were working," Steve commented.

"This *is* working," Cory replied, flashing a smile at Renee. "It's my job to keep my customers happy."

A waitress arrived a few moments later and Cory ordered six margaritas.

"So, first, here are my estimates." Sherman tapped on his tablet and the screen came to life. "Of course, it all depends on finishes and final permits etc. If you want, I know a few good interior designers – some of which owe me." Carmen and Tamara, who were sitting on either side, leaned in a little closer to see the screen while he explained the details.

The waitress came with their drinks. After Cory told her to add it to his personal tab, he turned to Renee. "Can I give you a tour? I'm sure you're not that interested in all their business talk."

"Sure. I'd like that," Renee agreed.

Sherman and the rest watched as Renee allowed Cory to pull out her chair and lead her away with her arm tucked safely into the crook of his.

"Looks like Casanova is at it again." Steve shook his head and laughed.

"Should I be worried?" Carmen directed at Sherman.

"She's a big girl." Three surprised gazes turned to Tamara. She raised her brows questioningly. "What? He looks good enough to eat. Let her have some fun while she's here."

Steve scowled and took a gulp of his drink. A coy smile formed on Tamara's lips.

Carmen focused on the tablet. "So what do you think the timeline will be like once we acquire the property? We don't want to be closed for too long, do we Tamara?"

"If we have to close at all," the other woman said.

"Depends on a lot of things." Sherman pushed his glasses up. "Contractors, permits… the scope once we actually open the walls and see what we're dealing with. Some people try to stay open during a major reno, but you would probably have to scale back your services. We'll cross that bridge when we get to it, though. Now that I'm not going anywhere, I'll be there to help you all I can."

"Thank you. We really appreciate it." Carmen's eyes flickered downward and then up to meet Sherman's. "I know you're very busy, but it's a relief to know you're not going anywhere."

Sherman could have lost himself in Carmen's gaze but a hand on his shoulder brought him back to reality and he turned his head.

"Hi, guys. Am I interrupting?"

"Hey!" Both Sherman and Steve stood up and in turn gave the newcomer a hug. "This is my sister, Sherri. Sherri, meet Tamara and Carmen."

Sherri nodded at both women and then took the seat Cory had vacated. "I believe we've met before. You two own The Brew downtown, right?"

Both Tamara and Carmen nodded. "You look familiar to me, too," Tamara said.

"And what brings you here?" Sherman asked.

Sherri's eyebrows rose. "I'm not allowed to socialize? Sheesh!"

Sherman laughed. "That's not what I meant. Just surprised to see you here, that's all."

"After the last time, you mean?" Sherri challenged with a stare.

Steve smirked. "That was quite a show if I recall."

Sherri frowned. "Were you even there?"

Steve nodded. "Oh yes. It was quite the show."

Sherri gave a little huff and directed her gaze at the other women. "Don't let them influence your opinion of me. I hardly drink – ever."

"You don't have to convince me," Tamara cut in with a smile. "You're a grown woman and don't have to answer to anyone, least of all a couple of men."

"Ouch. I think that was an insult," Steve said.

"Anyway, I figured this was the best option if I want to see you," Sherri directed at Sherman. "You're a hard guy to pin down these days. So busy all the time."

Sherman just shrugged.

"Your mom recover from the shock yet?" Steve asked Sherri. "Of you and Clarke, I mean."

"I'm not sure she'll ever get over it." Sherri let out a self-deprecating chuckle.

Carmen leaned forward, concern written on her face. "Oh dear. What happened?"

Sherman and Sherri exchanged a glance. "Oh, she wasn't too happy when I broke up with my fiancé. That's all."

Steve sported a mild grin. "You've got to understand Mrs. Chan. I love her to death, but she's got some pretty entrenched ideas about whom her children are allowed to marry."

"Shut up, Steve," Sherman said. It wasn't unkind, but held just enough authority to make Steve clamp his mouth shut.

"That's a mother's job. To look out for her children," Tamara piped up.

"It's okay," Sherri said. "She just has her heart set on us marrying good Chinese boys – or girls, as the case may be. She wants grandchildren."

"Oh." Carmen grabbed her drink and took a sip.

"Thanks a lot, Sis." Sherman said under his breath.

"Did Sherman tell you about the crazy accident on the job site last week?" Steve asked brightly.

Sherri frowned and looked from Steve to Sherman. "No. What accident?"

"A guy fell three stories and survived. Pretty lucky," Steve said.

"I remember that," Tamara said. "You were in the café when you got the news. He wasn't hurt?"

"Nothing major. He's fine," Sherman said with a dismissive wave.

"That cowboy of yours is one lucky guy." Steve shook his head.

Sherri narrowed her eyes. "What's that?"

"Oops. I'm sure putting my foot in my mouth tonight." Steve grimaced.

Sherri turned her full attention onto her brother. "What aren't you telling me?"

Sherman concentrated on swirling the remnants of his beer around in the bottom of his glass.

Steve turned to Tamara and Carmen. "Hey, what do you ladies say we go find Cory and Renee? Check up on Casanova."

"Sounds good." Carmen gave Sherman's shoulder a small squeeze as she left.

It brought little comfort. "What was he talking about Sherman?" Sherri demanded. "What did he mean, 'my cowboy'?"

"That guy you were hitting on a while back. Lester Tibbett. He works for me, remember?"

"And?"

"He's the one who fell down the elevator shaft. Three stories."

Sherri gasped sharply and her hands flew to her mouth.

"But he's okay," Sherman assured, placing a hand on her shoulder. "It's some kind of miracle, but he survived without any broken bones. As far as I know he'll be back to work next week."

"And you didn't think to tell me?" Sherri's voice squeaked.

"I didn't think it was important." Sherman shrugged. "He was the catalyst that made you see you didn't love Clarke, but I didn't think there was anything more to it. Besides, I didn't want to worry you." Sherri dabbed at the corner of her eyes. Was she crying? He placed his arm around her shoulder and squeezed. "Hey, I'm sorry. I didn't know you'd be so upset. Honestly."

Sherri took a deep breath and shook off his comforting arm. "Of course you're right. There's nothing between us, so it doesn't matter." She flashed a bright smile. "I see you've finally decided to make a move with Carmen. I think she's perfect for you."

"You think?"

Sherri nodded.

"Now I just need to convince Mom. After I convince Carmen, of course." They both laughed.

"And Steve and Tamara? Are they a couple now, too?" Sherri asked.

"I know Steve hopes so, but Tamara is a little harder to read. And then there's Cory and Carmen's niece Renee."

"The three Musketeers falling in one fell swoop. Who would have thought?" Sherri laughed.

Who indeed.

It was past midnight and Sherri had long since gone home in a cab. Renee and Cory had also disappeared - together. Sherman was tired of the club atmosphere and had curbed his own alcohol consumption so that he could offer a ride to Carmen.

Steve obviously had the same idea. "Since neither of you two lovely ladies own a vehicle, it behooves us gentlemen to give you a ride," he offered.

Tamara looked at Carmen with a twinkle in her eye. "Shall we draw straws to see who gets to go with whom?"

Steve frowned. "Not exactly what I had in mind."

Sherman laughed. "My car is only about half a block away. First one there gets to ride with me."

All four of them were already sauntering toward the exit, the women slightly ahead of Steve and Sherman. Sherman stopped Steve's progress with a hand on his sleeve. "Hey? You sure you're okay to drive?"

Steve nodded. "I only had two drinks all evening. But then I guess you didn't notice since your attention was focused elsewhere."

"Good. Just checking. And you're okay otherwise?" Sherman persisted. "I saw you talking to Vinny Kirkpatrick earlier but didn't get a chance to talk to you about it."

"Just working a story, that's all. Nothing to worry about."

Sherman didn't buy it. "I saw that other guy earlier, too. The one who looks like he just broke out of prison."

"Don't judge a book by its cover," Steve said.

"Just be careful."

"You know me."

Sherman did know Steve – all too well. He would go to any lengths to get a story, even if it meant putting himself in danger.

The girls were waiting by the door. Steve got there first and held it open until all of them had exited.

"Talk to you tomorrow," Sherman called as Steve and Tamara started walking in one direction while he and Carmen headed the other.

"I wonder if Renee is at home by now." Carmen's heels clicked on the cement as they walked.

Sherman stuffed his hands in his pants pockets but couldn't help the smile. "Why? Were you going to invite me in?"

Carmen's eyes widened. "Oh! Well, no. Not this time... I mean, it seems a bit early for that, don't you think?"

Sherman chuckled. "Just joking. I totally agree. Although I have a feeling Renee won't be home, anyway..."

Carmen puffed out a white cloud. The temperature had dropped considerably. "I know I shouldn't worry, but I hate to see her get hurt. She's only twenty-one."

"But an adult none-the-less." Sherman shrugged. "I don't know what else to tell you. Cory is a good guy, but not exactly the kind to make promises, if you know what I mean."

"He is your friend, so I don't want to sound rude. It just seems like they..." she hesitated, "hit it off a bit fast, don't you think?"

"Well... that depends." Sherman measured his next words carefully and looked at her out of the corner of his eye. "Do you believe in love at first sight?"

"Um, oh dear! This is making me uncomfortable." Carmen stopped walking.

"Not what I meant for it to do." He stopped also. "I wish I could reign in my feelings a bit more, but I've already been bottling them up and I'm going to explode. You must know that I really like you. A lot."

Carmen bobbed her head up and down. "I got that."

"And?"

"I like you, too."

Sherman let out a sigh. "That's a relief. Okay, now that that's out of the way...?"

"We could start by getting to your car. It's freezing out here!"

Sherman laughed. "Good idea." He grabbed her hand and they started trotting the rest of the distance to the vehicle.

Sherman started the engine from several yards away with the automatic start on his key toggle. He helped Carmen into the passenger side door, and once inside the car himself, he turned the heat up and waited. "Now, where were we?"

"We established that we mutually agree on one particular topic," Carmen said.

"Right." Sherman rubbed his hands together to get them warm. "Maybe we should take a play out of the Cory and Renee playbook and just throw caution to the wind." He looked over at Carmen hopefully.

She shook her head. "I told you. One night stands don't interest me."

"Me neither."

"Good. That's two things we agree on."

"Okay. How's this for a third?" Sherman shifted his body so that he was looking straight at her. "Can we agree that it's time for a kiss at least?"

Carmen wrinkled her forehead. "Um... okay. Maybe just one."

They both leaned over the console in the middle of the car. When their lips came together it was just as wonderful as Sherman had imagined it would be. The kiss was light and not too long, but when he pulled away his heart was racing. "That was nice. Again?"

Carmen nodded. This time their lips lingered until passion ignited. Carmen pulled away first. She patted her head, even though her short curls defied getting mussed. "We're acting like teenagers, making out in a car."

"How many teenagers do you know drive a Lexus?" Sherman raised an amused brow.

"Good point."

"So now that we got the first kiss over with, maybe it's time for the next step." Sherman took his glasses off and squinted through the lens at a smudge created during their kiss.

"I told you I didn't do one night -"

Sherman chuckled as he cut her off. "I was talking about coming to meet my family." He rubbed his glasses on his pant leg.

"Oh." Carmen sat back against her seat.

Sherman held up the glasses for a second inspection. Satisfied that they were clear enough to see through, he slid them into place on his nose. "We have dinner every Sunday night together at the family restaurant. I would just love to see my mother's face when I show up with a date for the first time ever."

"Are you sure?" Carmen's brow was furrowed into a worried line. "I heard what your sister said earlier about your mom wanting you to… well, you know. Only wanting you to date Chinese women."

"I love my mother, but she doesn't control my life," Sherman said with more assurance than he felt.

THE 'FORTUNE COOKIE FAMILY RESTAURANT' was run by Sherman's extended family. Sherman couldn't remember a time when the family didn't gather there for their regular Sunday family dinners. In many ways, it felt more like home than the apartment his parents kept over their convenience store. He, Sherri and their three cousins had worked, eaten and done homework many a night at one or more of the restaurant's tables.

Sherman picked Carmen up at her apartment and they chatted all the way to the restaurant. After Friday's revelation, they had spent almost all day Saturday and Sunday together. He learned that Carmen had been hurt badly in a previous relationship, so he was determined to do everything in his power to reassure her of his sincerity. He was surprised by the certainty of his own feelings for Carmen. It wasn't that long ago that he was among those of his species who had sworn off serious relationships. Funny how the right person could change all that.

He swung his Lexus into the almost empty parking lot behind the restaurant and cut the engine. "This is it." He glanced over at Carmen and offered a smile that he hoped had masked the tension he suddenly felt inside. Bringing a member of the opposite sex home to 'family dinner' was a big deal, and despite his assurances, he wasn't sure how his mother would take it.

Sherman helped Carmen out of the car and grabbed her hand in a firm grip as they walked around to the front door.

"Are you sure this is okay?" Carmen asked. "You seem kind of nervous."

"Just be yourself. They'll love you," Sherman said.

"What's not to love?" Carmen joked.

"Exactly." Sherman flashed her a smile and then dove in for a quick kiss before they reached the flashing 'closed' sign that lit up the glass entrance. Sherman rapped on the glass with his knuckles and an aging Chinese man came to unlock the deadbolt.

"Carmen, this is my Uncle Dave," Sherman introduced.

Dave bowed and then turned his attention to locking the door behind them. Things hadn't changed much. Dave had never been a talker and as a bachelor, he had become even more introverted as the years went on.

They entered the dim interior of the restaurant. Chinese lanterns illuminated the alternating red wallpaper and dark wood paneling. The place needed a facelift, that was certain, but the older members of the family wouldn't hear of it. It would cost too much to close down for repairs.

The distinct singsong cadence of Mandarin could be heard from the kitchen along with the clatter of pots and pans. Nobody but Uncle Dave was in the main part of the restaurant. "We always eat in the dining room," Sherman explained. "We'll go in there and wait."

His grip on Carmen's hand tightened as he swung through one of the red panelled doors into the dining room reserved for groups and special guests. He breathed a sigh of relief when he saw Sherri sitting with his grandmother, Nai-Nai.

"Wow! Well, hello!" Sherri said, standing up. "This is a surprise."

"Hi." Carmen waved tentatively.

Sherri hugged first Carmen and then Sherman. "Does Mom know you're coming?"

Sherman shrugged. "I assume she does since I visited earlier in the week. I didn't call or anything though."

"Oh." Sherri's one syllable held a wealth of meaning.

Carmen turned a worried expression toward Sherman. "You mean you didn't tell her I was coming?"

"Relax. It'll be fine," Sherman assured. He turned his attention to his grandmother. "Nai-Nai." He bowed and then said something else in Mandarin and drew Carmen forward. The old lady squinted her eyes as she tried to focus on the newcomer. "This is Carmen."

The old lady nodded and bowed her head in a gesture of respect. Carmen did the same. Grandmother said something in Chinese.

"What did she say?" Carmen asked.

"She says you look like an African princess." Sherman smiled.

"Tell her thank you."

Sherman repeated the request in Chinese and Nai-Nai bowed again. Then she patted the chair beside her. Carmen looked at Sherman for his approval and he nodded, so she sat down.

Lily, Sherman's eighteen-year-old cousin, scurried into the dining room with dishes and cutlery. She stopped in her tracks when she saw Carmen but then she continued with her duties and scurried out again.

"That was my cousin Lily," Sherman informed. "Auntie Jo and Uncle Ed's daughter. I'll introduce you to everyone else when we're all together."

"Do they need a hand in the kitchen?" Carmen asked.

Sherman shook his head. "Special guests aren't allowed to help. It's custom and it would offend my mother if you did."

"Oh. Well, I don't want that," Carmen said and smiled.

A middle-aged woman entered the dining room. She stopped and took a good look at Carmen and then said something to Sherman in Mandarin. He nodded and turned to Carmen. "My Auntie Joanne says my mother needs to talk to me in the kitchen." He leaned in and whispered. "Maybe she saw us come in together."

Carmen's eyes widened. "Is that a bad thing?"

"Leave it to me. " He squeezed Carmen's hand and then released it. "Keep Sherri and Nai-Nai company," he said as he backed away toward the kitchen doors.

"But I don't speak Chinese."

"Doesn't matter," Sherman said. "Nai-Nai is mostly deaf anyway."

He entered the kitchen through the right hand swinging door and sought out his mother. She was ladling hot broth from a large pot into an ornate tureen. She squealed and almost dropped the ladle when she saw him. "Sherman! You still here! Naughty boy! You haven't called all week. I make dumplings. Your favourite."

Sherman glanced from his mother's rapt features to his Auntie Jo. The latter's were quite stern.

"I've been busy. Auntie Jo says you wanted to talk to me?"

"No," Auntie Joanne corrected. "I said you needed to talk to your mother. What are you trying to do? Give her a heart attack?"

Lani set the ladle down and frowned. "What is this?"

Sherman approached his mother and started with a giant hug. Then he cleared his throat. "I should have told you sooner, but I wanted to make sure everything would work out first. I'm moving back to Calgary." He smiled broadly, hoping this news would soften what was to come next.

As expected, Lani squealed again and clapped her hands. "Did you hear that? My son is moving back home where he belongs! When? When you moving back?"

"Right now." Sherman accepted another squeeze from his ever-affectionate mother.

Joanne just shook her head and went back to her work.

"I am so happy." Lani clapped again. "Now you settle down. Your sister is not even trying to find a nice husband."

"How would you know?" Sherman asked.

Lani made a scoffing sound. "I know your sister. She tries to spite me. That's why she left poor Clarke – such a nice man!"

Sherman laughed. "I doubt that she left Clarke to spite you."

Lani ignored him. "Next thing you know she will show up here with some white man. I just know it."

Sherman took a deep breath. "Mom. A person's skin colour doesn't determine whether they're a good person or not. You know that."

"You children! What will become of you? My daughter with a white man and my son with no one!"

"Actually..." Sherman adjusted his glasses. "That's another thing I have to tell you. I did bring someone to dinner tonight."

"Ah!" Lani clasped her hands to her chest.

"But you need to prepare yourself."

Lani's hands dropped to her sides. "Why? I suppose she is white woman, too?"

Sherman shook his head. "No..."

Lani clapped her hands. "Hooray! Take me to meet her right now!" She scurried forward, heading straight for the swinging doors.

"Mom..." Sherman trailed after her but it was too late. His mother had already opened the doors. When he joined her, he could see that she was standing still, speechless, just staring at Carmen.

"I said she wasn't white," Sherman said in Mandarin. "I never said she was Chinese."

Sherman's mother let out a blood-curdling scream and proceeded to throttle him with the oven mitt she had carried with her from the kitchen. A barrage of Mandarin spewed from her lips with each blow.

"Calm down!" Sherman shouted, dodging to the left.

The rest of the family had gathered by this time, even the sedate

Uncle Dave. Sherman's father, Joseph, pulled the wild woman away from Sherman and back through the doors of the kitchen.

Sherman straightened his shirt and glanced at where Carmen sat. Her eyes were wide with shock and Sherri had an arm around her shoulders.

Without a word, Sherman spun on his heel and headed back into the fray. The door reverberated behind him as it swung on its hinges. "What kind of way is that to treat a guest?" he shouted, not caring if Carmen could hear him.

"You disgrace me by bringing her here!" Lani shouted back. Joseph had his arm around her, presumably to contain another outburst and she shoved him away.

Sherman stalked within inches of his mother, staring down at her quivering form. "No, you disgrace yourself by acting like a spoilt child every time things don't go your way." His voice was calm now – eerily so.

"Your mother is sorry for -"

Lani cut her husband off in mid-sentence. "I am not sorry." Joseph stepped away and folded his arms. Lani continued. "I ask only one thing of my children. That they marry nice Chinese boy or girl."

Sherman threw his hands in the air. "Can I help it if I love someone who isn't the right skin colour for you?"

Lani let out a disgusted grunt. "Love? What do you know of love? Real love is obeying your parents, even when you have to leave your own home and family and travel far away to be with the one chosen for you."

"Things aren't done that way anymore," Sherman said. "It's archaic."

"Archaic?" She waved her hand and didn't wait for an explanation. "What colour will my grandchildren be? At least with a white man, they will look normal. But with that one?" She gestured with her head to the door that had just finally quit swinging on its double hinges.

Sherman shook his head, a wave of sadness suddenly overtaking him. "You are a racist."

"I will not have that one here, at family dinner. No!"

"Then I guess this is good-bye." Sherman turned and marched toward the door. His father intercepted him.

"I am ashamed. Tell your lady friend that I am sorry." Joseph's eyes were rimmed with tears. It was the most emotion Sherman had seen from his father in a long time.

Sherman narrowed his eyes. "Why won't you do something then? Put a stop to this ridiculous behaviour."

"You know your mother. She can't be forced. When she is ready she will recant," Joseph said.

Lani was wailing in the background like she had lost her only son. She had. Sherman flicked his gaze away from the pathetic sight of his mother's doubled over posture. "And then what? Carmen and I are supposed to pretend like nothing happened? I don't think so." Sherman pushed past his father into the dining room.

It was a scene from a funeral. Everyone was sitting or standing perfectly still. Tears were streaming down the faces of both Carmen and Sherri.

He crossed the room in three strides and held out his hand for Carmen. She took it and stood up. He enfolded her in a hug and kissed her by the ear. Her kinky hair tickled his lips as he pressed them to her temple. "I'm so sorry," he whispered. "It wasn't fair to bring you here like this."

He stepped back to face the rest of the group. "I'm sorry for what just happened. I'll probably be seeing most of you around, but I won't be coming to family dinner anymore."

Lily and her two younger brothers started to protest.

"The same goes for me."

Sherman swung his gaze to his sister. "You don't have to do that, Sis. This isn't your fight."

Sherri's voice was like steel. "Maybe not today. But who knows?"

NAVIGATING THE NEIGHBOURHOOD

*L*ester rolled his head to one side and winced. It was hard to concentrate on what Reverend Wallis was saying when his neck felt like it was seizing up. He cupped the back of his neck with one hand and tried a side-to-side motion. The doctor said the stiffness in his neck and back would keep cropping up for the next several weeks. Not bad for a guy who'd fallen three stories down an elevator shaft. A fall like that could kill – or at the very least put a person in a wheelchair for the rest of his life. If a few aches and pains were the worst he had to deal with, then he wouldn't complain. In fact, his near brush with death had put a few things in perspective.

First, he needed to spend more time with his sister Patsi. Even though she was in college, she was young and naïve and needed his guidance.

He looked over at where she sat next to him, her eyes glazed over with boredom.

True, the church they had been attending since moving to the city wasn't the most exciting. The pews were filled with mostly old people and the song service was rather stiff, but Reverend Wallis's messages were suitably pleasant. In the few Sundays they'd attended, Lester noticed that the young man of God avoided topics that might be controversial or offensive. It was all about love, love, love, which was all well and good, but sometimes a little fire and brimstone helped to liven things up a bit. The pastor seemed eager to please, no doubt fearing that his already small congregation might dwindle if he got carried away.

Lester sighed. Maybe they needed to try a different church after all. One of those big ones in the suburbs with modern music and a youth program. It might help Patsi adjust better if she met some Christian friends. She was spending too much time with her city friend Megan. He'd only met the girl once, but Patsi seemed awfully naïve next to her. The girls always went elsewhere to hang out, and he couldn't blame Patsi since their apartment was nothing special, but he worried. Their neighbour Goldie had mentioned a different church when they'd had dinner at her house a while back. It was the one she and her son Jason attended and she had invited him and Patsi to come sometime to check it out.

The only problem was that Lester had the distinct impression Goldie liked him in a man-to-woman kind of way. He'd suspected it on more than one occasion, but when her son Jason asked if he'd like to be his new dad, that about took the cake. Lester had been avoiding them ever since – not an easy task when he was bound to run into them since they lived in the same apartment building.

When the service was over, Lester and Patsi waited in the customary line to shake the reverend's hand at the door. Another neighbour, Millicent Peacock, was in front of them, her silver head held erect, her nose in the air. Now there was one person he wouldn't miss if they started attending a different church. The woman was downright nosy. She never failed to make some snide comment each and every time he ran into her, either at church or in the apartment hallway. She lived directly below and her habit of banging on the ceiling with a broom handle was getting annoying. He wished she'd just jump on the thing and fly away.

The thought made him smile.

"You're looking smug this morning, Mr. Tibbett." Ms. Peacock cocked one eyebrow, a skill she had evidently perfected with practice.

"Just glad to be alive." The grin wouldn't be suppressed. Trust Ms. Peacock to make a comment just when he was thinking the worst of her.

"I heard about your little mishap. You're a lucky man."

"That I know, Ms. Peacock. I feel very lucky. And thankful."

"As you should." She sniffed, her back stiffening as her chin tilted up. "Just make sure you don't waste God's grace."

"Thank you for your concern. I will certainly try not to." Lester gave a slight bow.

Ms. Peacock made a little 'harumphing' noise and turned to shake the Pastor's hand. Patsi rolled her eyes at the older woman's back.

Lester and Patsi walked home from church – one of the advantages of their current place of worship. It had become a brisk walk now that the weather had turned cold, and Lester stomped his feet in the lobby to warm them as soon as they entered the apartment building. Their neighbour Jed Malloy was standing by the mailboxes.

"Did you say a prayer for me?" Jed asked with a roguish smile. His voice was loud, even when he didn't mean for it to be.

"You know it," Lester returned. "You could always come with us sometime."

Jed let out a depreciating snort. "The place would collapse if I walked in."

"You're not so bad as all that. Half of it is for show," Lester said.

"I'm not gonna test that theory. Say, youse two want to come up for some grub? I'm makin' Newfie breakfast."

"Breakfast?" Lester asked. "But it's past noon."

"So? Any time's the right time for Newfie breakfast," Jed declared.

Patsi frowned. "Newfie breakfast? What's that?"

"It's 'eaven on earth, little lady, that's what it is."

"What's an 'Evan'?" Lester asked, just to get under Jed's skin. He was used to Jed's way of dropping the 'h' at the beginning of words, but it was fun to tease him about it. Jed just ignored him.

"I have some homework to do," Patsi said. "I'll just make myself a sandwich."

"Suit yourself. What about you?" Jed nodded toward Lester.

Lester rubbed his chin. "Newfie breakfast, eh? Why not."

"I hope you like bologna, cause that's the main ingredient," Jed said as he pushed the 'up' button on the elevator.

In a few moments they arrived at their destination. "Enjoy your Newfie breakfast," Patsi called as she stepped out of the compartment. She headed in one direction while Jed and Lester went toward Jed's door.

Once inside, Jed gestured for Lester to take a seat at the kitchen table while he went to work, clattering about as he retrieved a large frying pan from the cupboard. "Good to see ya up and about. The doc clear ya to come back to work soon?"

Lester nodded. "Tomorrow. No point missing any more work when I feel fine."

"That was some close call you 'ad there, b'y. Guess all that church goin' came in handy. Somebody upstairs is lookin' out for ya." Jed started slicing potatoes into chunks.

"I certainly feel lucky, that's for sure."

Jed paused in his preparations, pinning Lester with his eyes. "Ever consider it wasn't an accident?"

Lester frowned. "Of course it was an accident."

Jed went back to chopping. "Not the impression I get from some of the guys on the crew."

"What have you heard?" Lester leaned forward in his chair.

Jed shrugged his massive shoulders. "They say Titan has a few enemies. Rival construction outfits that might like to shut 'em down."

"And 'they' think these rivals would stoop to killing a man?" Lester shook his head. "I can't believe it. You've been watching too much TV."

"Just tellin' ya what I heard, that's all." Jed threw the potatoes into the frying pan and went to work on the next ingredient – bologna. "Lots been goin' on since you been laid up. At work and around here."

Lester smiled. If there was one thing Jed liked, it was gossip. "Oh yeah? Might as well tell me all about it since you're going to anyway."

"First of all, did ya see that new gal that's just moved in? She's a bit big boned, but then who don't like a gal with a bit of meat on 'er? I like 'em curvy, myself."

"Good for you. You should date her."

"Me? No, I was thinkin' of you. She's a hairdresser or esthetician or cosmetician or whatever the heck you call it. "

"Why would I want to date her? You think I need a haircut?" Lester rubbed his curly brown hair.

"No, but that kind would probably be good with Patsi. See?" Jed tapped his head with his free hand. The other one still had a knife in it. "I'm lookin' out for ya."

"Yeah, thanks for that," Lester said dryly. He watched as Jed continued to fry up his creation – potatoes, eggs and bologna – all cooked in the same pan.

"And here's the other piece of news. The boys down at the Urban Cowboy are puttin' on a bull riding competition. Cash prizes and everything." Jed slid the concoction onto two plates along with some buttered toast. He set one in front of Lester and then went to the refrigerator for the ketchup. "You'd clean up except for the fact that you just 'ad an accident." Jed plunked himself down opposite Lester and proceeded to smother his entire plate with ketchup. "If it was an accident, that is."

"How can you even taste your food with that much ketchup on top?" Lester asked.

Jed rolled his eyes heavenward as he took a huge bite. "The nectar of the gods."

Lester just smiled and took a bite of his own food. It was surprisingly good and he ate in silence for a bit.

"So? What do ya think of the tournament?" Jed asked, his mouth full.

Lester frowned. "I don't know. I'd like to, but I'm not sure how smart that would be after what happened. I'd have to get clearance from the doctor." He rolled his neck to one side, testing how it felt.

"I saw that pretty little Chinese gal again, by the way. She was there with her brother, the architect."

Lester felt his body go still. "Is that so?" He focused on eating the next bite of his breakfast.

"Judging by your reaction, I'd say you 'ave a little thing for 'er." Jed pointed his fork at Lester and raised his brows.

Lester blew the comment off. "Don't be stupid. I don't even know her. Besides, she's engaged, remember?"

"Not the last I heard. I heard she broke it off."

"You are a fount of information, you know that?"

Jed shrugged. "Just thought you'd like to know. I seen the way you was lookin' at her that time. And I think she might 'ave taken a liking to you as well."

"You're delusional. First of all, she was plastered drunk and second, her brother is the main architect of the building we're working on."

Jed's eyes narrowed. "Maybe he was tryin' to get rid of you. Sabotaged the site 'imself to protect 'is sister."

Lester laughed outright and almost choked on a piece of bologna. He coughed into his fist and then took a drink of water.

"Easy, there, b'y. You okay?" Jed surveyed Lester over the table, fork poised.

Lester took another swallow of water and shook his head. "You really are a piece, you know? That was just about the stupidest thing I've ever heard in my life."

Jed shrugged. "Nothin's impossible, I always say. Scared is what I think."

"Scared of what?"

"Findin' a woman who'll put up with ya."

"Says the guy who is scared of serious relationships."

"Not denying it. I'm not the settlin' kind. You, on the other 'and, seem like the type who needs a bit of bossin' to keep 'im in line."

Lester snorted his disagreement and kept on eating. Sure, he'd been thinking about the 'pretty little Chinese gal', as Jed put it. But thinking about her and having leeway to do anything about it were two different things. He needed to forget he'd ever laid eyes on her. She wasn't his to pursue and even if she was, there were probably certain complications, like different cultural backgrounds and a belief in God. He'd actually checked in the phone book once and there were literally hundreds of S. Chan's listed. The chances of finding her were minimal, and even if he did get lucky, what could he say? That he thought she was pretty and sometimes she visited him in his dreams? It sounded sappy just thinking about it. He needed to figure out a way to get his life back into balance. And as far as his accident being anything other than that, he refused to even entertain the idea.

He finished his food and pushed the plate away, needing to think of a way to change the subject. "That was actually pretty good, if I do say so."

"Never underestimate the power of bologna. Course, it'd be better with toutons but only my ma makes 'em right."

"What on earth are toutons?"

"Fried bread dough." Jed sighed and rolled his eyes. "If my sis comes for a visit, I'll get 'er to make some."

"Your sister is coming for a visit?" Lester asked.

"Talkin' of it." Jed shrugged. "I got more than one, but the youngest, Reba, she's kind of a wild one and wants to come out west. My ma's not in favour but Reba's never been one to listen to no one."

"Must run in the family. How many brothers and sisters you got anyway?" Lester folded his arms in front of him on the table. If he could keep Jed talking about family he might drop the 'Chinese gal' thing.

Jed cocked his head to one side. "Well, there's Fanny – she's the oldest and is married with three kids. Then there's me. Then there's Zeb, Mary, Sissy, Bo, Will, Reba and Pip. He's the youngest – twenty-two."

Lester's eyebrows rose. "Quite the brood. And who names their kid Pip?"

Jed laughed. "Watch it! His real name is Steve, but we call him Pip. Short for 'Pip-squeak'."

"Ah. I should of guessed."

"Four girls and five boys. Nine kids in all." Jed's mouth twisted into a grin. "Small family by Newfie standards. You're not considered big until you hit the double digits. My ma was one of sixteen and Pops came from a family of twenty-one."

"You're joking. Nobody has twenty-one children."

"Tell that to Nan. She says she spent 'er whole adult life either pregnant or nursing a baby so she deserves to get taken care of now she's old. Of course, she still gardens and cooks like the dickens. Won't slow down for nobody. We breed 'em tough on the rock."

Lester shook his head. The 'rock' was the nickname given to the island of Newfoundland. Even though it was part of Canada, it had joined the confederation later than most. A distinct culture had flourished due to the isolation and the people there were very proud of their heritage. "That's an awful lot of Malloys. It's kind of a scary thought."

Jed laughed. "Just wait till my brother Zeb comes for a visit. He works in Fort Mac. My brother Bo was thinkin' of looking for work, too – that's where Reba got the notion - and if they come west, Zeb'll probably come down to see 'em on his time off."

Lester laughed. "Not sure this city can handle too many more of you."

"You won't know what 'it once Zeb gets 'ere."

"Crazier than you?"

"A real party animal."

"Wow. I can hardly wait." Lester stretched and slapped his knees. He wondered how Ms. Peacock would take the addition of more Malloys. "Well, thanks for the food – and for the gossip. I better get going now, though." Lester picked up his plate and took it to the sink. There was nowhere to set it, so he perched it on top of another pile of dirty dishes.

"Just leave it. I'll get to them dishes one of these days." Jed stood and followed Lester to the door. "Don't forget about that bull riding tournie."

"I'll see what the doctor has to say."

Jed winked. "I know a pretty little Chinese gal that might be there watching."

THE NEXT DAY AFTER WORK, Lester stopped by the mailboxes in the front lobby to get the mail. He rolled his shoulders and arched backwards before inserting the small key into the lock. He'd been on light duty all day, but his back muscles were protesting none-the-less.

"So good to see you up and about. You had us all worried."

Lester knew who had spoken without having to turn around. Goldie Harper. "Um, yeah. Still a bit stiff, though, but I'm sure I'll be good as new in no time." He reached into the small box and pulled out a few letters and a flyer. He clicked the door back into place and removed the key. "Um, thanks for the food you sent over. It was real thoughtful." He turned his whole body to face Goldie. His neck was stiff and it was easier than trying to turn his head.

"It was the least I could do once you got home from the hospital. I hope the casserole wasn't too spicy."

"It was real good and I do love a good brownie. Patsi appreciated not having to cook while I was laid up." Lester let his eyes wander to the floor.

There was an awkward silence until Goldie spoke again. "This might sound like a silly question, but does Patsi have a boyfriend?"

Lester looked up sharply and then winced at the pain the sudden movement caused. "Not that I know of. Why?"

"Well, I don't want to alarm you, or anything, but Jason mentioned that there was a boy over once while I was on nightshift."

Lester's brows descended over his eyes. "Is that so?"

"It's probably nothing. When I asked her about it she said it was just a school friend dropping something off for a project."

"I'll ask her about it," Lester said.

Goldie's lashed fluttered. "Oh dear. I hope I haven't gotten her into trouble."

"If it's as you say, then there's no trouble at all."

"I wouldn't even have mentioned it, but having male guests over when I'm not home is one of my rules." Goldie's eyes shifted to the right as a newcomer came into the front entry.

The woman looked to be in her mid-twenties with a pretty round face and luxurious chestnut brown hair that fell halfway down her back in calculated curls. Her rather tight red knit dress revealed a curvaceously full figure with plenty of cleavage showing and ample padding on the backside. Must be the new tenant Jed had mentioned yesterday. She had on a little too much dramatic makeup, but then he'd also said she worked in the esthetics industry, so it probably made sense.

"Excuse me," the newcomer said. Immediately Lester and Goldie stepped to the side to let her near the boxes.

Strong perfume wafted past and Lester averted his eyes. He and Goldie waited silently until the girl left with her mail. Finally, Lester cleared his throat. "Thanks for telling me. About Patsi."

"Of course. I like her. She's a good sitter and Jason really likes her, too."

"Okay. Well, nice talking to you." Lester touched the brim of his cowboy hat and strode to the elevator. He was definitely going to have a little talk with his sister.

AFTER A QUICK SHOWER, Lester made supper - tuna casserole. It was one of Patsi's favourites, and he wanted to make sure she was in a good mood before he asked about the boy Goldie had mentioned. He stirred the cooked macaroni in with a can of tuna and the other ingredients and then turned it into a baking dish. He topped it with grated cheddar cheese and popped it into the oven. It would be ready in forty-five minutes and Patsi still wasn't home. He checked the time on the stove clock and then double-checked by comparing it to his watch. It wasn't like Patsi to be so late and it certainly wasn't like her to not call if she was out longer than usual.

One hour later, Lester decided to eat. 'Murphy's Law' stated that as soon as he started, Patsi would show up. It didn't work. After he ate, Lester cleaned up and then turned on the TV. He really couldn't focus on the show, a silly sit-com that made males look like idiots. He clicked it off in frustration. Where could Patsi be? He'd already left several texts but there was no response. At what point should he call the police?

He was just about to take action when his cell phone chimed. He grabbed the device out of his shirt pocket and brought up the incoming text. It was from Patsi.

"On bus. Running late. C u soon."

It was already dark in the apartment when Patsi arrived home. Lester had purposely left the lights off and was sitting in the shadows, waiting. And seething.

"Anybody home?" Patsi called when she entered. She threw her purse and backpack on a kitchen chair and turned on the kitchen light. Lester watched as she lifted the lid from the casserole dish and smelled its contents. She then fixed herself a plate and put it in the microwave. When it dinged she walked to the small table and was about to sit down when she saw him for the first time. "Oh!" she squealed. "You scared me! What are you doing sitting alone in the dark with all the lights off?"

"Really? That's the first thing that comes to your mind?" His voice was tight.

"Sorry." Patsi shrugged a nonchalant shoulder. "I lost track of time. But I did text you. Didn't you get it?" She began eating.

"Yeah, I got it, but it's pretty late. I was worried."

"Well, you need to get over that. I'm a big girl now, remember?"

"Patsi, a little common courtesy is all I ask. This is a big city. And there are lots of crazy people out there. You shouldn't be traveling alone after dark."

"Technically, it wasn't dark. Just dusk. And how am I supposed to get that extra help I need in Math if I can't stay after classes?"

"Is that what you were doing?" Lester asked. "Getting extra help?" She nodded. Her mouth was full.

"Well, I suppose if that's the case… but I want you to come right home afterwards. And let me know which days you're staying so I won't be expecting you before a certain hour."

"Okay." She took another bite.

Lester frowned. She seemed quite agreeable to his suggestion. Compliant. And that worried him. His sister was never compliant. "You sure there's nothing else you want to share with me?"

Patsi sat for a moment, fork poised. Then she shook her head. "No, that's it."

"You're sure?"

Patsi laughed. "I said so. Sheesh."

"Okay. Well, there is something else I need to talk to you about, though."

"What's up?" Patsi continued eating.

Lester stood up with a grunt and walked to the kitchen table where he slowly lowered himself into the chair across from his sister.

"You okay?" she asked. "You look like you're hurting."

"I'll be fine." He waved a dismissive hand. "I saw Goldie Harper today. She said you had a boy at her apartment." He waited.

"A guy just needed to drop off some stuff for a project. It was nothing. I already explained it to Goldie. Why? What did she say?"

Was that a tick in her jaw?

"Basically what you just said. As long as that's all there is to it."

"You're getting paranoid in your old age." Patsi stood up and took her plate to the sink. "Now, if you're done interrogating me, I have homework to do."

Lester watched as she rinsed her dish and then sauntered to her room. He stood, his back protesting painfully, and walked on jerky legs to his easy chair. Once he'd lowered himself into it he picked up the remote control and flipped the TV on again. Why did he feel like there was more to this than she was letting on?

"Sorry, bud. The doctor said it wasn't a good idea." Lester cradled a beer between his hands and made eye contact with Jed in the mirror across from them on the other side of the bar. The Urban Cowboy was filling up.

"I was hoping for a few side bets. My chances of making money on the deal are gettin' slimmer by the minute." Jed scowled and took a swig of his own brew.

Jacques the bartender was wiping down some glasses a few feet away. "It'll keep the bosses insurance costs down. He doesn't need a liability entering the tournament, anyway."

"Insurance costs? What odds!" Jed sputtered a derisive laugh and drank some more.

"Well, I'd say the odds are pretty good I'd get hurt," Lester said reasonably. "And that is not something I'm willing to risk. It is my neck we're talking about."

Jed looked sideways at Lester, like he'd suddenly grown two heads. "I knows yer not stun, but yer some contrary."

"What?" Lester screwed up his brow. "Sometimes I'm not sure you're even speaking the same language."

"Better brush up on your Newfie," Jacques advised. "What odds means 'who cares?' and I think in that last part he just called you stupid."

"Yes, b'y. Youse a smart one fer a frog." Jed sent his now empty beer stein sailing down the polished counter top and straight into the backstop of Jacques' waiting hand. "I'll 'ave another."

Lester rolled his neck to one side and held it there for a second. "How soon is that tournament?"

"Not for another three weeks." Jacques plunked another frothy draft down in front of Jed.

"I might be up for it in that amount of time."

"Now yer talkin'" Jed slapped Lester across the back, making him wince. "A late entry'll make for more suspense."

"I'm not promising anything." Lester rubbed his neck. "I just said I'd see."

"Speaking of see, there's that new gal what moved into our building." Jed gestured with his head to the front entrance. The buxom chestnut haired woman had entered and was scanning the room. Her attire was somewhat less revealing than it had been the other day when Lester had seen her in the lobby of the apartment building, and her makeup was much less dramatic. Maybe she just dressed that way for work.

"So?" Lester turned back to his beer and noted that Jacques was watching the woman intently from behind the bar. From this vantage point, facing the mirror, he could see that she had joined someone at a table.

His attention was taken from the new tenant when Cory Roberts, one of the owners of the establishment, joined Jacques behind the bar. "Glad to see you out and about again," Cory directed at Lester. "That was some fall, I hear."

"Word sure gets around," Lester said with a shrug.

"This town isn't as big as you might think. I had hoped you would be entering our little tournament, but maybe that's out of the question now."

"We'll see," Lester hedged.

"I been tryin' to convince 'im," Jed said. "Then again, if there was foul play on the job site, I don't blames 'im if 'e feels nervous about bull ridin'."

"Foul play?" Cory and Jacques tuned their full attention to the big Newfoundlander.

"Active imagination," Lester said with a laugh. "Ignore him."

An older black man approached and sat on a stool next to Jed. He was broad and looked to be in good shape and his head was cleanly shaven. Cory looked at the newcomer, forgetting his other customers for a moment. "Dad."

"Hello, Son."

"I wasn't expecting you this early." Cory gestured to Jacques. "This is Jacques Marcett, one of the best bartenders in town. Jacques, meet my dad, Tad Roberts."

The older man reached across the counter to shake Jacques hand. "We've already met. I'm glad to know my son has good employees. Somebody has to keep the business going."

"What is that supposed to mean?" Cory asked, the good-natured smile never leaving his lips. Lester wondered if there was more behind it.

"Just that you're not here as much as I would expect. Always off playing that party music, or so I hear."

"Who told you that?" Cory asked.

"I have my sources." Tad smiled.

Cory glanced at Jacques, who just shrugged his shoulders. "My dad is not a fan of electronic music. Says it's not real music if it doesn't have guitars and a drum kit."

"I never said that," Tad countered. "I just don't care for it. And as the principle financier of this place, I want to know my business is being run efficiently."

"So you're the other owner?" Jed joined the conversation. "I always wondered who'd trust Cory 'ere as a business partner."

Tad turned slowly to face Jed and Lester. He smiled, the gesture not quite reaching his eyes. "Hello. Who are you?"

"Just regular payin' customers. Name's Jed and this 'ere is Lester." Jed lifted his mug and took a long swallow, ending with a satisfied sigh.

Tad smiled and this time the look appeared to be genuine. "Pleased to meet some paying customers. I'm just down from Edmonton. Thought I'd check up on the place. See if things are running as smoothly as he says." He flicked his head toward his son.

"May I say your son does a fine job, Sir, so there's no need to worry one bit," Jed said.

Tad nodded. "Good to know. I'd hate to see my retirement fund go down the drain."

"There's lots goin' down the drain in this joint." Jed lifted his ale. "But it ain't your retirement fund." He laughed at his own joke.

"You didn't have to lend me the money," Cory said quietly from behind the counter.

Tad shrugged. "It's what parents do. Support their kids whether they agree or not."

There was an awkward moment of silence. Far too much personal history had been revealed in the short conversation. More than Lester – or apparently anyone – felt comfortable with.

Jed lofted his beer mug again. "Cheers to the Urban Cowboy. May the ale flow as long as a dinosaur's -"

Lester cut in. "To the Urban Cowboy." He lifted his almost empty stein as well.

"Why'd ya cut me off, there b'y? I was about to say a dinosaur's neck, not something crass."

"Oh. Well, I'm never sure what's going to come out of your mouth next," Lester said.

"I 'ave some manners."

Everyone laughed. "A round for our paying customers," Tad said to Jacques.

"And what will you have, Sir?" Jacques directed at the elder Mr. Roberts.

"Nothing. I don't drink," Tad replied.

"Now that is a shame," Jed said and clapped Tad on the shoulder. The older man looked at where Jed's hand had made contact and for a moment, Lester thought he might get upset.

Instead he smiled. "Actually, make that a tea, Jacques. Chamomile, if you have it."

Jacques nodded. "One chamomile tea, coming up."

WHEN LESTER ENTERED his apartment building the next day after work, he was surprised to see both Tad Roberts and Jacques Marcett standing in the lobby, chatting.

"Well, hello." Tad greeted Lester. "Do you live here, too?"

"Yes." Lester stopped a few feet away and waited.

"It's a small world, isn't it?" When Lester didn't do anything but nod, Tad continued. "Jacques has offered to let me stay with him for the week instead of checking into a motel."

Lester's eyebrows rose. "You aren't staying with your son?"

"It was... awkward."

"I see. Well, nice to meet up with you again." Lester nodded and headed toward the mailboxes. Awkward because they didn't get along or awkward for other reasons? Either way it was none of his business.

He and Jed had stayed and chatted with the elder Roberts last night after Cory had begged off. Tad Roberts turned out to be an interesting man. An ex-army officer, he and Cory's mother had split up when Cory was young. Cory and his mom had stayed in Calgary and Tad continued with his military career, finally settling in Edmonton after early retirement. Apparently, father and son were trying to reconnect after years of distance. Cory seemed happy enough to take his father's money, but beyond that Lester was doubtful how much the younger Roberts really cared for his father.

It was too bad that families sometimes fell out with one another like that. Not so with his own parents. They'd always had a solid relationship. Then again, it had never really been tested since they had been taken away from him far too early. Perhaps God in His wisdom knew he would need the good memories of them to get through the years raising Patsi.

Lester busied himself with the mail just as Goldie Harper and the new female tenant entered the building together, the latter back to her rather provocative attire instead of the demure outfit from the night before. Goldie was carrying on with some friendly chatter, which was a relief since it meant she couldn't corner him. He'd had enough awkwardness of his own where she was concerned.

"Hello, Jacques," Goldie greeted the men. "Have you met Angela Carravagio yet? She just moved in."

Jacques, Tad, Goldie and the new girl, Angela, exchanged introductions. Lester focused on sorting his mail. For some reason he felt tired and wasn't in the mood for small talk. He had no interest whatsoever in getting to know Angela Carravagio or furthering his relationship with Goldie, for that matter. And while Tad Roberts seemed like a nice man, Jacques Marcett had always appeared aloof. Lester was surprised that Jacques had offered to let Tad stay with him.

On his way by, Lester tipped his cowboy hat, purposely avoiding eye contact.

"Lester." Goldie reached out and stopped him by putting her hand on his arm as he went by. "You haven't met Angela yet."

Lester pasted on what he hoped was a suitable smile. "Hello."

"I was thinking," Goldie continued. "We should have a social of some kind for the people living here in the apartment complex. Like a block party only a building party. What do you think?" She seemed enthralled with the idea as she looked from Lester to Angela to Jacques. "It would be a nice way for newcomers to get to know people."

Lester just shrugged. To his surprise Jacques spoke up. "I fancy myself a bit of a chef. I could make some appetizers." The Frenchman smiled at Angela, his eyes roaming from her face to parts below and back again.

"Sounds wonderful." Angela flashed a smile at Jacques. "I can help organize. I'll give you my number." She was talking to Goldie but her eyes never left Jacques. Goldie retrieved her phone from her purse and Angela recited the number, all the while maintaining eye contact with Jacques.

"Well, I better get going," Lester mumbled and turned to leave.

"Oh! Just a minute," Goldie said.

Lester waited.

"I invited Pat to my church on Sunday night. They have an evening service geared more toward young adults. She didn't commit, but if you went, too, I think she would." Goldie turned to Angela and the rest. "You are all invited as well, if you'd like."

"Church? I don't think so." Jacques's smile looked more like a sneer. "Besides, I'm Catholic."

"Thanks, but I don't think so, either," Angela responded. "I'm not much of a church goer." She and Jacques shared a look.

"Well, I am. A church goer, that is," Tad said. All eyes turned to him. His brows rose. "What? That surprises you?"

Goldie was beaming. "I am so pleased to hear it." She turned her attention to Lester. "So? Will you come?"

Lester rubbed the back of his neck. "Um, I'll talk to Patsi."

With Tad along as a chaperone, maybe he could deflect some of Goldie's attention onto the older man.

THE FIRST THING Lester noticed when he entered his apartment was the blinking light on the answering machine. He pressed the button and listened half-heartedly as the mechanical voice droned on about the number of messages. The first said he'd won a trip to the Caribbean. He deleted it. The next was someone doing a survey. Another delete. The third one caught his attention.

"This message is for Miss Patsi Tibbett. This is Professor Chan. It has come to my attention that you signed up for a tutorial block, but have not been attending. Since there are other students waiting to get into these very valuable sessions, may I suggest you start attending or withdraw your name from the list so that others may take advantage of this service? Your attention to this matter would be appreciated."

Lester frowned and rewound the message, listening to it again. Patsi had told him she was going to tutoring after classes and that things were making sense now, especially since she'd gotten the initial help from Goldie. Apparently, the only thing she'd really figured out was a way to pull the wool over his eyes. He felt anger bubbling up inside. This was the way she repaid him for all the sacrifices he'd made? And just where was she going when she claimed she was getting Math help?

He waited in his armchair, trying to focus on the sports show that was on TV. She was apparently at one of her tutoring sessions now and he would have longer to wait than usual. The longer he waited the more livid he felt.

Finally he heard the front door open and Patsi entered. "Getting some help with Math again?" he called from his chair, his voice laced with sarcasm.

"Yes. I told you earlier." She already sounded defensive.

"Is that so?"

"What's that supposed to mean?" She came and stood right in front of him, arms folded across her chest.

Lester faltered in his resolve for a moment. She seemed genuinely confused by what he'd said. "There's a message from one of your professors. Listen for yourself." He gestured toward the answering machine.

Patsi strode to the phone and hit the button. When the message came on, her face changed. First dismay then outrage flashed across her features. "She has no right calling my home. This isn't high school."

"Apparently she's conscientious."

"This is just stupid!"

"Are you even passing?" Lester asked.

"It's none of your business."

"Oh yes it is," Lester countered, his voice rising just a notch. "Who is paying for your education?"

"The trust fund you set up after Mom and Dad died, remember?" She stuck her chin out. "So don't lecture me about spending your hard earned money. I should just quit school and then you wouldn't have to worry about it."

"You are not quitting school."

"Why not? It was your idea, not mine." Patsi strode from his presence and slammed her bedroom door behind her.

Thumping ensued from below. Lester sighed. Millicent Peacock was letting them know she had heard every word. Using her broom handle, no doubt.

Lester hoisted himself from his chair and followed Patsi's footsteps to her bedroom. He rapped on the closed door with his knuckles. "If you're not going to your tutorial, where have you been going?"

"Go away," was Patsi's muffled replay.

"Not until you tell me where you've been." Lester crossed his arms.

"No."

"I can wait all night. You know I will. I'm a very stubborn man." He looked up at the ceiling and noticed a cobweb.

A few minutes later Patsi came to the door. Her eyes were red from crying. "Promise me you won't flip out."

"I'm not promising anything until I know what you've been up to."

Patsi stood for a moment and then opened the door wider so that Lester could enter. She flopped down on her bed and he carefully sat down on its edge.

"Spill it," Lester demanded, not unkindly.

Patsi stared at the ceiling for a moment. "I got a part time job."

Lester's eyebrows rose. "Come again?"

Patsi sat up and clutched one of her pillows to her middle. "I got a part time job at a coffee shop."

Lester could feel his anger rising and had to take a steadying breath so that he could speak calmly. "I thought I said that was out of the question. That it would be difficult to arrange transportation, not to mention it would affect your school."

Patsi looked down at her hands. "I know. But as you can see, it's not so bad. Most days I'm home before dark."

"Most days. Not acceptable."

Patsi's gaze swung upward, pleading. "I really like it. Tamara and Carmen are really nice bosses."

"Wait a minute." Lester held up a hand. "Tamara and Carmen? Are you talking about The Brew?" Patsi nodded. "That's right downtown!"

"Most of the time I catch a ride home with Tamara. I've only had to ride the bus a couple of times."

Lester frowned. "Who put you up to this? Jed?"

"Don't be silly," Patsi said. She actually smiled. "Tamara mentioned it the first time I babysat for Goldie. Jason and Tamara's son Matonabee are friends and Mat was over playing when I got there. Tamara was only there for a few minutes to pick him up before Goldie had to go to work, but when she asked me, I knew it was like a gift."

"A gift?" Lester raised a skeptical eyebrow.

"Yes," Patsi persisted. "You know how you're always saying God works things out?"

"And you think this is from God?" Lester couldn't help the skepticism in his voice.

"Why not?" Patsi lifted her chin. "I know you work hard and I don't like asking you for money for things. This way I can make my own spending money, plus I'm contributing."

He couldn't argue with that. "What about school? The very thing I was afraid would happen is happening. You are failing your Math class. You should be spending that extra time getting help, not worrying about a part time job."

"I hate Math. I'm no good at it and I want to drop it," Patsi declared.

"No."

"But Lester! Math is not my thing! It's like Chinese torture." She stopped and giggled.

He glanced sideways at Patsi's profile. She looked so young. Like the little girl he still imagined she was. "What's so funny?"

"Nothing. Just that my Prof is Chinese, so it really is like Chinese torture."

"I thought you said you were figuring it out."

Patsi sighed. "I went once to the tutorial. The first time. But it was horrible. I didn't understand a thing and the assistant was no help at all. He was really rude and treated me like I was a moron. Not to mention the fact that he kept checking me out the whole time." She emphasized that last part and made sure she made eye contact

This made Lester frown. He knew she was playing him, but the thought of some sleazy university senior making a pass at his little sister made him see red.

"Please let me drop the class. Please? I promise I will do super good in every other class. Just don't make me go back to Math with the dragon lady!"

"No promises. Let me think about it first." He rose with some difficulty and straightened as best he could. His back was killing him and those painkillers the doctor had prescribed were calling his name.

"But I can keep the job?" Patsi asked hopefully.

"I'll think about that, too."

She jumped off her bed and squeezed him around the middle. He winced but couldn't help but soften just a bit. "Please, please, please can I keep the job? Pretty please?"

"Tell you what. Goldie invited us to her church on Sunday night. If you go with me I'll think about it even harder."

Patsi's brows descended for a moment and she sighed. Almost instantly her face cleared and she nodded. She stuck out her hand. "Deal."

Lester took her smaller palm in his and gave it one decisive shake. "Deal."

"Hooray! You're the best brother ever." She flung her arms around his neck and he gasped with pain. She jumped back. "Sorry. I forgot you were still hurt."

He rubbed his neck. "I didn't say you could keep the job for sure."

"But you're thinking about it…" She smiled coyly. "I actually feel a lot better now that you know."

"Get some sleep." He tousled her hair. "Love you."

"Love you, too."

Lester turned and left the room with stilted steps. Teenage females. Who could understand them? He knew he was already giving in to the job thing. If she really could catch a ride home with the owner then that would solve one problem, and earning her own spending money would be a good lesson in responsibility. He would have to talk to Tamara Spence to make sure the rides were a for sure thing. And as for going to church with Goldie, it didn't mean he would have to date the woman. Patsi needed more spiritual guidance and he wasn't sure he was living up to the task.

Tomorrow he would pay a visit to the college and talk to this Professor Chan. Something had to be done to salvage Patsi's grades as well as his frayed nerves.

LESTER ARRANGED to leave work early the next day so he could get over to the college in good time. He'd phoned ahead and scheduled an appointment with the Math department secretary.

Patsi didn't know he was going to see her Math professor. He needed to get a good read on the woman without Patsi along.

Once in the Arts and Sciences Building, he made his way to the appropriate floor and waited in the designated lounge area that the receptionist had indicated. It was large with overstuffed furniture that was wearing in spots. Still, it looked like it had been refurbished sometime in the last decade. No oranges and olive greens to be found here. Everything was a neutral taupe, charcoal grey or black.

After just a few minutes, a middle-aged secretary came out to greet him and ushered him along a dimly lit, quiet corridor lined with wooden doors. The private recluse of academia's elite. She stopped at one with a nameplate that read 'Professor S. Chan' and rapped lightly with the back of her hand. "Enter," was the directive from within. The secretary swung the door open and gestured for Lester to do as he was bid.

Lester removed his cowboy hat and ran a hand through his hair. It probably stuck out in places but there wasn't much he could do about it now. He nodded to the secretary on his way by and then turned his head. He stopped and his eyebrows shot up as he recognized the petite Asian woman sitting behind a menacing piece of oak furniture that served as her desk. Her eyes were wide and her mouth had formed a silent 'O'.

"Sherri Chan?" He felt rooted to the spot. "You're my sister's Math professor?"

The woman behind the desk blinked, obviously at a loss for words.

"Is everything alright?" the secretary asked.

"Oh yes. Fine, thank you." Sherri Chan nodded to the office assistant and straightened her back. The other woman closed the door and her muted footfalls retreated down the hall.

Lester's fingers worried the brim of the hat in his hands. "I can't believe I didn't put two and two together before now." His gaze ventured upward to connect with Sherri's.

"Please sit down." Sherri gestured to the chair opposite her desk and then immediately focused her attention on her computer screen.

She waited for him to sit and then cleared her throat. "So… about your sister's Math mark… I explained to her the importance of -"

Lester leaned forward and stopped her in mid-sentence. "I know my sister's education is important, but frankly I'm having trouble concentrating at the moment."

Her lashes fluttered but her eyes never left her laptop.

"Did you know?" he asked. "That Patsi Tibbett was my sister?"

She shook her head. "No. It never occurred to me." She inhaled sharply and ventured a glance in his direction. "Should it have?"

He smiled. "I suppose not. It just seems like more than a coincidence. You being Patsi's teacher. Your brother being the architect on the project where I work…"

"I'm so glad you weren't hurt too badly." She looked up and then down again.

"You heard about that?"

She nodded. "Yes."

"And then there's the fact that we've run into each other a couple of other times…"

Lester could swear Sherri blushed. "Oh that. Please forgive me for my behaviour. I had a little too much to drink."

"It's okay. I was kind of flattered, although it was probably just the booze talking." He surveyed her features, hoping for a sign of something else. She definitely seemed flustered if the way she kept avoiding eye contact was any indication. "I hope your fiancé wasn't too upset."

"Oh… we broke it off anyway."

Lester knew as much thanks to Jed but it was good to hear her say it. "I hope it wasn't my doing."

She shook her head vigorously. "No, no. It just… we weren't… it's for the best," she finally finished with a shrug.

Lester nodded, a smile of satisfaction creeping unfettered across his features. He cocked his head to one side. "Would you like to go out to dinner with me, Miss Chan?" He laughed outright at the startled expression that passed over her features.

Her eyes flew up to meet his and she blinked several times before answering. "Yes, actually. I think I would like that very much."

EPISODE 7

SKELETONS IN THE NEIGHBOURHOOD

*S*teve Russell rubbed his chin between his thumb and index finger as his eyes scanned the computer screen in front of him. It illuminated his face with an eerie blueness in the now empty newspaper office, which was dark save for the emergency light over the exit. The whiskers on his chin made a rasping sound as he rubbed back and forth. It was late in the afternoon and he should be heading home. Or over to The Brew to see Tamara. But an anonymous tip had his mind elsewhere.

In front of him were three screenshots from his own newspaper sent from an unknown email address. One was a headline about a company called Nudara Oil making some significant inroads in the industry, despite being the new kid on the block and relatively small next to other big oil companies. The second shot showed a local government official, Sean Fasburger, promising an even 'closer relationship' between the city and the oil and gas sector. The last was the report about a recent accident on a construction job site downtown. The message in the email read, "Connect the dots."

Steve wasn't sure what that meant, but he intended to find out. As a journalist he often relied on anonymous tips, but they always needed to be backed up with facts. And he knew just the person who could help - an ex-cop turned Private Investigator named Vinny Kirk-patrick. Vinny was good at what he did. He might look like a has-been straight out of a seventy's TV drama, but the guy had connections.

Political backroom deals and profit skimming among the business sector were nothing new to Steve. It was the reference to the accident that really got his attention. Monetary kickbacks just gave way to attempted murder. And that had him worried. His friend Sherman Chan was the chief architect on the building project.

If there was something going on, Steve was certain Sherman had nothing to do with it. He intended to do his homework before alerting his friend to anything shady. The poor guy had enough on his plate these days since being alienated from his family.

Steve shook his head. He and Sherman had been friends since grade school. He had always known that the Chans were quite traditional. Old fashioned was more like it, especially when it came to some of their cultural traditions. Still, he couldn't believe that Sherman's mother had severed all ties with her only son simply because he was dating a black woman instead of someone Chinese.

Speaking of dating, he better give Tamara a call if he didn't intend to get over to her coffee shop before closing time. He'd been giving her a ride home from work most days since they started seeing one another, about the same time that Sherman and the other owner of the shop, Carmen Lamont, had been dating. Of course, in his case, it was all 'unofficial' and Tamara didn't use the term 'dating'. She said it sounded juvenile not to mention colonial – whatever that meant. She insisted it was a casual, non-committed relationship, despite the fact that they'd found themselves engaging in some steamy good-byes when he dropped her off at her apartment building. Sometimes he couldn't read her. One minute she was a woman on fire and the next she was as skittish as a virgin.

Steve picked up his cell phone and hit Tamara's number. When she answered he transferred the phone to his right ear so that he could still use his dominant left hand on the computer keyboard. "Hey, gorgeous. Just thought I'd let you know I won't be making it over before closing. I have a lead I need to check. Hope you don't mind."

"I never asked you to be my taxi service," Tamara responded matter-of-factly.

Steve smiled. Tamara's independence was one of the things he admired about her. "I know. I just like giving you a ride. It's what a guy does for his girlfriend."

"Please! That sounds so juvenile!"

"Sorry. Woman friend, then? Does that sound better?" He smirked, knowing full well she would hate that just as much.

"It makes me sound ancient."

"Anyway, if it's not too late, I can stop by your place after." He waited a beat before responding to the silence. "One of these days you're going to have to let me come up."

"Not tonight... Mat will probably be in bed by that time."

"Sounds like a good opportunity for some alone time, then."

She laughed into the receiver. "Nice try."

"Well, you can't blame a guy for trying." The smile faded from his lips. "I'm not sure why you're being so over protective. He's going to have to find out about us sooner or later."

"Stop pressuring me. I will be the one to decide if and when my son gets to meet you." She sounded miffed.

Steve rolled his eyes toward the ceiling. "Okay, okay. Forget it. When you're ready for him to know you'll tell me. Anyway, gotta go. I'll see you tomorrow at the shop."

With a sigh, Steve hung up. As if by reflex, he smoothed his brown hair into place. Even if he didn't always feel like he was in control, he might as well look the part.

Tamara was being awfully paranoid when it came to her son Matonabee. He understood that she didn't want the boy to get attached to a strange man just in case things didn't work out between them. On the other hand, Steve felt like she was using Mat as an excuse. One of these days he might just show up at her apartment without notice.

For now he needed to concentrate on figuring out the anonymous puzzle. He reached for his phone and dialed again.

~

THE URBAN COWBOY held its usual bustle of patrons – denim clad cowboys - or perhaps just look-a-likes, office drones escaping the stress of the day, and girls dressed up like country music stars in skirts that were too short to be decent. Steve perched on a stool in his usual spot at the bar.

Jacques the bartender placed Steve's brand of beer in front of him without waiting for him to order. "Haven't seen you around much. Your new woman got you on a leash?"

"Hardly. Just busy." Steve took a swing of his beer.

"You know what they say. Too much work makes Jack a dull boy." With his French accent, it almost sounded like Jacques said his own name.

Cory Roberts, the owner and Steve's friend, came up behind Jacques and slapped him on the back. "What's this? Talking about yourself again?"

"I said 'Jack', not 'Jacques'." Jacques shook his head with an amused smirk on his face. "He says he is too busy with work but I say it's better to be busy with a woman. No?"

"You're learning under my tutelage," Cory said with a laugh. "Now we just need to find a woman who will put up with you."

Jacques frowned. "Mon dieu! As if I need your help!" He turned away and started polishing glasses.

"Not what I heard." Cory turned to Steve and leaned on the counter. "My father says Jacques' got his eye on a someone who lives in the same building. She's been in here a couple of times, too. If he doesn't hurry up someone else is gonna beat him to it."

Jacques said something in French under his breath – probably explicit and derogatory if Steve wasn't mistaken. Cory just grinned.

"Your dad?" Steve furrowed his brow. "What's your father got to do with it?"

"Jacques' putting the old man up while he's in town. My extracurricular was making him uncomfortable. His new found religious beliefs have made him a bit of a prude."

"You're still seeing Renee, Carmen's niece?" Steve asked.

Cory frowned. "Of course. Who else?"

Steve shrugged one shoulder. "You've never been one to stick with one woman for too long."

Cory shifted his stance as well as the subject. "Coming to the bull riding competition? It's next week."

"Probably. Are there lots of entries?"

"Not as many as I'd hoped, but there's still time."

Steve glanced to the left and noticed a face that was becoming familiar. One that, for some reason, made him uncomfortable. He turned back to Cory. "You know that guy?"

Cory leaned a bit to the left and squinted. "He's been in here a fair bit, recently. Why?"

The man in question had the look of a seasoned bouncer, or maybe someone fresh out of jail. He had a shaved head, a goatee and enough tattoos to make any biker proud. Steve shook his head. "Forget it. I just get the feeling that he's watching, that's all. Every time I come in here he's not far behind."

"Maybe it's the company you keep." Cory gestured with his head toward Vinny Kirkpatrick, who had just entered through the front door.

Steve downed the rest of his beer and slipped off the barstool. "All part of the job. Talk to you later."

"Stay out of trouble," Cory called to Steve's retreating figure.

VINNY KIRKPATRICK WAS in his fifties with a greying moustache that was far too bushy to be fashionable and rumpled clothing that sported the odd coffee stain. For all Steve knew, Vinny slept in his clothes, although he doubted the older man actually slept much. The guy ran on caffeine and always seemed jittery. Legs bouncing, eyes twitching, fingers drumming... Good thing he had more contacts than a rock star and was a literal fount of information.

Steve leaned forward across the small table they'd found tucked in a corner. "Before we start, do you know that man sitting alone with the bald head and tattoos?"

"Should I?" Vinny asked, glancing sideways.

"Just checking. There's something about him that I don't trust. He's familiar somehow, but I can't put my finger on it."

Vinny's eyes twitched. "Probably nothing, but I'll check him out if you want."

"Thanks. I'd appreciate it. Now, what have you got for me?"

Vinny drummed his fingers on the tabletop. His coffee jiggled in the cup, splashing over the sides. "The three stories seemed unconnected at first glance but it didn't take much to find a connection."

"I'm all ears." Steve leaned in even closer.

"For starters, Nudara Oil is helping to finance the Titan project." Vinny took a noisy slurp of his coffee.

"I thought Northstar Holdings was building the tower," Steve said. He watched as Vinny proceeded to add more sugar, stirring it vigorously with his spoon.

"Northstar Holdings is actually a conglomerate, and Nudara is the principle shareholder." Vinny crossed his legs to the side, the bottom one bouncing to an inner rhythm only he could hear.

"When I tried to get a list of shareholders, the information was denied," Steve said. "Confidential."

Vinny just smiled in his usual nonchalant way. "Which is why you need me." He took another long slurp of his coffee.

Steve returned the grin. "Fair enough. So there's a connection between Nudara Oil and Titan. Titan is contracted to build the tower and Nudara is part of the group financing the project. Why would they want to keep that information hidden? Why not be the flagship company and plaster their own banner on the side of the building?"

"Unless they don't want people to know how profitable they really are," Vinny offered. He waved to a passing waitress to get a refill. As a former alcoholic, Vinny didn't drink alcohol, but he made up for it in caffeine.

"Which could have something to do with Fasburger's promises to ease taxes for start-up resource based companies. If Nudara is actually a bigger company than they appear, maybe he's taking kickbacks. Lining his own pockets with what should be going into public coffers."

"I suspect it's something along those lines. Never met a politician yet who was immune to lining his own pockets." Vinny's leg continued to bounce. His index finger joined in, tapping on the table-top. "Might take some digging to prove it, though. They'll have a boat load of fancy lawyers."

"That's why I pay you the big bucks." A slight smile played at the corner of Steve's mouth.

"Hm. And when can I expect the check?" Vinny cocked an eyebrow and grinned. Vinny and Steve had a relationship that had nothing to do with money. Vinny shared what he knew pro bono, like a public service. It stemmed back to the days when Steve's father and Vinny were partners. Steve Russell Senior was the crusty older cop and Vinny the rookie. When Steve's dad had passed, Vinny took the younger Russell under his wing.

They waited for a few minutes while the waitress filled Vinny's mug. He then poured an obscene amount of sugar into it and stirred.

"And what about the accident?" Steve asked once the waitress was out of earshot. "Was that just a reference to Titan? A way to point to the relationship between the three?"

"Word on the street is it might not be an accident." Vinny took a tentative sip of his coffee and smacked his lips.

Steve frowned. "I was afraid of that. It doesn't make sense, though. Nudara wouldn't sabotage their own project, especially if there is something going on behind closed doors. They wouldn't want the publicity."

"And Titan wouldn't sabotage their own site, either. Maybe it's the competition."

"Whose?" Steve asked. "Nudara's or Titan's?"

"Either one. Or it could be an enemy of Fasburger. If someone found out about a deal between him and Nudara, they might be trying to make a point. Politicians tend to make a lot of enemies."

"Strong enough to kill an innocent person?"

Vinny shrugged. "Wouldn't be the first time. People get radical."

"Maybe it was just shoddy workmanship," Steve suggested.

"Doubtful. Big companies like Titan have a reputation to uphold. They have safety checks and inspectors coming out the yin-yang. If it was shoddy workmanship, somebody got paid off to turn a blind eye."

"Another way for someone to make an extra profit?"

"Like I said, if that's the case, it's doubtful it would be the higher ups in either Titan or Nudara. Nobody wins when bad publicity is involved. Probably someone lower on the rung, if you ask me."

Steve rubbed his chin thoughtfully. "It was deemed human error on the part of the man who got hurt. Apparently all safety checks were still in place. There was hardly even a blip in terms of production. The site was only shut down for three hours."

"Which is suspicious in itself," Vinny pointed out. "These things can shut a site down for days. Weeks even."

"So it could have been a pay off after the fact. Shoddy workmanship, human error, sabotage... doesn't matter as long as they pay off the safety inspectors to keep the bad press away." Steve looked directly at Vinny. "Seems we have more questions than answers."

"Ain't that always the way?" Vinny shook his head. "I'll keep my eyes and ears open. Ask around a few more places. I didn't have time to do a thorough check on any of it."

"I appreciate it," Steve said.

"Meantime, you should talk to your contact at Titan. But don't let him know too much just yet. We don't know who can be trusted."

Steve's mouth became a clenched line. "If you think for one second that Sherman Chan has anything to do with any of this, you are plain wrong. I've known Sherman since we were kids. He's clean as they come."

Vinny shrugged. "There isn't a person on this planet that can't be bought."

Steve narrowed his eyes. "Even you?"

"I have my weaknesses the same as any man." Vinny's eyes met Steve's, Vinny's twitching and blinking like Christmas lights while Steve's remained steady. "For some people it's about money. Some it's their good name. Or family. That's always a big one. There are many ways to motivate a person. Just sayin' is all. Don't let your personal feelings get in the way of finding the truth."

Steve let out a gust of air. "I won't. You know me better than that."

"I know you better than you think." Vinny downed the rest of his coffee and set the cup on the table with a thump.

"What is that supposed to mean?"

"Nothing. Just keep an open mind." Vinny gave one last tap with his hand on the tabletop and then stood up. "Well, I better get goin'. Thanks for the coffee."

STEVE WATCHED Tamara from his usual perch - one of the high tables at The Brew. He'd been coming to the coffee shop for months now to have coffee and to read the *Globe and Mail*. If the truth be told, it didn't take him long to realize the real reason he kept coming back was Tamara. She was beautiful in an exotic sort of way with long black flowing hair, wide dark eyes and flawless skin. She was so much more than a pretty face, however. She was a woman of deep passion, dedicated to her beliefs. Now that he had finally convinced her to give him the time of day, he longed to see that passion turn toward him.

Sherman Chan entered the establishment, waved to Steve and went to the counter to place his order. His girlfriend, Carmen Lamont, stretched across the counter and greeted him warmly with a quick kiss. Steve smiled. He couldn't imagine Tamara going for that kind of public display of affection.

Several minutes later, Sherman joined Steve with his coffee, a panini and a cookie on the side.

"Hungry?" Steve commented.

"I could get used to Carmen's cooking." Sherman grinned and then took a huge bite of his Vegetarian Panini.

"How is that going?" Steve asked. "With your parents I mean. Has your mom come around yet?"

Sherman finished chewing before answering. "Dad stays in

touch, but you know how he is. Afraid to rock the boat. He says Mom is coming around. I told him I won't break up with Carmen regardless, so we'll see. She doesn't like to admit it when she's wrong, but I have hope that she'll smarten up in this case."

"And she's worth it, I take it?" Steve gestured with his head to where Carmen was adding fresh cookies to a stack under a covered glass container.

"Absolutely," Sherman stated emphatically. "There's no doubt in my mind."

"Then she's the one."

"A bit early for that, but yes, I think so." Sherman looked at his friend curiously. "And you? Have you finally found the right one?"

Steve shrugged. "From my perspective, I'd say, yeah. I'm about 90% sure. From her perspective, I'm not so sure."

"Give her time. Carmen says she's doesn't open up that easily. Just be patient."

"Thanks." Tamara made him feel things he didn't know he was capable of feeling, but in many ways she was a closed book. He looked at Sherman who was now devouring his cookie. "I'm thinking of doing a follow up piece on that guy who had the accident on the Titan job site. What else can you tell me about it?" Steve watched closely to gauge Sherman's reaction.

"Um, why? Have you heard something?" Sherman's features had a closed and wary expression. He took another bite of his cookie.

"Not particularly." Steve shrugged, looking at Sherman out of the corner of his eye. "Just thought a human interest story – something positive and upbeat - might be nice for a change. The 'Miracle Man'. Something along those lines."

"Hm." Sherman didn't sound convinced. "We've been friends too long for me to buy it."

"Humour me," Steve said.

Sherman set the cookie down and picked up his napkin, twisting it between his fingers. "Not much to tell. Safety inspectors deemed it human error. The guy is lucky he didn't get canned all together. Don't get me wrong. I'm glad he's okay, but that kind of negligence could shut a project down for good."

"Only this time it didn't." Steve's gaze held Sherman's in a lock.

"Right." Sherman's eyes shifted downward and he reached for his mug.

"I almost get the feeling you aren't convinced." Steve raised an eyebrow.

Sherman shook his head in protest. "Forget it. All the necessary paperwork was done and inspectors cleared the site in record time. I'm glad it worked out for the best." He hesitated. "For everyone."

"Except?" Steve prompted.

Sherman expelled a heavy sigh. "Except, I can't help thinking there is more to it. Some of the workers are talking, saying that Titan has enemies and that the accident was sabotage."

"You buy it?"

"Not really. It seems kind of extreme."

"What about the guy who fell? Does he have any enemies?" Steve asked.

"Lester Tibbett?" Sherman gave a sheepish laugh. "I hope not."

"Why's that?"

Sherman looked down at the coffee cup cradled in his hands. "He took my sister out for dinner the other night."

"The plot thickens." Steve took a sip of his own coffee.

"No kidding. Remember our rodeo bull riding cowboy?"

Steve's eyebrows rose and he nodded. "Ah, yes. I remember."

"Seems they found each other after all. Sherri thinks its karma or fate or something like that."

"Can't argue with that, I suppose, if you believe in that sort of thing," Steve said.

"Sherri didn't even want to tell me when I found out she'd been on a date, but I dragged it out of her." Sherman sighed. "Here is where it gets complicated. I want to see my sister happy. But I don't actually know much about this Lester Tibbett fellow other than the former cowboy part. For all I know he could have lots of enemies."

"Deep enough to want to kill him?"

"I hate to think so, but the accident theory is hard to swallow. The safety checks and balances are very strict for a reason. A man doesn't just fall down a shaft unless it was tampered with. The best scenario is that Lester was doing something he shouldn't have been doing and was just lucky he didn't die for it."

"Either way, he must have friends powerful enough to go to the trouble to cover it up," Steve observed.

Sherman nodded. "It sounds worse when you put it that way."

"I think a chat with Mr. Tibbett is in order."

STEVE AND TAMARA sat outside her apartment building, the engine on his silver sedan idling. "Why can't I come up? I don't understand why you don't want me to meet your son."

"I never said I don't want you to meet him. I just said not yet." Tamara leaned to the side as she looked out the window to get a better view of some of the upper stories in the building. She sighed and sat back against the seat. "Ms. Peacock is spying again. I better get going." She reached for the door handle.

Steve extended his arm across her body to stop her from opening the door. "Just a minute. I want an answer, Tamara. Why is it that every time I suggest it, you have an excuse? I'm beginning to think you've got some horrible secret stashed in your apartment."

"Don't be ridiculous." Tamara swept a strand of long black hair off her shoulder.

"Am I?" Steve surveyed Tamara for a moment. "You're scared."

She released a small laugh. "I'm not scared."

"No? Prove it. Let me come up. Right now."

"Mat's over at his friend's house right now anyway, so you won't meet him."

"I thought you picked him up from the sitter as soon as you get home," Steve countered.

"I do, but..." Tamara wrung her hands. "He's... it's a school night. He has to go to bed early."

Steve checked his watch. "He goes to bed at seven?"

"Well, no. But he goes to bed at eight and he might need me to help him with homework."

"Perfect. I'm good at homework."

"No, I don't think..."

Steve shook his head. "See what I mean? Excuses."

Tamara let out a sigh. "I just don't want him to get hurt. He's not used to men, at least not ones that are with me. I don't want him to get attached to you if we..."

"If we break up," Steve finished for her.

"Yes. Although, technically, we aren't really dating so it wouldn't really be a break up."

Steve moved closer and put his arm around her shoulder. "Why isn't it dating? I want to get closer to you, Tamara. I wish you'd trust me enough to know that I'm not out to hurt you - or your son." He tried to convince her with a kiss, which she seemed eager to accept at first.

Then she tore herself away and pulled her bottom lip into her mouth. "I better go. Mat is waiting and that nosy Ms. Peacock is watching out the window."

Steve watched her exit the car. After slamming the door she trotted to the entrance and let herself in, not looking back. How was he ever going to get her to trust him? To realize he loved her enough to love her son, too?

The thought startled him. Love? It was the first time the word had popped into his brain. Steve put the car in gear and pulled out of the parking lot with a screech.

STEVE GRIPPED the guardrail with both hands and gave a little shake. The street was only one story below, but seeing as he was investigating an accident at this very job site, it didn't hurt to take precautions. The noise of traffic as it passed reached up to meet him as he watched the cars and trucks through the open sides of the building, still under construction. The November wind whipped his face with a gust of cold air and he stepped back, hunkering down into the collar of his overcoat. He clamped one hand onto the top of the hardhat he'd been forced to wear to keep it in place.

He heard footsteps echoing across the cement and turned to watch Lester Tibbett's approach. The other man had the swagger of a cowboy even in steel-toed work boots and a padded plaid jacket.

"Steve Russell?" Lester came to a halt a few feet away and nodded to the pass dangling around Steve's neck from a lanyard.

"That's right. Thanks for taking the time during your break to talk to me." Steve extended a gloved hand.

Lester's grip was strong through his work glove, his handshake firm and quick. "I'd rather answer a few questions myself than leave it for the gossip mill." He hesitated and surveyed Steve with narrowed eyes. "Just to set the record straight, I don't want any sensationalism. I only agreed to talk to you if you promise to keep it low key."

"Of course." Steve smiled encouragingly and reached into his overcoat and drew out a pad of paper and a pen. "I still do it old school," he said, holding the paper aloft in his gloved right hand. "Now, can you explain to me again what happened exactly?"

Lester adjusted his hardhat, the earflaps of the liner dangling over his ears like an Orthodox Jew's payot. "I leaned on the safety gate blocking the shaft and fell. Simple as that."

"Interesting. It's my understanding that those gates only open out. How is it that the gate opened in, over the shaft?" Steve looked up and smiled.

"This one was a scissor gate."

"I see. And it just gave way? Or was it was unlocked?" Steve scribbled a few notes while he talked. "Those gates can only be unlocked with a special key and only when the elevator is present, correct?"

"The elevator wasn't in place yet," Lester explained. "But you're right about the key." He leaned his back against the railing overlooking the street below, and hooked one booted foot over the other – a brave stance considering his recent fall. "Apparently the safety lock was in place when the inspector came around before the accident and again after when the safety team came to investigate. To me it felt like it gave way and I told them that, but…"

"It felt like it gave way?"

Lester just nodded.

"Doesn't that seem strange to you?"

Lester shrugged. "It happened pretty fast. I know I didn't vault over the thing, but if they say the gate was secure then I believe it."

"Can you think of anyone who might… have something to gain by sabotaging the site?" Steve gestured with the pen in his left hand. "Enemies of Titan? Personal enemies?"

Lester looked Steve square in the eye and crossed his arms over his chest. "I'm not buying into the sabotage theory, if that what's you're trying to get me to say. I'm new at this and I need the job. If they say it was human error – my error – I accept that."

"You don't intend to do anything about it? It seems to me legal options are well within your rights."

"I intend to be very careful, that's all." Lester pushed off from the railing. "And I also intend to get back to work. I haven't said anything other than what I said in my initial statement, so I better not read any crazy theories in tomorrow's paper."

"I am a newsman after all, but I promise I won't print anything that isn't one hundred percent verified. If you could just give me a few more minutes?" At Lester's scowl, Steve added, "I'd like to hear more about your miraculous escape from injury."

Lester visibly relaxed and he consulted his watch. "Two more minutes. That's all I've got time for."

"So, can you tell me more about that? How does a man fall three stories without getting hurt – or killed?"

"I like to think the good Lord was looking out for me," Lester replied with the first hint of a smile pulling at the corners of his mouth.

"O-kay…" Steve's hand hovered over the notepad. "Beyond that, how can you explain it?"

"Let's see. There was some scaffolding that broke my fall half way down and a huge pile of insulation bats directly at the bottom. Still, I like the miracle option better. It's certainly helped put a few things in perspective."

"Like...?" Steve glanced up.

"The importance of family, faith and the like. Life is short and it's important to live it to the full. No point in wishing things were different. Seize the day, as they say."

"Carpe Diem," Steve added. With a smile he flipped the little book shut. "Thanks for your time, Mr. Tibbett. I can't guarantee a story will come out if it, but I appreciate it none the less."

"Don't do me any favours. I'd be as happy without the story," Lester said. He shifted from one foot to another and looked up sheepishly. "Are you a man of faith, Mr. Russell?"

Steve blinked, not used to being the one interviewed. "No, not really. Why?"

Lester shrugged. "Oh, I don't know. Just a thought that came to mind, that's all. That happens to me sometimes, since the accident. Like God is talking to me and I should listen."

"And what did he say?" Steve asked.

"Be patient. Something like that." Lester shook his head. "Forget it. I'm kind of new at this. Sharing my faith, I mean." His eyes narrowed and he snapped his fingers. "Say! Now I know!"

"Pardon me?" Steve raised his eyebrows at the strange reaction.

"I've been trying to place where I know you, that's all, and now I remember."

Steve's smile was patronizing. "We know one another?" Steve knew where he had seen Lester before, but he doubted the other man had any reason to recognize him.

"I live in the same building as your girlfriend, Tamara Spence." Lester smiled. "Owner of The Brew," he added for good measure.

Steve's eyebrows rose involuntarily. "You know Tamara?"

"In passing. I've seen you in the parking lot, dropping her off."

Steve frowned. Making out might be more like it. Tamara had been right to be paranoid about the neighbours, although she hadn't mentioned this one. "Right. Well, I better let you get back to work."

"Okay. Do you think you could run the story by me before you print it? If you decide to, that is."

"That's not usually the protocol, but I promise I will not say anything that will put you in a bad light," Steve assured.

Lester extended his hand for another handshake. "Alright. I'll take you as a man of your word." He didn't let go as quickly this time and Steve wondered if it was his way of sealing the promise.

Lester touched his hardhat as a sign of farewell and Steve watched him as he strode away. Steve shivered, noticing for the first time since the interview began just how cold it was in the open shell of a building. Somehow he had to get to the bottom of this mess without causing any more harm to the man. Lester was innocent, Steve had no doubt, but too trusting for his own good. Something was amiss and Steve was no closer to the truth than he had been earlier that day. Only now he had a reluctant prophet to watch out for as well.

THE URBAN COWBOY was not exactly the place Steve had wanted to take Tamara on a date, but it seemed like fate had other plans. Convincing her to leave Matonabee with a sitter was difficult in itself, so he couldn't very well say no when she suggested meeting Sherman, Carmen, and Renee at the pub. He would take what he could get. Be patient, that's what Lester Tibbett had said, and that is exactly what he was trying to do.

The five of them found a large round table and soon a waitress came to take their order. Along with their drinks they ordered a plate of the Urban Cowboys latest appetizer offering: Nacho Poutine. Cory joined them a few minutes later and bent down to give Renee a lingering kiss before pulling up a chair himself.

"Taking another night off?" Steve directed at Cory.

"Afraid not." Cory stretched his arm across the back of Renee's chair. "I'm short staffed at the moment and I need to keep Jacques happy. I'm helping him behind the bar. Just thought I'd say hi before I get back to work."

"I thought maybe your business partner was keeping you in line," Sherman teased.

Cory laughed. "You mean my dad? That too. I get regular reports from Jacques. I wish the old man would just head back to Edmonton and let me run things without looking over my shoulder." Cory shook his head. "Parents, eh? Gotta love 'em, but sometimes..."

There was a moment of awkward silence when all eyes turned toward Sherman.

"Sorry, man," Cory said.

"Forget it." Sherman shrugged. He straightened and placed a careful smile on his face. "When's your next DJ-ing gig and when are we going to get invited?"

"Soon. I'll let you know, although I thought you'd all be sick of it by now. Just because we're friends doesn't mean you have to come to every gig to be supportive."

"You're forgetting that I just moved back and haven't seen you play for a while," Sherman said.

Tamara looked at Carmen. "Isn't Pat's boyfriend a DJ?"

Carmen furrowed her brow in thought. "Yes, I think so. I think she mentioned it once."

"Who's this?" Cory asked. He was always interested when it came to keeping up with the local music scene.

"One of our waitresses, Pat Tibbett. I think she said her boyfriend was into electronic music," Tamara replied.

Steve frowned. "Tibbett? Any relation to Lester Tibbett?"

"Sister," Sherman answered.

"And her boyfriend's name?" Cory asked.

"Brett or Brent or something like that," Carmen said. "He's been in the shop to pick her up a few times but I forget exactly. Early twenties, nice looking..."

"I think his parents are corporate lawyers or something," Tamara added.

"Brett McMillan?" Cory asked.

Tamara shrugged. "Could be. You know him?"

Cory laughed. "Small world if it is. Brett McMillan and I do some

DJ-ing together. He's just getting into it and I let him use my equip-
ment sometimes. He's done a couple short sets at some of my gigs."

Steve's cell phone vibrated in his suit pocket and he reached in to
retrieve it. A quick glance told him whom the message was from.
"Um, if you'll excuse me for just a minute?"

"I thought you said no business tonight," Tamara reminded.

"I know, but…" Steve glanced over his shoulder and then back to
the group. "It won't take long. I promise."

"Can't guarantee there will be any Poutine by the time you get
back!" Cory called to Steve's retreating figure.

Steve spotted Vinny Kirkpatrick at a small table near the front
door and slid into the seat opposite. "Make it quick." Steve gestured to
where his friends were sitting. "I'm trying not to mix business with
pleasure."

Vinny's leg jiggled under the table. "This is something I think
you'll want to hear. Especially since it might involve her."

Steve frowned. "Who?"

"Your girlfriend."

Steve's eyebrows rose. "You've got my attention. Shoot."

"Your girl might be involved in the Titan sabotage somehow."

Steve's eyes widened even further. Then he laughed outright. "You
had me there for a second."

"I'm serious."

Steve sobered almost instantly. He glanced over at where Tamara
sat, her beautiful long hair hanging down her back, her perfect
aquiline nose and chin tilted ever so slightly upward, her posture and
poise the picture of pride and humility wrapped into one. He turned
back to Vinny. "This better be good."

"She's a bit of an activist." Vinny reached for his phone to scroll
through some pictures.

Steve snorted. "Tell me something I didn't know."

"I've got pictures of her at a rally outside city hall. Found them
online on that social site. " Vinny held the phone out for Steve to see.
"Obviously posted by someone who doesn't value privacy."

Steve glanced quickly at the pictures and then sat back in his chair.

He gave the older man a withering look. "So what? Where's the connection?"

"This particular one was against government tax breaks for big oil companies - a.k.a. Fasburger and crew. Seems she was very vocal about the inconsistencies given to small business owners in the city compared to what the oil companies are getting."

Steve shrugged. "Makes sense. She hates it when big brother doesn't play fair. And she's a small business owner, so she has a vested interest."

"Threats were uttered."

"What kind of threats?"

"Against various corporate businesses. Sabotage. Vandalism. Things like that. Said they wouldn't stop until someone started paying attention. Not saying she was directly involved, but she was there," Vinny added quickly at Steve's deepening frown. "The cops had to come and break things up."

Steve shook his head. "So?"

"She was arrested along with several others."

Steve blinked, suddenly at a loss for words.

"I take it she never mentioned that to you," Vinny noted dryly. "She was released right away with no charges against her. I'm not surprised she didn't tell you." Vinny's body had become still and he surveyed Steve thoughtfully out of the corner of his eye. "I knew you'd be interested."

Steve shook himself, as if trying to wake from a dream. "I'll ask her about it."

"I'd advise against it. For now, anyway. You might be able to get more information out of her if she doesn't know you know."

"I won't lie," Steve said.

"I never said lie. Just forget to mention it until it suits you." Vinny shifted in his seat, his leg taking up its standard jiggling rhythm again.

"And for the record, getting arrested at a rally doesn't mean she's involved or that she even knows anything," Steve pointed out.

"True, true." Vinny tapped on the tabletop. "I found out the name of Nudara's lawyers, too. They use a firm called McMillan and McMillan."

Steve looked toward the ceiling and laughed. "Kidding, right?"

Vinny frowned. "No. Why?"

"There are just too many connections here for my comfort level." He leaned forward. "I was just talking about them with Cory and the others."

"What about them?" Vinny asked.

Steve shrugged. "Not much except their son is a friend of Cory's. They play music together." Steve shook his head with a laugh. "And get this. His girlfriend is the sister of the infamous miracle man, Lester Tibbett."

"A tangled web indeed," Vinny said softly.

STEVE PULLED into the apartment parking lot and, as per usual, put the car in park without shutting off the engine. The weather was too cold to sit for long in a car that wasn't heated.

He and Tamara leaned toward one another for a goodnight kiss, but he didn't let it go on for too long. The thought that she was hiding something from him had tamped his desire - slightly.

"I've been thinking," Tamara said, her eyelashes fluttering downward. "About me making excuses."

Steve's brows rose. Was this finally the night? When he wasn't sure he was in the mood? A small, sardonic laugh escaped his lips.

Tamara frowned. "What's so funny?"

Steve schooled his features. "Nothing." He leaned over and gave her another peck on the lips for encouragement. "You were saying?"

"I think I'm ready to trust you. To let you meet Mat."

Trust. The word had a hollow ring. "Okay. When?" he heard himself ask.

"There is this party coming up. For people who live in the building. Sort of like a block party only a building party. I thought maybe you could come as my guest."

Steve nodded. "Okay. Where would they hold something like that?"

"In the common room on the main floor. At least that's what the posters say. My friend Goldie is helping to organize it."

"And Mat would be there?" Steve asked.

Tamara nodded.

The wheels began to turn in Steve's brain. "And anyone else from the building that wanted to? Like Jacques and Cory's dad, Tad?" And Lester Tibbett, but he didn't say it out loud.

"No one is obligated to come, of course, but Goldie is trying to get people to RSVP to make sure the numbers don't get out of hand."

"Don't you think it would be a good idea for me to meet Mat at least once before the party?"

"A public place might be best to start with. It will help me gage his reaction."

"And if he doesn't seem to take a shine to me? Then what?"

"We'll figure that out later." Tamara moved a bit closer despite the confines of the front seat. "I'd offer to let you meet him now except he's staying the night at his friend Jason's." Her mouth was only inches from his now.

"You are a cruel woman." Steve smiled when he said it and reached to stroke a stray strand of hair off her cheek. The way the light from the street lamp illuminated her features in the semi-darkness of the car had him forgetting about his earlier reservations. Who cared about her involvement at the rally? She was probably just embarrassed to mention it.

"Why is that?" Her voice suddenly seemed breathless.

"Because you're going to get me all turned on and then leave me out here in the car. Again." He smiled.

"Would you like to test that theory?"

Their lips came together with a passion unmatched thus far. When Tamara finally pulled away, Steve's head was reeling, his heart pounding. He could never believe she would be involved in willfully putting another human being's life at risk.

"Park the car," Tamara ordered with a coy smile.

"You sure?" Steve searched her face for any sign of doubt.

She shook her head. "All my excuses seem tired, even to me."

Steve put the car in gear and swung around to the visitor parking area. When he cut the engine he turned to look at her one more time. "You're absolutely sure?"

Her kiss was all the answer he needed.

STEVE LAY on his back in the dimness of Tamara's bedroom, one arm tucked behind his head and the other encircling Tamara's body, naked beside him under the covering of the sheets. Sure, it had been a while, but he honestly didn't remember sex ever being this good. His heart swelled with love for the woman who was curled into his side, her warmth radiating into his very being.

She stirred and then stretched, shifting away from the confines of his arm.

"Wait a minute. Where do you think you're going?" he asked, his voice amused and husky.

"Nowhere." She smiled and doubled up her pillow then turned so that she could look at him from her position beside him. "That was pretty amazing, you know that?"

"Maybe we just fit together. Like we were made for each other or something." He smiled back at her but was dismayed by the troubled look that crossed her features. "Sorry. Too much too soon?"

"Just don't make commitments you can't keep," Tamara responded.

"Who said I'm not going to keep them?" Steve asked. "I want to be with you. That shouldn't come as a surprise."

"Right now, because you want sex again."

"Don't you?" Steve looked into her eyes. "Cause I could swear just a minute ago you were thinking the same thing."

"That was just nature talking. A basic human need."

"Ouch. That hurts." Steve thumped his chest.

"Well? What do you expect me to say?' Tamara folded the sheet more tightly across her chest and propped herself up on one elbow.

"I'm just trying to be honest. What happens when the novelty wears off?"

"Is that what happened before? With Mat's father?" Steve tucked a strand of hair behind Tamara's ear.

"I don't want to talk about it." She lay back on the mattress.

Steve sighed and forced her to look at him by tilting her face toward his. "What is it going to take to convince you I'm the real deal? That I think I'm in love with you, in fact." There was silence and Steve surveyed Tamara's features.

At first she seemed to not register what he had said. Then tears rimmed her eyes and she turned away.

"Wow! That's the first time in history that the words 'I love you' brought that reaction. Hey, forget I said it if it makes you uncomfortable. I'm moving too fast, I know, but..."

Tamara shook her head. "No. It's just that... oh dear! How can I explain it to you?"

"You can tell me anything. You know that." He hesitated. "I wish you would tell me everything."

"It's just that no one has ever said that to me before. Except my mother, but she doesn't count." Her smile wobbled.

Steve's eyes went wide. "No one?"

She shook her head. "My father left us when I was young. My mother had very hard feelings toward him and I grew up feeling abandoned. Unloved by him. I suppose it's why I've had trouble trusting men. Then my ex wasn't any better. Abusive, drank too much... I was glad to get rid of him, but even through the time we were together he never once said he loved me."

"He was a fool."

Tamara shrugged. "I'm glad he didn't. It made it easier to leave. To take Mat out of that situation. I've been very careful ever since." Her gaze sought his for understanding.

"I see. Well, let me assure you I am not going to do any of those things. I'm not perfect, but I will never abuse you and I certainly won't abandon you."

"It's easy for you to say that now, but -"

"Hush!" Steve a put a finger over her lips. Then he smiled. "Marry me."

"What? You're crazy." Tamara shook her head, but a smile had begun to form on her lips.

"I know I am, but so are you. Marry me, Tamara. I mean it."

Tamara shook her head. "Marriage is an old fashioned institution that just sets people up for divorce."

Steve rolled his eyes. "Not exactly the response I was hoping for…"

"Plus, it's very colonial. Not the way my ancestors did things at all. If two people are committed to each other they don't need a contract to prove it."

Steve shrugged. "Okay, have it your way. Let's just move in together."

Tamara frowned. "I can't. Matonabee…"

"I know, I know. Mat has to approve of me first." He kissed her on the nose. "Which just goes to show what a great mother you are, not to mention a great person."

Tamara laughed. "Not always. I have a few skeletons in my closet."

"As do I," Steve responded. He stroked her hair and then leaned in for another kiss. "Anything in particular you want to tell me?"

"I don't think so," she responded coyly.

"You sure?"

A slight line formed between her brows but she still smiled. "Like what? I almost get the impression you're baiting me."

Steve let his hand drop to the sheet. "A friend told me today that you were arrested recently after a rally."

"You're spying on me now?" She sounded indignant.

"Of course not. He just mentioned it in the course of the conversation. I just wondered why you didn't tell me is all." He reached to touch her hair again and she stiffened.

"I don't have to report my every activity to you. It's not the way this relationship works." She flung the sheet back and stood up. "And by the way, it's not the first time I've been arrested."

Steve sat up. All he wanted was to gaze at the glorious sculpture of her naked form, but he knew he had to say something to appease her that didn't reference sex. "Apparently threats were made against some of the big oil companies."

"What? You're on their side now?" Her eyes flashed, even in the dimness of the room. She thrust her arms into a fuzzy bathrobe and cinched the belt tight.

"No! I didn't mean to upset you. It's just the reporter in me got to wondering is all. I thought maybe you'd know something about it."

"So now you're using me for information," she spat out.

Steve sighed and ran a hand through his normally well-kept hair. "Of course not. Forget I mentioned it and come back to bed. Please?" He looked at her with his best puppy dog eyes.

"Not while you're in it. In fact, I would be highly appreciative if you'd get your butt out of my bed and leave. Now." She straightened herself to her full height, chin up, and perused him down the length of her nose.

With a sigh, Steve flung the covers off his side of the bed. He should have taken Vinny's advice and kept his mouth shut. So much for happily ever after.

EPISODE 8

LEAVING THE NEIGHBOURHOOD

*P*atsi clutched her books to her chest as she descended down the main isle in the lecture theatre. She slid into her seat beside Megan and set the books down on the small desk with a thunk. "I can't wait for this semester to be over. No more Math for me. Ever! No matter what my brother says."

Megan leaned closer, apparently unmoved by Patsi's heartfelt declaration. "Guess who I heard from last night?"

"Who?" Patsi straightened her books.

"Emmanuel."

Patsi stopped what she was doing and furrowed her brow. "Who?"

Megan rolled her eyes. "Don't you remember? Hunky foreign guy from that party?"

Patsi's eyebrows rose. "Oh, that Emmanuel! It's been a while, don't you think? And how did he get your number?"

"I gave it to him, of course." Megan flipped her perfectly styled hair off her shoulder.

"And?" Patsi prodded.

Megan's earrings dangled in time to her excitement. "We talked for like, an hour. His accent is just so sexy! We're going to meet up later on today."

"Do you think that's safe?" Patsi asked. "What if he turns out to be a psycho? I mean, to not call for so long and then out of the blue get in touch again? It seems weird."

"You've watched too many movies. Besides, we'll meet at a public place like a restaurant or a movie theatre." She tapped her palms together several times in a silent clap. "I'm so excited! Maybe he has a friend. I could call and ask."

"No thanks," Patsi whispered. The Math professor, Ms. Chan, had entered the lecture hall and the general chatter was settling down.

"I'll tell you more later," Megan said under her breath.

Patsi just smiled. She wondered what Megan would say if she revealed her own secret.

PATSI WENT STRAIGHT to The Brew from the college campus for a three-hour shift. She usually rode home after work with owner Tamara – one of Lester's rules since he didn't want her riding transit alone after dark, and darkness came early in the winter months. Tamara was busy today, though, so Brett was coming to pick her up – unknown to Lester of course. Lester still didn't know about their relationship. He and a few other people.

When Brett sauntered into the coffee shop, Patsi's stomach did a little flip flop. "Hi Brett." She wriggled her fingers in a pseudo wave. "Just grab a seat. I'm not done for another hour." It had been a month at least since they had been officially dating, but she still felt butterflies whenever he walked into a room. He was just so good looking with his blonde hair, dreamy brown eyes and sinfully long lashes, not to mention his toned and tanned body.

He found a seat at one of the high tables.

"Actually, it's pretty slow this evening," Carmen, the other owner, said from behind the counter where she was restocking some tea. "Why don't you take off early?"

"You don't mind?" Patsi turned to look at her employer.

"Of course not. You go on and I'll finish cleaning up." Carmen smiled, her teeth white against her dark skin and red lipstick.

Patsi undid her apron and hung it on a hook behind the counter and then went to the back room for her coat. Once she and Brett were outside, he grabbed her gloved hand and they trotted to his electric blue Mazda RX-7 parked on the street.

"So? Anywhere you want to go?" Brett asked.

"I should probably just go home," Patsi said as she got inside. "My brother will be expecting me."

"Not for another hour," Brett reminded. He started up the engine and pulled out onto the street.

"True." A warm fluttery feeling filled Patsi's chest. They drove silently for a few minutes as she looked out the window, trying to gather her scattered thoughts.

"So? Where will it be?" They were passing the large neon sign outside the Urban Cowboy. "Ever been there?" Brett asked.

"I'm still not eighteen, remember?"

"A minor problem." Brett laughed at his joke. "Get it... minor problem?"

"My birthday is soon, though. Next Friday." Patsi peered out the window. "Hey, I see my brother's truck." She laughed. "For someone who doesn't approve of my friends, he certainly has no trouble hanging out at a bar."

"So he obviously isn't at home." Brett glanced briefly at Patsi and then back at the street in front of him.

"Um, right." Butterflies of anticipation were dancing in her stomach. "Would you like to come over, then?" She wasn't a little kid anymore and it was time she stopped acting like one.

PATSI AND BRETT started making out almost immediately once inside the apartment doors. It was like a romantic movie and she was the heroine. Mouths connected, hands roaming, they stumbled out of their shoes and into the living room, landing on the couch in a tangle of limbs.

Patsi wasn't sure how much time lapsed – she didn't really care – when suddenly she felt Brett's hands straying lower than was comfortable. "Wait," she murmured, struggling slightly to get out of his grasp.

He kept on kissing her. "What's wrong? I want you so bad and I think you want me, too."

"I know, but -" She pushed with a little more force.

"Patsi…" he whispered into her ear in a singsong voice.

That was the last straw. She gave one violent shove and sat up, simultaneously straightening her blouse. "Who told you that?"

Brett's eyes were clouded and he sat up with a confused look. "Told me what?"

"That my name was Patsi. I hate that name."

His eyebrows rose as he registered what she was saying. "What? Your real name is Patsi? I was just saying it like 'baby' only 'Patsi'…" He rubbed a hand over his tousled hair.

Patsi blinked, still breathing hard – from anger, fear, or her own libido, she wasn't sure. "You didn't…? Oh." She looked down at her hands.

Brett smiled and took a few strands of her carefully straightened hair between his fingers and rubbed them together. "Patsi… it's cute. I like it."

She looked away. "You're just saying that."

"No I'm not. It suits you. For real."

She laughed derisively. "Actually, my full name is Patsi Mae, if you must know."

"Patsi Mae?" His eyebrows rose even further and a smile played around his lips, making him all the more attractive.

Patsi couldn't help her own smile. "I know. Horrible. Talk about country bumpkin. Now you know why I want people to call me Pat."

"Pat it is, if it makes you happy. I really don't care one way or another. Now… where were we?" He leaned in to once again capture her mouth with his.

Patsi put a hand on his chest. "Wait. I'm… I'm not ready yet."

"You're killing me. Don't you think it's time we took this to the next level?" He tried for another kiss.

She stopped him again. "I mean it, Brett. This is too fast."

He sighed and flopped back against the couch cushions. "An old fashioned girl to go with the old fashioned name. Okay. I can wait. Whenever you're ready." He grinned and looked at her out of the corner of his eye. "As long as you don't make me wait too long."

Patsi's eyelashes fluttered down. "Actually, there's something you need to know." She blushed. "I'm a virgin."

"Oh." He took the information in, nodding.

"So if you don't want to see me anymore, I'd understand." She looked over at him for his reaction.

"Why wouldn't I want to see you?" His brows had become a furrowed line.

Patsi shrugged. "I don't know. Cause I'm inexperienced." She looked away again, really blushing now.

"I don't mind." He leaned in and gave her another kiss. This time she let him. It was gentler and sweet and when he was finished he sat back and smiled. "Whenever you're ready, I would be more than honoured to introduce you to those particular pleasures."

"Thanks." She initiated the next kiss and it soon became more urgent.

It was Brett who pulled away this time. "But not tonight." He reached into his pocket for his cell phone. She frowned, but he continued talking as he showed her the time on the screen. "The last thing I want is for your brother to walk in on us – especially if it's your first time. I want it to be special, with no rush. Okay?"

She felt cheated but exhilarated at the same time. Brett was such a gentleman. Definitely not the player Megan had warned her about. "Thank you."

They kissed again and then Brett stood up. "You are making this awfully hard, you know that?"

"Sorry," she said and giggled.

Several kisses at the door and Brett finally left. It was none too soon either, as Lester was home within fifteen minutes of Brett's departure.

"Hi, Sis." Lester hung his jacket up in the closet and set his boots neatly side by side on the mat by the door. "How was your day?"

"Fine," Patsi replied. She sat on the couch, hugging one of the cushions to her stomach.

"You worked after school today?" He sauntered into the room and sat in the chair opposite.

She just nodded.

"And that was good, too?"

She nodded again. She broke into a grin when he kept looking at her. "What?" she asked with a laugh.

He shrugged. "I don't know. You just look different. More grown up."

"It's my hair. I bought a better straightener." She flipped her hair off her shoulders.

Lester surveyed her more closely then nodded. "Yeah, that's probably it."

Patsi watched him wander into the kitchen and open the fridge. She knew exactly why she looked different. She was in love.

"You're coming to the block party, I hope."

Patsi blinked, only just then registering her neighbour Goldie's voice. "Pardon me? I didn't hear you."

Goldie laughed. "I can see that. I said, are you coming to the block party?"

"As long as I'm not working," Patsi replied. Goldie Harper, a resident of the apartment building and also the mother of one of the boys Patsi often babysat, was planning a party for residents of the apartment building sometime before Christmas.

She and Goldie were standing in the foyer of the large church that Goldie had recommended. Goldie thought it might be a better fit for her since there was an active youth program. Lester had agreed –

somewhat reluctantly – and they had attended for the past couple of weeks. Patsi looked over at where her older brother was in an animated conversation with Tad Roberts, another man from the apartment who had also started coming to church with them. Lester seemed happier about the change in churches, but Patsi herself didn't really care much one way or the other. She knew she should be more interested in religion. It would make Lester happy. But right now God didn't seem all that important. She had other things on her mind.

Jason, Goldie's seven-year-old son, came running up to his mother's side. "Can we go out for lunch? Please? My friend Kaydn is going to that new place with the indoor play park attached."

"I'm not sure we can afford it this week." Goldie placed a hand on Jason's kinky black hair.

"Aw!" The little boy scowled. Just as quickly, his face broke into a smile and he turned toward Patsi. "Maybe Pat and Lester can come, too."

"That doesn't change the fact that I can't afford it, honey," Goldie said.

"And Mr. Tad?" Jason raised his brows hopefully. Apparently, the addition of the older Mr. Roberts would clinch the deal.

"What's this?" Tad Roberts and Lester had sauntered over to where Patsi, Goldie and Jason stood.

"You should go out for lunch with my mom and me," Jason stated. "She can't afford it but maybe you could pay."

"Jason!" Goldie scolded, a pink glow staining her dark cheeks. "It's not polite to ask someone else to take you out for lunch."

Tad laughed. His head was as round as a bowling ball and it shone just as black. "I think Jason might have a good idea. I could go for a burger. What do you say?"

Patsi's cellphone beeped and she glanced at the caller. It was Megan. She turned away from the group to answer it. She vaguely heard Lester making some kind of excuse about not joining them, which was just as well. She had no desire to go out for lunch with a bunch of old people and a kid. "Hi Megan," she said into the phone.

"Oo!" Megan squealed into the phone and Patsi held it slightly away from her ear. "I can't wait to tell you about my date with Emmanuel. We met once after school and again on Saturday." She squealed again.

Patsi glanced at the group of adults to her left. "I can't really talk about it now. I'm still at church."

"Church?" Patsi could hear the frown in Megan's voice. "That sounds boring."

"I should be home soon. I'll text you when I get there and then we can talk."

"Alright. All I'll say now is the sex was amazing!"

Patsi glanced nervously at Lester and the others and moved further away. "What? You had sex already?" she whispered into the phone.

Megan's laugh tinkled in Patsi's ear. "That's what I love about you. You're just so... old fashioned!"

"Well? Isn't it kind of soon?" Patsi asked, a defensive edge to her voice.

"Why? After we went to the movies, he showed me where he works at his uncle's dry cleaners. We went in for a tour and one thing led to another. Then I met him again on Saturday. I can't tell you everything over the phone, but it was hot, believe me!"

"What if your parents find out?"

"They won't. They're totally preoccupied with work." Megan paused. "But speaking of my parents, next weekend I need you to vouch for me. I told them I'm staying at your house."

Patsi furrowed her brow in confusion. "Okay... it is my birthday next Friday and you could stay over if you want. My place is nothing fancy, though..."

There was a long pause on the other end and Megan's voice lost its normal sing-song quality. "Next Friday is your birthday? Really?"

Patsi nodded, even though Megan couldn't see her. "Yes. My eighteenth."

"I'm the worst friend ever," Megan moaned.

"No you're not."

"Yes, I am. I totally forgot. Emmanuel and I are going away for the weekend. It's all arranged. I bought the tickets and everything. That's why I need you to vouch for me in case they call and ask."

"Oh." Patsi blinked. She felt deflated inside, like the wind had just been knocked out of her.

"When we get back, I'm going to throw you the biggest party ever," Megan declared in a rush. "Promise."

"You don't have to do that. Lester always makes a cake and he promised he'd take me to the Urban Cowboy after."

"I am so sorry that I forgot about your birthday. But I'll make it up to you. I promise."

Patsi smiled, despite the fact that she felt a little empty inside. She knew Megan meant well, even if she didn't always follow through. "I gotta go. Lester is waiting."

AT WORK THAT WEEK, Patsi was surprised when Ms. Chan, her Math professor, entered The Brew and went straight to the table occupied by Carmen's boyfriend, Sherman Chan. Carmen had been dating the good looking architect for a while now, and he had become a regular at The Brew. The thought that he had the same last name as her Math prof, and that there may be a connection, had never occurred to Patsi before. In fact, the idea that the straight-laced professor had any kind of life outside the college had never dawned on her.

"Hello Ms. Chan," Patsi ventured as she gathered up some dirty dishes from a table nearby.

"Hello." The petite Chinese woman nodded in Patsi's direction.

"I'm in one of your classes," Patsi explained, pausing for a moment with the dishes in hand.

"Yes, I know. Pat Tibbett, correct?" Ms. Chan smiled.

Patsi's brows rose slightly. "That's right. I'm surprised you remembered my name. You have so many students."

"You're quite memorable, believe me." Ms. Chan smiled again and then turned to her companion, apparently ending the conversation.

Patsi turned and marched toward the dish cart behind the counter, depositing the dishes with more clatter than necessary. The woman was probably referring to her poor marks. Well, she'd been turning things around lately. Why hadn't she mentioned that?

"Watch it." Tamara Spence cautioned from behind the counter. She had just walked in from the back room in time to hear the noise. "We can't afford to replace too many broken dishes. I might have to start taking it out of your pay." She turned on her heel and stalked back out again.

"Sor-ry." Patsi extended the word under her breath, her tone anything but sincere. When she glanced to the side, she noticed Carmen, the other owner, staring at her from behind the counter where she was positioning some freshly baked goods under a clear display tower. Patsi wiped her hands on her apron and straightened her back. "Sorry," she repeated, much more meekly this time.

"Just be more careful, okay?" Carmen smiled and kept her voice low. "And cut Tamara a bit of slack. She's having some personal issues..."

Patsi nodded and scurried to clear the rest of the tables. She knew that Tamara and her boyfriend Steve had been having problems simply because Tamara refused to talk to him every time he came into the restaurant. He was a newspaper journalist and still came in like clockwork, but Patsi had witnessed Tamara giving him the cold shoulder recently. Who knew what kind of spat they'd had? Patsi just wished they could get over it so that she wouldn't have to bear Tamara's foul moods at work or on the way home.

Brett came to pick Patsi up after work. While driving in his car she mentioned her birthday again. "Maybe it would be a good time to introduce you to my brother. He wouldn't be able to get too mad since it is my birthday and everything."

Brett's eyes stayed glued to the road in front of him. "I'm really sorry, babe, but Friday isn't good for me. I've got a DJ-ing gig that night. It's been planned for months."

"Oh. Well, maybe I can come and see you, then. Since I'll be legal and everything."

"What about your brother?"

"He's not a total ogre." Patsi tilted her chin up. "Besides, I'll be eighteen so I can do what I want."

Brett cleared his throat. "Actually, it's kind of a private party. Something Brian and Scott have been planning for a while. I'd love for you to come – and your brother, too – but I don't think it would go over too well with the others." He glanced her way before focusing on driving again. "I'm really sorry. I hate missing your birthday and you know I really want to meet your brother..."

"No big deal." Patsi felt the sting of hot tears forming and she kept her eyes focused to the right on the view out her side window so that Brett wouldn't see.

"I'll make it up to you. I promise."

"Sure." Patsi swallowed hard. They were almost the exact words his sister had used.

ON FRIDAY EVENING, Lester invited some of their friends from the building to share Patsi's birthday cake - Jed Malloy, Goldie Harper and her son Jason, and Tad Roberts. He made his usual simple white cake, an old recipe handed down from their mother and about the only kind of cake he knew how to make.

"After you blow out the candles I 'ear we're takin' you to the Urban Cowboy to get drunk," Jed said. Jed was an import from Newfoundland; a big man with massive hands and dark curling hair that was mostly hidden by a ball cap. His thick accent, much like that of an Irish brogue, accentuated his sense of humour.

"I never said that," Lester countered. "Besides, there's a kid present."

Jed frowned. "I could a sworn..."

"What I did say was, since she's probably going anyway, I might as well be the first to take her."

"I'm not a baby," Patsi put in, her mouth forming a pout.

"I never said you were. Just that it might be best for me to supervise," Lester clarified. He caught and held her gaze and Patsi felt her chin lifting in defiance.

"Can we have cake now?" Jason interrupted.

Thankful for the change in topic, Patsi let out a sigh and pasted on a smile. "Of course. Let's get this show on the road."

Lester lit the candles and a ragged rendition of 'Happy Birthday' followed. Patsi closed her eyes and then blew, extinguishing the flames in one swoop. A smattering of claps accompanied the cutting of the cake while Lester scooped a large spoonful of ice cream onto each slice.

Goldie, Jason, and Tad left shortly after and Lester, Jed and Patsi piled into Lester's truck and headed for downtown.

The Urban Cowboy was different than Patsi had expected. The neon sign out front gave it a retro feel and the interior didn't disappoint. A long bar on one wall was lined with stools and around the corner it opened up to a large area with pool tables and an old mechanical bull. "So this is where you're planning on killing yourself," Patsi murmured, looking around.

"I never said I was entering the contest," Lester said.

Jed elbowed Patsi as they sat up to the bar. "Your brother's enterin', don't you worry. I see 'im eying up that mechanical bull every time we're in 'ere. Jacques! Our usual beers and something fancy for the young lady!" he called to the bartender.

"This is my sister, Patsi," Lester introduced. "It's her eighteenth birthday today."

Jacques, a rather lanky man with a goatee and a French Canadian accent, leaned over the counter toward Patsi. "May I see your ID, please mademoiselle?"

Patsi was happy to comply. She dug in her purse and handed the document over to Jacques. "Here you go."

Jacques squinted at the plastic card, making a show of it. "If I'd known Lester had such a pretty sister I would have been nicer to him."

"Watch it, b'y!" Jed teased. "I'm 'er honorary brother since I left me own sisters back 'ome. And I'll 'ave yer head on a platter if there be any funny business."

"Shall I make you something special?" Jacques asked Patsi with a wink. "A Bellini, perhaps? They're on special tonight."

"Uh, sure. Whatever you think." Patsi grinned as Jacques set to work.

The trio continued to joke and banter through the first drinks and Jed and Patsi ordered another. Lester was driving so he only had one. It was fun to hang out with Jed and Lester but they were a lot older and Patsi couldn't help wishing she could be with some of her own friends, namely Brett. She glanced to one side and stopped short. "Wow. No way."

"What is it?" Lester asked, swivelling in his own seat.

"It's my prof, Ms. Chan. That's the second time I've seen her this week. What's she doing in a place like this?"

Lester pivoted with deliberate slowness to look at the college professor. His features were schooled into a neutral mask. He turned back to Patsi. "Professors have lives, too, you know."

"I guess, but Ms. Chan? I just never thought I'd see her here."

"Don't judge a book by its cover." Lester downed the rest of his first beer and set the bottle on the counter with a thump. "I think it's about time to head home."

"So soon?" Patsi frowned.

"I think that's enough for your first time," Lester said.

"You're no fun at all." Patsi pouted. "Some birthday."

"Agreed," Jed said. "The night is young, b'y. I'm stayin'."

"Suit yourself. I'm leaving so you'll be taking a cab." Lester slid off the stool and threw some bills on the counter.

"I'd offer to escort Patsi 'ome, but somehows I think that wouldn't be goin' over so good." Jed winked at Patsi and took a swig of his beer.

When they exited the building, Patsi could have sworn Lester made eye contact with Ms. Chan and nodded when they walked past. For her part, she tried to avoid looking at her teacher. It would be far too embarrassing come Monday morning.

"I'M GOING out later with some of my friends," Patsi announced the next morning before she left for work. "So don't expect me home right away and don't wait up."

"Which friends?" Lester looked up from the morning paper he was reading at the breakfast table, his empty cereal bowl off to one side.

Patsi shrugged. "Megan."

"And?" Lester prompted.

Patsi rolled her eyes. "Just some of her friends. Geez."

"Watch your language. And just cause you're legal doesn't mean you should stay out all night and get hammered."

Patsi folded her arms over her chest and eyeballed Lester with a tilt to her head. "Says the guy who goes out to the bar every other night."

"You need to learn to drink responsibly."

"I'm not stupid."

"What time will you be home?"

"Lester!" Patsi wailed. "I'm not a little kid."

"No, but while you're under my roof, you're still my responsibility."

"Midnight?" She suggested.

Lester's brows furrowed in thought. "Make it one," he countered with a grin. "You're not a little kid anymore."

Patsi laughed and planted a kiss on his cheek before heading out the door.

PATSI CHANGED in the washroom at The Brew after she was done her shift. Brett was coming to pick her up right from work. She wasn't sure of his plans, but he said he wanted to do something nice in honour of her birthday the night before.

"So? Where would you like to go?" Brett asked once they were driving.

"You pick," Patsi said. "You probably know more places than I do."

They were driving past the Urban Cowboy and Brett gestured

with his head. "Want to try it? It's not very fancy for a birthday but I hear it's good. And my friend Cory runs the place."

"No thanks," Patsi said hesitantly. "My brother goes there a lot and I don't want to meet up with him. Besides, I went there last night with him and his buddy."

Brett's eyebrows rose. "You did? Should I be jealous?"

Patsi laughed. "Of my brother?"

"Of course not. Of the friend."

Patsi shook her head, the smile still playing on her lips. "Jed is even older than Lester, I think. Definitely nothing to be jealous of there."

"Good."

She looked sideways at him. "Would you be jealous? Of another guy?"

Brett reached over and squeezed her hand. "Of course I would. You're very sexy."

Patsi looked down at their intertwined hands. She felt like a fraud. "Not really. I'm kind of plain."

Brett shook his head. "You really have no idea, do you?" He turned a corner. "So where is it going to be? We should decide before we end up in the suburbs."

"I was thinking…" Patsi looked down at her lap, her voice suddenly catching in her throat. "Maybe we should just skip dinner. Now that I'm eighteen, I think I'm ready to… well, you know." She flushed and was glad for the cover of darkness in the interior of the car.

Brett raised a brow. "You sure about that?"

Patsi just nodded.

"Okay. But my parents are home tonight."

"We can go to my place." Patsi didn't recognize the squeak in her own voice.

Brett gave her hand another squeeze and then disengaged it for the rest of the drive to the apartment building. The silence that enveloped the car was palpable. Patsi felt the flush of heat deep within her core as her stomach turned itself inside out. Was she really ready for this?

When they got there, Brett left the car idle as he stopped in the visitor parking area. "What if your brother is home?"

"He's not. His truck isn't here." Patsi leaned over and gave Brett a lingering kiss. She suddenly felt bold. Powerful. Wicked. She could hardly believe she was going to sleep with a guy for the first time in her life.

She finally disengaged herself and slipped out of the car. The December air assaulted her with its cold, accentuated by the contrast between it and the heat of her own blood. Brett cut the engine and scurried to join her on the sidewalk and they walked hand in hand up to the building.

Once inside, he kissed her in front of the elevator, which made her giggle with nerves. "Let go of my hand in case there's someone in the elevator, and pretend we don't know each other, okay?"

"Okay," Brett agreed, but stole another kiss just before the doors swooshed open. Fortunately there was no one inside and they scrambled in.

As soon as the doors were closed they started kissing again, but had to stop when it came to a halt at the next floor. Anyone waiting on the other side would think they were total strangers when the door opened. As it was, Patsi recognized Jacques, the French bartender from last night, but he was obviously going down since he didn't get in.

Finally, they reached Patsi's floor and they strode from the elevator to her apartment. With trembling hands, Patsi unlocked the outer door. Once it was shut behind them another tango of kisses and roaming body parts ensued.

"Don't take your shoes off. Bring them into my room," Patsi gasped between kisses.

"Why?" Brett managed.

"Just in case."

Brett didn't argue. Once the door to Patsi's room was closed behind them, she knew there would be no turning back. And it was exactly what she wanted.

PATSI LAY ON HER BACK, Brett's head cradled on her upper arm. He was breathing softly as she played with a few tendrils of his hair that she could reach with her fingers. She was sore in places she previously didn't know about, yet she'd never felt more vibrant and alive. So this is what it felt like to truly be a woman. She smiled.

Lester would be disappointed if he found out, and there was just a twinge of guilt somewhere in the pit of her own conscience, but for the most part she was glad they had done it.

She lifted her head slightly to check the clock beside her bed. Brett would have to leave soon. There was no telling what time Lester would be in and she couldn't have him finding them like this. Patsi moved her arm out from under his head. "Hey. You have to go," she whispered.

"Huh?" Pleasure drunk eyes met hers and he smiled.

"My brother Lester might be home soon, so you have to go," she repeated.

Instead, Brett rolled on top of her.

Panic that Lester would arrive any minute and a desire to please Brett were at war. Finally, the latter won out.

Spent once again, they lay in each other's arms. Patsi went to say something about leaving again when she heard a noise in the apartment, like the rattling of keys in a lock. She immediately stiffened. "Sounds like Lester is home," she said, barely whispering. "We'll have to sneak you out once he goes to bed."

"We could just tell him," Brett suggested.

"Sh!" She held her index finger to her mouth and then pointed to the narrow stretch of carpet between her bed and the window. "Get on the floor. He might check on me."

Brett didn't look too pleased, but he did as he was told.

Several agonizing minutes passed as Patsi deciphered the sound of the door closing and the hall closet being opened and then shut again. She heard Lester's low voice, maybe as he talked on the phone or to himself. And then she heard something she wasn't expecting. It was the distinct sound of a feminine voice.

Patsi sat up and strained to listen.

"What is it?" Brett whispered, his head popping above the surface of the bed.

She just put her finger to her mouth and kept on listening. She slipped from the tangled sheets and tiptoed to the back of her door where she kept her bathrobe on a hook. She was so intent on being quiet that she didn't even notice that she was naked until she was covered up again.

A quick glance toward Brett told her he had definitely noticed. She motioned for him to lie back down and then she put her ear to the doorframe.

Again, she could differentiate between the low timber of Lester's voice and that of a woman's - musical, light and slightly familiar. She heard Lester laugh softly followed in kind by the female voice. Patsi stepped back and put her hand over her mouth and grinned in shock. Lester had brought a woman home!

Unsure what to do next, Patsi turned around and almost squealed. Brett was standing right behind her. It was his turn to tell her to shush.

"What should we do?" Patsi mouthed.

"I'm not staying on the floor all night," Brett said.

"I wonder who it is?"

Brett shrugged. "Take a look."

Patsi eyed the closed door and looked back at Brett. "Should I?"

"Why not?"

Patsi thought about it for another second. "You stay back," she directed, waving her hand.

Brett moved into the shadows while Patsi opened the door a crack. Just that tiny bit of unimpeded airflow was enough to increase the volume and clarity of the voices.

The woman laughed again and then realization hit. Patsi stood stunned.

Without thinking further about the consequences, Patsi opened the door and stepped out into the hallway. The slight movement was enough to alert Lester to her presence, but the apartment was small and she was already in the living room before he could remove his arm from around the woman's shoulders. "Ms. Chan?" Patsi squeaked.

"Patsi! What are you doing home?" Lester jumped to his feet.

"I live here," Patsi said dryly.

Lester ran a hand over the back of his neck. "I thought you were staying out late. I didn't see your shoes at the front door."

"Obviously." Patsi looked from Lester to Ms. Chan who was still sitting on the couch, her feet crossed neatly at the ankles. Besides the prim set to her tiny mouth, she hardly looked flustered. "How come you never told me?" Patsi asked, starting to feel angry.

"I didn't want to distract you from your schoolwork."

"I guess I should be the judge of that. I'm not a baby." Patsi folded her arms.

"We were going to wait until after the semester. Easier that way," Lester added.

"And why is that?" Patsi asked. For once she felt as if she had the upper hand. Imagine her, questioning Lester about his personal life! How the tables had turned.

"It's complicated." Lester looked down at his sock feet.

A conversation she'd had with Megan came back to mind. "Does your fiancé know?" Patsi's gaze slid from Ms. Chan back to Lester with a triumphant look.

"I'm no longer engaged," Ms. Chan said simply.

"That happened before Sherri and I started seeing each other," Lester said, his tone defensive. "There are other complications with Sherri's parents that we have to consider." His eyes narrowed, his countenance once again becoming that of the controlling older brother. "I just heard something. Is someone in your room?"

"Um…" Patsi glanced toward her open bedroom door.

The next thing she knew, Brett was standing in the doorway, fully dressed, thank goodness, but clearly coming from her bedroom.

Other than to blink, Lester became still as a statue.

To his credit, Brett walked forward, extended his hand, and introduced himself. "Brett McMillan. You must be Pat's brother."

Their hands pumped in slow motion. Lester was still staring a Brett.

"I think I should probably go now." Brett retrieved his hand and looked at Patsi.

"I'll walk you to the door." Patsi scurried after Brett and followed him into the hall.

"That was awkward," Brett said. "Is he really mad? Is that why he didn't say anything?"

"Probably, but don't worry about it. I can handle Lester." Patsi straightened her shoulders just a bit. "Call me tomorrow."

Brett gave her a quick kiss on the lips before he turned and strode down the hall. Just as he disappeared into the elevator, Lester and Ms. Chan showed up in the doorway.

"We'll talk when I get back." Lester's tone was clipped. He moved past Patsi without a glance, his hand guiding Ms. Chan by the elbow.

Patsi shut the door to the apartment with a click. She closed her eyes and leaned her forehead against its coolness. She wanted to know about Lester and Ms. Chan, but the last thing she wanted was to discuss the intimate details of her own relationship with Brett. With a sigh she pushed off the door and headed for her own room. If she pretended to be asleep, she might not have to deal with it.

No such luck. As soon as he was home, Lester rapped on her door, entered, and came and sat on her bed. The springs creaked under his weight. "So? How long has this been going on?"

Patsi expelled a huge sigh and opened her eyes. There was no point pretending. "By 'going on' do you mean dating or sleeping together?" She waited while Lester digested her frank response.

"Both I guess," he finally said.

"Quite a while for the first one. Almost since we moved here. Tonight was the first time as far as the second question goes."

"I see."

Patsi couldn't really see his facial expression in the dark but she imagined he was frowning. "I didn't tell you cause I didn't want you to freak out." She paused. "You can hardly get after me when you've been sneaking around with Ms. Chan."

"There is a difference. You're still living under my roof."

"Would you prefer the back seat of a car?"

Lester was silent.

"I didn't think so." The small triumph held little satisfaction.

"Who is he, exactly? Is this the same guy who came to Goldie's?"

Patsi ignored the second half of the question. "He's Megan's brother. His parents are fancy lawyers."

"That doesn't make it okay. You know it's not what Mom and Dad would have wanted."

"Cut with the guilt. It's not very Christian of you," Patsi flung back.

Lester sighed heavily and rubbed the back of his neck. "I guess it's just hard for me to accept that my baby sister is growing up." His profile turned toward her in the dark. "I hope he's worth it."

Patsi tamped the guilt down with indignation. "Why didn't you tell me about Ms. Chan?"

"Honestly, I thought it would be awkward for you. And she didn't want anyone to think she was giving you privileges."

"Why would anyone think that?"

"You know how people are," Lester said with a shrug.

"My marks have come up," Patsi offered. "Did she tell you that?"

"We've only been out together a few times and you aren't the only topic of conversation between us." He paused and Patsi could tell he was smiling. "You know, I'm actually really proud of the way you've adjusted – despite tonight. You've managed to go to school, work, and find a boyfriend. All without my help." He patted her hand. "But I still expect you to come to church."

It was Lester's way of offering a truce. She sat up and hugged him around the middle. "Thanks for not freaking out – too much."

"Exams aren't over yet," he teased.

"I love you." She squeezed and then released him.

"I love you too, little sister."

"I'M QUITTING SCHOOL," Megan said on the phone the next day.

"What? Why?" Patsi was lying on her bed in her room, rubbing the spot where Brett had lain the night before.

"I hate it and it's a waste of time. I've been looking online and I found a really great esthetics program. Mom and Dad will just have to get used to it."

"If that's what you want to do." Patsi hesitated. "Um, Megan. There's something I need to tell you."

"How was your birthday?" Megan asked, ignoring Patsi's statement. "I hope you went out and got drunk or something. I'm going to plan the biggest party ever."

"Megan," Patsi interrupted. "My birthday was fine and I don't want the biggest party ever. Stop for a minute and listen."

"Okay."

Patsi took a deep breath. "Brett and I have been… well, we've kind of been seeing each other."

There was silence for a few moments. "Pat! Didn't I tell you to stay clear of him? I know he's my own brother, but trust me, he's a jerk when it comes to girls."

"Well, we kind of… slept together." There. It was out.

"Pat!"

"What?" Patsi defended. "I like him. And I don't think you're being fair. You slept with Emmanuel on the first date."

Megan sighed into the phone. "Whatever. Just don't say I didn't warn you."

ON MONDAY MORNING, Patsi sat alone in Ms. Chan's class for the first time in weeks. Obviously, Megan was serious about quitting. Even though Patsi didn't like school either, it didn't make sense to quit now when it was so close to the end of the semester.

When Ms. Chan entered the lecture hall, Patsi sank a little lower in her seat. Knowing her brother was seeing the woman romantically was awkward in the light of day. Patsi purposely avoided eye contact. She just needed to make it through the class.

Once out of the lecture theatre, Patsi checked her phone for messages. It had been turned to silent during class and when she saw that she had an unread message from Brett, her heart did a little flip flop. She'd texted him several times yesterday but he still hadn't gotten back to her. She scurried to a bench in the hallway and sat down to read it.

With a scowl, Patsi perused the message a second time. It was awfully short. Cryptic even. No declarations of love or even an 'I've been thinking about you.' Just 'busy will call later'.

Patsi stood up with a sigh and pocketed her phone. There was no time to worry about what it meant – or didn't mean. She worked at The Brew today and couldn't miss her downtown bus connection.

NEAR CLOSING TIME, Megan rushed into the cafe. Judging by the puffy, red-rimmed eyes, she had been crying. Patsi set the dishcloth and spray bottle on the nearest table and headed straight for her friend. "What's wrong?"

Megan burst into tears and threw her arms around Patsi's neck. "They said they're going to kick me out if I don't break up with him."

Patsi disengaged herself and led Megan to a seat. She pushed her into a chair. "Who? Emmanuel?"

"Of course, Emmanuel." Megan sniffled. "They said if I don't break up with him they're kicking me out of the house."

Patsi pulled a napkin from the dispenser and handed it to Megan before sitting down in the chair opposite. "What are you going to do?"

"Pretend to break up with him. At least until after the holidays." Megan dabbed at her eyes, careful not to ruin her mascara. "By that time I can register for my esthetics course and they will already have paid for it."

"And then what?" Patsi asked.

Megan shrugged. "Move in with Emmanuel, I guess. His uncle says we can rent the apartment over the dry cleaning shop. It's vacant in January."

Patsi frowned. "Won't that be kind of hard? I mean, you're not exactly used to slumming it."

"I know, but I'll learn. True love will do that to you." Megan sighed dramatically and turned watery eyes to Patsi. "Someday you'll understand."

Patsi's jaw clenched but she didn't say anything.

"Is my brother behaving?" Megan asked, flipping her hair back.

"I guess." Patsi looked down at her clasped hands on the tabletop. "He... we've both been kind of busy these last couple of days."

"In other words he's been avoiding you since... well, since the big night." Megan reached out to pat one of Patsi's hands.

"I'm sure that's not it," Patsi bit back. "We've both just been busy."

"Don't worry. It's not you, per se. He has commitment issues." Megan flipped her hair again and sat back against the seat. The tears from just a few moments before had vanished.

"That seems kind of insensitive."

"You can't say I didn't warn you."

Patsi straightened. "I don't believe you. Not until I hear it from his own lips."

"Suit yourself."

Patsi inhaled a frustrated breath. Megan was just so smug.

"I'm kind of excited about moving in with Emmanuel. The look on my parents' faces when they realize will be priceless." Megan gazed off into the distance and smiled.

So. It was back to talking about herself again. Suddenly Patsi wondered what she had actually seen in Megan. The other girl was so superficial. So self-absorbed. Patsi pasted on a smile, trying to appear as unflustered as Megan. "Well, I really should get back to work, now." She stood up and straightened her apron.

"When are you done? I can give you a ride if you want," Megan offered.

Patsi blinked. "Um... okay." She'd been hoping that Brett would show up, but after what Megan said she wasn't going to hold her breath.

~

MEGAN'S WORDS played over and over in Patsi's mind as she lay on her bed trying to study for one of her exams. Had getting her into bed really been Brett's only purpose? Had he intended all along to drop her once he'd reached his goal? She couldn't – wouldn't – believe it until she talked to him herself – a task that seemed difficult since he wasn't returning any of her messages.

And what about her life aspirations? She was quitting school after this semester, of that she was certain. There was no point paying for something she had no interest in. But the thought of being a waitress for the rest of her life was equally unappealing. Maybe she'd been hoping that Brett would just take care of her. That they would get married and have a house full of kids. That dream was crumbling around her faster than she cared to admit.

Even Megan had more direction than she did, albeit somewhat unrealistic and certainly foolish. At least Megan was passionate about something. What was she, Patsi Mae Tibbett, passionate about?

Patsi closed her eyes and rolled onto her back. If she could picture herself doing anything in the whole wild world, what would it be? A magnificent stallion galloped by in her mind's eye and she smiled. The only thing she really liked – had always loved – was horses.

Patsi sat up and tossed the textbook she'd been reading aside. She reached for her laptop and googled 'horse careers'. Now this was something Lester could understand, and if she had a plan he might not be so sour when it came time to telling him she was quitting school.

~

THE NEXT DAY AFTER SCHOOL, Patsi walked to the nearest transit station and hopped a train. She wasn't heading downtown to work, as she normally might. She was commuting the considerable distance to Brett's part of the city. He couldn't avoid her forever. They needed to talk.

When she reached the sidewalk in front of the McMillan home, she stopped and just stood there for a few moments. The front yard was covered in snow but the walkway was cleanly shovelled and there was a large wreath hanging on the front door. It looked homey and welcoming. She just hoped the reception she received was the same.

With determined steps she approached the door, took a fortifying breath, and expelled it with a cloud into the crisp air. A few seconds after she rang the doorbell, a surprised Mrs. McMillan opened the door. "Yes?"

"Is Brett home?" Patsi smiled at the older woman.

Mrs. McMillan blinked. "Who may I say is calling?"

Patsi hesitated. Was she kidding? "Pat."

Mrs. McMillan apparently had a sudden memory recall and nodded. "Oh, of course. Megan's friend." She didn't move to let Patsi in. "Megan's not at home, I'm afraid."

"That's okay. I'm not here to see Megan. I need to talk to Brett."

"Oh. I see." She still didn't move.

"It's kind of important..." Patsi said.

With a sigh the older woman swung the door wide enough for Patsi to pass. "He's out back. In the hot tub."

"Hot tubbing at this time of year?" Patsi asked in surprise as she followed Mrs. McMillan through the house to the family room.

"It's quite refreshing." Mrs. McMillan opened one of the French doors that led out onto the deck and gestured for Patsi to exit.

Patsi stepped out onto the deck and immediately heard the sound of voices muffled by the noise of the hot tub jets. Seated around the outer rim were Brett, his friend Scott, and a girl whom she had never seen before. All of them were wearing knitted hats and steam billowed up from the surface of the bubbling water.

Déjà vu hit. This was the first place she had seen Brett. Another feeling – namely jealousy – punched her in the gut. The girl was snuggled up awfully close to Brett and was giggling at something he said.

"Pat." Brett sat up with a splash and slid slightly away from the female. "What are you doing here?"

"Does that mean I'm not welcome?" Patsi's voice remained controlled.

"Of course not. Hey, Scott. Pass me that towel, will you?" Brett stood, the water dripping off his perfectly sculpted body. He stepped over the edge of the tub and then wrapped the towel around his torso. Flip flops were waiting by the edge of the tub and he slipped them on. "Be right back," he called as he shuffled to the French doors and opened one with a yank. Patsi could see he was already getting cold, despite the warm water. She followed him inside.

Brett glanced at his mother who was sitting at the kitchen island flipping through a magazine. His gaze swung back to Patsi. "Hang on while I get some clothes on. I'll be right back."

Patsi wanted to follow him; wanted to ask him why he hadn't answered her messages. But she could tell that he expected her to stay put, so she perched on a stool opposite Mrs. McMillan and waited. The silence seemed to stretch on so Patsi tried for some small talk. "I like your home. It is very nicely decorated."

Mrs. McMillan replied with a cryptic, "Thank you."

Patsi scanned the room for something else to say. "Our house back on the farm had a big kitchen like this. Not as nice, but it was big at least."

"You're not selling him drugs, are you?" Mrs. McMillan asked, barely looking up from her magazine.

Patsi's eyes widened. "Pardon me?"

"You heard me."

Patsi's gaze fluttered down. "No, no! Of course not."

"Well that's good to hear." The other woman flipped to the next page in her magazine. "Exactly what is your relationship with my son?" she asked without looking up.

"I, um… we're friends…" Patsi said.

"My son seems to attract girls like you, but you must know that he would never consider a serious relationship."

Patsi frowned. "What do you mean, girls like me?"

Mrs. McMillan looked up for the first time in the conversation.

Her gaze was icy. "Insignificant girls. Girls with no future. Oh, I'm not naïve enough to think he doesn't enjoy variety, but in the end he needs a woman who has similar life plans."

Patsi blinked, stunned into silence.

Just then, Brett returned, looking more handsome and virile than he had any right to. "Tell Scott I had to go. He can give Vanessa a ride." He turned to Patsi. "Come on. I'll give you a ride home."

Patsi's brows furrowed but she clamped her mouth shut and followed him to the front door and out onto the front stoop. "What's going on? Why didn't you answer my calls?" she demanded.

"We can talk on the way." He skipped down the steps and walked to where his car was parked in the driveway. When he opened the passenger door, he gestured for her to get in and waited expectantly. "Get in."

"I'll do no such thing until you tell me the truth." Patsi crossed her arms over her chest. "Megan says you have commitment issues and that's why you didn't call."

Brett threw his arms in the air. "Are we going to talk about it here? In the cold? It's freezing out. At least get in the car." He pointed to the open door once again.

Patsi expelled a puff of air. With reluctance she slid into the passenger side of the blue Mazda and Brett shut the door behind her.

In a moment he was sitting in the driver's seat. He turned the heater on but didn't put the car in gear. "There. That's better. You don't know my family. We have to take it easy."

"Which doesn't explain why you didn't return my calls. And don't say you were busy. I can see by today that you've had a bit of time on your hands."

"Vanessa is an old friend."

Patsi let out a derisive snort. "Of course she is."

Brett turned puppy dog eyes toward her and reached for her hand. "Come on, babe. She's nothing. And I really was busy…"

Patsi snatched her hand away. "Maybe you just like variety, as your mother said."

Brett frowned. "What exactly did my mother say to you?"

"She said you would never have a serious relationship with a girl like me."

"She's a snob. Besides, what she doesn't know won't hurt her." He reached for her again, this time tracing a finger down her cheek. "You're pretty when you're mad."

Patsi stiffened. "Stop it. You're just as big a snob as she is."

Brett's hand dropped to the seat. "That's not fair. You don't know what it's like."

"Then tell me."

"My folks are…" Brett hesitated. "They put a lot of stock in appearances. In knowing the right people. They've told me more than once that I need to have a plan ready for the coming year if I don't want to get cut off financially."

"And would that be such a bad thing? To have to get a job and actually take care of yourself?"

"On the oil rigs? As a labourer on a construction crew?" Brett laughed. "No thanks."

Patsi's mouth stiffened into a line. "My brother works as a labourer on a construction crew. You know that."

"Sorry. Bad example." Brett shrugged. "I refuse to work in retail or the service industry, so my only choice is to go back to school. And my parents won't pay unless I follow their rules. They would never approve of a relationship between us."

"Wow. I don't even know what to say to that." Patsi sat back in her seat and blinked.

"It's not that I don't want a relationship with you," Brett said. "We'd just have to keep it quiet, that's all. Now, come on. Kiss me and I'll take you home." He leaned toward her.

Despite her better judgment, Patsi found herself being drawn to Brett like metal to a magnet. The moment their lips met all thoughts of her hurt and frustration vanished.

Brett broke the kiss and his lips hovered over hers. "Is your brother at home?"

Lucidity burst into her brain and she pulled away. "Stop. Now."

"But why? We were just getting to the good part."

Patsi let out a frustrated sigh and she turned her head to avoid looking at him. "Your sister has a lot more guts than you."

"What does that mean?"

"Just that she plans to follow her dreams, not be kept like a puppet on a string."

"I'm not a puppet," Brett countered, his voice taking on a defensive edge. "I'm just a realist. I'm not cut out for manual labor and I've grown accustomed to a certain level of comfort. What's wrong with that? I don't see why you have to make a big deal about everything. No one needs to know we're seeing each other and we can have the best of both worlds."

"You are a piece of work." Patsi shook her head and reached for the door handle. "Call me when you grow up." She hoisted herself from the car and slammed the door, probably harder than Brett would have liked.

Almost simultaneously, Brett jumped out of the car. "Wait a second. Where do you think you're going?"

"Home."

"But I was going to drive you." He leaned over the top of the car, looking at her from the opposite side.

"I'll take a bus."

"Don't be crazy. It's cold and it's getting dark. Lester won't like it," he added for good measure.

Patsi laughed. "Since when do you care about what my brother thinks?" She strode to the end of the sidewalk.

He caught up to her, grabbed her hand, and swung her around to face him. "This isn't how I meant for it to end."

Gazing into his eyes, she believed him. "I know. But you did mean for it to end, didn't you? You had no intentions of a committed relationship between us."

"I'm sorry." He looked down at his feet.

"It's okay. I'm all grown up now and I can take it." She turned on her heel and walked away.

∾

LESTER SAT ACROSS FROM HER, finishing off the last piece of quiche she'd made for supper that night. "This is good. Where'd you find the recipe?"

"Goldie gave it to me. When I got home today I thought I'd make something to use up some of those eggs in the fridge." Patsi sat for a moment longer, gathering her courage. She cleared her throat. "Lester? I have something to tell you."

He looked up, his fork poised in mid-air. "There's more? I thought you'd about knocked the wind out of me for the last time." He set his fork down on the plate and leaned his elbows on the table. "Okay. I'm ready."

Patsi took a deep breath, focusing on the tabletop to avoid his intense gaze. "You already know that college isn't where it's at for me."

"So you've said. Go on..." He sat back and crossed his arms.

The rest came out in a rush. "I've answered an ad for a ranch hand down in the southern part of the province. It's a place where people send their horses for the winter months if they don't have their own stables."

Lester's eyebrows raised a notch. Then he sat back and laughed out loud.

"What's so funny?" Patsi demanded.

"The way you were so serious I thought you were going to tell me you were pregnant or something."

"Lester!" She threw her napkin at him.

"Well? You've been putting me through my paces lately. What was I supposed to think?"

"You're terrible." She smiled in spite of herself.

"So. Tell me more about this job offer. I thought you liked the excitement of the city now that you're here." His eyes narrowed. "And what about the boyfriend?"

Patsi shrugged and kept her gaze down. "It didn't pan out."

"Are you okay?"

Patsi ventured a glance his way but quickly lowered her eyes when she saw the intensity of concern written there. "I'm fine. It was better to find out now than later."

Lester was silent for a moment then nodded. "That's too bad." He sat forward and cleared his throat. "That kind of work is seasonal. What about when spring comes?"

"If they like me, they'll keep me on, I hope."

"When do you start?"

"Right after Christmas."

Lester was silent for another moment. When Patsi looked up she saw tears glistening in his eyes. "I knew you'd be leaving some day. I just wasn't expecting it to be this soon."

Patsi rose with a clatter and rushed to the other side of the table. She flung her arms around Lester's head and shoulders and squeezed. "I love you more than I can say. And I'll miss you terribly. But for now, I need to leave this place."

EPISODE 9

THERE GOES THE NEIGHBOURHOOD

The general hum of voices, accentuated by the occasional burst of laughter, almost drowned out the country music playing in the background. A waitress sidled between two full tables, a large tray laden with glasses lifted surprisingly high as she maneuvered through the crowed bar. Just another night at the Urban Cowboy. Or not.

"Mind if I join ya?"

Lester looked up to see his friend and neighbour Jed Malloy standing over him. "Of course not. Have a seat." He grabbed the cowboy hat that rested on the empty chair beside him and set it on the table instead.

Jed lowered himself into the empty chair and nodded to the women also seated at the table. "Good to see you both. Here to cheer on our b'y, eh?"

"Since I couldn't talk him out of it, I thought I better be here to pick up the pieces." Sherri Chan, Lester's girlfriend, smiled at Jed. Her straight black hair framed her petite face, and she and Lester were holding hands on top of the table.

"Atta girl. And sis is 'ere, too, I see," Jed directed at Patsi with a

233

wink. "Not letting any grass grow under yer feet now that you're legal."

"I used to watch Lester ride broncs when I was a kid. A mechanical bull should be easy." Patsi gave Lester a sly smile. "As long as he isn't too out of shape, now that he's so old." She put her lips around the straw protruding from a frothy pink drink and took a sip.

"Thanks for the vote of confidence," Lester snorted. "I'm not sure how I got talked into this in the first place." He looked pointedly at Jed. He still suffered from a stiff neck after his accident on the construction site, and entering the mechanical bull riding competition at the Urban Cowboy was probably a really bad idea.

"Don't look so nervous, b'y!" Jed slapped Lester on the back, nearly sending him off his chair. "I knew ya'd enter after all, and you'll take the prize, too, if you don't let nerves get in the way. Let me buy ya a pint of liquid courage."

Lester shook his head and laughed. His big Newfie friend had already had more liquid courage than was necessary. "After, maybe. I might need it to kill the pain."

Jed shrugged one shoulder. "Suit yerself."

"I distinctly remember the first time I saw you ride that thing," Sherri said, her mouth forming a petite bow. "You scared me to death."

"I only fell off cause you distracted me," Lester replied. An intimate look passed between the two, not lost on the others at the table.

Lester counted the day he'd first met Sherri Chan – and subsequently been tossed off the mechanical bull – a blessing. He'd take more knocks for her, if necessary, although entering the competition was not her idea. Sherri didn't care about that kind of thing. Showing off wasn't her style. It wasn't his, either, but Jed's incessant hounding had whittled his resolve. At least that's what he told himself. The lure of competition might have had something to do with it. Or pride.

"At least ya got yer cheering section." Jed gestured to the group. "That ought to soften the fall."

"And there are lots more people coming," Sherri said. "My brother Sherman and his girlfriend are on their way, as well as a few other people we know."

Lester rolled his eyes. "Great." Maybe he could use some of that liquid courage after all.

∿

"So, the big day is finally here." Steve Russell sat up to the bar and leaned his elbows on the polished counter. He'd shed his suit jacket and tie earlier, and had his shirtsleeves rolled up. His version of relaxed.

"Just hope it pays off. I was expecting a bigger crowd." Cory Roberts had his dreadlocks pulled back into a clump at the nape of his neck. The ends bobbed in time to the shake of his head, visible in the mirror at his back behind the counter.

"It's early yet. They'll come. I'd be more worried about liability issues once it's over and done with."

"Handled." Cory's dreadlocks did a little dance as he bent to retrieve a bottle from underneath. "Relax. You're beginning to sound like my business partner." He set the bottle of Scotch whiskey on the counter with a thud.

"Your dad has a good head for business," Steve said.

"How would you know?" Cory poured two shots, one for himself and one for Steve.

Steve shrugged. "Just a hunch." They clinked glasses and downed the shots in unison.

"Ah!" Cory let out a satisfied sigh and set the glass down before his attention turned to an approaching group. He scooted around the counter in time to greet them. "Hi babe." He graced his girlfriend, Renee Tucker, with a quick kiss. Then he turned to the others – Sherman Chan and Carmen Lamont. "Where's Tamara?"

"She's not coming." Carmen pursed her ruby red lips and glanced quickly at Steve before her gaze shifted downward.

Cory furrowed his brow and let his eyes settle on Steve. "You two have a falling out?"

"You could say that." Steve absently rubbed the rim of his empty shot glass with his finger.

"What happened?"

Steve shook his head. "I let business get in the way."

Cory leaned on the counter with one elbow. "There must be more to it than that."

Renee flashed Steve an apologetic smile and placed a hand on Cory's arm. "He obviously doesn't want to talk about it, and it's none of your business anyway."

"I see my sister over there," Sherman cut in. He gestured toward the table where Sherri sat with Lester. "We should go say hi."

Steve squinted in Lester's direction. "Ah yes. The infamous miracle man. Don't tell me he's entered?"

"Can't keep a good man down, or so they say." Cory slung an arm around Renee's slim shoulder and drew her to his side.

"Or a stupid one," Steve muttered. He faced forward again and surveyed his group of friends in the mirror. Sherman had Carmen, Cory had Renee, and right now he had no one. He sighed heavily. C'est la vie. It was the story of his life.

"I'd agree but I feel obligated to stick up for the guy," Sherman said. "My sister seems to think he's okay so I'm trying to be open minded." He smiled and then turned to Carmen. "Do you want to come or would you rather stay here?"

"I'll come." Carmen tucked her arm into the crook of Sherman's elbow. Her teeth flashed whitely against her red lips and dark skin.

"Not before getting a drink." Cory lifted the bottle of Scotch. "This one's on me."

"Your business partner isn't going to like that." Steve pointed to the bottle. "Giving away all your profits."

"But he isn't here, is he?" Cory winked and reached under the counter to retrieve more glasses.

"Did I mention two of me brothers is coming down? It'll be a right family get together, it will." Jed slapped his knee.

"I remember you mentioning it," Lester said.

"Bo's trip got delayed so 'e decided to wait till Christmas time, much to me mother's dismay. Zeb's comin' down from Fort Mac and Reba wants to come in the worst way but me ma won't 'ave it. Not till after the 'olidays, anyhow." Jed's accent eliminated the 'h' sound at the beginning of most words.

"Look out Calgary," Lester said under his breath, but he smiled.

"Ya got that right, b'y." Jed's laugh was robust. "She won't know what 'it 'er, especially if the entire bunch come for a visit. We'll turn this town upside down."

"Remind me to take a vacation," Lester said. He paused when he noticed the approaching couple and then waved. "Grab a chair," he called.

Sherri twisted in her seat to see whom Lester was talking to. Her face broke into a smile. "Sherman! Carmen! So good to see you."

The group at the table shuffled to one side while Sherman found two empty chairs and pulled them over. He held one out for Carmen until she was seated and then he sat down himself.

"I'm not sure you know everyone." Sherri's eyes roamed from person to person.

"Carmen knows me." Jed leaned forward in his chair. "Best pastrami sandwiches in the country."

"Thanks." Carmen's large earring danced against the dark skin of her neck. "You're one of our best customers."

"And we've met on the job site." Sherman gestured toward Jed and Lester. He turned to Patsi. "You look familiar, too, but I'm not quite sure if I can place why."

"Pat is Lester's sister," Sherri supplied. "Plus, she works at The Brew, so you may have seen her there as well."

Sherman nodded his understanding. "Pleased to officially meet you."

"Miss Chan – I mean, Sherri – is also one of my profs at college," Patsi said.

Sherman raised his brows and glanced over at Sherri. "It is a small world, isn't it?"

 ∾

"WHAT DO you mean you're leaving for Vancouver at the beginning of next week?" Cory grasped Renee by the arm, his gaze searching her face.

Renee's eyes darted to Steve, who was sitting beside her, and then back to Cory. She lifted a slim shoulder. "Just what I said. The play is over and my contract is up. I'll be heading home for the holidays."

"But…" Cory looked puzzled. "I thought…"

"You though what?" Renee interrupted. "You knew I was only here temporarily."

"Let me get this straight. You're just up and leaving. Just like that?"

Renee narrowed her eyes. "You act like it's a big surprise. You seem to be forgetting that I live in Vancouver. My agent said he has something lined up that might be promising."

"Can't you get a job here?"

"I'm an actress." Renee rolled her eyes. "It's tough enough to make a living in this business. Vancouver is the place to be."

"But what about us? I thought we had something special." Cory reached out to grab her hand and stroked the back of it with his thumb.

She watched the movement for a moment. "You want me to give up my career?" She pulled her hand out from his grasp and looked away. "Don't ask me to do that."

Cory blinked. "I would. For you."

Steve cleared his throat. "This seems kind of private. Maybe I should leave."

Cory straightened. "Forget it. Here comes my dad. We can talk later."

Steve turned to see Cory's father, Tad Roberts, approaching with a pretty black woman.

Before the couple arrived, Renee stood up and smoothed her palms over her form fitting dress. "There's nothing more to say. I'm leaving now."

Cory hustled around the bar after her and Steve watched as Renee shook off the hand that Cory placed on her arm. A few minutes later Tad and his lady friend had joined them and although Steve couldn't hear the conversation, he knew it wasn't necessarily pleasant. He swung around on his bar stool and met Jacques the bartender's questioning gaze.

"What's going on?" Jacques tilted his chin in the direction of the squabble.

"More trouble in paradise." Steve plunked his empty glass down on the counter and stood up to leave.

"DID I tell you I bought a lot for Mom and Dad's new house?" Sherman asked Sherri. The siblings had finally found a few minutes to speak privately. Jed had vacated the table, Carmen had rushed off to the washroom to console a crying Renee, and Patsi and Lester were deep in conversation with Goldie and Tad.

"You're still going ahead with it?" Sherri's almond eyes opened wider. "After everything?"

"Of course. They're still our parents." Sherman pushed his glasses up higher on the bridge of his nose.

"But will they accept it?"

"Not sure. We'll cross that bridge when we come to it."

Sherri rested her chin in the palm of her hand and sighed. "Christmas just isn't going to be the same if we can't be with the family."

"Nobody is forcing you to stay away." Sherman gestured toward Lester, who was in conversation with Tad. "Do they know about...?"

Sherri shook her head. "No."

"Chicken." He smiled.

"I know. I admit it."

Sherman stared past her for a moment. "Maybe we'll have to start our own family traditions." He sat up straighter and looked squarely at Sherri. "You, me, Lester and Carmen. I'm not backing down. Until they accept her - apologize - I'm not going back."

"That might never happen," Sherri said. She could see the determined glint in her brother's eyes - a mere fraction of the stubbornness their mother possessed.

"I'm prepared for that. And you?"

"I think so. I mean, if things…" she hesitated, "progress between me and Lester, I might have to be."

"I HEAR you're starting a new job after Christmas." Goldie placed a hand on Patsi's paisley sleeve. "Jason and I will certainly miss you. You're such a good sitter!"

"Thanks. I'll miss you, too." Patsi smiled back at the older woman.

"What is it you're doing again?" Tad leaned forward.

"I'll be working in a stable down south that winters horses. There's a chance I could stay on in the spring, too, if things go well." Patsi grasped the end of her braid and twisted it between her fingers.

"I hope it does, although we're very sorry to see you go," Goldie repeated. She turned to Lester. "I'm surprised you're letting her out of your sight."

"She's not a kid anymore, so I guess I have to stop acting like she is." Lester flashed Patsi a brotherly grin.

Patsi smiled back when all of a sudden her gaze caught something in the distance and her face fell. "What's he doing here?" She turned her back to the entrance and grabbed for her drink.

"What's the matter?" Lester's eyes searched the room until they focused on Brett McMillan. "Oh. I see."

Tad looked in Brett's direction. "He's a friend of my son, Cory. They play music together - if that's what you can call it." He turned back to the group. "He seems nice enough. Is there something wrong?"

Patsi sighed and her shoulders sagged. "I used to go out with him, but we broke up." She turned pleading eyes on Lester. "Any chance I can get a ride home before the tournament?"

Lester frowned. "It's going to start soon and I probably

shouldn't..." His face broke into a grin. "Unless I use you as an excuse to back out."

"Nonsense!" Goldie spoke up. "You don't need to run away. Just hold your head high. You have every right to be here - just as much as he does."

Sherri leaned forward to join the conversation for the first time. "Maybe Lester was looking for a way out." She smiled coyly.

"Not a chance." Maybe he was but he wasn't about to admit it. "Well, I guess I better go get my number." He grabbed the cowboy hat that had been languishing on the table all this time and jammed it on his head. "A kiss for good luck?" he directed at Sherri as he stood up.

Sherri went on tiptoe and he turned his face to the side, expecting a kiss on the cheek. "That won't do. What if you break your neck?" she asked.

He looked at her and before he knew what was happening she'd placed her hands on either side of his face and gave him a lingering kiss on the lips. He felt his face heat and his senses soar. He wasn't much for public displays of affection, but risking his neck was worth it if it meant receiving that kind of send off.

When Sherri had reseated herself, a pert smile playing on her lips, he tipped his hat to the group in general and strode away.

Cory had wisely hired a professional to run the machine. Someone who would know when to speed up, change the spin, and generally look out for people's safety as much as provide a good ride. Stan was leaning on the controls, a low riding 'poor-boy' hat shading his eyes.

Quite a few people had paid the registration fee already but by the looks of the line-up at the registration table there were quite a few more who were last minute entrants. Lester sized a few of them up. Most looked to be amateurs – both women and men who were looking for a thrill, or maybe entering on a dare. He could tell by the stance even more than the clothes. Anyone could put on jeans and a cowboy hat. The real telling feature was the posture – the way they held themselves.

Lester narrowed his eyes at one man who was just paying the fee. His cowboy hat was tipped back on his head and he was firmly built.

Not too heavy but arms roped with sinewy muscle and legs slightly bowed from riding a horse from a young age.

Lester tipped his hat when he went forward to get his number, a fabric tunic that went over his western shirt – his best one with the red plaid cuffs and embroidered shoulder plackets. The other man returned the greeting but they didn't speak. Somehow they each knew they were looking into the eyes of the competition.

A crowd had gathered around the roped off area and Lester glanced among them to see the faces of Sherri, Patsi and the others. He wouldn't make the same mistake of looking for them during his ride. One had to stay focused, even during the easy rounds.

Round one began and one by one the contestants jumped on the back of the 'bull' and went for a ride. Each person rode for the same eight second count at a slow but steady pace. The bull only spun in one direction – as easy as a merry-go-round. But even then, a few contestants fell before the allotted time and were eliminated.

Lester shook his head. No one had told them they needed to use their legs. Trying to hang on with your hand spelled certain failure. One had to squeeze tight with the thighs if there was any hope of staying put without getting hurt. The best strategy was to try to point the heels and lean back when the bull dove forward to counter its momentum. When the head came up, the rider folded forward. It was a simple matter of compensating for the shift in the centre of balance as the bull moved. Of course, spinning was another thing altogether. But for these preliminary rounds, a two year old could have stayed on top. At least that's how Lester saw it.

When it was his turn, Lester gripped the padded handhold with his right hand, palm up, and settled himself on the bull's back, getting ready to squeeze his thighs as soon as the machine started. As expected, it was a slow and easy ride, like a Granny in her rocker.

In round two, the bull went a little bit faster, and by round three the spin of the bull became a little less predictable. Several more people were eliminated, and the crowd had become more boisterous. Lester easily survived both rounds and took a moment to search for Sherri's face when he dismounted. She waved and he raised a hand in acknowledgment. He stepped to the sidelines to watch the final contestant in that round – the cowboy he'd noted earlier.

Weston Drake, as Lester had come to find out, rode the bull with the ease of experience. In fact, he was a bit of a showboat. He clutched his cowboy hat in his free hand, waving it high above his head and then sweeping it forward with each buck of the mechanism. The free hand was actually necessary to maintain balance, but the graceful swoop of the hat added flair to the ride and the crowd clapped appreciatively. Show off.

Round four saw several more contestants fall as the bull's erratic movements increased. Lester felt the back of his neck starting to seize up. Not a good sign, since remaining loose was key to staying on the bull. He gritted his teeth for round five and made it through. After that there were only two contestants left.

"We're gonna take a little breather so these two fine cowboys can take a rest." It was Cory on the microphone. "Then we'll come back for the final round. And may the best man win!" The crowd cheered like they were witness to a real live rodeo event. The amount of alcohol consumed by the onlookers probably helped.

Lester took his cowboy hat off and wiped his brow with his sleeve. He winced, rubbing the back of his neck and then rolled his shoulders a few times.

"You're amazing!" Several skimpily clad cowgirls had taken a sudden interest. One clutched his arm.

"Thanks," he said over the tops of their heads. His eyes scanned the room for the one woman he really wanted to see. His lips split into a smile when he saw Sherri pushing past the crowd. He disengaged himself from the clinging female, none too delicately, and rushed forward to meet Sherri.

"Are you alright?" she asked, concern written on her petite features. "Come and sit down."

He took her preferred hand and followed closely on her heels as she led the way to their former table. "I'm fine. Have you been watching the whole time?"

"Of course, although I don't know why." She shook her head and pursed her lips. "It hurts me to see you in pain up there. And for what? It's not like the prize money will amount to much."

"It's the bragging rights." Lester huffed as he sat down, suddenly feeling much older than his years.

Sherri looked into his eyes, genuine concern for his wellbeing in hers. "This is silly. You can stop now. You're going to hurt yourself."

"And let the other guy win? Not a chance."

"'Ow's about that beer now?" Jed interrupted, coming to tower over Lester's seat.

"Not yet. I have to win first. Then you can be the first to buy me one." Lester took off his hat and set it on the table.

Patsi threw her arms around Lester's neck from behind. He grimaced and gave a little 'oomph'. "I'm so proud of you, big brother. You're gonna clean up."

"Not if you squeeze the life out of me." Not if he broke his neck doing it.

STEVE SLIPPED into a seat across from Vinny Kirkpatrick. The older man was wearing his customary rumpled suit complete with loosened tie slightly askew. "See that? He's here again." Steve had his back to the man in question but he knew Vinny understood exactly whom he was talking about. The rough looking guy with a shaved head, an armload of tats, and a long goatee that tapered off to a scraggly point.

"Rocky Carrvagio." Vinny took a sip of his steaming mug of coffee.

Steve frowned, reaching back into the recesses of his memory. "Rocky Carravagio…" he pronounced the name slowly. "Sounds familiar." He glanced at Vinny for enlightenment.

"Made the back page a few years ago. Ex-military man who got into trouble and was dishonourably discharged." Vinny was sitting side-saddle in the chair and his crossed leg swung back and forth rhythmically to one side.

"For what?"

"Possession of drugs. Barely a pinch of marijuana, but in those days it was a big deal. Nobody even confessed to doing it in a former life if you were in the army and wanted to keep your job."

"And?" Steve prompted.

Vinny shrugged. "The drugs were found. He says he was framed. No criminal charges were laid, but he got canned. End of story."

Steve drummed his fingers on the tabletop and then risked a glance in the man's direction. "So why is he always hanging around? I keep bumping into him and it's starting to make me nervous. What if he has something to do with the Nudara-Titan scandal?"

"Maybe it's not you he's interested in." Vinny took another slurp of the dark brew in his mug.

Steve squinted at Vinny, trying to read the older man - not an easy task. Though he was rumpled in appearance, his demeanour was not easily ruffled.

"I know you're about to ask, so I might as well tell you." Vinny set his mug down. "I think he's following me."

Steve's eyebrows shot up in surprise. "You?"

Vinny nodded, his leg still swinging.

"I suppose you've made a few enemies in this business over the years. But why you and why now?" Steve rubbed his chin thoughtfully.

"My questions exactly. We have no connection that I can recall. Then I got to digging a little deeper." Vinny's leg suddenly stopped.

Steve felt a shiver run down his spine at the sudden stillness between them. "And?"

"Remember me telling you one time that any man can be bought? Everyone has an Achilles heel? Remember that?" Vinny's leg started up again.

Steve nodded. "Yes. I remember."

"I think Mr. Carravagio is on the verge of discovering mine."

Steve blinked. "Can you be a little more specific?"

Vinny smiled. "Ah. Nice work. You want me to tell you my weakness."

"How can I help you if I don't know how?" Steve countered.

"Your father was a good man." Vinny stared into the distance for a moment and Steve let him. When his gaze returned to Steve's, the younger man was waiting, patiently. "Your dad told me once, when we were still on the force together, that he would look out for me and my family like they were his own. And I said the same to him, only I was a lot younger than he was then and it didn't seem as real. As necessary. Later, when he died, I took it to heart, and I've been trying to keep an eye out for you ever since."

"Thanks. I appreciate it. I always have." Steve waited, knowing there was more.

"Somewhere along the way, while looking out for others, I forgot my own responsibilities. My own family."

Steve knew that Vinny had divorced many years before and that he only had one son. Their relationship had not always been good. "Is this about Lenny?" Steve asked.

"You know Lenny and I haven't always seen eye to eye. His mother poisoned him against me, although I don't totally blame her. I was never at home and he needed a father, not a hero."

"But he's a man now. Surely you can put that behind you."

"He's twenty-eight and never had a real job, at least not to my knowledge. Rumour has it he sells drugs for a living, but it's easier for me to turn a blind eye. I know he lives off his girlfriend. She got some kind of settlement after having a car accident. Anyway, he may have had something to do with Rocky Carravagio's discharge."

"As in supplying the drugs?" Steve's eyes narrowed as he considered this.

"Something like that." Vinny glanced at the man with the biker tattoos.

"What can I do?" Steve asked.

"Nothing. The next step is up to him."

Brett McMillan stepped right into her path, blocking Patsi's way to the ladies' room.

"I have nothing to say to you," Patsi bit out between clenched teeth.

She sacheted sideways in an attempt to move past but Brett countered her movements.

"I've been thinking about what happened between us and I'm sorry." He surveyed her up and down. "You look nice. I like the country vibe."

Momentarily off guard, Patsi looked down at her boot cut jeans and cowboy boots. She'd purposely dressed like a cowgirl for the occasion in her favourite cowboy shirt in a paisley print and a straw cowboy hat. She steeled her features and raised her head to meet his lingering gaze. "You had your chance and now I'm leaving Calgary."

"When?" He seemed genuinely surprised.

"Right after Christmas." She folded her arms and lifted her chin, planting her feet in a more solid stance.

Brett was silent for a moment. "I didn't know. Megan didn't say anything."

"I didn't tell her yet." Patsi hesitated and she let her arms drop to her sides. "How... how is she?"

"Mom and Dad kicked her out as soon as they found out about Emmanuel."

"I thought she was going to wait until after Christmas to tell them?" Patsi furrowed her brow and tucked a piece of stray hair behind her ear.

"Mom found out somehow and that was it. Out on her ear." He put his hands in his pockets and swayed back on his heels. "They're hard line, like I said."

Patsi couldn't help but follow his movements, a sudden longing to touch him filling her. She shook her head. "I can hardly believe it. Couldn't they at least wait until after the holidays?"

"Now you know what I'm up against." He gave a hopeful little smile, still rocking in place.

Patsi stiffened her posture. "That's too bad. I'll give her a call tomorrow or something and maybe we can have one last visit. She needs to know that not everyone has abandoned her."

"That's nice of you. And what about me? Can you find a way to include me in that generosity?"

"I don't think so, Brett. Now, if you'll excuse me, I need to use the facilities." She pushed past him and swung into the ladies' room.

~

CORY'S VOICE boomed over the loudspeaker, making the announcement for the two remaining contestants to come back to the arena.

Lester looked over at Sherri. "Another good luck kiss?"

"A prayer might be more useful." She laughed and then complied with a quick kiss on the lips.

It would have to do for now. Lester hoisted himself from his chair and made his way to the arena. Weston Drake was already waiting by the ropes.

"This is going to be the final round. Each rider will have the opportunity to ride the bull one more time and Stan, the operator, has been instructed to pull out all the stops. This one won't have a time limit. They'll stay on just as long as they can and the man with the longest time wins."

"What if neither of them fall?" someone called out.

Cory looked to the operator for guidance.

"I've never seen a man stay on for longer than two minutes. It could be done I suppose, but…" Stan shrugged. "I think that'd be a record."

"Fine. We'll have a… three-minute time limit. If both stay on for that length of time we'll have to call a tie. Sound fair?" Cory looked around the crowd and there was an accenting cheer. "Alright! Let's ride some bull!"

They drew for who would ride first and Weston's number came up. The operator didn't have to do much since the machine was set for full speed and spin – just hit the stop button should he fall off.

The bull jerked Weston around like a rag doll. He was no longer the graceful rider putting on a show for the ladies. He was holding on for dear life. Finally, at around one minute ten seconds he'd taken one too many jolts. He flew sideways and Stan hit the stop button just as Weston tumbled onto the mats. He got up slowly, retrieving his hat on the way and then lifting it high for the onlookers. The crowd clapped and whistled their appreciation. The poor guy had taken a beating and Lester had no doubt they'd both be suffering from a mild bout of whiplash come morning.

Lester sighed. What a person didn't do for pride.

He strode to the machine and mounted with one fluid jump. On a last minute decision, he took off his hat and tossed it into the crowd, right at Sherri. She caught it and placed it on her head. It was far too big and almost covered her eyes, but she tilted it back and waved. Another cheer went up.

"You ready?" Stan called.

Lester gave one quick nod, his balancing arm already up in the air.

The bull started with a jolt. Lester focused on his centre of gravity, allowing his body to become one with the erratic twist and buck of the machine. Using his thighs, he squeezed the flanks of the robotic animal for all he was worth. Soon he had no other sensation than the pain in his neck, a knifepoint of agony that stabbed with each jerk and twist.

His mind numb, his body no longer his own, he felt his resolve slip and he tilted too far to one side. Head over rump he toppled to the mats.

Lester lay there for a second, catching his breath while the room spun around him. Then he heard a shout and someone was pulling him up by the arms.

"Ya did it, b'y! Ya beat 'im!"

Lester's legs felt like jelly and he leaned into Jed's strong side as the other man maneuvered him off the mat and into the crowd of well-wishers.

One minute and fifteen seconds. That's all it took to become a hero in these parts.

FROM ALL THE COMMOTION, Steve knew that the winner had been declared. Lester Tibbett had guts if not brains. Maybe it would make a good follow up story in next week's paper. 'Miracle Man Can't Be Beat'.

Cory had put on a good show, too, despite the fact that his heart had just been ripped out. Steve shook his head. There was too much drama in this world. Like a reality TV show, only worse.

He glanced over at Vinny Kirkpatrick. They were still sitting together at the table that Vinny regularly called home. They'd forgone conversation while the tournament was taking place, listening to the proceedings instead of trying to talk over them.

Steve frowned. Vinny was staring at something and the look on the older man's face was one of guarded apprehension. Steve turned to see what had grasped his friend's attention so thoroughly. When he saw, his own eyebrows shot up.

Tattoo man was almost upon them.

"Mind if I join you?" Rocky Carravagio had a gravelly voice to match his appearance.

"Go ahead," Vinny responded with an aloofness that Steve knew came from practice.

Rocky swung one of the vacant chairs around and straddled it, resting his heavily inked arms across the back. "I need to deliver a message."

Steve shifted in his seat. "If this is a private conversation, I can leave."

Rocky shrugged. "Doesn't matter to me. The message is for Vincent, but it might be good to have a witness. Stay if you want."

"Alright, I'll stay." Steve glanced at Vinny to make sure it was the right decision but the other man's expression was a mask of stoicism.

"What's on your mind?" The rhythm of Vinny's leg under the table had slowed in pace, a sure sign that he was using every faculty to remain calm.

"I need to ask for your forgiveness," Rocky said without preamble.

Steve blinked and he could see that Vinny's armour had also slipped just a notch.

"Excuse me?" Vinny managed after a moment. His leg had taken up frenetic speed.

"I need to apologize," Rocky repeated.

"For what, exactly?" Vinny eyed the other man warily.

"Your son, Lenny. He did me wrong. But you know that. For a long time I spent my days and nights planning how I would get my revenge. On him. On you…" Rocky hesitated in his speech and held Vinny's gaze. "See, I blamed you almost as much as I blamed him. You knew I was innocent – that your own son framed me for money. I lost everything. My career. Respect. You were a cop. You should have done the right thing."

"I didn't know all the details," Vinny said. "That's the truth."

Rocky waved the statement away. "I get it. Blood is thicker than water. Anyway, that's not why I'm here."

"Then why are you here?" Vinny asked.

"I want to say I'm sorry for hating you for so long. For hating your son. It didn't solve anything and all it did was make me bitter. I realize now he was just a pawn, like me. Used by someone higher up to get me out of the picture. It's over now and I need to move on with my life. That's what the padre says. If I want healing," Rocky thumped his chest with a fist, "I have to forgive."

"The padre?" Steve couldn't help asking.

Rocky looked over at Steve for the first time and nodded. "Army chaplain. He still talked to me even after I was canned. He's the one who told me about Jesus. But in order to move forward, I have to let go of all my anger. It's what I'm trying to do."

"But… you've been following me," Vinny said. "I thought you were out for revenge."

Rocky smiled. There was a gap in his teeth where a tooth was missing. "I was trying to get up the nerve to talk to you. Now that I have, I realize I should have done it a lot sooner. I feel free, man, just like the padre said I would." A tear glistened in Rocky's eye and he swiped at it with the back of his hand.

Vinny cleared his throat. "I, um… I accept."

"Thanks." Rocky stood up and placed the chair back in its rightful position. Then he reached out and grasped Vinny's hand in a firm handshake.

Steve glanced at Vinny, who was sitting open mouthed and speechless and then over at the retreating biker. If the old cliché 'You can't judge a book by its cover' was dead, it had just been resurrected.

~

LESTER CLOSED his eyes and slowly lowered himself into his armchair, wincing until he was settled. Although victory was sweet, he was paying for it the morning after. He'd even put his whiplash collar on for comfort. A visit to the doctor might be in order, but he hated to make a fuss. Things would probably sort themselves out in a couple of days.

The intercom buzzer sounded. "Patsi? Can you get that?" he called. There was no answer. Right. She was at work already. Maybe if he ignored it they would go away.

The annoying buzz went off again. With a sigh and a grunt Lester heaved himself from the chair, his back ramrod straight. He walked to the intercom and hit the little talk button. "Yes?"

"Lester Tibbett?"

"Right." He waited.

"It's Steve Russell. Can I come up? I learned something you might want to know."

Lester frowned. They had enough mutual contacts these days that Lester didn't have to think hard about how Steve had found out where he lived. He hit the entrance button to open the front door and waited. No point in getting settled back in his chair if he just had to get up again.

Several minutes later a knock sounded at the door. Lester swung it wide for the newsman. Steve's overcoat covered most of his clothing, but Lester wasn't surprised to see him wearing dress pants, even on a Saturday. "Throw your coat on a chair if you like. My neck's too stiff to offer to hang it up for you." Lester turned without moving his head and led the way back to the living room.

Steve trailed behind. "Thanks. I see you're still recovering from last night. I hope you didn't do any serious damage." He took his coat off and slung it over the arm of the couch then sat down next to it. "Congratulations, by the way."

Lester had already lowered himself into his armchair. "Stupid is as stupid does. So? To what do I owe the honour of this visit?"

"I'm here to give you a heads up. I just found out this morning that the police are planning to open an investigation into some shady dealings between Nudara Oil and city hall."

"What does that have to do with me?"

"There might be a connection to the accident on the Titan project. I though you should know. You might be called as a witness."

Lester frowned. "What kind of connection?"

"Let's just say I've had my suspicions and they seem to be verified."

"You can't be more specific than that?" Lester asked.

"Nudara Oil is a principle shareholder in Northstar Holdings, the conglomerate that is financing the project. They obviously didn't want people to know how big they really are, because they got in on some pretty hefty tax breaks." Steve paused and leaned forward, his hands clasped between his knees. "Rumour has it Fasburger knew all along and was taking kickbacks. Local activists got ahold of it and started making a fuss. Police think they might be responsible for the accident – to make a point."

"They'd put someone's life on the line just to make a point?" Lester's brows descended over his eyes.

Steve shook his head. "Unbelievable, I know."

"I guess I shouldn't be surprised. People will do anything to save a tree but turn a blind eye to killing an unborn child."

"I don't want to get into those politics right at the moment." Steve looked down at the floor.

"But what about the safety inspectors? You mean they're in on it too?"

Steve shrugged. "That will all be part of the investigation, I imagine. My guess is somebody got paid off to avoid bad press."

"Hm. Pretty sobering." Lester sat for a moment in thought. "And how do you know this?" He glanced at the other man without moving his torso.

"It's my job to know." Steve smiled. "Although, if it makes you feel better, that piece I ran on you helped put the matter back in the spotlight."

"It was a good article. Not too flowery and no finger pointing."

"I had a ton of feedback. Wait until I run a follow up on how you cleaned up at a local mechanical bull riding event." Steve grinned.

Lester raised his brows. "I never agreed to another article. Is this the real reason you came over this morning?"

"Maybe."

"Let's get it over then," Lester said with a sigh. "Just don't mention the fact that I might land in the hospital with permanent whiplash."

"My lips are sealed."

"And hey." Lester held Steve's gaze. "Thanks for letting me know."

"You sure you want to do this?" Sherman glanced at his sister's stoic profile, seated across from him in the passenger seat of his black Lexus. "This doesn't have to be your fight."

"It already is. You know that." Sherri placed a hand on Sherman's right arm where it rested on the seat between them. "Maybe I can talk some sense into her."

"Let's hope so. I'll be waiting right out here. If it takes more than ten minutes I'll take it as a good sign."

Once outside the car, Sherri hunched further into the collar of her black wool jacket. With a deep intake of breath, she looked up at the neon sign that declared 'Open' in the window of the family convenience store. She expelled the warm air from her lungs in a thick white cloud and with determined steps she approached the entrance and opened the heavy door. The little bell overhead announced her arrival.

Her cousin Lily was sitting behind the long glass counter beside the cash register. "Hi Lily. I'm surprised to see you working here today. Where's Dad?"

The teenager looked up from her tablet. "Uncle Joseph took Nai-

Nai to the doctor." Lily was taller and slimmer than Sherri and her features less refined. Her long, straight black hair was pulled back into a ponytail, and as was her habit, she was dressed all in black.

Sherri furrowed her brows. "Is Nai-Nai sick?" Not only was she concerned for her grandmother's health, but it was uncharacteristic for her mother to shirk her duties by allowing Lily to man the store in her father's absence.

Lily shrugged a shoulder. "Not sure. It might just be a regular appointment."

"I see. Is my mom upstairs?"

"Not sure about that either. Maybe she went with Uncle Joseph since he phoned and asked me to work for a couple of hours. That's the best I can do. Sorry." Lily smiled and went back to her tablet.

Sherri headed toward the back of the store and pushed through the storage room door. The dark backroom connected to a narrow set of stairs that lead to the upstairs apartment where she had grown up.

Sherri pushed the apartment door open and stepped inside. "Hello? Mom? Are you home?" The smell of cooked vegetables immediately assaulted her nose. The cramped and outdated kitchen – her mother's usual domain - was directly to the right, but Lani Chan was nowhere in sight.

A muffled, "Hello? Who there?" drew Sherri's attention and she tiptoed down the narrow hall with its darkly stained wood trim and peeked into her parent's bedroom.

Lani Chan was lying on top of the embroidered coverlet that graced the double bed. She was on her side, facing away from the door. "Mom?" Sherri asked quietly. "Are you not feeling well?"

At the sound of Sherri's voice, Lani's head popped up and she peered around to see who was talking. "Sherri?"

Sherri entered the small room and when she sat on the mattress it sagged beneath her. "What's wrong?"

"Very sick." Lani let her head fall back upon the pillow.

"What kind of sick? Can I get you something? A glass of water?"

"A headache. Always a headache." Lani sighed heavily and closed her eyes.

"Have you seen a doctor?" Sherri asked.

"Poo!" The little woman let out a disparaging snort. "What do doctors know? Stress he says. Everything is stress. What I have to be stressed about?"

"Mom." Sherri's tone was gentle yet firm. She laid a hand on her mother's shoulder and she felt the older woman stiffen beneath her touch. "You know as well as I do what there is to be stressed about."

Lani sniffed. "Your brother stubborn. Is that my problem?"

"Are you sure it's Sherman who is the stubborn one?" When Lani didn't respond, Sherri took a deep breath, choosing her next words carefully. "Sherman loves Carmen. If you'd let yourself spend even a few minutes with them, you'd see that."

"But… but she not Chinese girl!"

"So? Is that really so important?" Sherri rubbed her hand against her mother's shoulder in a circular motion. "You've always wanted for us to get married. That's been your dream. For us to find a nice husband or a wife and for you to have grandchildren. Don't spoil it now that it's so close to happening."

"But… what kind of children they have?"

"Very adorable children, I should think." Sherri kept on rubbing. "Sherman is out in the car right now. It's killing him. He doesn't like to disappoint you and he wants to make up. But he loves Carmen, too. You're the one who is going to have to come to terms with it and accept her if you ever want to see him again."

Lani rolled over. Sherri could see the tears glimmering in her eyes as she sought her daughter's gaze. "She a good woman, this Carmen?"

"I think so, and more important, Sherman thinks so."

"Hm. Maybe I see him today. He outside?"

Sherri nodded, a smile forming on her lips. "Yes. He'll be very glad to hear it."

"I never said I accept her. I just talk to Sherman. Then I decide." Lani pursed her lips in that familiar, yet endearing, way she had when she was about to give into something, but still had to save face.

Sherri nodded and stood up, the bed creaking as it strained to spring back into place.

"And what about you? When you going to find a man again?"

The question brought a smile to Sherri's lips. The meddlesome mother she knew and loved was back. "Actually, I've been seeing someone, and I think it might be serious."

"Oh?" Lani struggled to sit up, her face suddenly alight with anticipation.

Sherri took a deep breath. "His name is Lester and he's a rodeo cowboy."

"Jumpin' Jehoshaphat! Would ya look at this?" Jed shook the weekend edition of the newspaper and stabbed at the front-page headline. "Nudara Oil Caught in Bed with Fasburger. More like caught with their pants down, I'd say."

Lester smiled at his friend, who had just joined him in the large common room downstairs in the apartment building. Today was the big 'Block Party', which had become more of a Christmas party for those that wished to attend. Because of his stiff neck he had been relegated to sitting at a table looking for burnt out bulbs in a string of lights while Goldie, Tad and Patsi were busy hanging them up. "Let me see."

Jed jammed the rumpled paper into Lester's hands.

Information has been leaked about a possible backroom deal gone bad between Nudara Oil and Councilman Sean Fasburger. Fasburger was quoted not long ago that a 'closer relationship' between start up resource based companies and the city is part of the new economic realignment. This was welcome news for small companies like Nudara Oil, a relatively minor player in the oil and gas sector. After benefiting from some hefty tax exemptions, news leaked that Nudara might not be such a small fry after all.

Nudara Oil is one of the principle shareholders in Northstar Holdings, a conglomerate of investors currently funding the construction of a new highrise office building in the downtown core. Titan Construction, the company responsible for constructing the new tower, was recently in the news when an employee survived a miraculous fall down a three-story elevator shaft. Police are reopening the investigation, suspecting foul play on the part of local activists who may have been leaked information pertaining to Nudara's connection to the project. A police investigation is pending.

"So? What do ya make of that?" Jed asked.

"I'd say I'm glad the truth is going to come out." Lester folded the paper and set in on the table.

"My thoughts exactly." Jed grabbed the lapels of his plaid shirt and tugged proudly. "Thanks in part to yours truly."

"Come again?" Lester shifted his gaze from the page of type to Jed's sparkling blue eyes.

"It was me who gave that anonymous tip to that newsman, Steve Russell." Jed tapped his temple with a finger. "Got the ball rollin', I suspect."

"I see." Lester was genuinely surprised.

"Course I can't take all the credit. I'm sure there's lots more nastiness to come out of it." He leaned forward and lowered his voice. "For instance. Did ya 'ear that the lawyers for Nudara Oil might be under investigation, as well." Jed waited for a reaction and when he didn't get one he went on. "Are ya daft as well as dumb?"

Lester frowned. "What do you mean?"

"McMillan and McMillan. You'll be thankin' yer lucky stars now that your sister dumped that boy. They're 'is parents, or so I 'ear."

Goldie approached the table and pinned Jed with a playful but stern gaze. "No sitting around, Mister. We need a hand finishing up with these decorations. People will be arriving soon."

"What about 'im?" Jed pointed at Lester with his thumb.

"You wouldn't want an injured man to climb one of these ladders, now would you?" Goldie scolded.

Lester grinned. "You heard her. I'm an injured man."

Jed slapped his knees and stood up. "No rest for the wicked, me ma always says. Okay. What'd ya need?"

Lester watched Goldie lead Jed to a stepladder and hand him a string of lights. Tad Roberts slid into the chair vacated by Jed.

"Better be careful," Lester advised. "The taskmaster won't like to see you sitting down on the job."

Tad laughed. "I don't mind. She can boss me around all day long."

Lester kept his eyes focused on the bulb he was replacing. "Are you planning on sticking around Calgary a while longer then?"

"That's the plan. Especially since my business partner says he's moving to Vancouver in the new year."

"Is that so?" Lester looked up briefly, trying not to move his head too much. "Cory is moving to the coast?"

"So he says." Tad sighed. "I should have known. I'm not the best bet for running a club, but I suppose I can hire someone. Or sell. Know of anyone who would like to run a bar?"

"Not off the top of my head. I'm surprised, actually. I thought the Urban Cowboy was Cory's dream."

"It was, once upon a time. But love will do that to you. Make you chase someone across the country."

"I guess." Lester didn't say any more on the subject. He didn't doubt he'd follow Sherri to Timbuktu if necessary. "Will you be looking for your own place?"

"Maybe. Unless I make... other arrangements." Tad's gaze flickered over to Goldie, not unnoticed by Lester.

"I see."

"I didn't mean to say I'd be moving in with her," Tad clarified quickly. "I am a Christian. I just meant, maybe in time things would progress to a point where we could make it legal."

Lester's eyebrows shot up. "Really. That seems fast. I take it you two are getting along well."

"I would say so. I'm not sure if she's quite there yet, but I can be very persuasive when I want to be. I'm getting too old to waste my time on games." Tad hesitated. "Can I ask you something?"

Lester slowly raised his eyes. "Sure."

"At one time I thought that maybe you and Goldie were... well, had something between you. Just the way she talked about you at first, and Jason mentioned something once. As if there was more to it than that." Tad rubbed the smooth surface of his head with his palm and then let his hand drop as he looked directly at Lester. "Am I wrong?"

Lester chuckled. "I think it was just wishful thinking on Jason's part. We've only ever just been friends." Lester glanced to where Goldie was instructing Jed on how she wanted the lights draped just so. "She's a good woman and I wish you all the best."

"Good." Tad nodded to no one in particular. "I know it's not very Christian to be jealous. And of course, you have a girlfriend, so I shouldn't have worried. By the way, is Sherri coming to the party?"

"No, she had something going on with her own family," Lester replied. She hadn't told him much other than that it was an important family meeting and if everything went well, he'd be invited to the next family dinner at the Fortune Cookie Restaurant. He wasn't sure if he should be happy about that or scared out of his boots.

"I know it's foolish to be insecure, but I'm older than she is," Tad continued. "And... I've been out of the game for some time now. I just needed to know."

Lester looked into Tad's eyes. "I think you and Goldie are going to be just fine."

"Tad! I need your help with this one," Goldie called. "It's all tangled."

"Coming," Tad called back. He stood up and smiled at Lester. "Thanks. I better get back to the taskmaster now."

THE SOFT GLOW of mini-lights illuminated the crowd that had gathered for the evening, casting festive warmth over the room. A long table was laden with all kinds of casserole dishes, bowls and desserts. Lester surveyed those present from his vantage point at one of the far tables. He'd never laid eyes on some of the people, but most he'd at least seen, either entering or leaving the building, even if he did not know all of them by name. By all accounts, the event was a success. He imagined there were more people in attendance than even Goldie had hoped.

Jed and Jacques plunked down on either side of Lester, a heated conversation already going on between them.

"A little respect is all I ask," Jacques said, his nose slightly in the air and his goatee jutting out.

"All I said was 'Nice view'. Ya can't fault a man for 'aving eyes." Jed's gaze strayed to the right.

Lester let his own eyes follow those of Jed. Angela Carravagio was talking to a rough looking man with a lot of tattoos. Her full figure was not lost on him, squeezed as it was into a rather form fitting knit dress with a plunging neckline. She was pretty, no doubt about it, but perhaps a little too artificial.

"See? Even Lester can't 'elp but take a peek!" Jed elbowed the air near Lester. "Guess it's hard not to when she dresses like that, eh?"

"So this argument is about Angela?" Lester asked, an amused smile on his lips.

Jacques pointed a finger at Jed. "You are crass."

Jed shrugged. "I'll take that as a compliment."

"By the look of it you're both out of luck," Lester said. Angela was laughing quite boisterously at something the man with the biker vibe had said.

Jacques scowled. "Women. Never trust them."

"They 'ave their uses." Jed took a drink from the large travel mug he'd brought to the table. Lester wondered what was in the mug. Goldie had insisted on no alcohol at the event since there would be children present, but that probably didn't stop Jed from mixing his own drink upstairs in his apartment.

Jacques threw up his hands. "See? Crass, just like I said!"

"Well, here she comes, so you better play nice," Lester warned under his breath.

"Hi boys." Angela slid into the chair next to Jacques', her thigh almost touching his. She smiled widely at all the men in turn. "I'd normally ask if someone was going to buy me a drink, but I guess that's out of the question."

"You can 'ave a little sip of mine." Jed winked and slid the clunky mug in front of her.

"Thanks." Angela tipped the mug back and took a sip. Her eyes widened and she blinked before setting it down again. "My goodness! That was... potent."

"My secret ingredient."

Jacques blew out a frustrated breath and rolled his eyes.

Angela didn't seem to notice. She smiled and reached over to lay a hand on Jed's arm. "Jed, right?" She giggled. "By the way, I just love your accent!"

"Do ya now?" Jed tipped his ball cap onto the back of his head. "Well, that might be a first. Did ya 'ear that Jacques?" He looked pointedly at the other man. "Someone likes me Newfoundland accent."

"I 'eard." Jacques own French accent seemed more pronounced, laced as it was with indignation.

Angela focused on Jacques and patted his hand with the same one she'd used to touch Jed. "Yours is hot, too. But then everyone adores a French accent." Angela batted her enhanced eyelashes and took another sip from the drink, looking from man to man over the rim of the mug.

"Yes, well, I'm kind of tired." Jacques stood abruptly. "But I guess you won't mind, since you have other admirers."

The rest of the group watched Jacques strut to the exit and disappear.

"What's gotten into him?" Angela turned wide eyes toward Jed, her perfectly arched brows rising delicately. "I was just about to ask if our date was still on for tomorrow night."

"Probably jealous," Lester said. Jed's chest ballooned.

Angela giggled and looked from Jed to Lester. "Of who?"

Jed blinked, at a momentary and uncharacteristic loss for words.

Angela's laugh tinkled. "I didn't mean for that to sound the way it did. You're both big and strong and I'm sure you have to fend the girls off with a stick, but neither one of you are my type."

"Is that so? And what is your type?" Jed raised his brows.

"Someone sensitive. Passionate about life." Her glance flickered to the exit where Jacques had disappeared.

"I'm sensitive." Jed thumped his chest with his fist.

Lester laughed outright. "Now I've heard everything."

"Jacques is all yours, then. Ya just don't know what you're missin', that's all." Jed straightened and took a swig from his mug, avoiding eye contact with either Lester or Angela.

"Maybe he's not jealous of us." Lester nodded toward the biker who was talking to an older man in a rumpled brown suit.

Angela's well made up features crinkled in confusion. "What do you mean?" Her gaze followed Lester's and in a moment her face broke into a grin. "Do you mean the guy in leather?"

Lester nodded.

"That's my brother." Angela waited smugly for a response.

"Jacques will be relieved to hear it," Lester said.

"Maybe I won't tell him right away. A girl needs to have some tricks up her sleeve." Angela stood up and flicked her long brown curls off her shoulder. "Well, I guess I better move on. My goal is to talk to every person here before the night is through. Thanks for the drink." She waved and sauntered away.

"If that don't beat all," Jed muttered.

"What? That the biker dude is Angela's brother?" Lester asked.

"No. That I wasted good screech on a woman like that."

STEVE HESITATED outside the entrance to the party room. It was as bright as ever in the hall, but beyond the door, decorated with faux pine boughs, the soft glitter of Christmas lights made it difficult to identify the occupants within. He took a step inside, gave his vision a moment to adjust, and scanned the room for Tamara. Maybe she wasn't here yet. Or maybe she wasn't coming. Either way, arriving at the party uninvited was a long shot, but he just couldn't stay away anymore. Somehow he needed to make amends. Make her understand that she could trust him with her heart.

Someone tapped him on the shoulder and Steve spun to face whomever had touched him. "Vinny," he said with surprise. "What are you doing here?"

Vinny gestured across the room to the now familiar figure of Rocky Carravagio. "Rocky invited me."

Steve frowned. "He lives here?"

"Not exactly. He's staying with his sisters for the time being." Vinny adjusted the tie at his neck that was actually tightened, although still somewhat crooked. His hair looked slicked down as well. The Private Investigator had obviously taken some extra time with his grooming, for a change.

"And you felt obligated to come," Steve stated.

Vinny shrugged. "The least I could do. Say, want to head to the refreshment table? I could use a coffee."

Steve followed Vinny, keeping an eye out for any sign of Tamara. They reached a long table where a severe looking woman with a perfect grey pageboy hairdo was standing guard over the punch. Her mouth was pinched into a straight line.

"Got any coffee?" Vinny smiled at the woman.

Her stern expression didn't change. "Certainly." She handed Vinny a paper cup and he proceeded to fill it from a large urn. Then he added several packets of sugar and she raised a brow. "I don't recall seeing you before. Do you live in the building?"

"No, but my friend Rocky invited me, so I thought I'd drop by." Vinny stirred vigorously and some coffee splashed over the side and onto the white tablecloth.

"I see." The two words held a wealth of disdain. "I hope we have enough food and refreshments. If everyone off the street decided to just 'drop by', we might run short." Her eyes shot darts, first at Vinny and then Steve.

Steve held up a hand. "I already ate, so not to worry."

"Name's Vinny Kirkpatrick, by the way." Vinny held out his hand, apparently oblivious to her scorn. "What's yours? I didn't catch it." She ignored his outstretched hand and he finally dropped it to his side.

"I'm Miss Peacock." Her chin tilted upward.

"Do you have a first name, Miss Peacock?" Vinny's gaze held hers over the rim of his coffee cup.

She blinked rapidly, almost as if she hadn't heard him correctly. "Of course I have a first name. It's Millicent."

Vinny nodded. "Millie. I like it."

Steve suppressed a smile. If he wasn't mistaken, his old friend was trying to impress the lady. Well, to each his own.

Steve turned as someone placed a hand on his shoulder. "So glad you could come," the pretty dark woman said. "I'm Goldie Harper. And you are?"

Steve's brain clicked into overdrive. Goldie Harper. Tamara's friend. "Steve Russell."

Goldie's brows rose a notch. "The newspaper columnist?"

Steve smiled and shrugged. "One and the same."

"I read your column faithfully," Goldie said. "I especially enjoyed the pieces about our mutual friend, Lester Tibbett. You did a wonderful job of exposing the truth."

"Time will tell," Steve said.

"Did Lester invite you?"

"Um, sort of." It was a lie, but Steve wasn't sure how much Tamara had confided in her friend.

"Mom, can we open the gifts from Santa now?" A little boy was tugging on Goldie's sleeve. Another boy of about the same age with dark hair and olive skin was with him. "You said I had to wait until Mat got here and he's here now."

"It's not time yet," Goldie said. "Be patient." She turned to Steve. "Well, enjoy yourself. I've got some other people I need to talk to."

Steve waited until Goldie was out of earshot and then he turned to the little boys. "Let me guess. Your names are Jason and Matonabee. Am I right?"

Both boys' eyes got round. "How'd you know?" Jason asked.

"I'm a reporter. It's my job to know." Steve's eyes roamed the room, looking for Tamara.

"My mom said I'm not supposed to talk to strangers," Matonabee said.

"I'm a friend of your moms," Steve replied, focusing on the boys again. "Didn't you see me talking to your mom?" he directed at Jason.

Jason just shrugged. "I guess. Hey, come on, Mat. Let's go look at the presents."

Jason took off but Steve laid a hand on Mat's shoulder before he could follow his friend. "Say, Mat. Is your mom here?"

"We were on our way but she forgot her casserole. She said I could come by myself as long as I came straight here and didn't talk to strangers." Mat looked Steve square in the eye as if to make sure he didn't fit into that category.

"Good advice. How has your mom been, anyway?" He tried to make it sound casual.

"My mom's sad a lot," Matonabee responded with the candidness of a child. "Sometimes she even cries and she never cries."

Steve blinked and his chest squeezed in on itself. "Sorry to hear that. Tell you what. You go help Jason look at those presents and don't talk to any more strangers, got it? I'm going to go help your mom with that casserole."

Mat frowned. "It's not a very big dish. I don't think she needs help."

"Don't worry about it. And thanks man."

Steve positioned himself by the bank of elevators, one eye on the stairwell just in case she chose to go that route. He heard the rattle of the elevator's approach even before the numbers changed. The instant the doors began to open, Steve slipped inside and hit the button to close them again.

Tamara stood wide-eyed, her hands thrust into red oven mitts, holding a pottery casserole dish. "What are you doing?" Her voice rose slightly.

He took several seconds to just drink in her presence. She was as exotically beautiful as ever with her flowing black hair, aquiline nose, and large brown eyes. Her body was draped in a full-length dress that clung in all the right places.

"Answer me," she demanded a little more forcefully.

"What do you think? I needed to see you, that's why I'm here." He jammed his hands in his pants pockets but maintained eye contact.

"But… Mat. He's downstairs. I have to get to the party." Her eyes flickered from Steve's face to the closed steel doors.

"Mat's fine. I talked to him already."

"But…"

"Here, let me take that from you." He gently placed his hands over top of the oven mitts and took the casserole dish from her as she slid her hands out from their confinement.

"Careful. It's my favourite curry recipe. And my favourite dish."

He set the dish on the floor and laid the mitts on top. "Should be safe there for a few minutes." When he straightened he took her hands in his. "I'm here to tell you I'm sorry for everything that made you lose faith in me. My feelings for you haven't changed and I'll do whatever it takes to make you believe that."

Tamara's eyes flickered to the side. "I want to believe you. I'm just…" her voice trailed off.

"Afraid?" Steve finished for her. She nodded her head. "Look at me, please," he pleaded. She complied, turning wide, dark eyes toward his. "Trust me. I'm not saying I won't make mistakes, but I want to spend my life trying to make you believe in me."

Her mouth turned up at one corner. "Maybe if you kissed me I could start believing. Just a little."

He chuckled and then lowered his head to claim her mouth. When he pulled away her eyes fluttered open.

"I hardly remember what I was so upset about," she said.

Steve grinned. "Let's try that again and maybe you'll forget all together."

The evening wound to a close. Most of the guests had taken their dishes and gone home already. It would be up to the committee – as in Goldie and any that would help her – to finish the clean-up. "The custodian says we can leave the decorations up until after the holidays," Goldie informed those still present. "So there really isn't that much to do."

Sure, sure. That was the problem with these kinds of events, Lester decided. Somebody had to stay behind and do the dirty work.

His cell phone buzzed and Lester took it out of his pocket to check the number. He quickly pushed the button and put it to his ear. "Hi beautiful. What's up?"

"I'm right outside. Let me in and I'll tell you," Sherri said on the other end.

Lester strode from the party room straight to the front doors. Sherri was waiting on the other side of the glass and he could see by the excitement on her face she had news.

As soon as she was inside she grabbed his hands. "It's a miracle!"

"What's a miracle?"

"What happened tonight with my mother!" she exclaimed. "I can't wait to tell you!"

"Can I at least get a kiss first?" he asked with a grin.

She complied with a quick peck – hardly satisfactory, but Lester could see she couldn't hold her excitement in much longer.

"Let's go into the party room and sit down. You can tell me all about it." Lester suggested.

"I just want to tell you a little bit first, here in private." Sherri took a deep breath then burst out. "My mother apologized."

Lester's eyebrows rose. "Oh?" He didn't want to sound unimpressed, but it seemed rather miniscule, considering all the fuss.

"You don't seem to understand. This is a big deal. My mother is never wrong. At least she'd never admit it." Their hands were still clasped and she gave Lester's a squeeze. "But she apologized to Sherman for disowning him and says she'll give Carmen a chance."

"Wait a minute." Lester shook his head. "Your mother disowned Sherman? For dating Carmen?"

"Maybe we should sit down after all." Sherri led Lester into the party room to a chair that was away from the others. When they were both seated she continued. "My mother is very traditional and it's very important to her that we – Sherman and I – find spouses. Nice *Chinese* spouses." She emphasized the word 'Chinese' and held his gaze for a moment. "Don't you see what that means?"

Lester blinked and then nodded. "So that's why I've never met anyone in your family besides Sherman."

"Yes. Choosing to be with you meant choosing to alienate my family."

"Wow. I never knew." Lester saw tears glimmering in Sherri's eyes and a lump formed in his throat. "That's a tough choice."

"Not really." She squeezed his hand. "It was one I was willing to make."

Lester was humbled beyond words. An overwhelming love for this woman welled up within his chest. He felt his eyes begin to burn and he cleared his throat. "I'm glad you didn't have to do that."

"Me too."

"I think I'd like a proper kiss now," Lester said, leaning toward her.

"Lard thunderin' Moses!" The booming voice had a familiar cadence, but was different at the same time. All eyes turned to the entrance from where it came. "You call this a party? There's nobody 'ere!"

Jed was standing in the doorway with another man who was just as tall and possibly even broader across the shoulders. His full beard had a slightly reddish tinge and he wore a sheepskin vest over a lumberjack shirt. If Lester had seen him on the street, he'd have thought Paul Bunyan had materialized from the pages of folklore.

"Quit actin' like the redneck you are," Jed scolded, just as loudly. "Everybody!" he called. "This is me brother Zeb, come for a visit."

A chorus of 'hellos' echoed from Goldie and Tad while a few others just waved and kept on tidying up. Lester flashed Sherri an amused smile. "I guess we should be sociable." They didn't have much choice since Jed and Zeb were already headed in their direction.

"Lester!" Jed slapped him on the back. He turned to his brother. "This is the fella I was tellin' you about. The bull rider."

"Pleased to meet ya." Zeb's grip on Lester's hand was like a vice and he pumped far longer than necessary. "Zeb Malloy."

"I've heard a bit about you," Lester responded. He rubbed his now free hand.

"Don't believe a word my brother said about me," Zeb said with a wide grin. "He's a lyin' son of a -"

"Watch yer mouth!" Jed interrupted. He gave Zeb a thump across the back of the head. "There's kids present."

Lester could just imagine the wrestling that took place in the Malloy household when they were younger. Perhaps it still did. "Here for the holidays?" he asked, trying to keep the conversation on an even keel.

"That's right. Our brother Bo and sister Reba are comin' too. Be on tomorrow's flight from Newfoundland," Zeb said.

"Ma agreed to let Reba leave before Christmas?" Jed whistled. "I can 'ardly believe it!"

"We'll put on a regular Malloy Christmas, won't we, b'y?" Zeb grabbed Jed around the shoulders and the brother's jostled one another while they laughed.

"Should we be worried?" Sherri asked, smiling.

"Nah! Bo's the quiet one of the bunch and he won't stay unless he finds a job. Not sure about Reba, though." Jed shook his head. "I'm 'oping she's grown up since last time I saw 'er."

"Not to my knowledge," Zeb said.

"You've been in Alberta for a while, isn't that right?" Lester asked. "Down from Fort Mac?"

"True," Zeb replied. "Although I'm gettin' tired of workin' in the oil sands. I might look around for something to do here. If I like it, that is."

Lester's eyebrows rose slightly. "Is that so?"

Jed slapped Lester across the back again. "Pretty soon you could 'ave a whole truck load of Malloys for neighbours! What do ya think of that?"

Lester opened his eyes wide but smiled. "What can I say? There goes the neighbourhood!"

❖ ❖ ❖

NEIGHBOURHOOD CAST

Lester Tibbett: former rodeo cowboy who moves to the city for work.

Patsi Tibbett: Lester's younger sister who is tired of being under his control.

Sherri Chan: college professor who feels trapped by family expectations.

Sherman Chan: Sherri's twin brother, an architect, who moves back to Calgary.

Tamara Spence: First Nations' activist, single mother, and co-owner of the Brew.

Carmen Lamont: co-owner of the Brew café.

Steve Russell: Newspaper columnist with a nose for a scoop. Best friends with Sherman Chan and Cory Roberts.

Cory Roberts: runs the Urban Cowboy and a DJ on the side. Best friends with Sherman Chan and Steve Russell.

Jed Malloy: a redneck from Newfoundland who befriends Lester.

Jacques Marcett: manager of the Urban Cowboy, originally from Quebec.

Millicent Peacock: nosy neighbour who lives in the same apartment building.

Lani Chan: Sherri and Sherman's somewhat controlling mother

Joseph Chan: Sherri and Sherman's father

Megan McMillan: rich girl who befriends Patsi.

Brett McMillan: Megan's playboy brother who is interested in Patsi.

Goldie Harper: A nurse who lives in the apartment building.

Renee Tucker: Carmen Lamont's niece.

Tad Roberts: Cory's father and financier of the Urban Cowboy.

Vinny Kirkpatrick: retired newspaper reporter turned private investigator.

Minor Characters

Reverend Wallis: pastor of the church that Lester and Patsi attend

Ed Chan: Joseph's brother helps run the family businesses.

Joanne Chan: Ed's wife and mother three.

Dave Chan: Joseph's brother helps run the family businesses.

Nai-Nai: Sherri and Sherman's elderly grandmother

Lily Chan: Sherri Chan's cousin who works at the family restaurant, daughter of Ed and Joanne.

Clarke Ling: Engaged to Sherri Chan.

Elaine and Bruce McMillan: Brett and Megan's rich lawyer parents.

Scott and Brian: Brett McMillan's friends

Angela Carravagio: new to the apartment building.

Rocky Carravagio: Angela's scary looking brother.

Weston Drake: a cowboy

Emmanuel Fernandez: Megan's love interest.

Matonabee Spence: Tamara's young son.

Jason Harper: Goldie's young son.

Zeb Malloy: Jed Malloy's brother is rough around the edges

~

MORE IN THE SERIES!

Did you enjoy reading *NEIGHBOURS SERIES I*? An honest review is always appreciated. **AND THERE'S MORE!** *Neighbours Series II* is coming your way with lots of mischief and mayhem featuring the entire Malloy family. That's right, Jed Malloy and his siblings take over the neighbourhood in *KEEPING UP WITH THE NEIGHBOURS*.

https://www.tracykrauss.com/books/keeping-up-with-the-neighbours-a-contemporary-christian-romance-series-2/

OFFER

Join Tracy's mailing list and get up to date info on all new releases, promos and giveaways when they happen. You'll also get a free book!

https://tracykrauss.com
- fiction on the edge without crossing the line -

If you enjoyed this novel, or any of Tracy's books, please consider writing a review online. Reviews help readers find books they'll love and are tremendously helpful for today's authors. Thank you in advance!

ABOUT THE AUTHOR

Tracy Krauss writes contemporary Christian romance with a twist of suspense and a touch of humour. Her books strike a chord with those looking for a hard hitting yet thought provoking read. She also writes stage plays tailored to a high school audience, and has contributed to several anthologies, devotional books, and one illustrated children's book. Tracy has a Bachelor's degree from the University of Saskatchewan and taught secondary school Art, Drama and English – all things she is passionate about. She is a member of ACFW, The Word Guild, and is on the executive of Inscribe Christian Writers' Fellowship, a Canada wide organization for writers of Christian faith. She and her husband have lived in five provinces and territories including many remote and unique places in Canada's far north. They have four grown children and now reside in beautiful Tumbler Ridge, BC where she continues to pursue all of her creative interests.

Visit her website for more:
https://tracykrauss.com

ALSO BY TRACY KRAUSS

<u>Novels</u>

Wind Over Marshdale

Lone Wolf

Play It Again

Conspiracy of Bones (And the Beat Goes On)

My Mother the Man-Eater

Neighbours Series I

Keeping Up with the Neighbours Series II

Three Strand Cord

Blood Ties

Tempest Tossed

Aliens Among Us

Out of This World

Whispering Winds

<u>Stage Plays</u>

Dorothy's Road Trip

Ebenezer's Christmas Carol

Hook's Nemesis

Ali and the Magic Lamp

Mutiny On Mount Olympus

A Midterm Eve's Phantasm

The Western Tale

Little Red In the Hood

King William Travels The World

Non-Fiction

Life is a Highway: Advice and Reflections On Navigating the Road of Life

Thirty Days of Targeted Prayer

Divine Appointments: Daily Devotionals Based On God's Calendar

Children's book

The Sleepytown Express

BONUS RECIPES FROM THE NEIGHBOURHOOD

Urban Cowboy Buffalo Wings

Approx. 2 lbs of chicken wings (12 wings)

3 Tbsp butter

1 Tbsp Paprika

½ tsp cayenne pepper

4 Tbsp Hot sauce (bottled variety of your choice)

¼ tsp black pepper

Cut the wings at the joint. (Cut off the wing tips first and discard)
Melt butter and combine all other ingredients to make a sauce. Thoroughly coat wings in sauce. Broil for twenty minutes - ten minutes on each side, or until chicken is cooked and meat is no longer pink.
Brush the tops of wings with more sauce before serving. (Do not use sauce that has touched the raw chicken.) Serve with blue cheese dressing, sour cream, or ranch dipping sauce.

Urban Cowboy Garlic Ribs

Approx 4 lbs of pork ribs, cut into bite size portions
1 cup soya sauce
3 tsp garlic powder
1 tsp onion powder
¼ tsp black pepper
Vegetable oil for frying (2 to 4 cups if using a pan)
2 cups flour
Garlic salt in a shaker

Combine soya sauce, garlic powder, onion powder, and pepper. Marinate ribs in this mixture for at least half an hour. Drain off excess marinade and thoroughly coat individual pieces in flour. Deep fry in the heated oil, or use a deep fat fryer, until they are crispy and brown. Shake another sprinkling of garlic powder on top once they are cooked.

Lester's Homemade Beef Burgers

2 lbs lean ground beef
1 egg
½ cup oatmeal
Salt and pepper to taste

Mix all ingredients together and form into balls. Press each ball into a patty, smoothing the edges to make them uniform. Barbeque on a gas or briquette grill covered with tin foil. (The foil keeps the fresh meat from sticking.) Once the burgers have formed a crust, they may be transferred directly onto the grill if desired. Once cooked, serve on a bun and top with your favorite garnish and condiments.

Double Decker Pastrami Sandwich

1 lb thinly sliced beef pastrami, warmed
6 slices rye or whole wheat bread
4 slices havarti cheese
Prepared sweet hot mustard
mayonnaise
Thinly sliced sweet onion
2 – 4 dill pickles (Optional)

Warm pastrami on grill or in microwave. Lightly toast and butter bread. Spread a layer of sweet hot mustard on four of the bread slices and mayonnaise on the other two. Arrange equal portions of pastrami on the slices with mustard, topping with havarti cheese and one or two rings of onion. Stack 2 and use the mayo covered bread as a lid. Garnish with pickles. Makes two sandwiches.

Lani's Vegetable Pork Soup

2 lb pork
8 cups water
1 celery heart (including leaves)
½ head of Chinese cabbage
1 large onion, chopped
1 clove garlic, minced
2 Tbsp Soya sauce
½ tsp salt
¼ cup rice
1 Tbsp oil

Cut pork into small pieces and lightly fry in oil. Add onions and garlic and toss until they begin to cook. Add water and rice. Bring to a boil. Chop the entire celery heart (including leaves if desired) and half a head of cabbage. Add vegetables, soya sauce and salt. Simmer for half an hour, or until rice is fully cooked.

The Fortune Cookie's Special Chop Suey

½ lb of chicken, cut into small pieces
¼ c oil
1 tsp salt
1 Tbsp soya sauce
1 clove minced garlic
½ c onion, chopped
½ cup celery, chopped
½ cup broccoli
½ cup baby corn (canned)
¼ cup water chestnuts, chopped
½ cup mushrooms, chopped
1 cup bean sprouts, fresh
1 tsp brown sugar
1 Tbsp cornstarch
¼ cup water
1 Tbsp slivered almonds

Fry meat and garlic in oil along with salt, sugar, and soya sauce. Add chopped vegetables, tossing constantly. Don't overcook. Mix cornstarch and water into a paste and add to pan. Cook until thickened. Sprinkle with almonds. Serve over noodles or rice.

Peking Duck

1 whole duck (approx 3 lbs)
4 Tbsp Salt
1 tsp five-spice
4 Tbsp Sugar

Preheat oven to 350 degrees. Rub the entire bird, inside and out, with a mixture of the sugar, salt and five-spice. Place duck in an open roasting pan and put in the oven. Render off the fat as the duck cooks so that the skin becomes very crispy. Cook for approximately 2 hours or until the leg comes off the bone.

Caribbean Sunset (Non-alcoholic version)

1/3 Cranberry cocktail
1/3 Orange juice
1/3 Lemon-lime soda
1/2 tsp coconut extract
Maraschino cherry
Orange slices
Ice

Add coconut extract to cranberry cocktail and stir. Place ice cubes in a large glass. Slowly pour equal parts soda, cranberry cocktail, and orange juice into the glass. Do not mix. (This allows for the 'sunset' effect.) Top with a cherry and a slice of orange.

Japanese Vegetable Rolls in Rice Paper

1 package round rice paper wrappers
1 package rice vermicelli (noodles)
4 tsp soy sauce
1 tsp lemon juice

    1 small cucumber, cut into thin wedges
    1 carrot, peeled, cut into matchsticks
    1 red pepper, cut into thin strips
    1 cup bean sprouts
    1 small bunch of mint or cilantro (optional)
    soy sauce and/or sweet chili sauce, to serve

Place the vermicelli in a medium-sized bowl and pour over enough boiling water to cover. Set aside for 5 minutes or until the noodles are tender. Drain well and return noodles to the bowl. Combine the soy sauce and lemon juice, add to the noodles and toss to combine. Set aside to cool.

    Fill a large bowl with very warm water and dip rice-paper wrapper into the water until pliable but not too soft (10-30 seconds). Remove the wrapper from the water and place a little of the vermicelli across the centre of the wrapper, leaving about an inch at each end. Top with 2 wedges of the cucumber, a little carrot, pepper, bean sprouts, and a few mint or cilantro leaves. Fold in the ends of the wrapper and then roll up tightly to enclose the filling. Place on a plate and cover with damp paper towel. Repeat with the remaining wrappers and filling ingredients. Serve cut in half with soy sauce and/or sweet chili sauce (or a combination of both).

Chai Latte
    2 cups milk (or soy)
    2 cups water
    2 Tbsp loose leap Chai tea OR 2 Chai tea bags
    Sugar or honey to taste

Whisk all ingredients in medium size pot. Heat and steep to desired strength. Strain, then use a frother to make foam. Sweeten to taste and serve.

Goldie's Macaroni Casserole

1 lb. lean ground beef

1 box Kraft Dinner© or other macaroni and cheese

1 can 'niblets' corn, drained

1 package taco seasoning mix. (Use half the package for a less spicy version)

½ cup grated cheddar cheese.

Brown the beef in a skillet. Add the taco seasoning mix. In a separate pot, cook macaroni and cheese according to package directions. Mix together beef mixture, macaroni and cheese mixture and corn. Turn into a casserole dish and top with grated cheddar. Bake for 30 minutes at 375 degrees.

Goldie's Apple Crisp

Six apples

¾ cup brown sugar

¾ cup flour

½ cup quick oats

½ cup butter (softened)

1 tsp cinnamon

Preheat oven to 375 degrees. Peel, core and slice the apples and put them in a casserole dish. Combine all the other ingredients and layer it over the apples. Bake for 40 minutes.

~

Vegetarian Pea Soup
   1 large onion, chopped
   1 Tbsp olive oil
   1 ½ teaspoons sale
   1 tsp pepper
   3 or 4 carrots, diced
   1 lb of dried split yellow peas
   8 cups water

Sautee the onions in oil. Add water, salt and pepper, carrots and about half of the peas. Bring to a boil and then simmer for 40 minutes. Add the rest of the peas and continue to simmer for another 40 minutes. This allows the soup to thicken but keeps some of the peas in tact. Stir frequently.

~

Carrot Cake
   2 ½ c flour
   2 tsp baking powder
   2 tsp cinnamon
   1 tsp baking soda
   ½ tsp salt
   4 eggs
   2 cu brown sugar
   1 ¼ c oil
   8 oz can crushed pineapple 1/2 c chopped walnuts
   2 c grated carrots

Mix the first five ingredients well (dry ingredients). In a separate bowl, beat eggs and then add sugar, oil and pineapple (partially drained). Mix dry ingredients with the liquid mixture. Last, add the walnuts and carrots. Bake in a 9 x 13 pan in a preheated 350 degree oven for 45 minutes or until a toothpick comes out clean. Ice with cream cheese icing when cool.

Icing:
    4 tsp butter
    ½ block of cream cheese
    icing sugar to form a semi-stiff icing

Goldie's Glazed Beef Ribs
    4 – 5 lbs short ribs (beef)
    ½ cup ketchup
    ½ cup honey
    1 small onion minced
    1 clove garlic, crushed
    1 tsp cayenne pepper
    ½ tsp Salt
    ½ tsp Pepper
    1 Tbsp prepared mustard

Clean ribs by removing excess fat and any silver skin. Steam cook the ribs for 2 to 2 ½ hours in a 300 degree oven. (Use a large roaster or cake pan with a rack in it. Add water to the roaster, keeping the ribs above the water on the rack. Cover with lid or tin foil.) Combine all other ingredients to make a glaze. Remove ribs from roaster and coat with glaze. Return to oven using the roaster minus the rack and water. Cook at 350 for another hour, tossing the ribs once or twice to keep from sticking.

Goldie's Oven Roasted Potatoes

    1 small bag of baby potatoes (or five or six regular sized potatoes)

    ¼ cup olive oil

    ½ tsp black pepper

    ½ tsp salt

Wash potatoes and pat dry. Cut baby potatoes in half. (If using large potatoes, quarter or cube them.) Pour olive oil into a shallow baking dish (approx. 9"x12"). Add potatoes and seasoning and toss until covered in oil. Spread the potatoes out evenly and bake at 375 degrees for 45 minutes or until golden brown.

Lani's Chinese Dumplings

    Dumpling dough:

    3 c flour

    1 to 1 ¼ c water

    ¼ tsp salt

Filling:

    1 c ground pork (or beef)

    1 Tbsp soya sauce

    1 Tbsp rice wine

    ¼ tsp pepper

    1 tsp salt

    3 Tbsp sesame oil

    1 green onion finely chopped

    1 ½ c shredded Chinese cabbage

    4 Tbsp bamboo shoots – shredded

    2 slices ginger, finely chopped

    1 clove garlic, finely chopped

Combine salt and flour for dough and slowly stir in water, only adding as much as needed to make a smooth dough. (Don't add too much – you don't want it to be sticky.) Knead dough into a ball. Cover and let it rest for thirty minutes.

Mix filling ingredients together. Once dough has rested, divide it into small balls – this makes approximately 60 dumplings. Roll each ball out to a circle of about 3 inches in diameter. Put a small portion of filling (approximately one level teaspoon) onto each circle. Wet the edges with water and fold over, pinching the edge together to make a crescent shape.

Place dumplings in boiling water – not all will fit at once. Stir gently while boiling, until they float – approximately five to seven minutes. They may be pan fried after this if desired.

～

The Brew's Orange Date Muffins
　　1 orange (cut and remove seeds) include the skin!
　　½ c orange juice
　　½ c chopped dates (or substitute raisins)
　　1 egg
　　½ c butter
　　1 ½ c flour
　　1 tsp baking powder
　　1 tsp baking soda
　　½ tsp salt
　　¾ c white sugar or substitute Stevia for a healthy alternative.
(Follow substitution chart on packaging)

Blend orange in a blender with ½ c orange juice. Drop in dates, eggs, butter and whirl. Stir together dry ingredients. Combine all. Bake at 375 for 15 to 20 minutes

～

Cory's Signature Margarita (Virgin Style)

    1 1/3 c orange juice

    1 c lime juice

    2 tablespoons powdered sugar

    8 cups crushed ice cubes

    2 limes, cut into wedges

    ½ c coarse salt

    1/8 c agave (or to taste)

Place ingredients in blender or food processor and blend until smooth. Squeeze lime onto rims of glasses and coat the rim in salt. Pour mixture into glasses.

Auntie Joanne's Fried Eggplant

    2 medium eggplants

    3 teaspoons garlic – minced

    1 green onion chopped

    1 teaspoon minced ginger

    3 Tbsp soy sauce

    1 Tbsp rice vinegar

    1 Tbsp rice wine

    ½ teaspoon sugar

    1/3 cup chicken broth

    Pinch of pepper

    1 Tbsp peanut oil

    1 tsp cornstarch

    1 Tbsp water

Cut the eggplant into cubes. Combine soy sauce, vinegar, wine, sugar, pepper and broth. Heat oil in wok or frying pan. Sauté ginger, garlic and onion. Add eggplant and stir fry for one minute, then add sauce mixture and cook another minute. Turn pan down, cover, and simmer for ten minutes. Thicken with cornstarch and water mixture.

~

Jed's Newfie Breakfast

3 eggs
3 or 4 pieces thick sliced bologna
1 or 2 leftover baked potatoes
butter
Bread for toast

Cube potatoes into good sized chunks, skin on. (Left over baked potatoes work best.) Fry in butter until almost crispy. Cut bologna in half.
Fry in the same pan with the potatoes. Bologna may have to be 'but-
terfly' sliced to make it lie flat. (Make little incisions along the edges)
Once it gets a crust on both sides, stack it off to one side of the pan.
Spread the potatoes out evenly in the pan, and make three 'wells' in
the potatoes. Add more butter and crack an egg into each well. Cover
if desired. When the eggs are done to your liking, serve over toast.

~

Tuna Casserole

3 cups elbow macaroni
1 can celery soup
½ cup frozen mixed vegetables
1 cup milk
salt and pepper to taste
1 Tbsp Miracle Whip salad dressing
1 cup grated cheddar cheese

Cook macaroni and drain. Combine all ingredients except cheese and
put into a greased casserole dish. Top with cheese and bake for 45
minutes at 350 degrees.

~

Goldie's Enchilada Casserole

2 lb ground beef – browned
1 large onion, chopped
1 can mushroom soup
1 can cream of chicken soup
1 c green chilies, chopped
2 Tbsp chili powder
1 tsp cumin
1 lb of grated cheddar cheese
2 – 8 ounce cans of tomato sauce
1 can tomato paste
1 pkg of corn tortillas

Put one layer of tortillas in a large baking dish. Layer ingredients with tortillas much as you would for a lasagna. Top with more cheese. Bake at 350 for 45 minutes.

Never Fail Brownies

½ c margarine
1 c white sugar
2 eggs
¼ tsp salt
½ tsp vanilla
½ c flour
½ c cocoa
½ c chopped nuts (optional)

Combine and bake for 25 minutes at 350.

Avocado Vegetarian Panini

Panini press

Your choice of whole wheat, rye, flax or other whole grain bread
Butter (optional)
Avocado
Provolone cheese
Cherry tomatoes
Fresh spinach

Prepare vegetables: mash avocado, chop the tomatoes, and wash spinach if it is not already washed. Slice the cheese into thin slices. Spread butter on the outside of the bread (optional – it works just as well on the press dry, but butter adds flavor.) Spread avocado on both slices of bread. Top with sliced tomatoes and spinach and finish with cheese. Put the other bread on as a lid. Grill in the Panini press until golden.

~

Favourite Oatmeal Cookies
½ lb margarine or butter
¾ c brown sugar
¾ c white sugar
2 eggs
1 ½ c flour
3 c oatmeal
1 tsp salt
1 tsp baking soda
1 tsp vanilla
1 c chocolate chips

Mix butter, sugar and eggs. Combine dry ingredients and then add to the mixture along with the vanilla and chocolate chips. Make into balls. Leave plenty of room on the cookie sheet and do not press down. Bake at 350 for 8 minutes

~

Nacho Poutine (A Mexican Twist on a Quebecois favourite)

    French fries – either frozen prepared or fresh cut potatoes
    Beef gravy
    Cheese curd (traditional) or grated mozzarella cheese
    Tomatoes, chopped
    Green onion, chopped
    Prepared salsa
    Ground beef – cooked and drained
    Taco seasoning mix
    Tortilla chips - crushed

Prepare the ground beef as you would for Tacos. Drain and add taco-seasoning spice. Grate mozzarella or crumble the dry cheese curd. Chop green onions and tomatoes into fine sections. Heat beef gravy use prepared gravy or make your own)

Deep fry the French fries. Top with generous amounts of gravy and cheese to make a traditional Poutine. Sprinkle taco beef, salsa, onion and tomato on top. (Not too much) Finish with a garnish of crumbled tortilla chips.

Carmen's Peanut Butter Cookies

    ½ c butter (or margarine)
    ¼ c brown sugar
    ½ c white sugar
    1 tsp vanilla
    1 c peanut butter
    1 egg
    1 ½ c flour
    ½ tsp soda

Cream butter and sugar. Add wet ingredients and then dry ingredients, making sure to mix the soda in with the flour first. Roll into balls. Press with a fork. Leave room for expansion on the baking sheet. Bake for 8 minutes at 350.

Lester's White Cake

   1 c. white sugar

   ½ c. butter

   2 eggs

   2 tsp. vanilla extract

   1 ½ c. all purpose flour

   1 ¾ tsp. baking powder

   ½ c. milk

Preheat oven to 350 degrees F (175 degrees C). Grease and flour a 9x9 inch pan or line a muffin pan with paper liners. In a medium bowl, cream together the sugar and butter. Beat in the eggs, one at a time, then stir in the vanilla. Combine flour and baking powder, add to the creamed mixture and mix well. Finally stir in the milk until batter is smooth. Pour or spoon batter into the prepared pan. Bake for 30 to 40 minutes in the preheated oven. For cupcakes, bake 20 to 25 minutes. Cake is done when it springs back to the touch.

Goldie's Quiche

   Quiche Crust

   1 ½ c. flour

   ¼ tsp. salt

   ½ c. cold unsalted butter

   3+ Tbsp. cold tap water, milk or buttermilk

Mix flour and salt. Cut butter into slices, cut in. Stir while adding liquid 1 Tbsp. at a time. Gather in a ball. Roll and form edge on pie plate.

Gruyere Quiche Filling

    1 quiche crust (homemade as above or store bought)
    1 Tbsp olive oil
    3 c. diced onion
    ½ tsp. salt
    ¼ tsp. dried thyme
    ¼ tsp. dried sage
    1 tsp. dry mustard
    1 Tbsp. balsamic vinegar
    1 c. red pepper, thinly sliced
    1 c. (packed) grated Gruyere cheese
    3 large eggs
    1 c. milk
    Black pepper

Preheat oven to 375 F. Half-bake pie crust (about 10 minutes).

Sauté onions and oil for 5 minutes. Add salt, herbs and mustard. Cook 15 minutes. Add vinegar and pepper and cook 5 minutes. Combine eggs and milk and beat. Sprinkle cheese into partially cooked pie crust. Spoon in onion mixture and then cover with egg and milk mixture. Bake 35-40 minutes. Cool 10 minutes and serve hot.

The Urban Cowboy's Peach Bellini

    2 medium sized peaches, peeled and diced
    1/2 cup water
    1 teaspoon lemon juice
    pinch of sugar
    1 bottle dry sparkling wine

Puree peaches, water, lemon juice and sugar in a blender until smooth.

Fill a champagne flute a quarter full of the puree and then top off with sparkling wine. (Makes approx. 6 drinks)

Tad's Favourite Burgers

    Whole beef burgers
    Red onion, sliced
    1 cup white vinegar
    1 tbsp white sugar
    ¼ tsp celery seed
    Thousand Island dressing
    Tomatoes
    Lettuce
    Cheddar cheese sliced
    Kaiser rolls
    butter

Slice read onion into rings and marinate in a brine made from the vinegar, white sugar and celery seed. Cook the burgers in a frying pan or on the barbeque. (Use ready-made or make your own using your favourite recipe.) Melt a slice of real cheddar cheese on top before removing from heat. Cut Kaiser buns in half, butter and lightly toast on a grill or in the oven. (Watch to make sure they don't over brown.) Assemble the burger using Thousand Island dressing, the pickled onion, tomato and lettuce.

Old Fashioned Baked Beans

1 lb beans
1 quart water
1 small onion, chopped
½ tbsp. salt
2 tsp vinegar
½ tsp mustard
1 tbsp brown sugar
¼ cup molasses
½ cup ketchup
pepper to taste
¼ lb bacon – chopped (optional)

Soak beans in water overnight. Skim off foam. Bring to a boil and simmer for 30 minutes. Drain but save the water. Put all other ingredients in a casserole dish or crock pot. Add enough of the hot water to cover. Bake in a low over (250) for 7 hours or in a slow cooker. Before serving, you may remove a cup of beans and mash, then re-add them to the mixture.

Curried Grain with Vegetables and Tofu

1 c whole grain (brown rice, millet, quinoa…)
1 c chopped broccoli
1 c chopped vegetable of your choice (carrots, mushrooms…)
½ to 1 cup cubed tofu
4 Tbsp olive oil
6 Tbsp flour
2 tsp curry powder
1 tsp salt
3 cups milk or soya milk

Cook grain as directed. Steam vegetables. Lightly fry tofu chunks in a little bit of oil. oil. Heat rest of oil in a saucepan over low to medium heat. Add flour, curry powder and salt to make a white sauce. Gradually add milk until it thickens. Spread rice on a platter. Cover with vegetables, tofu and finally curry sauce.

Multi-Layered Salad
    1 medium head of lettuce
    1 c sliced celery
    6 hard boiled eggs, chopped
    10 oz cooked peas. (frozen or fresh not canned)
    ½ c green pepper chopped
    8 green onions, sliced
    6 oz of water chestnuts, chopped
    8 strips of bacon, cooked and crumbled
    1 c mayonnaise or miracle whip
    1 c sour cream
    2 tbsp white sugar
    2 c grated cheddar cheese

Mix mayo, sugar and sour cream. Break lettuce into small pieces. Layer all vegetables etc. starting with the lettuce. A large bowl or glass cake pan works best. Spread the mayo mixture over the top, being careful to 'seal' the mixture right to the edges of the pan/bowl. Scatter cheese over the top. This can be stored for 24 hours before serving in covered with plastic wrap and it will remain fresh and crisp.

Crazy Chocolate Cake

- ½ c marg or butter
- 1 c white flour
- 1 egg
- 1 tsp vanilla
- pinch salt
- ½ c cocoa
- 1 ½ c flour
- 1 tsp soda
- 1 tsp baking powder
- ½ c milk
- ½ cup boiling water

Important: Put all ingredients in ONE mixing bowl IN THE ORDER GIVEN. Do not mix until all ingredients are in the bowl! Beat until smooth. Bake at 325 for 40 minutes.

www.ingramcontent.com/pod-product-compliance
Lightning Source LLC
Chambersburg PA
CBHW031336020726
47499CB00005B/1290